BROKEN BONES and BROKEN HEARTS

TWO CLASSIC NOVELLAS:
THE HI LO COUNTRY AND
BOBBY JACK SMITH YOU DIRTY COWARD!

MAX EVANS

J
JOVE BOOKS, NEW YORK

This Jove Book contains the complete text of the
original hardcover editions. They have been
completely reset in a typeface designed
for easy reading and were printed from new film.

BROKEN BONES AND BROKEN HEARTS

A Jove Book / published by arrangement with
the author

PRINTING HISTORY
The Hi Lo Country was published by The Macmillan Company in 1962
Bobby Jack Smith You Dirty Coward! was published
by Nash Publishing Corporation in 1974
Jove edition / November 1995

ISBN: 0-515-11794-3

A JOVE BOOK®
Jove Books are published by The Berkley Publishing Group,
200 Madison Avenue, New York, New York 10016.
JOVE and the "J" design are trademarks
belonging to Jove Publications, Inc.

PRINTED IN THE UNITED STATES OF AMERICA

10 9 8 7 6 5 4 3 2 1

The Author
Looks Back a Bit

I must confess that this book was damn near as hard for me to put down on paper as it was for its characters to live it—and there was a lot of fun, and problems, in both cases.

First of all, the book was inspired by my best cowboy friend getting himself killed by five .38 bullets. At the time, of course, I didn't know I was inspired. I was just shocked numb.

Shortly before this shooting took place, I had sold my modest-sized cowranch near Hi Lo and moved to Taos, New Mexico, to become rich and famous. What I did, with great rapidity, is become a pauper and slightly infamous. It took me several years of living and learning—and three other books—before I started putting this particular story on paper. When I was about halfway through it I decided it was time to stop for a deep breath and celebrate a bit. I went to my favorite bar where the events of the evening led to a very short fistfight with a fine and brilliant artist who had a skull like a Neanderthal man. I swung. He ducked, and I instantly found out that the bones in my right hand were far less solid than the top of his head.

Now I had to decide what the best course of action from this point would be. If I took my shattered hand to the local hospital, they would apply a cast and it would be a long time before I could use it. So, I decided to go to my friend the Indian medicine man. I had witnessed some of his miracles and had deep faith in his healing powers.

After hearing some mumbling explanations on my part, he reluctantly agreed to try to fix the hand so I could soon go on writing. He applied a mixture that looked like ground-up fish guts (it may have been), and then straightened the two most damaged fingers using popsicle sticks for splints and expertly tied it all up. This left me two swollen, unbroken fingers and two swollen, broken fingers on my right hand which made me mostly a left-handed typist for awhile.

I finally finished the book and mailed it to New York. My agent liked it and sent it to an editor. The editor liked it, and when it was published it just naturally called for another celebration—but I really should have just gone fishing instead. Well, unfortunately, another fracas started, this time over a friend's bar bill. When it ended there were seventeen people involved. Three went to the hospital. Three of us went to jail. The battered condition WE three were in must have created a puzzling situation as to whom was to be hauled where.

The jail was an underground dungeon at that time. They've rebuilt it since then, I'm told.

My failure to arrive home that night made my wife Pat pretty upset. She thought I was out running around getting into some kind of orneriness. When we finally got word to her that I was merely incarcerated for simple brawling, she became angry at the other side. She showed up at the jail noticeably agitated, with a clean shirt for me—mine had vanished during the flurry of activity—and a basket of fried chicken that we shared with the other inhabitants.

The trial was held that afternoon. The three of us were fined all the law would allow, plus damages for broken glasses, etc. I borrowed the money for the fine, which took me a year to repay. This, however, was a small penalty compared to what came down in New York regarding my new novel as a result of this.

Unbeknownst to any of us there was a UPI man in the courtroom. He sent out a wire describing the battle in terms that would have made Zane Grey jealous. I also didn't know that my editor was in London and had just sold the British rights to my book before its American publication. He was having a sedate breakfast in Brown's Hotel when he saw this little UPI item in the London *Times*. He was incensed by it for some reason and wrote me a long, nasty, lecturing letter. I returned the favor with one of righteous indignation, strongly feeling it was too late for a lecture and suggesting that what I needed was a little compassion. Our previous, fine relationship had ended. Inside sources later revealed to me that this editor had sent down orders that only fifteen review copies of my book were to go out and no advertisement for it at all.

In my mind *The Hi Lo Country* appeared to be as dead as last year's plans.

It wasn't. A "hot" young director named Sam Peckinpah read *The Hi Lo Country*, called my agent, and said he wanted to meet the guy who wrote it. We met in an Oriental restaurant in Studio City, had a fine old time and he optioned the book for a movie. Sam had three pictures booked ahead, so the option on the book ran out.

By now several other people had miraculously gotten copies. Among the many actors who wanted to be part of the film were: Brian Keith, Lee Marvin, Charlton Heston, Robert Culp, Slim Pickens, Ali McGraw, and others. Some of the producers and/or directors, besides Peckinpah, who wanted or tried to get it made were: Saul David, Buzz Kulick, Tom Gries, Marvin Schwartz, David Dortort. I sold so many options and there were so many scripts written and so much money spent that I truly have lost track. I horse-traded it back and forth so many times to Peckinpah that we once had to hire two separate firms of lawyers to find out who owned it. The book was batted around like a rock 'n' roll groupie, or the shifting wind of Hi Lo. Now, after almost two decades, I finally own the film rights clean and clear as distilled water. My agent thinks we'll actually get it made into a movie now, but I'm just happy to have it back in book form again.

Most of my novels and short stories are set in the country around Hi Lo. The geographical Hi Lo country covers the northeastern half of New Mexico, a lot of southern Colorado and extends over into far West Texas. The indomitable spirit of that land should cover the world and beyond.

In my early writing career I was aware that all the millions of words—mostly myth—from around 1870 to 1900, had been overly covered. From then through the '20s the myth continued, but at least Will James told about the real West during his time. I became obsessed with the fact that the West of the '30s, '40s, and '50s would also slip by and become mythologized out of recognition as the previous two periods had. I have nothing against the myth any more than I do fairy tales. However, I feel it is crucial that history be recorded close to the time it happens or the mists of legend alter it beyond recognition.

Since I had been brought up—or more properly "kicked up"—by several remaining old-time cowboys, and had been made a cowhand under them, I chose myself to attempt to put this period in time on paper, and I chose to try it in fiction. It seems to be more personal and more fun that way. So from *My Pardner* (1963) which was set in the '30s, through the early '40s and '50s with *The Rounders* (1960; Gregg Press edition 1980), *The Great Wedding* (1963), *The Hi Lo Country* (1961), *The One Eyed Sky* (1963), *The Shadow of Thunder* (1969), along with many short stories and novellas, I attempted to show what the American cowboy truly was during those three decades and still is to a lesser degree today.

In the '30s the cowboys were still under the influence of old-timers and their ways in spite of the barbed wire. There were only a few old, flatbed trucks in use and hauling was still mostly done by wagon and team. The massive and final transition to the pickup truck was just getting started in the early '40s when World War II caused a postponement of the inevitable. After that terrible conflict the nation got slowly back into peacetime production; the pickup became more and more dominant. By the end of the '50s just about every ranch in the West had at least one. The transition was completed by Detroit, Michigan. Now this is not to say that the horse isn't used and needed on isolated ranches today, but the total dependence on the horse, and an era, is gone forever. I lived it and I've tried to write that period as straight and true as my ability allows. How well the words are strung out, only the readers can judge, but the actuality of those times are sure as hell there.

These deep emotions created by great transitions had always attracted Sam Peckinpah. In *The Wild Bunch* the railroads, automobiles and armies are going to crowd the horse-powered "Bunch" into eventual oblivion. In *The Hi Lo Country* we see the post-war pickup truck and societal changes doing this to the mind of its hero (anti-hero?) Big Boy Matson. I know that the drive to reveal this next great change in the West also drove Sam Peckinpah—for over twenty years—to spend more time, love, agony and his own money on this book than any other.

Over and over it would be scheduled for filming and then one of his wars would break out with the studio . . . you know the rest. It is hard for me to grasp, but now Warner Brothers is releasing the *uncut* version of *The Wild Bunch* in special showings in New York, Los Angeles and San Francisco. A month later they will have a complete retrospective (TV work and all) at Lincoln Center in New York and in London. Then the greatest Western ever made will be released worldwide.

By the time you read this we will know if the world will still go for the best. If so, I strongly sense that someone will come along and film *Hi Lo* in the great Peckinpah's memory. That would be artistic justice done. Let us all dream on anyway.

The younger cowboys I worked, sweated, fought and played with are aging now. They will soon disappear just as most of the old-timers have who influenced them. Just the same I will always remember a few things. On a real working ranch the rope and "cow savvy" were always more important than the gun. Another thing—in my young cowboying days, I cannot recall a single cowhand sitting in a bar feeling sorry for himself. He was there to drink, try to find a woman, dance, gamble, have fun, and for a spell, get in out of the wind. The fistfights were just something to add to the short time of relief. Few held grudges and most were buying one another drinks before they could wipe the blood from their faces.

In the Hi Lo country the wind blows hot or freezing about three hundred days a year. Fighting just that alone would cause a man to have a tendency to turn loose when he had a chance, not to mention the bucking horses, the kicking calves, the poor wages, the fence building and windmill repairing, the hay hauling in blizzards, and the chopping of ice with an axe from a tank so the stock could water. Then there are the droughts that shrivel everything on the earth: the grass, the wild animals, the cattle, the horses, the insects, the birds, bank accounts, and of course, the men and women responsible for the survival of all.

The Hi Lo country is not just made up of cowboys. There are merchants, mechanics, railroaders, miners, bartenders, poets, inventors, whores, semi-whores, and elegant, dedicated, long-suffering women, every kind that's anywhere else on the globe. I think here, though, the land and the elements are finally in control. It is a country of extremes. You adapt or die, in body or spirit. Because of this, the inhabitants laugh and play to extremes; they speak with descriptive comparisons in extremes; and as some old cowboy once said, "What the hell, you just live till you die anyway, and the rest of the time you spend shoveling manure so you can get the cows in the barn."

I don't know if God ever intended to give his blessings to the Hi Lo country, but I lived it, loved it and wrote about it. With all the high winds, broken bones and hearts, I'd like to do it all over again. Since I can't, here it is on paper the best I could do at the time.

Max Evans
Albuquerque, New Mexico

PART ONE

The Hi Lo
Country

Good Read
Wayne

Leo

For patience, loyalty, and understanding, I hereby dedicate *The Hi Lo Country* to Henry Volkening, Ada Dryce, Al Hart, and Chuck Miller.

Max Evans
Taos, New Mexico

Chapter One

I watched them lower Big Boy Matson into his grave. It was a large coffin, and yet I half expected it to burst apart from the weight and size of the man. Not only his physical bigness but from the whole of his being.

I stood above the crowd of big-hatted men and dark-dressed women. I stood alone. Not very long ago I had been one of them, but I had left and gone to another part of the land. The people were fast becoming strangers to me as I to them; but the land, the great swelling earth under my feet, was mine, and I belonged to it even as the man it now reclaimed.

As the preacher said his last words and the coffin sank out of sight, I looked down from the wind-stroked hill to the town, Hi Lo, New Mexico. It didn't seem to be affected by the death of its strongest son. Maybe the event had been anticipated for so long it had lost its impact.

Even I, his best friend, felt no sadness. No tears. There was only a vacancy, as if the bicep of my arm had been torn away.

He had died very young, but nothing seemed to have been wasted. This was strange, for he had had so much to give. The violence of his death had been no surprise, but the way it had happened was. It was as if a village had been vacated because of an impending flood, and had been destroyed by an erupting volcano instead.

I walked to my pickup truck, got in, and looked back at the scene for the last time. I said, "Goodbye, you old son of a bitch; I hope they have broncs in hell."

The town of Hi Lo squatted, hugging the earth as if at any moment the constant wind would blow it into the dust of the arroyos. But as doubtful as it appeared about its geographical position, it seemed even more uneasy about its social standing.

3

Its frame and adobe houses were scattered untrustingly over a relatively large area. Long ago, in the early 1900's, the homesteaders had settled the land and merchants had come from far places to build the town. Rock and mud houses had sprung above the natural contours of the mighty grass-covered hills like trees in an orchard.

The inhabitants of these homes filled the town with trade, and the councilmen planned for a city. Building jammed against building, while in the country, across several million acres of grassland, neighbor joined neighbor on every 160 acres.

The plows dug into the grass, and horses lunged against their traces, drawing the furrowed lines behind them. Trees were planted, wells dug, children sired, and the torn land was sown with beans, corn, cane, and wheat.

Some prospered for a time. The crops were harvested and sold. New rooms were added to the new homes. New plows were bought, and bigger and stronger horses to pull them. The men with the best crops bought land from those with the poorest. Little by little, unnoticeable at first, the number of farms shrank as the size of a few others increased.

But then the land rebelled against this violation—although in her own subtle way she assisted the strong in overtaking the weak by deceit: gradually at first, then with mounting force, the furrows blew level in the drying wind. The deserted homes fell, one rock, one adobe at a time. The men who survived let the plows rust away, and stem by stem, acre by countless acre, the grass returned. It was a land meant for livestock. Cattle country. And so in the end it was.

The great ranches took hold. Thousands upon thousands of cattle ranged its hills, its mountains, its brush-covered canyons. The people were scattered thinly across the land, and the town, most of its trade gone, shriveled to only five hundred inhabitants.

It was a lonely land, and its people came to the dying town of Hi Lo to visit, to talk cow talk and horse talk, to get drunk, to gamble, to whore around. Hi Lo was the hub of the limitless grasslands and wild gorges. But the land had left its curse upon it too. For over three hundred days a year the wind drilled at it and sucked at it as a reminder of the desecration of the plow.

The men of the ranches remembered and understood, and suffered the wind with amazing forbearance.

Hi Lo has its business section, though small, like all its counterparts. Every shop of the town fronts on the highway that runs parallel to the railroad. In the summertime business is brought by tourists who stop for gas, food, or liquor between the widely scattered oases of New Mexico.

In the fall the ranchers drive their cattle into the stockyards and load them on the trains for Denver or numberless feed lots in Texas, Illinois, Oklahoma, and Kansas. The profits determine the well-being of the ranchers, the cowboys, and the citizens of Hi Lo throughout the sharp, bitter winter.

The everlasting wind naturally creates great thirst. Hi Lo has two establishments for the relief of this torture. The Wild Cat Saloon is on the south side of the highway, and directly across the street stands the Double Duty Saloon. The two places eye each other like two young herd bulls. The former is managed by a short overstuffed man called Nick Barnes. He serves his drinks slowly, methodically, invariably saying: "Drink up, you bastards, and order another round. You didn't come to stay, you came to play." The latter is managed, so to speak, by Lollypop Adams. No one knows the reason for this name. Lollypop is tall and skinny, like a reared-up greyhound, and all bones except for his stomach, which has a slight swelling. This slight paunch comes from joining the boys too often in their festivities. Everybody comes here to drink and play cards, tell lies, and get out of the goddam wind. A man really has to be in bad shape to be thrown out of one of these places. Business is not always good, and fistfights from pure boredom and wind-tense nerves are as common as gnats after a pig's rump.

Down the street a way is the general mercantile, Hi Lo's supermarket. Everything a man needs to fight this country can be found here if he has the money or the credit. Nearly everyone has credit at least for a year—from one shipping time to the next. Mitch Peabody, a beady-eyed little man, owns the store. But it's his wife, twice as heavy, who runs it and sees to the profits. Rose is her name, and her bountiful breasts are her fortune. One rancher said that in the past twenty years he had bought over a thousand pounds of female breast from the Peabody mercantile. Rose, when weighing nails, beans, sugar, or anything else that's sold by the pound, always manages to have one breast on the scales. This is partly unavoidable because of their size. But when Abrahm Frink once said, "Two dozen bolts and a pound of teat," his credit was cut off forthwith.

There are three gas stations, one with a fair-to-less-than-average mechanic, and a small hotel with a restaurant, The Collins Hotel by name. And there is a moneylender, Steve Shaw, who is not exactly a fixture of the town because he owns a ranch and spends as much time in the country as he does at his office in Hi Lo.

There are others, of course, but it is not these I am mainly concerned with. They are so close together they no longer have individual personalities, but have intermingled and welded into one lone identity—just simply Hi Lo, New Mexico. It is the people scattered out across the land that make Hi Lo whatever it is. They are strong and weak in varying degrees. They all contribute something to the town, something of themselves and each in his own manner. Hi Lo may not see some of these people for months. But she waits, knowing they will come. I think the one she looked forward to seeing most, and dreaded most, was Big Boy Matson. But this is not just the story of Big Boy or myself or the woman Mona, with her terrible gifts of love and guilt and grief. No, this is not enough to give you a complete picture of the Hi Lo country. I have to include many others—cowboys, cattle barons, farmers, inventors, artists, sheepherders, thieves, drunkards, killers. All these are the spokes projecting from the hub, which is the town.

An eagle flying straight out above Hi Lo as high as his wings could carry him would see red and white cattle, heads down, grazing in every direction. To the south, on the edge of the desert, were innumerable sheep, with the herders alert for the wild marauding creatures lurking around the edges of the flock. Here the grass struggles to move out into the eroded desert, and the cactus and sagebrush thrust themselves back in pincered stabs at the grassland. It is a static battle, and has been so for thousands of years.

To the east and the west, for thirty or more miles, the gramma and buffalo grass carpet the land except in those places where flint-hard malpais mesas ripple across the earth like huge, flattened snakes. The same grasses blanket the rolling hills for fifty miles to the north. Here the hills mesh with mountains, and the cedar and piñon change to pine and spruce. All the smaller animals of the open range live here— the coyote, the bobcat, the fox; here, too, are the bear, the deer, and the mountain lion.

Although Hi Lo has tried hard to act civilized, it can never quite escape the wildness of these wild creatures. Often during Sunday-evening prayers at one of the churches the monotonous, mumbling tones of the congregation will be shattered by the yapping, unsynchronized howling of a pack of coyotes hunting right to the edge of town. And then on the opposite side of town another pack will answer, and yet another some distance beyond. On and on.

So is it with the people of this land. They listen, and hear the call of the beast.

Chapter Two

The first time I saw Big Boy was at a country dance. I was giving it. It was a short while after the dust bowl of the early thirties had reduced almost everyone to the same low level. We were all broke and half starved. But now the grass was beginning to return, and a man could latch on to a dollar here and there. I'd hired a couple of Spanish musicians; one sawed on a fiddle and the other pounded a guitar. Everybody was dancing, stomping, yelling, drinking homemade whisky and raising general hell.

Almost everyone had come in a wagon or on horseback. There were just a few old cars and a couple of pickups outside.

Big Boy came up to me, introduced himself, and said, "If you ever need any help around here, just yell."

I didn't talk to him again that night; but he lit in and had as fine a time as anyone. It did strike me as odd that a total stranger should make such an offer. Later I learned how much he meant just what he said.

I had heard about the Matsons when I first came here, years back, but I'd never met any of them before. Big Boy had two younger brothers, his mother and an old grandmother on the Matson outfit. When Big Boy was just a kid his father had died from a bullet in his lung. The bullet had been put there twenty years before by a rancher in a dispute over the exact location of a fence line. Just the same, it was the bullet that finally killed him. I heard that Big Boy's grandfather had died the same way down in Texas for whipping a man with a loaded quirt. Instead of lasting twenty years, though, he'd died before his heavy frame hit the ground.

Big Boy had grown up fast, taking over a man's job at fourteen and learning to do it right. Being head of a family at that age was quite a calling, and I think that even then black things hovered around him like an invisible spray—felt but never quite seen.

Time passed and things gradually got better. The price of cattle moved up; the rains came in grass-growing torrents; and a man could begin to plan once more. I hadn't seen much of Big Boy for several months. We were all too busy trying to make a living. My next meeting with him was because of a horse.

I had bought a four-year-old sorrel from the C-Bars. He had been broken by their foreman and had a good rein and stop on him. He traveled smooth, with a running walk, and was already developing good cow sense. It was about a month before I got to bring him home with me. I saddled him up and started for home. I noticed some healed-over spur marks on his shoulder that weren't there before and I wondered about them. In a couple of days I stopped wondering.

I rode the sorrel (and that's what I called him, Old Sorrel) out after some springing heifers about two miles from the house. I took him to a shallow, muddy spring to let him water. I put one leg up over the swells of the saddle and lit a smoke. I was about half asleep. Old Sorrel finished drinking, raised his head, and when he pulled his foot up out of the mud the suction made a popping noise. That's all the excuse he needed. Down between his front legs went his head, and a thousand pounds of horse flesh jumped right straight up in the air. I was caught completely off guard, and on the third jump I went down on my left shoulder into the mud.

By the time I got up and scraped the mud out of my eyes, Old Sorrel had bucked to the top of the hill and was now in a dead run for the ranch house. I was afoot with a two-mile walk ahead of me. I may say that I was unhappy with that horse.

Every time I rode him something drastic happened. The mere shadow of a fence post would start him bucking, and the son of a bitch always threw me. He bucked crooked, twisting, gut-wrenching jumps that I just couldn't handle. He was more of a horse than I was a cowboy, and that's all there was to it. I tried every trick I knew. It didn't do any good.

Now I understood about the spur marks. The foreman was mad because his boss had sold Old Sorrel, so, before I came after him, he deliberately spoiled the horse by spurring him viciously in the shoulders and making him buck. It was a shame, too, because he had the makings of a fine animal.

I told Lollypop Adams, the bartender at the Double Duty Saloon in Hi Lo, about this and I guess he told Big Boy. Anyway, Big Boy and his brother Sykes, who was just a year or two younger than him, rode up one day. People called Sykes Little Boy. He was as tall as Big Boy but much lighter.

"Pete," he said, "I hear you got a spoiled horse on your hands."

"Yeah, that's right. He's out there in the corral now."

"Let's go look at him," he said. We all went out to the corral, and Big Boy walked around Old Sorrel twice.

In a few minutes he asked, "How much you want for him?"

"My money back," I said.

"How much is that?"

"Seventy-five dollars."

"I'll take him," he said, and counted out the money.

I was sure glad to make that sale. Big Boy proceeded to unsaddle the black he was riding.

"You going to ride mine home?" I asked.

"That's what I bought him for," he said.

Little Boy hadn't said anything but "howdy" since they got

there. But he got down, tightened up his cinch, and made ready to haze Old Sorrel if need be.

Big Boy caught the horse and tied him to the snubbing post in the center of the corral. Then he saddled him up, climbed aboard, and started off. I waited for the action to begin, but nothing happened. That horse just plain knew better. Between him and Big Boy it was "no contest."

He said quietly, "Let's go, Little Boy."

His brother, leading the black, opened the gate and they rode off together. I stood watching them go, feeling kind of funny. The picture of him saddling that outlaw horse with such ease and total confidence was stamped on my mind.

Though Big Boy was only about five foot eleven, he gave the impression of being taller, and he looked thirty pounds heavier than the two hundred he actually weighed. An impression of terrific reserve power, just barely held in check at all times, was given by the way he talked and moved. I thought of him as being dark, but this wasn't so: his hair was light brown, and he had a strange kind of skin, almost white but with just the faintest touch of olive, that never tans or burns but always stays the same, indoors or out. He had a long, broken nose, not flattened but twisted a little to the side by a horse's hoof.

I just couldn't handle mean horses as casually as he did, and I had to admit I admired his talent. If only people were more like horses, Big Boy would have lived to a ripe old age.

Chapter Three

A couple of months later I spotted Big Boy in the Double Duty. We had a drink together and I asked about Old Sorrel.

"He's goin' to make a horse yet," he said and bolted a shot of bourbon. "So far," he went on, "he's behaved like an old-time cow pony. He's reining good and works a rope like he invented it. But I still don't entirely trust him. Ever since I bought him I've been too scared to talk and too ignorant to spell."

He said this with little change of expression, but you could sense the affection and respect he felt for the outlaw horse. He was that way about most wild things, but it was a long time before I knew it.

Well, the war came. I hated it for more reasons than the wholesale killing. The land was making a slow but steady comeback from the plow, the drought, and the consequent depression. Everybody was gradually gaining. The price of cattle had eased upward year by year. Things were breaking just right for the land and its people. Then the cattle price went up overnight. The value of land and grass rose like dead weeds in a cyclone. The land was overstocked again. It would take a few years to show, but it was as inevitable as love and hate. Men that couldn't operate a ten-furrow garden found out they were cattlemen. All they had to do was borrow from the bank to buy the cattle and get some grass. They couldn't miss. The rise in prices took care of that.

The old, the lazy, and the lame stayed behind and got rich. The rest of us went overseas to fight. I didn't want to. I still can't understand why I did, considering I was already running 150 head of good white-faced cows when it all started and could have gotten a waiver.

I told Big Boy, "I wish I had a wife and eleven kids; then maybe I could stay here and feel right about it."

"No," he said, "you wouldn't."

We both went.

We were just average soldiers, maybe less. It was hard to adjust to all that army business, used as we were to living eighteen miles from the nearest village and never having anyone tell us what to do but the weather.

We came back. That is, most of us came back. Big Boy returned to the ranch, but Little Boy had been in charge so long that he just left things as they were and went to work for Jim Ed Love, who owned the biggest ranch around.

We didn't talk about the war much. We knew *that* war was everybody's war, but the one here around Hi Lo was ours, and it would be until we left or died, both of which we thought about from time to time.

I suppose it was the spoiled sorrel I sold Big Boy that started our friendship. It gave us an excuse to talk and have a few drinks together. He liked to brag about how Old Sorrel was learning. And I liked to listen.

"By the Lord A'mighty, Pete"—I don't know where he got this expression; he claimed to be an agnostic—"that old pony hasn't forgot a thing since we left."

Well, we got to talking horses, women, rodeo, and a lot of other things. He said: "There's goin' to be a two-day show over at Ragoon. Let's try to make it."

"Suits me," I said.

The day of the rodeo we loaded my roping horse, a little bay weighing about nine hundred, and his dogging horse, a black about the same size, into the pickup and took off.

I don't know why I let Big Boy talk me into getting into the bareback-bronc riding because I am not by nature a bronc rider. Roping is my shot of whisky. I reckon I did it just to please him.

He entered the bulldogging, bareback-bronc riding, and the bull riding, but not the roping. As good a roper as he was out on the flats and up in the brush, he was helpless in this event in a rodeo arena.

There was a big crowd as usual, and what seemed like a million horses from all over the country. It was our first show after the war, and I was excited as a country boy the day of his wedding. When I eased down on the raw-boned back of that old bucking horse, I felt every nerve in my body stand at attention. I tried to swallow, and nearly strangled. The sweat ran down my arms and into my eyes.

I nodded for them to turn him out, because there was no workable alternative. I rode three jumps with my left hand welded to the handle of that bareback rigging. It wasn't any use at all. I flew off to the left and rolled over a couple of times, eating dirt. I got up and looked for my hat. The bronc was still slamming his hoofs into the ground at the other end of the arena.

It was a good day for Big Boy. He splayed the steel in his bronc's shoulders like a hammer after a nail, and took first money. In the bull riding he drew a whirling, spinning, hard-bucking animal and rode him to the whistle for second place. I hazed for him in the bulldogging. He was down, twisting his steer's neck, before we'd hardly started. Eight seconds flat and first money again. For an amateur rodeo hand this was one hell of a day.

I took third in calf roping. I made a bobble on my tie and missed first money by four seconds.

That night we celebrated and got pretty drunk. About two o'clock they ran us out of the bars. We drove over to the all-night restaurant. It was full of cowboys and cowgirls and a lot of other kind of people. We ordered ham and eggs and were minding our own business when this Art Logan, from up in Colorado, walked over. He was running a close second behind Big Boy for the two-day average.

"Hello, you hook-nosed son of a bitch," he said.

Now, in our country the word "son of a bitch" can be a friendly greeting, affectionate, really, or it can be a terrible insult. It's all according to what's in the voice. This time it was an insult. There was no mistake about Art Logan being jealous of Big Boy—probably had been for a long time. A lot of people were.

Art wasn't as tall as Big Boy, but he had a set of shoulders like a young buffalo and a neck thick as a gallon bucket. Now, when Big Boy Matson doesn't like a man he gives him a damn good leaving-alone. He tried this with Art. It didn't work. Art kept on.

"Hell, man, you must have your brother-in-law for a bronc-riding judge. You was marked at least twenty points too high."

And so it went. Big Boy put down his fork, pushed his chair back, pulled his hat down tight, and got up. He didn't say a word. He just went out to the sidewalk, and waited. Everybody in the place started getting up, and a lot of Art's buddies followed him out. The two of them walked side by side down the walk looking for someplace besides the concrete street to fight.

Suddenly Art whirled and smacked Big Boy in the side of the face, knocking him off the curb. Big Boy was up on his knees when Art hit him with both fists full in the face. Big Boy made it to his feet just the same.

I ran over, yanked a shovel out of the pickup, and turned to Art's friends. "Now, stand back and keep the hell out of this!" I yelled.

Art was swinging so hard that when he missed he fell down. When he connected it sounded like a flat board swung up against a hindquarter of beef. Big Boy was bleeding badly. I'd heard a lot about Big Boy's prowess as a fighter, but he sure was a slow starter. He kept measuring his man calmly and taking his beating.

Art got a little desperate and began swinging more wildly. No doubt he was wondering why Big Boy didn't go down—or when he intended to start swinging back.

Well, it came, and it came so fast it took most of the suspense out of the thing. Big Boy caught Art with a big right fist as he went by. You could hear the ribs snap like breaking pencils. Big Boy reached down and pulled Art halfway off the street and flailed down into his face about six times. Then he dropped Art and turned around to look for his hat.

Art stayed where he was a good spell.

The next day he came to the rodeo as a spectator. He didn't see much of the show because only one eye was operating, and you couldn't tell that from over a yard away. Art Logan was supposed to be the roughest man on the amateur rodeo circuit, but that reputation was now badly dented. And when Big Boy went on to win the all-around championship the next day, he didn't inspire any special love in the hearts of Art and his bunch. But he got from them the same thing he was accorded in Hi Lo—fear and respect.

Chapter Four

There isn't too much social activity in our country. That's one reason we usually drank enough whisky, played enough cards, chased enough women in one weekend to last us six months. It might be that long before we'd get together again.

Things happened pretty fast on this particular night: Big Boy and I fell in love with the same woman.

We decided to go to a fiesta dance down south at the Mexican village of Sano. The road leading to Sano is not calculated to warm the heart of the AAA. It is neither paved nor maintained. Twice a year a delegation of politicos descends on the county seat of Ragoon and raises hell about the road. Since a small but important block of votes exists there, the road gets graded, with many promises of improvements, but these never come to pass.

Cactus, chamisa, and reptiles inhabit the rolling hills. Here and there in a little valley a few sprigs of grass push their thin way out of the hard dry ground and afford some pasture for a limited number of sheep and goats.

The village of Sano itself is made of mud from the very earth it rests on. It seems to have sprung up as haphazardly as the grass in the valleys instead of having been made by man.

The people in Sano live off tiny patches of beans, corn, and squash irrigated from a lazily flowing desert creek that expends itself in the sand only two or three miles from the village. They sun-dry the squash and corn for winter use. The beans are dried and wind-threshed and are a stabilizing factor in an otherwise hopeless economy. Nearly all the food is stored in an airy room in gunny sacks for the long winter ahead.

To the west of Sano the purple hills are spotted with scrubby piñon trees. A wood road winds from the village into the hills, and several excursions yearly are made over this wagon trail for firewood. If by chance a wood hauler happens upon a browsing deer, he will usually come up from the floorboard of his horse-drawn wagon with a thirty-thirty, especially if the local game warden is in another area. This meat is also dried for the family larder. All in all, the people barely manage to get by.

One definite advantage exists: there is little work to do, for there is little to work on. What small amount of cash that does filter into the village comes from old-age pensions, those who can qualify for relief and from relatives who are away or in the army. Most of this is spent on clothing, wine and beer.

The school bus makes the road five days a week to Sano and takes the children into Hi Lo for their education. After they quit or finish school, most of them go to Albuquerque, Santa Fe, Utah, or California. So by and large Sano is inhabited by the old and the very young. But for the annual fiesta dance they come from Hi Lo, Ragoon, and the surrounding ranches by the score.

I looked out at the cactus as Big Boy herded the pickup along the bumpy dirt road. A great cloud of dust rolled away behind us and gradually settled back onto the dusty earth. I wondered what was in the far distant purple hills. It was certain there must be tons of gold, just waiting for discovery. And I was equally certain that back in the interior of the mountains lay a peaceful valley of rich grasses and tall trees.

I started to ask Big Boy if he had ever ridden in these desolate mountains when the village came into sight. We were early, still an hour until sundown. The town was full of cars, most of them parked in front of Sano's one bar.

Old Delfino Mondragon, rip-roaring drunk, came running over to us yelling, "Amigos! A drink for my amigos from Hi Lo!"

We took it. Then we bought a round of drinks, and then two more. Now it was night. The sun's heat had faded and the night air was cool. It was time for the dance.

I thought of going down the street and picking up Josepha O'Neil, a half-Spanish girl whose father ran the one and only grocery in Sano. Jim O'Neil had married a beautiful Spanish girl long ago. Six children had resulted, all of them gone now but Josepha. Many people wondered why anyone as pretty as she should remain in this lonely, isolated place. I, too, wondered. I had gone out with her off and on since before the war. There were times when I felt I might be falling in love with Josepha, but I could never say for sure. I decided not to mention her to Big Boy. She would be at the dance anyway.

We drove across the street and up from the bar about two blocks to what had once been the town hall. The dance was on. The orchestra consisted of a guitar, a violin, and a banjo. They were playing an old Spanish love song when we walked in. The lights from the lanterns were as soft as the music. At once a mellow feeling, part whisky and part atmosphere, stole over me.

I glanced across the half-filled dance floor to the benches against the wall, where a couple of dozen señoritas and ranchers' wives were sitting. The ranchers were still clustered in small lots talking shop and slipping out now and then for a drink. In an hour or so they would be dancing on till daylight, yelling and having a big time.

I saw Josepha; she was looking at me. She was lovely with her dark Mexican hair and light, slightly freckled Irish skin. Her eyes were big and lustrous with a sweet tenderness to complement her almost lush body. I was on my way toward her, when I saw Mona.

Mona Birk, wife of Les Birk, foreman for the C-Bars outfit northeast of Hi Lo. I had seen her around for years, had danced with her a few times, but I didn't really know her. Her hair was almost as black as Josepha's, but it had a reddish cast to it. The lines of her face were more pronounced—definite high cheekbones and a flowing jaw line that made me think of the head of an ancient statue I'd once seen in a magazine. Her eyes were medium size but gave a feeling of great depth and perception. I always felt after I'd looked into her eyes that if she cared to make the effort she could answer any question in the world. Her skin was white and transparent, as if the blood coursed very near the surface, flowing not through veins, but in a solid mass.

When she stepped in front of me and said in that soft voice that seemed always to whisper, "Hello, Pete," I just grabbed her by the arm and steered her out on the dance floor.

"How've you been, Mona?" She came to me like silver foil.

"Fine," she said, "just fine."

"Kids all right?" I asked.

"Yes."

I couldn't think of anything else to say. She was all fragrance and warm pressure. I suddenly felt hot. I danced with her off and on for an hour. Then I decided I'd better give it a rest. Her husband might get the idea I was enjoying myself.

I went outside with Big Boy. He was beginning to feel his whisky, and reared back and let out a yell you could have heard all the way to Hi Lo if the wind had been right.

"By the Lord A'mighty, Pete," he said, "this is one hell of a fine dance."

"Yeah," I said, and knocked back a big drink. Then I let out a yell myself. It sort of cleansed the soul.

Big Boy said: "The only time to take a drink of whisky or let out a yell is when you're by yourself or with somebody. It's a sure cure for ulcers."

I started to tell him about Mona, but nature called and I had to go around to the side of the hall for a visit with the weeds. That was a mistake.

When I got back inside, Big Boy had Mona, and there was no use kidding myself about the two of them. They went together like a span of black mules. Their cheeks were stuck together like a couple of copulating porcupines. But that invisible blackish mist that hovered over Big Boy seemed to envelope both of them as they danced.

It hit me right in the gut, as if I had swallowed a five-pound chunk of ice. I was in love with her. I had been all along but had fought it off because she was another man's wife—and he wasn't even my friend. But this wouldn't matter to Big Boy Matson. He had moved in and shot me out of the saddle just as I'd found out where I was riding. It hurt. Along with a lot of other people, I had my reason now to kill Big Boy. But he was my friend and saddle mate. Well, I should have told him. If I had he wouldn't have touched her, ever. That's the way he was about those he liked—those very few.

The night was warming up and so was the music. Everyone was laughing and yelling and there was no trouble except inside of me. I saw Josepha dance by with a drunk cowboy and motion for me to cut in. I turned and went out to the pickup and took a long pull from the bottle.

I stood there a few minutes and then I heard someone say, "Save one for me." It was Josepha. I handed her the bottle. She took a small drink. "Why haven't you danced with me tonight?" she said. "I've been waiting."

I looked away and said, "I'm sorry." I was, too.

"Mona Birk?"

"Hell, no." But I said it too quick and too loud.

"She's beautiful," Josepha said quietly.

"So are you," I said. "Come on, let's go." We got into the pickup. "Would you like to go to a movie?" I asked.

"In Sano? You're crazy."

"I know." I started the motor.

"Let's go to Ragoon," I said, forgetting I had Big Boy's pickup.

"Not tonight. I just want to talk to you."

We drove along in silence, and then I said, "You worry me. Why do you stay here in Sano? You're lovely and sensible. You could live better in Ragoon."

"Everyone asks me that."

"Well, why?"

"My father," she said. "He's happy here. In other places I see so much that is not happy, maybe I am afraid to leave."

I touched her hair. "It would be wrong for someone like you not to be happy."

"Why do you say so?"

"Because you're good. There are enough bastards in the world; they should take on all the suffering."

"We are all bad. The last time I danced with you in Hi Lo I had bad thoughts." She was smiling.

I stopped the pickup and pulled her to me. "That was good," I said.

Headlights shone down the road, illuminating our faces as if purposely searching us out. "Damn," I said, "there's no place in the world you can be alone."

"Yes, there is. Drive on, I'll show you. There's a road that goes to the river." A minute later she said, "Turn here."

It was only a narrow trail but it was passable. The cactus thickened and stood stark and black.

"Careful," Josepha warned. "Don't drive too near the bank. It sometimes caves off into the river."

"River? You call that a river?" I laughed.

"Well, to us it is. A little water seems like a lot."

The narrow stream disappeared into the earth here and there only to struggle upward again and again. The crickets drummed ceaselessly. Moonlight was tangled in the little ripples.

I held her tight, needing to. "Josepha, what do you think of me? Really?"

"It would embarrass me to tell you."

"Don't be embarrassed. Tell me, please."

She cupped my face in her hands. "If you should leave me now, I would be terribly unhappy."

"Are you going to stay here all your life?" I asked.

"I am not sure of anything right now. I'll know later."

"Let's walk by the river." I took her hand, and we stood looking into the water. A coyote howled.

"Listen," I said. "I love to hear them howl."

"Did you know the Navahos believe the coyote will be the last living thing on earth?"

I thought a minute. "Maybe they're right."

"Old Meesa says they are dead lovers come back as coyotes, and they are howling for a love they never found."

"Meesa?"

"She's a witch. She can heal or hex almost anything."

"You believe that?"

"Yes. So would you if you knew her."

"Come here; we'll talk about witches later."

She came. I kissed her a long time. I pressed the length of her harder against me; then I released her, took her by the arm, and led her back to the pickup.

I took Big Boy's heavy sheepskin coat from the seat and spread it on the desert sand. She waited silently. I took her hand and pulled her down across the coat.

"Promise me," she whispered. "Promise me one thing. If you can never really love me, tell me now, please."

"But I do, I do."

The coyote howled again, lonely and distant. A desert owl hooted. The cactus stood black all around. And I pretended that this sweet flesh beneath me was Mona's.

Chapter Five

I heard later that Mona's husband, Les, had tried to whip Big Boy that night. They had been pulled apart but the damage was done. The talk had started. Big Boy had said nothing about it on the way back to Hi Lo that morning, but I heard it around town a couple of times that Les had sworn to get Big Boy one way or another.

I thought a lot about Mona, and I remembered that she always had a lot of men giving her attention, even when Les was around. He hadn't ever paid much mind—at least, not on the surface. As far as I knew, she had never done any actual cheating; she—just sort of flirted. Maybe it wasn't even that. It was more like an instinct she had for men. At least the men felt that way. No doubt a lot of them entertained other thoughts about her, but at a certain point a coldness came over her and a man felt like he would be violating all the rules if he went an inch further. She had been that way with me. But with Big Boy it was different. With him the fences were down, the gates were open.

What she had was that indefinable thing that makes a woman stand out regardless of her beauty or lack of it. There was something deep about her, something untapped. I couldn't help wondering what she saw in Big Boy, and resented him for it.

A week later I saw Big Boy in Lollypop's and we had a beer together. He said, "I'm quitting that money-starved Jim Ed Love and going to work on Hoover Young's little outfit."

"The pay isn't as good, is it?" I asked.

"No, but he's an old-time working cowboy. That's the only kind that's worth a damn anymore."

"Lollypop, give us another beer," I said.

I wanted to ask him about Mona but didn't. Instead he got to telling me some yarns about Horsethief Willy, one of his favorite people around Hi Lo, and I got started in on old Abrahm Frink, my closest neighbor and one of the institutions in the area. We both got to laughing, and I thought that if Abrahm never did anything else worthwhile in this world, at least he gave me and Big Boy a lot of laughs.

When I first moved into the Hi Lo country and bought my little outfit, Abrahm Frink's name came up often. Things like: "That's a good place you've got there, but you've picked yourself one hell of a neighbor." Or, "Nobody can get along with that old buzzard. No one ever has." Or, "He's been there forty years, and all he's ever done is fight and make trouble."

So it went. I was determined that I would be the one to break him down.

Abrahm had a little two-bit bean and corn farm out in the middle of a lot of grass-covered ranch land. He had been offered twice what his place was worth just to get rid of him, but I don't think any amount would have bought him out. He enjoyed trouble too much. He was one of the last homesteaders left. Nesters, the ranchers called them. His house was only a half-mile down the hill from my place. The reason for this intimacy in such an isolated country was the water—springs on each side of the fence between us. It was a long way in any direction to another ranch house.

When I first met him he was about seventy-five years old, and half blind. He wouldn't admit to being either. He wore a pair of two-dollar glasses from the dime store when he wanted to see something bad enough. He was tall, skinny, and straight as a string. He was so straight he canted back a little bit and looked stiff and brittle, as if he would break long before he would bend.

His hat must have come to the Hi Lo country with him. Instead of the brim curling up, it curled down. When he stood out in the rain, water ran off it as it would off a steep pitched roof.

A Dutchman, who had been his neighbor twenty years before, had hit him in the profile with a two by four. This left him with exactly one half-set of upper and lower teeth all on the same side. He chewed tobacco all the time on the side with the teeth in it, and it ran out the other side in chocolate streams that he wiped off first on the back of his hand and then on his shirttail. This absence of teeth created an easy exit for a mouthful of tobacco juice, and he could spit five yards to the left without turning his head.

His wife was almost as tall as he was, duck-footed, big-ankled, and so dumb she laughed at everything you said. You could tell her that an epidemic of cholera had struck Ragoon and a thousand people had fallen dead the first day, and she would look at you, then slap her thighs, and laugh till she trembled. One morning I said "hello" to her, and it took her ten minutes to pull herself together. Maybe it was the only way she could survive after all those years on a bean farm and all those kids. They had kids running everywhere, aged from two to twenty-two. I never did try to count them. I don't think Abrahm ever did either.

They had me over to supper one night, and when we finished trying to beat the kids to what little there was on the table I was too tired to talk but willing enough to listen. Abrahm cussed out everybody in the country. To hear him tell it, there wasn't a half-honest man within a week's ride. Every last citizen of the Hi Lo country was a no-good, double-dealing cheat. Liars, thieves, backstabbers, blackmailers and rustlers were tame names, and they had done it all to poor old Abrahm. The government had ruined little men like him and given all the money to bastards like Jim Ed Love.

"But by gorry I'll show 'em, the no-good bastards! Them bastards will never get my place," he said. Then he spit the fresh juice of a new chew right out on the floor, and growled, "You goddam kids get to hell out of here so us menfolks can talk."

It sounded like the Chinese army in retreat. The little devils were snickering and whispering back over their shoulders at me as if they knew a big secret I wasn't in on. Little girls, big girls, little boys, big boys, and middle-sized boys and girls . . . How in the world that man had time to raise a crop of beans I don't know, but if there had been a good demand for kids he would have the market cornered.

Abrahm didn't slow down. He covered everybody an inch thick in vituperation until he got to Big Boy Matson. Then he paused and said: "Now there's a feller with enough guts to amount to something. The best cowhand in the country, when he likes his boss. The trouble with him is he don't like anybody unless they're a no-account something or other or an old wornout cowboy. No, sir, come to think of it, he'll never amount to a damn. Besides, it don't make no difference anyhow; somebody'll kill him before he's thirty. You mark my words." I wonder if he ever remembers saying that.

It was my turn to order a beer. I did and for a little we sat without talking, staring out the window at the little graveyard on the hill above Hi Lo. To get my mind off that well-populated piece of real estate, I recalled the time I had borrowed a so-called work team from Abrahm.

I figured the one way I could get along with Abrahm was to find and exploit something we had in common. So I told him I was thinking about breaking out a little patch of corn so I could have some horse feed through the winter. This seemed to go down well with him. He even volunteered to lend me a team of work horses and a two-wheeled plow. I decided that all these people who cussed Abrahm were wrong. Lending his work team was one of the most generous things one man could do for another. The trouble was, only two of the four horses had ever been hooked up to a plow before. It took me three days to get the harness on and hook the traces to the singletrees and get out to the field. But it only took about three minutes for them to tear off at a forty-degree angle in a dead run and rip down two barbwire fences for a hundred yards on each side, bust up a plow, and nearly cut off one horse's leg. By the time I got through paying for the damage on the worthless plow and the even sorrier horse, I was $150 in the hole, not to mention my lost time and the condition of my fences.

Abrahm said: "I just cain't figger what you did wrong. Never had no trouble with them old gentle horses in my life."

I just let it go. After all, *I* was the one who was determined to get along with *him*.

He went on to tell me that his system with horses was to keep them fat and then if they didn't act right just butcher and eat them.

"Yeah," I said, gritting my teeth.

Then I tried something else. I bought three sacks of beans from him at top market prices. If I had eaten nothing but beans for twenty-five years, there would have been plenty left over except for one thing: they were half dirt and small gravel.

All I said about this was, "Abrahm, you didn't do too good a cleaning job on those beans."

"What's that?" he said, throwing his head back and damn near drowning me in tobacco juice. "I cain't understand that," he said: "I cleaned them beans personally. You must of spilled some and when you was cleaning them up got a little dirt in 'em."

Before I could answer he was telling me about the time he had a fight with Tom Hall over on the main drag of Hi Lo.

"Tom accused me of having gravel in my beans. I knew it

was a lie and I told him it was his crooked scales that was bothering his conscience. I whupped old Tom all over Hi Lo and never did take the chewing tobacco out of my mouth."

So I let that go too. I told Abrahm I was going into town, and wondered if he needed anything. Well, he needed two more plugs of tobacco and a sack of flour.

I bought what I wanted, got Abrahm's order, then went a step further: I bought a big sack of candy for his kids. Those kids ate that candy like a hog does slop. It made me feel kind-hearted, and I thought maybe this special attention to his kids would put me in good with him. It seemed to work all right, but not half as good as the time I brought back a pint especially for him. It was getting a little expensive, having this bag of fancy candy and that pint of whisky added to my bill each trip, but I figured it was worth it to win his friendship. However, I did have to cut down on my trips to town.

Every time I saw Abrahm it was, "When you goin' into town again?" And when I saw one of the kids it was, "You goin' into town today?"

One day I rushed into Hi Lo to get some distemper medicine for my roping horse. I was kind of worried because it looked as if it might turn into pneumonia. I took care of Abrahm's usual order but I forgot the dessert.

He said, "Where's the whisky?" all reared back, glaring at me through half-squinted eyes, and not even chewing on his tobacco, he was so outraged.

"I'm sorry," I said. "I was in a tearing hurry."

Then the kids were all over my pickup, yelling and wanting to know where in hell their candy was. It was just too much. I had tried everything I knew to keep them happy.

Next time I was in town I bought a pint of whisky and got a little high. I drank it all and went over to the mercantile and got Mitch Peabody to fill the bottle up with turpentine.

I drove up to Abrahm's, and here he came dog-trotting out and salivating freely. He removed his plug with one hand while he felt around in the seat with the other until he found the pint. Since he had missed out on my last trip, he was mighty anxious to make up for lost time. He just unscrewed the lid and turned it up. I guess he intended to swill all he could before I asked for a crack at it. It didn't last that long, though. After about the third gurgle he kind of paused, as if struck by a serious thought, and then everything reversed course and sort of choked him. He looked at the bottle and dropped it like it was a scorpion. Then he grabbed his throat and fell down and thrashed on the ground, making strange noises.

In the meantime the kids had advanced in force for their sack of candy. When they saw their old man bellowing and writhing about on the ground they came to a shuffling stop. Their eyes bugged more than usual.

I said: "I think a mad dog's bit your pa. You better get a stick and knock him on the head before he bites one of you."

They all broke for the house at the same time. I gave the pickup the gas and got out of there. Me and Abrahm didn't visit one another after that.

But he got his revenge.

He had the scrubbiest half-breed bull I ever saw. He wouldn't have made a good sire for a mongrel dog. Abrahm found a fence post well hidden by brush, jerked the staples out, and pulled the wires to the top. Then he started turning his bull in with my well-bred Hereford heifers. I kept running him out and he kept turning him back in.

I finally caught the bull up near the corrals one day, penned him up, then roped him. He bucked and bellowed for a while, but finally he pulled over next to the corral fence. I got down off my horse and slipped around behind him. I gathered up a good strong piece of barbwire, wrapped it around his testicles, and tied it to a corral pole. Then I opened the gate, cut my rope from the saddle horn, and he was loose. I didn't mind losing an almost new rope considering the good cause in which it went.

When that bull felt the slack come in the rope, he lowered his head and jumped. Before he hit the ground he was a steer. He wasn't much good as a breeding animal after that, but he would have made every race horse in the world look silly on a downhill run. He went out through my corral like a jet, and when he hit the fence separating me from Abrahm you could hear barbwire snapping like lighting striking tall trees. He tore right through the garden fences, flashed by the barn and streaked on out across the mesa, telling the whole world his troubles.

Kids were climbing on top of Abrahm's house, kids were

swarming up the windmill, and Abrahm was running around in the yard waving his arms and trying to find out what the hell was going on. I wished he'd had better eyesight. However, a few days later I was glad he didn't.

It was almost sundown, and a coyote howled in the draw between our respective places. I kept about three running wolfhounds around for just such purposes as this. They jumped up and took off down the draw. I ran, grabbed a thirty-thirty, and made a dash myself. By the time I got where I could see what was happening, I was too winded to shoot straight. The coyote had led my hounds up on a little rocky mesa just behind Abrahm's house. The rocks were alive with coyotes. They had deliberately set a trap for the hounds. The dogs were fighting hard, working their way back down the mesa with coyotes all over them. I emptied my gun but couldn't shoot too close for fear of hitting the dogs. Then I heard something snap over my head. It was Abrahm shooting. *Bang! Bang! Blooey!* One shot dug up some of that bean gravel about six feet to my right. I hit the ground.

Abrahm was yelling: "I'll get them goddam coyotes! I'll kill every damn one of 'em! Don't you worry none, Pete!"

I was sure glad when he ran out of shells. If he'd had enough ammunition he might have killed one of my best dogs.

I set my empty glass down on the bar, stood up and stretched. "Big Boy, I've got to get my lazy ass home and get some work done for a change," I said.

"Well, Pete, I'll drop by and see you in a few days."

As I drove out of town I was still thinking of Abrahm Frink. He gave Hi Lo something to laugh about, and when people felt low, cussing him out brought them a measure of relief. Not such a bad justification for a man's existence, at that.

Chapter Six

I untracked Old Baldy, and mounted. I felt again to be sure the chloroform was in my chaps pocket. A week before, I had roped a big dry cow and jerked her down, breaking off one horn. The old fool had turned back time after time while I was trying to change pastures with a few head.

I had spotted her at the spring below the house the day before. She carried her head twisted oddly to one side. It meant one thing—she had worms where the horn had broken. The chloroform would take care of them.

It was a fine day. The grass was up eight or ten inches and waving in the wind. The last few years had been good to the country—no lushly wet ones but no scorching dry ones either. It was a little too dry now, though, and if the rains didn't come soon it might get serious. However, there was enough grass to carry the country through the winter if it was a mild one. If it was rough . . . well, we'd see.

The price of cattle was high, and everyone in the country had land stocked to capacity, draining from it every pound of beef and every possible dollar.

The clouds were piled up halfway to the sun over the mountains to the north. Here and there webs of blue rain spurted down into the canyons, but these were only showers that fell in the highest places. I could see the prairie dogs standing, fat and full, barking and carefree. I sat with my foot up over the swells of the saddle awhile and watched them play about. Then an eagle swept down and scooped one up as the rest of them dived, chattering wildly, into their holes. Always somebody eager to ruin a good day, I thought.

I really didn't feel that way, though, as I moved out through my cattle. The mother cows lay about so full they had hard breathing. A few grazed as if bored to death by the long grass. The calves bucked and played like the prairie dogs, watching me now and then with big deerlike eyes and white, startled faces. I made a count out of habit from the days I worked on the big outfits and you found them when and where you could. It was unnecessary here on my little place, fenced tight as it was.

I felt my old cowhorse stiffen under me; his ears were forward as he turned his head. About a mile off I spotted a rider: Big Boy. I could tell by the way he sat his saddle and wore his big old-time Western hat with the high crown pinched in on each side. The brim was at least two inches wider than the modern flat-topped cowboy hat. Big Boy's boots were old-style too—high-heeled and sloped under to hold a stirrup. I had noticed the many things he carried over into the modern West from his father. He seemed to hang on to the old ways, deliberately ignoring the new methods of modern cow ranching. I knew he was headed over to a lease held by Hoover Young to the south of me. Big Boy could have made the round in three hours in a pickup. It would take him three days horseback. But he and Hoover both *believed* this way. That's why they got along so well together. Besides, Hoover had the best racing quarter-horses, as well as cow ponies, in the country.

Big Boy told me many times, especially when he was drinking heavy, "To hell with cars and trucks and airplanes and paved roads and everything else but good horses and a handsome woman."

I knew now the singular approach to women meant one thing: Mona. When I thought of her it was hard to wave a welcoming hand and smile as if I meant it.

He was riding Old Sorrel, and as they came closer their mutual admiration was obvious. I don't think another man alive could have handled that horse.

"Howdy," he said.

"Where you headed?"

"Over to Hoover's."

"Glad you came along. I've got a cow with worms in the head, and you're just the boy to help me doctor her."

"Good, good." He was looking my herd over. "By the Lord A'mighty, Pete," he said, throwing his arms up as he always did whenever he felt strongly about something, "there's going to be one hell of a drunk in Hi Lo this fall when you ship those fat calves. Lollypop won't be able to throw you out of the bar; he'll have to pour you out."

"What'll they weigh by the middle of October?" I asked.

"They're going to go mighty close to four hundred, average . . . maybe a little more," he said.

We had a smoke and then rode out together, looking for the soreheaded cow. It felt good to have someone to work with even for just a little while. I wondered why in the dried-up world I didn't go ahead and marry Josepha and get it over with. Then I thought of Mona, and it wasn't so hard to figure.

We saw the sick cow standing in the shade of a scrub cedar. "Head or heels?" I asked.

"Heels," he said. "You're a lot better on the head than I am."

I eased her out into a flat while I took the leather strings from around my rope. Then I looped the hondo over the horn and pulled it tight. I shook out a loop, and Old Baldy bunched up under me, ready to go. I leaned over, and he jumped straight out in a dead run. The cow had already sensed something and was trying to head for the hills. I cut her back, and Baldy put me right up to her. I whirled the rope and let it sail. The loop reached out and curled around the cow's head neat as whisky. I jerked the slack and turned off. When the cow hit the end of the rope, she swung around half off the ground. I started dragging her toward Big Boy. He came riding by in the opposite direction and dropped a slow loop under her hind feet. She stepped in it. He jerked it tight and spurred Old Sorrel. When the slack came out of both ropes the cow was stretched out helpless between us. Damn, it was a good feeling to work things so right with someone you liked and who really knew what he was doing. I got down and walked over to her.

I took a little wooden paddle out of my chaps pocket and scooped the worms out of the hole. Then I poured it full of chloroform. I smeared a little pine tar over the wound and we turned her loose. She ambled off, shaking her head. She might look silly with just one horn, but the worms wouldn't be bothering her anymore.

We did up our ropes and reined the horses for the house. I asked, "You gonna stay all night?"

"What in hell you think I rode by this way for?"

We turned our horses loose in the corral and pitched them a little hay. We walked up to the house, and I built a cedar fire in the old iron range and put the coffeepot on.

"It's getting a little dry," I said.

"Yeah, it would. Jim Ed Love has got a million tons of hay put up that somebody's going to pay for with pure blood if another drought comes."

"Just like the old tight bastard," I said.

The wood was popping in the stove and the coffee started to

boil. When the grounds settled a little, I poured us a big cup apiece. We rolled us a smoke and I said, "How's Mona?"— trying to make it come out easy and conversational.

"Real keen," he said, "except that goddam husband of hers won't hardly let her out of his sight."

"Can't say as I blame him," I said, "with a rooster like you around."

"He ought to take better care of her then," he said, and took his hat off and banged it on the table. "She's away too much woman for him. Hell, he ain't even a good cowboy, much less a man."

"He's going to shoot your ass off if he ever catches you alone with her, though."

"Well, Pete, it's like my old grandaddy said after he robbed the First National: 'They've got to catch you first.' Besides, she's worth the risk."

"Yeah, I reckon that's right," I said.

"Every damn thing that's any fun or at all worthwhile is a risk," he went on. "Now, you take bronc riding: it's like I told that brother of mine; I said, 'By the Lord A'mighty, feller, quit worrying about what's gonna happen to you when you hunker down a-straddle one of them broncs—think about what *you're goin'* to do to *him*.'"

"How is Little Boy?" I asked.

"Aw, I don't know, Pete, whether he'll ever make much of a hand or not. He thinks the old-time ways are stupid and that a man ought to punch cows in a Cadillac. Seems like he's always resented me telling him anything. These young punks know it all before they start."

I knew that according to his dad's will Big Boy had complete charge of the home place, but I knew too that he had turned it over to Little Boy, his mother, and a younger brother, Pat, so they could have all the income from it. He didn't feel he should spend the ranch money on the poker playing, drinking, and such-like he was used to.

The next morning at breakfast he said, "Been getting in any roping practice lately?"

"Naw, I've just been hanging around here the last few days, patching up fences and so on."

"Say," he said, "why don't you come into town Saturday afternoon and we'll try to get up a little poker game."

"I'll be there," I said.

"We'll have us a real session," he said, "one of the all-day all-night variety, that separates the school kids from the old-timers. Meet me over at the home place," he said, "and we'll go on from there."

I agreed, but after he'd gone I wondered why I wasn't looking forward to it.

Chapter Seven

I drove up to the Matson place on Saturday as arranged. Big Boy's mother met me at the door.

"Come in, Pete."

"How are you, Mrs. Matson?"

"All right I guess. Getting a little dry, though, isn't it?"

"Yeah, it is," I said, "but the cows are doing fine. Well, we had a lot of early rain."

"Good thing," she said.

Mrs. Matson was a real Western woman; her worn, strained expression showed that she had already faced all the storms of life. From now on in, she would accept everything as it came, the good and the bad, without resistance or complaint. The years had knotted her hands and stooped her shoulders, but a calm strength deep in her eyes made you feel she was indestructible, and would endure forever.

"Big Boy's shaving," she said. "He'll be out in a minute."

Then I noticed the old woman sitting over in the corner, Big Boy's grandmother. I said, "Hi there, youngun."

She stopped playing solitaire and looked surprised, as though it was beyond belief that anyone would speak to her. "Hi there yourself, young feller," she said, her wrinkled face collapsing in a toothless grin.

"What are you doing," I said, pointing to the cards, "practicing up to take the boys in Hi Lo at poker?"

"Well, son, I tell you. This solitaire isn't much of a game, but it's the only one an old woman like me can play by herself."

We talked on about cards awhile, and then she asked: "When are you and Big Boy going to find you a woman and get married? A man needs a woman around. He ain't right with himself without one."

"I agree with you on that, Ma, but me and Big Boy are so particular we keep looking around for something special."

"That's no way to be," she said. "Better to find someone you can plain live with. That's the hardest part of all."

Big Boy stepped out all slicked up with clean Levi's, a freshly ironed shirt, and about half a shine on his boots. He dusted off his old hat, lit a smoke, and listened to his grandmother lecture.

His mother had picked up a shirt she was patching for Little Boy. I turned to her and asked, "Where are the boys?"

"Pat went over to spend the night with the Miller kids, and Little Boy has gone to Hi Lo."

"What's he doing in town this early?" Big Boy asked.

"Playing pool, I reckon," she said. "He's just learned how and that's all he can think about."

"Well, you tell him when he gets home he better start fixing up a few fences around here and patching up the corrals; then he can go play pool. This place is falling apart."

His mother sat silent and went on sewing.

Whenever Big Boy first lighted a cigarette he always coughed for a few seconds. Maybe this was another throwback to his dad and his bullet-punctured lung.

Grandma Matson said, "Is that a cigarette cough, Big Boy?"

"No, mum," he said, "that's a whisky cough."

"Oh, all right then. Tobacco's a killer."

As we walked out and left the two women, it struck me that both their men had died violent deaths. I heard the old woman remark, "Just like his grandad, that boy—the spittin' image."

We pulled at our hats to keep the wind from taking them as we walked to the pickup.

"Look at that yard fence," Big Boy said. "The wires are hanging as loose as Marie's drawers." (Marie was an old whore in town that just about every young whelp in the Hi Lo country had lost his virginity to.) He went on about Little Boy: "That kid is running around with gnats in his face. I'm gonna have to cut the seat out of his britches so they'll change locations."

Well, it didn't take us long to get into Hi Lo, and what with the dry wind and all, there wasn't much time lost in picking out a soft spot on Lollypop's bar for our elbows.

We downed a couple, and Big Boy threw his arms up in the air and said, "Come on, Pete, let's see if the wind's blowing as hard on the other side of the street."

Now, you never know in Hi Lo which bar will get the play. Today Nick Barnes' Wild Cat Saloon was going to get it.

Nick served us as if in no hurry to get us drunk but still fast enough to get the job done. Melvin Ball, a cowboy from over on the C-Bars, was finishing up a story to Nick.

"Then," he said, "she came down the street in broad daylight, mind you, her stockings torn and her dress ragged and twisted, with a twenty-dollar bill in one hand and a can of beer in the other, hollering, 'All you lawmen stare at my tail, you low-down chickenshit bastards.' Them's the very words she used. How she gets by with that kind of talk I'll never know."

Though Nick was trying to act interested in this yarn, he had already heard everything in the world, and his one real interest was selling the stuff that made the stories so easily available.

Big Boy looked up at all the bottles stacked behind the bar and said, "Hell of a lot of bright ideas up there."

"Let's take on some," I said. "I feel a little bit ignorant today."

"I don't know why," he said. "You're the only one around here with a college education."

"One year," I said. "College isn't too homey a place for a worn-out cowboy. But the government paid us heroes good beer money to go."

"Well, Lord A'mighty, Pete, look what just blew into town!" It was old Delfino Mondragon from Sano.

"Hey, Delfino!" Big Boy yelled. Delfino was a big kinky-headed Mexican with a sharp, mean-looking black mustache and tiny BB-shot eyes. "Come have a drink," Big Boy called.

"Sure, Beeg Boy," Delfino said, hurrying in out of the wind.

"What'll it be?" Nick asked.

"Double chot with water on the edge," Delfino said. "Thanks,

Beeg Boy. Hi, Pete." He put a hand on each of our shoulders. "Gotta great troubles." He downed the double and wiped his mouth with his sleeve. "Gotta great sorry today. My brother-in-law, she die."

I said, "That's too bad, Delfino."

"Sure," he said. "You know that model-A Fort I'm selling him? She no pay. Gotta great sorry in my gizzard," he said, hitting himself in the chest.

Delfino was not one of Hi Lo's favorite people, but he was one of ours. The first time I had seen Delfino I was standing in this very same spot, and he had climbed out of a truck with one leg in a cast. He had walked into Nick's on crutches. He had four or five, maybe six or seven double shots; then he said, "I gotta business to do for the boss. Sure." He said, "Nick, I come back one, maybe three minutes. You wait." As if Nick would leave with so good a customer loose in town.

Then he turned and walked out of the bar without his crutches. A little later he came walking back in with a hundred-pound sack of feed under each arm. When Nick reminded him of his crutches, Delfino stopped, dropped the feed, rubbed his scarred-up head, and said, "I be damn." Then he went limping like a three-legged dog.

Now, Delfino was one of the best hands in the country. He was strong as a Percheron stallion, and could do anything from working cattle to building a fine rock house, but he had what some considered a failing: when he got drunk he would crawl into whatever means of conveyance he was driving at the time, put it in reverse, and then feed it the gas till it stopped. This generally meant that he had run over or into something.

He had paid enough in damages and fines to have bought and stocked a good cow ranch of his own. Take that broken leg, for instance. The day he'd smashed it was a memorable one to certain parties in the area.

Delfino had been on wine and marijuana (he raised his own smokes), and when he left town in the power wagon with a load of cube cottonseed cake for his boss's cattle he had done so in his usual manner. Reverse. He backed fast across the highway, knocked over a gas pump in front of a garage, and crashed into a telephone pole. Then he got it in forward gear and out of Hi Lo he went. By the time he got to the bridge that crosses the creek about three miles this side of Sano, half of the power wagon was running along in the barditch. The truck turned a flip, cake sacks sailed out through space, and Delfino landed facedown with his head half underwater in the creek.

A rancher happened along and saw the wreck. He loaded old Delfino into the back of his pickup for dead. When he pulled into Sano he was somewhat surprised to discover Delfino sitting up and rubbing his kinky head. The road to Sano was so rough it had performed a pretty good job of artificial respiration on old Delfino.

I took another pull at my drink and remembered the time I had gone over to Ojo to the schoolhouse to a Mexican dance with Delfino. I was the only gringo there, which was a damn good thing. These people won't bother a gringo if he's by himself and minds his own business. Two or three gringos gathered together, though, and the trouble starts. I thought for sure Delfino would get us both killed that night. He was on his favorite wine-and-marijuana kick again. He got to dancing so wildly that he was knocking everybody else off the floor. He didn't mean to be rude; it was just a natural exuberance he was expressing. Some of the boys asked him to quiet down. Delfino resented this implied slur on his character and invited one of them outside, beating him to the door. The man hesitated. So Delfino says, "Two then, come on, sure, two *cabrónes*."

Everybody stopped in his tracks. Delfino was getting more impatient.

"Three, then!" he screamed. "Come on out, you yellow-bellies!" Then he got desperate. "Okay, chickens, all of you come on, sure. All the chickens come. Every son-of-a-bitching chicken come and fight Delfino!"

He had challenged the entire house—and no takers. It wasn't that a few of them couldn't have whipped him. It just wasn't worth the risk. Besides, most of these folks liked him.

I went on dancing, feeling more and more uneasy as I heard him screaming away outside. So I excused myself, picked up a bottle, and went out. I handed him the booze and said: "It's all yours, Delfino. Drink up."

He muttered, "Chickens!" and tilted it up and swallowed about seven times. Then he fell over on his face. I got some help and we loaded him into the pickup. Afterward I went back to the dance and had a nice time.

Well, things began to perk up in the Wild Cat. We forgot all about the poker game and just concentrated on our drinking. Every once in a while a man would have to go to the outhouse. This dry and windy errand would make him just that much more anxious to get back inside, away from the buffeting of that unseen, penetrating force.

Ramón Sánchez, who worked on the railroad, stopped by for a drink.

I said, "Howdy, Ramón. What are you doing in town today?"

"My day off," he said. "I come to get some nails to fix the leaking roof at my casa."

"Well, have another drink before you go," I said. He had a half-dozen. Then he went out to get the nails. Soon I saw him stop across the street at Lollypop's with his sack of nails. I figured he was going to borrow a hammer.

Then in walked Jim Ed Love, pushing his big belly ahead of him, all decorated with a gold watch chain. The diamond ring was shining on his finger like an empty whisky bottle in the sun.

Steve Shaw, the moneylender, was with him. I felt Big Boy tense up. It hadn't been too long since he had quit Jim Ed and told him where to stick his several hundred thousand acres, provided he could first get Steve Shaw's nose out of the way.

"Howdy, boys," Jim Ed said, smiling like a man who had just swallowed a sackful of gold nuggets.

Everybody nodded except Big Boy. He just humped over the bar.

"Well, hello, Big Boy," Jim Ed said. "On another drunk?" He laughed, making it sound like a joke, but you could sense the knives behind it.

Big Boy straightened up, raised his drink and said, "Hell no, it's the same old drunk."

There was a small silence while everybody shuffled around for position. Nick ran over and shoved a flock of dimes in the jukebox, and that did the trick. We all resumed our drinking.

Delfino had quit double shots and was on his favorite drink—muscatel. He walked over to Jim Ed and said: "I heard you need a hand for work with cows. How much you pay?"

Jim Ed glanced at Big Boy before answering. "Whatever you think you're worth, Del."

Delfino snorted and rubbed the top of his corrugated head and said: "I won't work for *that*. I'll telling you. Give me *hunnert* dollar by the month and I'll eat myself alone. Or give me seventy-five by the month and you eat me. You treat me right, you go to hell and I go with you; otherwise piss on you I quit."

Everybody laughed. Even Big Boy grinned down into his drink.

Delfino said, "More wine. More whisky," and he winked broadly at Big Boy. Justice had been served among friends.

Ramón came back in with his sack of nails and a smile as wide as a cowboy's loop. He walked up to me and Big Boy saying: "Too late to fix the leaking casa. It ain't gonna rain for many a sunny day anyhow." He opened up his sack of nails and passed them around, making everybody take a few. He said: "This is to nail down our friendships. Whoopee, let'er rain!"

Big Boy liked this and he threw his arms up and yelled, "Sing a song, you sons of bitches."

Nick Barnes gasped for breath and said: "Drink up, drink up, dammit. You didn't come into this world to stay, you came to play."

Jim Ed Love and Steve Shaw got ready to leave. Jim Ed walked over to Big Boy and said, "Well, son, have a good time," and stuck out his hand.

Big Boy looked up and said softly: "I'm afraid to take it, Jim Ed. I never know when it's got a knife in it."

I think I was the only one who heard him. The rest were too busy jawing to each other. Jim Ed got very red, turned and tromped out. Big Boy had now made another permanent enemy—this time one with money and power.

Delfino came over and said, "Let's us go rob a bank, run all the s.o.b.'s out of town, burn all the church down, buy a saloon, invite everybody, drink free on the house, have one hell of a big party all the time."

"Wait just a minute till I load my pistol," Big Boy said.

I went over and picked out the wildest tunes I could find on the juke and did a little jig just to get warmed up.

Melvin Ball was talking women again. He was telling Delfino, "This Marie, she cornered me in front of the public outhouse and read me off the almanac."

Delfino said: "Melvin, you got a crazy in the head. All the time you give women money. Crap, me give maybe-so one dollar is plenty. She get the same satisfy as the mans. Crazy Melvin. Anyway, everybody in Hi Lo has made the love to thees woman Marie."

Melvin looked kind of sad and said, "Well, hell, Delfino, Hi Lo ain't such a big town."

Delfino shrugged and turned to Ramón. "Gotta great sorry, Ramón. My brother-in-law, he die. He no pay for model-A Fort. Before he die he says to me: 'All time I walk to town. She broke the university joint. Before that I had one blows out and ruin one tube and the spikeplugs no gotta blaze.' That brother-in-law one no-good dead man."

Things were getting better all the time. A couple of sheepmen from below Sano came in with their wives and a whole herd of grown-up daughters. Everybody commenced dancing, jumping straight up and down and yelling.

After a while Melvin started kidding Big Boy about Mona and what old Les was going to do to him. Big Boy listened for a minute without saying a word. Then Melvin poked him in the ribs and said slyly, "I can't say as I blame you for takin' the risk; she's got the best-lookin' tail in New Mexico."

Big Boy turned halfway around, slapped him on the side of the head, and knocked him across the room into the corner by the jukebox.

The dancing stopped for a minute while Melvin staggered up and said: "Go right on, folks, it ain't nothin'. I just slipped on this damn slick floor." Everybody went back to dancing and drinking again.

After a while I got to thinking how nice it would be if Ramón would go home and get his violin and guitar and we could have some live music.

I said, "Ramón, how about some music from you?"

"Sure," he said, "go get my wife and my fiddle while I drink my beer."

"What if she don't want to come, Ramón?" I asked.

"Love 'er up a little, Pete; she'll come."

Well, I drove out to Ramón's place at the edge of Hi Lo. The kids were all in bed. Julia, his wife, let me in. I explained the situation and I could see she was willing to come whether I loved her up or not. I looked her over; she wasn't bad. Thickening just a little around the middle, but pleasingly enough constructed otherwise. I put my arms around her and inhaled her powerful, cheap perfume.

I said, "Let's make some fudge before we go."

She laughed and led me over to the couch. I took hospitable old Ramón at his word.

When we got back to the Wild Cat, a couple of the boys were fighting out in the street. I didn't pay much attention to who it was; I just wanted to get inside out of the wind. I guess everyone else felt the same way because they fought without benefit of audience.

Big Boy was now right out in the middle of the floor, dancing all by himself and waving his arms. Since he had started with Mona he wouldn't even dance with another woman, much less try to bed down with one. I never could figure that. Nick turned off the jukebox, and Ramón and Julia started playing the guitar and fiddle. I want to tell you, the cowboys, sheepmen, railroad workers, loafers, and drunkards of Hi Lo were having themselves a hell of a time.

Big Boy picked up a chair and broke it all to pieces over the top of a table. Then he jumped up on it to dance. The table collapsed under his weight and piled up alongside the chair. He fell down flat on his back, kicking and hollering.

Some narrow-minded bartenders might object to this sort of thing, but not Nick. He kept only cheap furniture around anyway. Besides, he was making enough profit every ten minutes to pay for the damages.

It wasn't long afterward that Delfino decided he was a tiger and went to snarling and trying to climb the wall. Then he ran his head through a large plate-glass window. The blood running down in his eyes from a three-inch cut in his scalp made him stop and consider.

He said: "I make my mind now. I go home."

There was a terrific jam-up as everybody hit the door at the same time to get their cars and trucks out of the way before

Delfino got cranked up. Motors were throbbing, gears grinding, and vehicles scattering like chickens before a hawk.

Delfino wound her up, and backward he went. He took about six inches off one corner of the Double Duty Saloon and was gaining speed all the time until he crashed through Mitch Peabody's henhouse. Then he changed gears with a terrible clashing and drove back through the same big hole he'd just made and hit the highway. You could hear him gaining speed as he headed south for Sano. It would take him six months to pay the damages, and Hi Lo wouldn't see him till he had the money.

The party was just about over. Besides, after Delfino knocked the window out the wind whooshed in and made conversation uncomfortable.

Chapter Eight

That party in Hi Lo held me for a while. I stayed home and worked—patching fences, repairing the barns, and hanging a new gate on the corral. Water in the spring was getting a little low from the dry spell, so I hooked up my work team to a fresno and cleaned and deepened it. The spring in my upper pasture had already gone dry, but the cows were taking care of themselves all right.

I didn't go into Hi Lo for about three weeks. In fact, I didn't leave the ranch. I thought about going to see Josepha but kept putting it off.

When I did get into town I kept an eye out for Big Boy's pickup. Finally I spotted it parked outside the two-room weed-wrapped shack of Levi Gómez. Levi was about the best friend Big Boy and I had in Hi Lo. In fact, Big Boy had told him one time, "Levi, you're the best damned Mexican in Hi Lo. No, come to think of it, you're the best damn Mexican in the whole state!"

Levi was a lot of things. He was a quarter French, a quarter Apache and half Spanish. He was a small, shy man with features that looked as if a famous sculptor had carved them as a working model for some future masterpieces. It was fitting because Levi was a good wood carver himself. Cedar, that was his medium. He made all kinds of standing saints the Mexicans called *bultos*. They had a real elegance about them, a grace and a special kind of dignity. Looking at several of them in a row, a man was tempted to believe in religion. But even more than that, Levi was a poet. People in our country thought that anyone who wrote poetry had to be a little crazy. But I figured a man had as much right to write poetry in Hi Lo as he did in Paris, France. When Levi met a friend, unless drunk, he wouldn't speak to him in the usual manner such as Hello or Howdy or How are you doing? If he liked someone he didn't say a word.

I walked in and took a seat. He bustled around the tiny little room getting me a cup of coffee. He poured himself one and then said, "Did you hear about Big Boy?"

Something cold twitched at my stomach muscles. I said, "No, what happened?" I just knew Les Birk had shot his heart out.

"He's in jail," Levi said in his unaccented English.

"What for?"

"Well, it's like this, Pete," Levi said. "He's been thinking about Mona a lot lately and he came into town the other afternoon—day before yesterday to be exact. He came over and got me and said: 'Come on, Levi. We're going over to Lollypop's and throw an old-time drunk.' Then he started telling me about him and Mona and how he didn't have any-place to go with her. He was wanting to run off with her, Pete. Right then. He said he didn't care what anybody thought. They were right for each other, and no man was going to stop him unless they killed him. Then he changed his mind and said he would just have to wait. He'd make a killing at gambling or something, and then leave with her in style. 'By the Lord A'mighty, Levi,' he said, 'you don't move a queen into a Navaho hogan.' He seemed to feel better, and we got to joking and having a good time when Martin Felder came in."

I thought of hulking, thickheaded Martin. It had always seemed to me his head was all bone except for a tiny hollow space right in the middle about the size of a midget walnut. He had been raised by his mother and an "uncle." He was around thirty-five years old and had never left home. He had tried to make it with a few girls, but hardly any of them suited his ma. Nelda Spruce was the only one she had ever approved of, and Nelda had run off to Ragoon with Big Boy for a weekend. That had culled her out as far as Mother Felder was concerned. It hadn't made Big Boy any too popular with Martin, either.

I asked Levi, "Was there trouble over Nelda?"

"Well, no. Not exactly. Martin came in and started chasing one whisky down with another like his guts were on fire. Then he began riding Big Boy and saying things like 'Some men don't know what's theirs and what's somebody else's.' And pretty soon Big Boy told him that some people were so small that when they came up out of their hole in the ground all they could do was blink their eyes and brood about what some other feller had that they didn't. Well, Martin was feeling pretty sassy by then, and he said: 'Some men are thieves. Some steal chickens. Some steal gold. And some steal other men's wives.' It was pretty obvious what he meant. I knew what was coming and sure enough, a few seconds later Martin is picking himself up off the floor. He got up and, without looking at anybody, rushed out to his car. He jerked out a thirty-thirty and started back. I yelled at Big Boy, who stepped around beside the door, and when Martin came through he grabbed the gun and jerked it out of Martin's hands. Then he cocked the hammer and marched him back out to his car. He got in the back and made Martin get in the front and drive. He yelled out the window: 'Don't nobody try to follow us. We are just going to have us a little private talk.' Well, he made Martin drive over a cow trail way out in the brush to a clearing and told him to get out. By this time Martin was whining and begging him not to shoot. Big Boy stood him out there and aimed that rifle right between Martin's eyes. He fell to his knees. Then Big Boy told him he was going to throw the rifle away and they'd have it out fair and square. So he did. Then he jerked Martin up and knocked him down. Jerked him up again and knocked him down again. Up and down, up and down. He kept this up until he was winded. Then he kicked Martin in the belly and broke a few ribs. Then he told him that the next bastard that butted into his affairs was going to get worse than that. I don't think Martin figured it could be any worse." Levi shook his head, took a swallow of coffee, and continued:

"Well, Big Boy came on back to town, and Deputy Tom Ezzard asked him what had happened to Martin. He said, 'The last I saw of him he was kicking a poor old crippled gopher out of his hole and pulling the dirt in after him.'

"They hunted for Martin all that day and night, while me and Big Boy got drunk and he told me all this. Then early this morning they found Martin down by the highway where he had crawled, pretty well busted up and out of his head. We were asleep when Tom Ezzard came over and got Big Boy."

"What are they going to do with him?" I asked.

"I don't know," Levi said.

"Come on," I said.

We drove down by Lollypop's, and I bought a half-pint of whisky for the J.P., Eldon Howard. He was a fine old Kentucky gentleman with a thatch of white hair that looked like a bleached haystack. I visited with him a lot when I was in town, and always took him a half-pint made back in his own country. We were old friends.

I went in and handed him the bottle and said, "Howdy, Mister Howard."

"Well, hello, son," he said. "Nice to see you."

I didn't waste any time. I asked, "What are you going to do with Big Boy?"

He said: "Nothing, son, but let him get sobered up. Everybody knows, although some folks are trying to say different, that Martin threatened his life with a rifle."

"What if Martin dies?"

"He won't. I just called Ragoon Hospital. The doctor said he'd suffer a while but live."

"Good," I said. "When will you let Big Boy out?"

"This afternoon, son. Why don't you see he gets out of town for a while?"

"I will," I said.

Levi and I moseyed around town to see what the sentiment was. It turned out to be mixed but not too violent. We stopped over at Nick's and had a light beer. We were waiting for sundown to get Big Boy out of town.

Levi said: "You know, I don't blame Big Boy one bit. Mona's a hell of a woman, and her husband is just chicken-shit."

"If he isn't chickenshit," I said, "he sure as hell's got henhouse ways."

"Did you know he was the one that spurred Old Sorrel in the shoulders till he spoiled him, just because you bought him?" Levi asked.

"No!" I said. "Well, of course, he was foreman of the C-Bars, but I had never suspected it was him. Now I agree with you. Does Big Boy know?"

"Yes."

"Well, I'll be an egg-sucking giraffe. If Big Boy don't steal his woman, I'm going to myself." I nearly choked on the blurted words. I could feel the blood rise up around my ears.

"Nick," I said fast, "another beer."

Levi looked at me kind of strangely. I was sure glad he was my friend. I thought back to the first time I had seen Levi after I moved into the Hi Lo country.

He was playing pitch in Nick's place. I noticed how his hands shook and I could tell that he was a sensitive man. He overplayed and lost heavily. I bought a bottle and took him home. He was section foreman on the railroad then and lived in a section house about four miles east of town. I heard he was the best hand on that line. I found out that night that when he had left for the war his wife had a baby by his blood uncle. Then she divorced Levi while he was still in Italy. They had fixed the court in some way or other, and she not only got custody of the child but everything else he owned. When he came home he took up his old job. But then he asked for a transfer to Hi Lo from Trinidad, Colorado.

He started gambling after all this, and drinking steady. He quit his job on the railroad before they fired him. After that he started studying art from mail-order courses and carving these saints. Lately he had started writing poetry. He damn near starved to death. And then one day a man from Dallas, Texas, drove up and bought fourteen of those saints for $200 each and told him that whenever he needed some cash just to ship him another one.

Well, the only thing Levi changed about his way of living after all this good fortune was to build an indoor toilet so he could keep in out of the wind.

I used to stay with him quite a bit when I was in town. Not that I didn't like the Collins Hotel, but I just plain enjoyed looking at those saints.

Levi would hibernate and work a while; then he would slip over to the express station with one of his saints addressed to Dallas. He would figure about how long it would take the package to get there and how long it would be before the check arrived; then he would ease over to the post office to get it. Mitch Peabody would cash it and sell him about a month's supply of grub, and Levi would head for the saloons to get drunk.

One time I drove into town and was actually having a Coke when I looked across at Nick's and saw Levi come busting out the door. He damn near ran over a couple of tourists heading in for a drink. They jumped sideways and crawled back into their big-assed jukebox of a car. Levi was yelling and running in a huge circle and waving his arms like a man roping something. He jumped off his imaginary horse and ran down the rope, and you never saw any rodeo hand in your life wrap a calf as fast as he did.

He headed for our door. Well, he got the door open and then fell headlong into one of the bar stools. It spun around like a runaway wagon wheel. He got up and ricocheted down the line till he came to me.

"Howdy, Pete," he said. "I'm Pancho Villa but I'm out of bullets."

I don't know what he meant by that and doubt if he did. He was always saying something unfathomable. Then he ran down the street to Mitch Peabody's and came back with a whole bundle of brand-new brooms.

He told Nick: "Give us a drink, Nick. The drought's on and clouds have gone out of style."

He downed a shot and ran out to the curb, dragging the brooms behind him. The blood was running down his cheek where he had cut it on the bar stool. Then he raised those brooms above his head and smashed them down across the curb, all the while yelling, "Whooooo-eeeeee!" and pieces of brooms were flying out in the road and all up and down the sidewalk. Finally he was out of brooms. He looked around, dusted his hands, and came back into Nick's. Nobody had said a word—just stared.

He stalked up to the bar. "Another round, Nick. I want you bastards to know that I ain't sweeping nobody's floors but mine. Nobody's!"

I believed him.

I tried to get drunk with him, but it was one of those times when a man just doesn't feel like it. I was too tired or something. We hung around until about ten o'clock that night, and finally I said, "Levi, I'm going over to your house and lie down a while before I drive back out to the ranch."

It was about two or three o'clock when I heard a moaning noise. I'd fallen asleep. I got up and stumbled over to the door. There sat Levi up against the house, baying at the moon. I got him up, hauled him inside, and turned the light on. His face was just solid dried blood. He must have been there quite a while before I heard him. I led him into the little bathroom he was so proud of, wet a towel, and eased it down across his face. I heard this funny noise—*ping, ping*. At first I couldn't figure it out. I made another swipe. *Ping! Ping! Ping!* By God, it was gravel falling out of his face into the washbasin! Somebody had literally stomped his face in the gutter.

It was the next morning before he could tell me it was Julian Cisneros and a couple of his buddies who had done it. He was swelled up like a snake-bit cow, and I had to get the doctor to come patch him up. I asked him what caused the fight, but he couldn't rightly remember.

He went back to work extra hard after this, and the word spread everywhere around Hi Lo about that crazy wood-carving poet. It was just natural for Big Boy and me to like him.

A couple of months later I walked into his little house, and there was a carving of the Lord's Supper all completed on a big flat board. I could tell he was really proud of it. There was a preacher holding a revival meeting over at the church, and he heard about this object and came over and visited with Levi.

They had a can of beer together and a good talk. Levi was so pleased he just up and donated the carving to the church. That was a prime mistake.

This preacher told the congregation that he had a precious gift that would be unveiled the last night of the meeting, a surprise from one of their local citizens. The preacher looked a lot like young Abe Lincoln and I presume he was just as good a talker, because before old Levi knew what he was doing, he had agreed to come to the final sermon.

Well, he didn't have the guts to go by himself, so he talked me into coming along. I didn't have guts enough for both of us, so I talked Big Boy into coming, too. I guess he had more guts than anybody could expect because he came without asking anybody else.

Well, we didn't know what time it started, so we were the first ones there. We didn't look bad either, if I do say so myself. Levi had on a pin-stripe suit and was pretty slick-looking. I had on clean Levi's and a new blue shirt. Big Boy had gone all the way with a solid black suit, a white shirt, and a bright red necktie. A Hollywood scout would have been flapping a contract at a hundred paces.

None of this primping did us any good, however. The people started filing in, one, two, three at a time, but every single one of them sat on the other side of the church from us. I looked at the empty benches in our vicinity to see if they had been freshly painted or something, but they looked all right. I inspected all the windows on our side to see if maybe there was a draft blowing, but every window was shut tight as a bulldog's jaw. Maybe these were reserved seats, I thought. I looked up to see if maybe the roof was sagging and about to cave in, but it looked as solid as a snubbing post. I felt like raising my hand and asking the preacher if the Lord had some rule against people sitting on the left-hand side of the church. Finally it dawned on me—those people just didn't care to be associated with us.

I was worried about how poor old Levi felt. Big Boy told me later it had bothered him, too. The preacher had a funny look on his face, but he nodded to us and smiled. The rest of the congregation did no more than glance at us as they came in.

After they were seated they suffered a collective crick in their necks and their noses pointed straight ahead.

The preacher went through the singing and such-like and then he got up in the pulpit. He said, "Brethren," being very quiet in his manner, "I am going to unveil before your eyes a magnificent work of art. God has inspired this object of ultimate beauty and he has given this talent to one of your own."

I thought, Levi may be one of their own, but they sure aren't about to claim him.

"Behold!" the preacher said, sweeping the tablecloth from around the Lord's Supper. "Behold, and feast your eyes upon the inspiration of God!"

Well, I have heard a lot of quiet things in my life, such as a kid that's just pooted at the Sunday table, a dog that has just swallowed a prize laying hen, or Hi Lo, New Mexico, the only time the wind stopped blowing. But they were all an ear-shattering, head-pounding roar compared to the silence that followed.

The preacher waited. The only reactions were one woman clearing her throat and another dropping her hymnal. I want to make one thing clear: this preacher was a real man, and the Lord sure gave him the power to get mad. He whirled on that congregation like a trapped lion, and said, "Mr. Gómez, stand up, please."

Levi was about to faint, so Big Boy and I took an arm apiece and raised him up between us. He came about shoulder-high to both of us.

In those same measured tones the preacher said, "I want every living soul in this church to stand up who believes this work of art is a thing of beauty and appreciates Mr. Gómez's generous gesture with all his heart."

Hesitantly, one by one, they rose. All but about a dozen.

"Now, all of you standing, move to the back of the church and stand against the wall."

They went.

"Now, I want to say," he went on in that same controlled voice to those still sitting, "that what you have done is bad enough, but it's not half as bad as these *hypocrites*"—he shouted the word—"standing there who have lied to save their faces right here in God's house."

And then he jabbed one finger at them. It looked like a wagon tongue, and some of the people ducked sideways. He spoke in a voice that boomed the wrath of God.

"Each of you—standing, sitting, no matter—each of you has committed a sin against God and your fellow man this night. It is such a small, measly, weasely little sin that I hate to talk about it. In fact, I won't because you are all aware of it. But I tell you this, brethren, you should get down on your hands and knees and pray for forgiveness, and though it is not my place to judge or sentence I would delight in your having to crawl through cactus and blazing rocks on your hands and knees to ask this young man's forgiveness."

We never did know if they got down on their knees or not, for Levi broke out from between us, streaked up the aisle, and out the front door. We followed.

Well, Nick kept setting the beer up and even bought a round himself.

"It's about time," I said, "to go down and get Big Boy out of hock."

Levi said, "Just a minute, I've got a new poem I want you to see."

He got up and dogtrotted over to his shack. In a minute he was back, and nervous. When he handed me the paper it was wet from his palm. I unfolded it and read:

> The Savage cried to the Moon Mother,
>   "I am great."
> The moon glistening in the heavens did
>   not answer.
> Again, louder, the Savage shouted,
>   "I am great."
> The silence was even more profound.
> Then in fury the Savage waved
> Sinewy arms and clenched fists:
>   "Oh, Moon Mother, is it that
>   you do not hear? I am great."
> Silence.

Softly, arms drooping:

> "What am I, then, Moon Mother,
> shattered voice though I am,
> Moon Mother? Speak to me.
> With your glorious light enfold
> me."

Silence.

The Savage hurled himself upon the jagged
rocks and beat them with fists of blood.

> "Moon Mother, after these next
> words, I can no longer speak.
> Oh, Moon Mother, I know what
> I am. I am nothing."

A deep and solemn voice roared from the skies.
The vines trembled in the wind.
Dust boiled up around the Savage;
The dust encloaked the Savage.
And he heard:

> "You have at this moment, O Savage,
> achieved the ultimate of flesh and bone.
> You are great!"

I sat very still for a while; then I said, "Levi, I like it." I
didn't know if it was a good poem or not but I knew I liked it.

He took the poem, folded it and put it in his shirt pocket.
"Let's go get our friend out of jail," he said.

Chapter Nine

I could wait no longer. I had to know. Jealousy ate at me like
a starved dog tearing at the belly of a fresh-killed rabbit. It
drove me to think about Josepha.

I would have to be alone with her, and sober, and give us
both time and a fair shake. I was not sure it was possible to love

her, but I wanted to very much. Certainly I felt a tenderness toward her and I felt comfortable in her presence. But that seemed pretty puny compared to the way I felt about Mona. She enveloped my being the way a shuck enfolds an ear of corn.

Anyway, I picked up Josepha in her native village of Sano, New Mexico. We, in this country, felt that Sano was a southern outpost for Hi Lo. It was still no place for Josepha. Did she hang on there because of me? The thought was pleasing. At the same time it made me uneasy. I couldn't ask her and she would never tell.

She said, "If you like, we could drive to Papa's cabin. It is ten miles into the desert. He has kept it since before I was born. It is an old mining claim, and he will never stop believing in its potential value."

"Yes," I said, "we could be alone there."

"Yes, alone," she echoed, so softly I could hardly hear.

We said nothing more as the pickup bounced along. It was nice not to *have* to talk. So many things were right about Josepha.

Ahead, and somewhat below on a long rocky shelf, I could see the cabin. It was lonely in the afternoon sun. It gave the appearance of never having been lived in. If someone were to open the door and step out, it would seem like a resurrection. The vast empty land around the cabin emphasized the fragility of man-made things. The wind would whip the dust into it and over it, and particle by particle, splinter by splinter, it would disintegrate. But today and tonight it would play its role.

Off to the northwest was a ridge a mile and a half long. Scattered about its length were rocks, cactus, and occasional bunches of grass. Under the shade of one projecting rock lolled a coyote, his tongue hanging out like a dog's. He panted and waited for night to come. By the light of the moon he would seek out the desert mouse, the rabbit, or anything else to fill his belly. If he had no luck, the following day he would simply dine on grasshoppers, ants, or weeds—anything to exist and avoid man.

Half a mile down the mesa in a shallow hole I visualized a cottontail rabbit slumbering in the cool of the earth. He, too, waited for night to nibble and scratch in the sparse vegetation for survival. He would listen and watch carefully for the coyote, the eagle, and the owl, but he would never die of old age.

Forty yards from the rabbit I could see in my mind's eye a lizard squatted motionless by a sun-soaked boulder. There was absolutely no movement. He blended into the earth as if part of it. If a stray bug or insect happened by, his sticky tongue would dart out in a movement so fast it would seem never to have happened. The next day and the next will be the same for the lizard, the rabbit, and the coyote.

The eagle circling high in the sky, slowly, smoothly, awful-eyed, would see the gleam of the sun on our pickup as we wound toward the waiting cabin. He would watch only from curiosity; we were not his meat.

We drove on, up and down ridges and gullies, twisting right, then left. The sound of the motor must have been noted by a thousand living creatures of this cactus-pronged land.

We stopped. I took her hand to help her out; it was warm and small. It was a hand made for touching, for holding.

We walked down past the cabin with wordless understanding. The spring was so small I wondered how it had ever been discovered at all. But it gave life to a mighty expanse of country. The tracks of the wild things in the shallow mud of its banks told the story. We sat in a small patch of grass and studied the water. From what depths did it come? And if the drought moved in on us as it threatened to do, would it last or would it hide in the guts of the earth to wait for the clouds to come and lure it out again? Or would it be brave and deny this drying, brown death and stay to give itself with courage and generosity to the wild things it sustained?

The wind came taunting, but not as strong as usual, whipping a tiny wave across the shallow water and blowing the long thick hair from Josepha's shoulders.

I buried my head in the sweep of her neck and held her a long while, savoring her smell. I was at peace for a moment. Slowly I sensed her blood come to life. I kissed her lips, and she held me close to her, without strain, with complete ease. A warmth, a sweetness as of all the fruits of the earth wrapped us around in our completeness.

We lay upon the barren land. The sun dipped and the wind died. Coolness came.

We arose and walked slowly to the cabin. Josepha unlocked the door. She lighted the oil lamp and looked around the room. There was a fine layer of dust over everything. She walked to the bed and pulled the top cover away, then she blew out the light and lay down.

I stood motionless in the middle of the room. The twilight cast blue shafts of light across the room. Out through the tiny window I could see the cactus standing dark green, almost black. It was still as life and death. Then I heard the subtle rustle of a woman undressing.

I followed and lay beside her. It was as nearly perfect as anything I ever knew, or will know.

Later we talked quietly, at peace with each other and ourselves.

"Tell me you love me, Pete. Say it."

"I love you," I said, and hoped to God I did.

With loving hands she pulled my head against her breast and caressed my temples. "Oh, darling," she whispered.

"I know," I said, but did not know.

The coyote raised his head, bared his fangs, and howled straight up to the heavens. Josepha shivered, and pulled me tighter against her.

But I knew it wasn't enough. Not yet.

Chapter Ten

When Big Boy Matson was ten years old, his father had started lending him out to other ranches. By the time he was twelve he was able to do a man-sized job of cowpunching.

One of the men he worked with was Horsethief Willy. Big Boy was very fond of him. A lot of his ideas on life originated with this man who had once been accused of stealing a horse.

They didn't prove the charge, but he got a nickname for life. To get acquainted with men like Horsethief Willy, Delfino Mondragon, and Levi Gómez is to begin to understand the Hi Lo country.

Horsethief had taken a liking to Big Boy and had taught him all the old-time tricks of horsebreaking and training. He also started him riding bareback broncs at rodeos.

Now, Horsethief was a good bronc rider, but if it was asked around Hi Lo what else he could do, a clear answer would be hard to get. One thing was certain: he could mess up worse than any man I ever heard of.

For instance, there was the time he took on a fence-building job for the C-Bars, and they lost three square miles of land on the deal. In the beginning, Horsethief had sighted the fence line out in good shape, but then he started drinking some of Vince Moore's bootleg whisky, after which the fence veered off about forty-five degrees in the wrong direction. Not only that, but before his boss caught on, he had dug holes and strung wire and posts for over a mile out into the middle of a section of land belonging to the Federal government.

Now, Horsethief had every right in the world to know what Vince's bootleg whisky would do to a man. He had been working for Vince about a month. One day Vince took the family into town for his daughter's wedding. He told Horsethief that it was time to start feeding some silage to the cattle. The grass had been a little short, and it was getting well on into winter.

Vince had a lot of sour mash soaking in his whisky still in preparation for later bottling and dispensing to a select clientele around Hi Lo. Horsethief, who had never had any experience with stills, mistook this to be silage. Wanting to do the best job possible, he fed a good bit of it to Vince Moore's scrubby old cows. The hound dogs got into it, too.

By the time Vince got home from the wedding his place had gone completely to hell. One old hound had passed out with his head hanging off the porch upside down; another thought he had something treed on top of the windmill and was stumbling round and round the mill, barking and falling down. The third dog had gone to help Horsethief control the riotous cattle. They were all over the place, butting heads like a bunch of young bulls. And there wasn't a fence left standing anywhere. Horsethief had ridden down two good cow horses and was started on a third when Vince showed up.

He told Vince as soon as he saw him: "By God, I quit! Every goddam critter on this place has gone plumb crazy!"

When Vince found out what had happened, it was unnecessary for Horsethief to submit his resignation.

But the thing that really made it hard for Horsethief to get work with cattle ranchers in the area was the deal he pulled on Jim Ed Love. Jim Ed would have killed Horsethief if he thought he could have gotten away with it. He had gone on a buying trip to purchase some high-powered bull calves to raise for breeding purposes. He went through the Northwestern states, as well as Canada, buying them up. Whenever he had a full carload he had them shipped back down to Hi Lo. On the way back home he stopped over in Denver for a few days to big-shot around, and got to telling some of his cattlemen friends about these bulls. The whole bunch of them loaded up and came out to the ranch to see these amazingly virile creatures.

Horsethief proudly escorted them out to the pasture, saying: "By God, Jim Ed, that was the best-looking bunch of calves I ever worked on. We didn't lost but two out of the whole bunch. Usually when a man castrates calves that age he has about a ten percent loss."

There sat Jim Ed and his *compadres* looking at the highest-priced pasture of steer calves in the entire world. Needless to say, Horsethief's employment was terminated on the spot. Everyone in the country laughed and kidded Jim Ed until he wouldn't come to Hi Lo for over a month.

Horsethief knew one thing and one thing only—horses. No one ever had a complaint about a horse he had broken. A horse would gentle down or Horsethief would kill him. And he would rein well or get his neck broken. And he would handle a rope or wish he had. But it was never more evident that Horsethief's talents did not extend to mechanical objects than when he bought a 1935 Chevy. The bowlegged, potbellied, badger-faced little devil looked as out of place working on this car as a brush-popping cowboy in an English tearoom. But work on it he did, just about day and night. Of course, it must be understood that Horsethief was on the road a lot, going from one job to another. Almost any time you traveled anywhere around Hi Lo, there would be Horsethief, pushing his car on foot or pulling it out of a ditch with a team of horses or changing a blowout or scraping the points.

When the radiator started leaking he just poured a sack of Bull Durham tobacco in it. When that didn't quite do the job, he told Big Boy, "Well, by God, I threw a double handful of horseshit in there and it ain't leaked a drop since. A man ought to start sackin' that stuff up and sellin' it for stopleak."

He didn't tell Big Boy that he had a hell of a time keeping the motor from catching on fire. The horse manure had stopped up everything else, too.

He had a neighbor clean the radiator out for him. In fact, everyone in the country at one time or another had worked on his car. How it kept on running was a mystery. It finally got to the point where the motor was so worn he had to carry a five-gallon can of used oil just to get into Hi Lo from his little two-by-four outfit about nine miles from town. Not only that, but he hauled a barrel full of water, too. What with jumping in and out, pouring water and oil in the car, it would take Horsethief most of the day to get to town. It's no wonder he would sometimes stay over two or three days, resting up for the return trip.

He finally had to give up and trade the Chevy in for a newer job. He crawled under the 1939 model one day to work on the clutch, and a snake bit him on the leg. By the time he got into town the car was smoking, the rods had beat their way out into the fresh mountain air, and Horsethief's leg was swollen and black.

They had to cut his leg off at the knee. It stopped his rodeoing for a while, but a year later the word got around that Horsethief was going to rope a bull from a Shetland pony in the next show. Everyone came.

Big Boy and I had bucked off that day and were sitting over on the fence when the announcer said: "Folks, we have a special act by one-time bronc rider Horsethief Willy. He is goin' to rope a thousand-pound bull fresh in off the range, wild as a tiger and . . . he's going to do it on a little old Shetland pony that don't weigh a third as much. Not only that, folks, but

Horsethief says he is goin' to jerk this bull down and get off and tie him up."

All of us had been used to seeing Horsethief around so long that we didn't even think about that wooden leg of his. Anyway, he didn't limp much. There were lots of people at the show from out of town and a number of tourists that had no knowledge of Horsethief at all.

"Look at that little potbellied son of a bitch," said Big Boy. "He's actually going to do it."

He rode out on the Shetland, and even his short legs nearly dragged the ground. He reined into the roping box and shook out a big loop. The chute hand turned the bull out. The bull took off in a high lope, and Horsethief spurred like hell after him. The bull didn't run very fast, not being too impressed by the opposition, but when he got to the other end of the arena Horsethief was still coming at full speed. The bull turned back, snorted, and tore off one way while the Shetland and Horsethief went the other. The loop went out and caught that big bull deep around the shoulders. Every cowboy there winced, knowing what a terrible stack-up there was going to be when the slack came out of that rope.

Well, I fell right off the fence at what I saw. The audience went wild. There were screams and shouts and eight tourists fainted. That bull just kept on going—and there on the end of the rope was Horsethief's leg banging along on the ground.

Horsethief had fallen off the Shetland and was yowling out there in the arena, taking on like a man in a tub full of scorpions. Then he stopped moaning and began to laugh.

Pretty soon everybody caught on. The ornery outfit had tied the rope to his leg on purpose and had even gone so far as to paint it blood red. He had only wrapped the rope around the horn of the saddle so it would be sure to pull loose. The applause was tremendous. It was a fine way to retire from the rodeo game.

Big Boy went to town and bought a whole case of whisky and brought it back to the show, and all of us cowboys saluted our most recently retired associate about two dozen times around.

Horsethief gave Hi Lo something to love in spite of itself.

Chapter Eleven

When Nick Barnes told us they had found Steve Shaw dead, Big Boy threw his arms up in the air and yelled, "By the Lord A'mighty, fellers, let's celebrate."

Nick said, "That ain't no way to talk about the dead."

"The world's a whole lot better off without him, Nick, and just because he's dead don't change what kind of a son of a bitch he was."

I had to agree.

Two nights before, I had sat in a poker game when Big Boy laid the wood to Steve Shaw. Usually Jim Ed played when Steve did, but Jim Ed had quit coming around Nick's when Big Boy was there.

Steve always had so much money in his pocket that he high-played and bluffed the working cowboys right out of the game. But Big Boy drew the hand in low ball he had waited a lifetime for: the best in the deck, an ace to a five. Steve Shaw had a six high, and I was stuck and went broke on an eight. Everybody else fell out. Steve was eyeing that money like it was a naked virgin queen. Finally Big Boy shoved a hundred more in the pot, and Steve hesitated.

Big Boy said, "Hell, I've got you beat. I've got a five high."

Steve glared at him and then squinted at his cards.

"Come on, Steve, decorate the mahogany so you can see this little beauty of a hand."

The sweat stood out on Steve's yellow, thin face, and his murky blue eyes glinted. He was scared. I would have mortgaged my ranch with a hand like his.

"You really got it, Big Boy?"

"You pay to look, Steve. Too bad Jim Ed ain't here to do your thinking for you."

That did it. Breathing hard, Steve covered the bet. I guess the pot was $400 or $500.

Big Boy didn't wait. He pitched the cards over to Steve face down and raked in the money. With trembling hands Steve picked up the cards and looked. He dropped them, stood up, and left without a word. He walked half a block down the street to the apartment he kept in Hi Lo and fell dead just as he closed the door behind him. It was two days before they found the body.

"Just think," Big Boy said. "I killed the son of a bitch without even firing a shot. Give everybody a drink on that."

It would be hard to understand his callousness unless you knew Steve Shaw. Jim Ed furnished the money and Steve did the lending. He was a walking bank. Between them they had taken over several small ranches and herds of cattle, as well as innumerable cars, trucks, and houses. Steve had a knack of getting notes signed by property owners who couldn't make payments.

He had lots of other talents along similar lines. For instance, if a valuable piece of land was involved Steve would make the borrower sign a deed and put it in escrow. If he failed to make payment, there was no long-drawn-out foreclosure battle. Steve merely went to the county courthouse, filed the deed, picked up the sheriff, and took over the land.

There was a dirt road—a short cut from one major highway to another—that passed right by the front gate of Steve Shaw's place. One day a sign appeared on the turnoff saying simply: *Save miles. Take the dirt road to Highway 286.* A lot of people did.

The road was rough and rocky most of the way, but the really bad spot was close to Steve's place. There was always a mudhole there regardless of the weather. Two cars out of three got bogged down to the axle. It was only natural then that they should seek help at Steve's place, his outfit being the only one in sight. And people often thought how lucky they were to have this misfortune with help so near at hand.

Steve was always willing. He had a good strong team of work horses ready at all times to perform a neighborly deed. Not only that, he had his hip boots which he'd obligingly pull on and then tromp right out in the mud like a Christian savior.

The team would leap into the traces with a 2,500-pound thrust, and out would come the car.

Naturally the poor boobs would say: "You don't know how we appreciate this. How much do we owe you?"

They didn't have to wait long for an answer.

"Five dollars."

This could add up fast when several cars a day would get stuck. Of course, Steve didn't get too much sleep during dry spells what with being up most of the night hauling barrel after barrel of water down to the mudhole to keep it ripe.

He and Jim Ed Love made a good team. Jim Ed was going to be awfully upset about Steve dying on him. Now he'd have to come out in the open and collect his money himself. It put a lot of little people in the country in better shape to negotiate.

Jim Ed was the biggest rancher around. His daddy had started putting the land together by selling groceries on credit to Mexican ranchers and sheepmen during the big drought of the early thirties. He had used the same methods Steve and Jim Ed were to use later. The Love ranch grew and expanded into a domain. Then the old man died, and Jim Ed inherited it all, along with the old man's touch for acquiring other people's property for nearly nothing. A lot of big ranches were built this way.

Jim Ed once sold a man five hundred head of steers, but only about a hundred head was actually involved in the deal. It was agreed that Jim Ed would gather the cattle and the greenhorn take the count; then the cattle would be turned loose for a few days while the buyers got ready to move them out. Jim Ed drove this one hundred head around the same hill five times. There was a lot of hell raised later, but Jim Ed said he couldn't help it if the man wasn't cowboy enough to gather his stock. This happened back in the twenties under his dear old daddy's direction.

And then the story went around that he had a formula that would constipate cattle for several days. People said that Jim Ed put heavier cattle on the scales than anybody in the country—until they took a crap a day or so later.

I had a feeling Jim Ed was going to make his move against Big Boy soon, and I was right. One way or another he was going to get Big Boy. And it wouldn't be out in the street with his fists, either.

Levi Gómez tipped me off.

"Pete, Les Birk has moved over to Jim Ed Love's and gone to work there."

"Well, I'll be damned," I said. "So that's it. The son of a bitch. I knew he was after Big Boy, but I never dreamed he'd do it that way."

"Les was in here about a week after they buried Steve," Levi said. "He was drunk and bragging about how he was working for the biggest outfit around and how he was going to be *paid* to get Big Boy. And he went on to say there wasn't a thing anybody could do about it. Jim Ed has enough money and pull to fix anything."

"Does Big Boy know about this yet?"

"I don't think so."

"Well, we'd better tell him, Levi."

"Yeah, we better."

I could see Jim Ed scheming and putting ideas in Les's head, and I had a feeling he was going to go to work on Mona. If she didn't take to his throat-cutting, he would start using his money on her. He was zeroing in on Big Boy where it would hurt the most. Somebody was going to get hurt. Hurt bad. The worst thing was that there was no telling when it might happen. It could be a month from now, or a year—or maybe tomorrow.

Chapter Twelve

I was glad to hear that Big Boy had gone over to Ragoon with some of Hoover Young's quarter-horses to wind up the racing season. I went over to see him. I found him back at the stables shooting craps with a bunch of horse trainers and a little Negro, one of the damnedest-looking men I ever saw in my life.

Big Boy said, "Pete this here is Whingo."

"Whingo what?" I said.

Whingo looked up and pushed a big blue hat (that's right, blue) back and grinned all the way around under his ears, showing a row of teeth that looked like an adjustable gold watchband.

"Just plain Whingo, man. That's all."

It was obvious that Big Boy was winning heavily. He sure had a string of luck going lately with the dice and cards. I got to thinking he might put enough together to run away with Mona yet. As much as I wanted to, it was impossible to wish him that much luck.

Something jumped out into the middle of the game, grabbed the pot, and went squalling off through the paddock. One of the horse trainers jumped up and said, "Whingo, I'm going to kill that goddam monkey!"

"You goin' to have to kill Whingo first!" he said, standing up about five feet tall. He had on yellow boots to go with the blue hat, and his britches were stuffed down into the tops.

Big Boy said, "Calm down. I'll make up the pot."

They all squatted back down, and Big Boy shot for his point. He made it and said, "You want in, Pete?"

"No, I don't believe so, Big Boy. I don't want to change your luck."

It took Big Boy about thirty more minutes to clean them out. The horse trainer left cussing the monkey as if it were solely responsible for his bad fortune.

Whingo reached down into the top of those yellow boots and pulled out a half pint of whisky. We all took a swallow.

"Where'd you get that monkey?" I asked.

"Alabama, boy, that's where. Stole him from a carnival."

Big Boy said: "Whingo ain't goin' to go hungry with that monkey around. Last week he stole three wristwatches, a diamond ring, and a box of sanitary napkins."

"Best goddam thief in seven states," Whingo laughed.

"What kind of monkey is he?" I asked.

"Hell, I don't know. He cain't talk. But I'll tell you one thing. Don't never get one of them red-ass monkeys." Whingo took another pull at the bottle, and his teeth nearly blinded me. "My old woman got one of them goddam things. Mean? And bite? Look here." He pulled up his sleeve. "Just bit the ligament in half right through my wrist. Had to quit jockeying on account of him. Every once in a while I goes home to see the old lady. Have to take a club with me. Seems like all that old woman does is sit on the porch rocking back and forth, back and forth, just waitin' for me to come home. Then that monkey jumps up and here he comes. It don't do no good to climb a tree with a red-ass monkey after you. All you can do is bust him over the head with a board and run for the house. I ain't sure I'm ever goin' back home again till I know for sure that monkey is dead. Man, I'm tellin' you, don't never get you a red-ass monkey."

"I'm sure glad you warned me, Whingo," Big Boy said. "A feller was trying to sell me a real keen one the other day. But I told him a friend of mine had advised against it."

"You was sure usin' your head there, Big Boy," Whingo said, emptying the half-pint. "That's another thing a man's got to watch is them red-ass monkey peddlers."

We all decided we would let the race horses take care of themselves for a while, and drive up to Ragoon. Whingo snapped a chain through the monkey's collar and took him along.

"What do you call that monkey?" I asked.

"Just plain Monkey Shine, man, that's all. Shine for short."

"Howdy, Shine," I said. Shine didn't pay any attention to me but looked snake-eyed down the road.

The first and last place we went before going to jail was the Chief Bar. It was a nice, cozy place and the bartender didn't seem to mind the monkey. In fact, he saw right away that the monkey was drawing lots of attention and attracting trade.

We'd been there guzzling for about an hour when a good-looking redheaded woman came over and began petting Shine. She had left a table of four men and two other women. They were watching us with looks on their faces that didn't leave any doubt about their feelings. But what started things popping was the necklace this gal wore that dropped down inside her low-cut blouse. All of a sudden Shine plunged an arm down in there to the elbow and jerked off the necklace. She screamed and ran backward with both hands on her breasts. I suppose it looked like somebody had gotten a little fresh.

Up out of their chairs came the four men and after us they sailed. The fight was on. One of them hit Big Boy on the side of the head, and when it didn't jar him much the man took after me. I was so busy with him for a while, and there was so much noise, that I can't remember it all any too clearly.

I finally got my boy off balance, knocked him down over by the jukebox, and whammed him a few in the face. He was peaceable then, so I looked to see if Big Boy needed any help. He had knocked one under a table and had another by the throat, choking the brains out of his ears. But Number Four was jumping up and down behind him, hitting him in the back of the head. I picked up a big glass ash tray and fitted him with a glass cap. This relieved the pressure some on Big Boy, and he started for the door with the other one.

In the meantime the women were screaming and raising hell and Whingo was chasing the monkey up and down the bar. Shine had knocked at least half the bottles off the back bar, and whisky was running out under the bar, making it a bit slippery underfoot. Whingo was skidding all over the place. This gave Shine a great advantage.

Big Boy had evidently disposed of his opponent, because he came back inside by himself, looking for his hat. About the time the others were getting up and Big Boy was pulling his hat down over his head, the bartender ran around from behind the bar screaming and waving a baseball bat at Shine. He chased him over to the front window. Shine was hanging from the curtains, chattering to beat hell and waving the girl's necklace. The bartender swung at him with the bat and knocked out the plate-glass window. Whingo ran over and started biting the bartender on the leg with his gold teeth. The monkey jumped on top of the bartender's head. The bartender dropped the bat and started to cry. Big Boy found a half-empty bottle of whisky, took a good slug, then handed it to me. "Come on," he yelled to everybody, "it's on the house. We're going to have to buy this place anyway."

They all came over and joined us. Big Boy said: "Let's be friends. A good fight now and then among friends just cements their loyalty."

Well, we found out a whole lot more about cement in a few minutes. The bartender had broken loose and gone out for the cops. Whingo ran around behind the bar and shoved a couple of pints down each boot top. We should have left that place while the bartender was gone, but all that free whisky kind of went to our heads.

Sure enough, here they came, filling up the door with their big dark blue uniforms and brass buttons.

The bartender pointed to me, Big Boy, and Whingo, who now had his monkey under control. "They're the ones! They started it!" he shouted.

Well, they hauled us around the block to the jail and threw us in the drunk tank. It was just after sundown, and we didn't have much company. They were puzzled for a while about what to do with the monkey, but finally one of them said, "Hell, they all look alike to me," and they threw Shine in with us.

It wasn't too bad, though that cement floor was kind of hard to sit on. But those bottles Whingo served up like magic out of his yellow boots kind of cushioned the shock.

We drank it down, and the next thing I knew I heard singing. At first I thought I'd died and gone to heaven: it was "Nearer My God to Thee." And then a lot of voices burst into "The Saints Come Marching In." I decided they were having my funeral and burying me half alive. I sat up, and what I saw made me want to lie right back down again. Big Boy was standing out in front of about fifteen drunks. He had them all lined up in rows and was leading a community sing.

Then Whingo, with Shine perched on his shoulder, got up and said, "Deacon Matson has done lifted your spirits to the glorious heavens with his singin', and now I am goin' to say a prayer for all you lost sinners." Whereupon he took off his hat and bowed his head. Before I thought I had bowed mine too.

"Dear Lord, forgive these poor stupid sinners for they know not what they do. They are weak and you have put the temptation of these heavenly spirits before them. Yeah, Lord." His voice, booming out of his tiny body, was like the sound of a cannon coming from a single-shot twenty-two pistol. "With all the troubles of your world upon their backs, can these poor unhappy souls be expected to do otherwise? Now, I ask you, Lord, can they? I hear you, Lord, and I know you are knowin' and forgivin' and I know you are goin' to help us get out of here and live in the light of righteousness. That's right, Lord, I hear you talkin'. I'll take care of that part, Lord. I'll deliver it myself. Praise the Lord and Jesus wept, Moses crept, and Peter come a-crawlin'. Amen." Whingo solemnly held his blue hat out in front of him, top down. "Get the other edge of the brim, Deacon Matson," he said. "The Lord done told me these poor lost souls is goin' to redeem themselves by contributin' to our cause."

"Get it up," Big Boy said, throwing one mighty arm in the air like Samson himself. The drunks muttered resentfully but shoved their hands in their pockets just the same. The bottom of the hat filled.

One wine-soaked old man said, "I had eight dollars and a pocket knife."

"Never mind the pocket knife," said Big Boy.

"But now I can't find it," he whined. "It's been stole. It's all gone, I swear it!"

Big Boy stuffed all the money he'd collected in his pocket and said, "Now, I'm going to try and make a deal with the judge for all you folks."

I went over to the door and yelled out through the slot, "Guard! Guard!"

In a minute somebody yelled back: "The judge won't be here till nine o'clock in the morning. Shut up or you'll spend a week in here."

It was a long night.

Nine o'clock finally came, and they took our bunch down first.

Big Boy paid our fines; then he pitched all the rest out on the judge's desk and said, "Judge, please be light on those poor sinners and apply this to their cost through the courtesy of Deacon Whingo."

The judge blinked unhappily, spotted Shine, and said, "Get the hell out of here!"

We went.

They don't feed you in the drunk tank at the Ragoon jail, so we hunted up a place to eat. We got settled down in a restaurant, and Whingo pulled out eight wrinkled one dollar bills and a pocket knife. He patted Shine on the head and said:

"This old monkey ain't never asleep, boys. The breakfast is on me." So we all ordered ham and eggs and hot black coffee.

Big Boy said to me: "Whingo is the only absolutely happy man I've ever known. He don't give a damn for nothing. He ain't afraid of being a fool or being wrong. That's what troubles the world, Pete. Everybody is afraid of being wrong." Then, as though there were a connection, he said, "Mona's coming in today. Ain't that keen?" and grinned.

I was hungry, but somehow I couldn't eat. Big Boy ate his and mine too.

Chapter Thirteen

Big Boy had neglected the ponies the afternoon before, so he had to ask me to take care of Mona. I got her a room at the same motel I was in. Then I went to meet her at the bus depot. She had driven in, but she'd written Big Boy to meet her there.

"Hello, Mona," I said.

"Hello, Pete, it's nice to see you."

I could hear the question in her voice, so I said: "Big Boy's stuck with Hoover's race horses. Said to tell you he was sorry and would be in later. Where's your car?"

"Just down the street."

"Would you like some lunch before you go to your room?"

"That would be nice," she said. She smiled and took my arm in her strong, soft hand.

I don't know how I felt walking along the street with her and I didn't come to myself until after we had ordered lunch. Then I got up nerve enough to look at her. I think I hid how I felt, but she was used to men staring at her anyway and probably didn't give it much notice. She had a way of gazing off into the distance until you asked her something; then she looked straight at you. And then she made you feel there was no one else in the world, and whatever you said was of the greatest importance. There was no half-attention from this woman. There couldn't be; she was so much woman that everything she did had to be whole. I thought it was pretty clear where this left me. She had had a rough time, kicking around from one cow camp to another with Les, living just any way that came along and on a salary that barely paid the minimum bills. That was the strange part. The black dress looked Neiman-Marcus, and she could just as well have been the mistress of the richest man in Texas.

"Have you seen Levi?" she asked, knowing Big Boy's fondness for him. "I've been dying to get in and see his carvings, but Les throws a fit every time I mention it."

"That's too bad," I said. "The boy's awfully good."

"I know. Big Boy told me. Oh," she said, "in case you're worried, I suppose I should tell you. . . . I'm in Colorado visiting my folks."

I didn't say anything. I hated being part of this rendezvous, and I wished with artery-tearing misery that it was me she'd come to see instead.

The waitress brought the baked salmon, and we ate for a while without talking. Then she said, "How is he, Pete?"

"Well, he's fairly happy with the race horses. You know any kind of horse will do as long as he's a good one, and if he's not, Big Boy will make him one. Look what he did with Old Sorrel."

"I know," she said, blushing slightly.

"I'm sorry," I said.

"There's no need to be sorry about the truth," she said. "Well, anyway, I'd like to see Big Boy with a little outfit of his own—no cattle, just horses to train and trade."

"I think he'd be happy if he just had you," I said.

She smiled, and put her hand over mine. "Thank you, Pete, that's awfully nice, coming from his best friend." She thought a minute and added, "You know, he will never be completely happy."

"No one is," I said.

"I know, but we all try to find some kind of middle ground."

"Not Big Boy," I said. "You know what he told me? He said nobody can be satisfied because everything in this goddam world is in competition with everything else. Every blade of grass is in competition with the one next to it and every coyote is trying to swallow more meat than the next one and every vulture is hoping to find more dead, and every stream is trying to beat the next to the ocean, and every goddam cactus is straining to plunge its roots deeper into the desert than the rest."

"A cowboy philosopher," she said without sarcasm.

"Yeah," I said. "But Big Boy wasn't complaining, you know. He doesn't mind these things. As far as he's concerned, they are the end of truth."

"That's one of the reasons I love him, Pete," she said. "But his main trouble is he's a man out of his time. He craves the old days, when a man's word had to be his bond because there was no paper around to sign. And he wants his justice to be personal. Pete, if things were like they were in his father's and his grandfather's time, Big Boy would already have shot half the people in this country. If a car breaks down, Big Boy is helpless, but let a horse outlaw and he's in complete control."

"The horsemen will come into their own again," I said. "He likes rodeo," I added, "but not enough to make a career out of it. He just gets a big bang out of it, that's all."

"I know," she said. Suddenly she was saying things I didn't want to hear. "Pete, I love him more than anything in the world. I'm ready to go with him"—she paused a moment—"anywhere, anytime. But he keeps telling me he wants to make a stake so he can take care of me right. Hell," she said, "taking care of me right is just his being with me, that's all. That's all it takes. No more, no less. We fit, Pete. There are no fancy words for it. We just mesh, that's all."

The truth of it hurt; but I was committed now, so I said: "Don't you see you're the only thing in this world besides raising hell and having fun that he can tie to the old ways? You're as special as a lone pioneer woman among a thousand rough-ass miners, trappers, scouts, and cowboys." I didn't know where these thoughts came from and I didn't know if it was right to say them, but it seemed to settle something in her mind.

We finished, and she followed me in her car out to the motel. I unlocked the Spanish-style room and pulled the curtains back. Then I got her bags out of the car, and she walked in ahead of me. The light through the window struck her hair and a soft copper glow shone out of its depths and I could see the swell of her body against her dress. I could smell the subtle aroma that was hers alone. Like a fingerprint, it was hers among one billion women. It was Mona.

I watched her move about the room in her sure flowing way, and I stared at the bed. For a moment I imagined being there with her, holding her with all the tenderness there could ever be. She caught my look, and I damn near dissolved. And then I did something I would never have believed myself capable of—but I just couldn't help it, not even if Big Boy had been pounding on the door: I grabbed her and pulled her mouth to mine. Without control I dragged her down across the bed by the back of her hair, crying. I kissed her face, her neck, and the top of her breast, feeling the world melt from under me.

Then her voice came to me, soft and calm. "Please, Pete, stop." Her hands were pushing me away easily and without violence. I stood up trembling, my chest heaving, feeling the tingling of blood spreading under the skin of my face.

She sat up on the bed and straightened her dress, perfectly composed.

"Hand me my purse, please," she said.

I picked it up from the floor where I must have knocked it. She took a tissue and a small mirror and wiped her mouth clean where I had mashed and spread her lipstick. Then she started combing her hair.

I stood rooted, trying to speak. Finally I said, "Are you going to tell Big Boy?"

She looked at me a moment consideringly. "No," she said quietly.

Suddenly my legs gave out under me and I sat down in the nearest chair. Well, she had saved a killing for now. Then it hit me in the solar plexus, where I believe a man's conscience hides: *Just how dirty could one man be to another? Take a man's trust, his friendship, and try to steal his woman—a woman he was risking his life for.* But wasn't I willing to do the same? No matter, I could not explain it away or escape the guilt I felt.

It was almost impossible, but I turned and walked to the

door. I said, "I'll tell Big Boy you're all set. He'll be in after a while."

"Thanks, Pete," she said, "thanks for everything." And she added, "Come and have dinner with us."

Big Boy finished working the horses about four, went in the tack room and washed, shaved, and put on clean clothes. We rode to the motel together. I got out and went to my room.

About an hour later Big Boy knocked and yelled, "Come on, Pete, we're going upstairs."

"No," I said, "you all go ahead."

"Hell no," he said, "come on along."

"Well, just a minute, let me wash up." I had tried to sleep and forget they were alone together in the motel room. I didn't want to go with them, but I didn't want to be alone either.

We went to this eating place with a cocktail lounge adjoining and had a few drinks before dinner. I drank about two to their one and was feeling somewhat better by the time we ordered steaks. Big Boy was smiling and talking. He polished off his steak before I got started. Mona ate slowly, relishing every bite, looking up at Big Boy with shining eyes. Big Boy was telling stories about people he liked and some he didn't like so well.

"Were you there, Pete, the time old Delfino was drunk and everybody was singing? He yelled out, 'Sing, you birds, before I tear up your nest.'"

"Yeah," I said, "that crazy Delfino."

"Did he ever tell you about his brother-in-law? He's always cussing his brother-in-law about something. He told me: 'I didn't see his face but I sure hear his tracks. He hits me right smack in the top side of my face when my back she turned.'"

We had another drink to wash down the steak, and Big Boy went on talking like he'd just learned how and liked it.

"I was sitting in the Hi Lo Café the other day with Levi. We were eating a steak about the size of this one, and in came Jim Ed Love with one of his hired hands. Old Levi looked up and said: 'Well, there comes old rich-ass Jim Ed with his hired hand. Watch him, Big Boy, he'll order *one* bowl of chili and *two* spoons.'"

After a while we went into the lounge. All the men stared hard at Mona. I didn't blame them. It was strange, her ability to capture the eyes and stop the breath of men and yet convey a very clear message: "Hands Off." I could never remember a man pawing her or getting fresh with her in public. I guess it was because she gave the impression when she was with a man she was sure enough with him.

I went over and played the jukebox, and Big Boy and Mona danced. I tried not to watch but I suppose I wanted to torture myself. They *meshed*, as Mona said. Two big fine people together. I, their closest friend, should have been happy for them. Well, I was trying.

They danced a long time. Then I saw Big Boy nod his head toward me, and I knew he had told Mona to dance with me. It was truly the last thing I wanted to do, but it would have looked wrong if I hadn't.

I tried not to hold her up against me, but she just naturally danced in the bend of a man. The sweat came in my palms and my lungs ached, as though I had just finished tying a five-hundred-pound calf. And that smell of hers just went right through my clothes and the pores of my skin to the marrow of my bones.

Afterward I had three more fast drinks. Then I felt sick. I told them I was going down the street and look up an old girl-friend. I caught a cab and went back to my room. Later on in the night Big Boy and Mona returned to theirs.

As dawns go, it was a pretty dawn.

Chapter Fourteen

Shipping time at Hi Lo. The cowboys rode in the hills and canyons, yelling, sweating, whipping coiled ropes and gloved hands against their chaps. Little bunches of scattered red stock were gathered into bigger bunches and then into the final count, according to the size and wealth of the ranch. The calves and the yearling steers were cut from the rest and loaded on trucks or trailed into Hi Lo, where stock buyers from Illinois,

Kansas, Texas, and all over, waited to weigh and load them onto cattle cars. They would be moved into feed lots and fattened further on rich, ripe grain. Then from the slaughterhouse they would go to cities all over America and from there to millions of dinner tables.

Hi Lo was busy as an ants' nest during this period. The stores were full of ranchers paying bills, some owed for eleven or twelve months, and buying things they had wanted for their families all year. The women planned excursions to Ragoon for a little fancy shopping.

The smell of money was everywhere. The bars overflowed, and the poker and pitch tables ran over with greenbacks. New cars and pickups were seen up and down the streets. Notes were paid at the bank and credit was reestablished. It was a time of plenty, and had been for some years now. The people were lulled into a sense of security. But they had overstocked their land to take advantage of these high prices. There had been plenty of grass to produce fat cattle this fall, but winter was just ahead. I must admit that this was as true of me as of anybody else. Even though the high wind had started cutting around the edges of the thinning grass, I bought only one stack of hay and said, "Hell, I'm ready for winter." I didn't think. For soon I would wish with all my heart that I had bought three stacks and let the new pickup and all the whisky and poker go by the board.

But now the beef flowed in like ants to pure honey, and the money flowed with it. Out in the hills and canyons, though, the mother cows responsible for all this meat and gold were beginning to find the grass stems harder and harder to find. It wasn't bad yet; they had their summer's fat to carry them awhile, but all the same they were having to work at grazing long before deep winter set in.

The men driving the cattle pulled at the brims of their hats, and their eyes watered constantly from the dust of the herds. The wind rose gradually, slackened, and rose again. It pushed across the rolling hills, bending the brown grass, and shoved on into the mountains, whipping the limbs of the timber and oak brush. Things were beginning to give before this dry, remorseless wind. It blew day and night, tearing at the very plant life it had once seeded. But who now worried about the wind? With a pocket full of money and our bills paid, we could afford to stay in out of it most of the time.

I helped Big Boy and Hoover gather their stock. We rode into the brush and rocks for three days, wearing down ten head of horses. The cows were fat and wild after being free all summer, and we lost a little weight chousing them into bunches big enough to move down on the flats and the gathering pasture.

Big Boy was happy. He was working with horses and cows and men who knew their jobs. The jeeps, the airplanes, and the laws of the land faded away. We came into headquarters at night, tired to the guts and half starved, and when we had filled our bellies we collapsed in our bunks.

At daybreak we were down in the corrals, skylighting our horses so we could catch them for a long day ahead. That's the way they had worked in the old days and that's the way Big Boy and Hoover wanted it now. When we had made the final gather and cut the calves from the mother cows, we trailed them all the way into Hi Lo swallowing dust, with Hoover losing $2,000 worth of meat from the drive. But that was the way they wanted to do it.

Jim Ed Love owned a small lot just a mile and a half from town. He had big stock trucks to unload his thousands of head there, and then it was only a short drive to the stockyards. For days a steady stream of cattle moved this short distance to the loading pens so that everyone could see the wealth and power of Jim Ed Love. It cost him a little in weight, this short move, but he figured he made it up in prestige. And though I hated to admit it, he was right.

Les Birk, Mona's husband, was there along with many other hands. But nobody thought to fight during this time. They were all too busy to hate. But later on, when the work was done, things would return to normal.

Chapter Fifteen

Big Boy dropped by to see me. "Listen, Pete," he said, "you know those hillbilly Adkins boys?"

"Clem and Ake," I said.

"Yeah. Well, they want us to pick up Uncle Bob and his hounds and come out to hunt. They say the coons are thick as clabber milk down there."

"How far do they live below Hoover's place?"

"About eleven, twelve miles, I guess," he said.

"Well, come on," I said. "By the time we get Uncle Bob and the dogs loaded and make the drive, it'll be time to hunt."

We took off in his pickup toward town and Uncle Bob's place. I knew Big Boy had gone to a hell of a lot of trouble to get permission for Uncle Bob to hunt there, but he felt a kinship thicker than blood with the old hunter.

Uncle Bob lived about three miles out of Hi Lo with a crippled wife and uncountable hound dogs. He had a prize fighter's face with a half-smoked cigar stuck in it at all times. He wore bib overalls and always smelled of coyote, coon, bobcat, or skunk. Sometimes I thought the odors of all these animals and many more had so impregnated his skin that the creatures of the wild just accepted him as one of their own. I know that when setting one of his steel traps he took very little precaution to stand upwind, and he always seemed to have exceptionally good luck anyway. He had running dogs for coyotes, and trail dogs for coons, bear, and mountain lion, but it was the coyote that fascinated him most.

Big Boy admired him a lot. In a way they were very much alike. If there was ever another man out of his time, it was Uncle Bob. He was as wild and free as the varmints he hunted. If he had lived in Kit Carson's day he would have been a wealthy and famous hunter. He had a lot of trouble, too, around

Hi Lo, like Big Boy. His brand of trouble was a little different, though.

Uncle Bob just couldn't help pinching women. His battered face testified to the times this had been violently resented. No matter; whenever the wind blew a female skirt or a quick movement pulled it tight, Uncle Bob just had to pinch. He had a thumb and forefinger that bit in like forceps, and the only way to stop him would be to cut his arm off. Most folks kind of indulged his weakness nowadays since he was getting so much older. In the past Uncle Bob had suffered innumerable beatings, but on the other hand he had administered just as many in defense of his dogs. A man that could stomp hell out of him for pinching a woman would find the process reversed if he insulted one of Uncle Bob's dogs.

Uncle Bob hunted every way but in an airplane. He hunted on foot, on horseback, and in his old Plymouth coupe. He kept a trap line every winter and made a little spending money this way, but it was the hunting, loose and free, that got his blood to moving. His main satisfaction in life was to be in on the kill. I damn near got killed once myself trying to keep up with him.

We were hunting horseback along a malpais-rimmed, oak-brush-filled canyon. Uncle Bob was riding his old bay mare, Mandy. The old mare had been on so many hunts that when the dogs took off she just naturally followed. It didn't make any difference where they went, Mandy went too.

I had a pair of staghounds with a rope strung through rings on their collars. I held both loose ends in my right hand. If we jumped a coyote, all I had to do was drop one end and the rope would pull out of the ring without ever checking their speed.

Uncle Bob held two greyhounds the same way. We worked slowly along the rim, looking for a place to get down. We decided one of us should be riding in the bottom. Just then a coyote jumped up and took off right along the rim of the canyon. The hounds leaped out with the horses pounding after them.

As the dogs closed the gap, I could see the coyote's tail start switching from side to side, which meant he was putting out all he had. This coyote knew it, too, for just as one grey made a lunge for him he dived off the side of the canyon.

Well, I didn't want to hurl myself off that pile of boulders and brush, but when old Mandy and Uncle Bob flew by, my little brown horse followed.

It was not a very pleasant ride. All I could see was Mandy's tail thrashing up and down and gaining a length at a time. Just when I began to think the brown would keep his feet after all, we hit a spot not far from the bottom that was almost clear of rocks, and that's where we rolled over and over at full speed. The momentum and force of the rolling horse sent me sailing through space. I hit the ground all right, but it was several moments later before I came to. I sat up and felt around and couldn't believe I had no broken bones.

I staggered up and stepped off the distance from me to the horse. To this day I have never told anyone how far it was. No one would believe me.

I got the brown up and we took a few deep breaths together. Then I got back on and rode to the top of the canyon. By that time Uncle Bob and the hounds were out of sight. About a quarter mile to the west I heard him yell. I spurred out on top of a little knoll. I could see the hounds, heads down and tails in the air, chewing the guts out of Mr. Coyote. Uncle Bob and Mandy were standing there, heads down and leaning forward, almost equally interested spectators.

An hour later, out in the flats, we jumped a pack of three. The dogs started to split up, then moved back together and singled out one lone coyote. He was moving off south, hunting a brushy canyon to hide in.

When we first spotted them they were about two hundred yards behind us. Now they moved out in long rhythmic strides that melted the ground from under them. The coyote strained, his small feet hammering the ground and his fur streaming back in the wind. His very life was running out with each yard, each foot, each inch he lost.

As they moved up beside him, one dog reached over and grabbed him in the neck. Down and over they went in a cloud of dust. The other three dogs sailed on past, then, braking and whirling, they leaped in on the coyote, biting down in the breast, the throat, and the entrails, clamping down and tearing his breath away.

We came to a fence—a four-wire fence. I rode down it looking for a gate. No gate. But Uncle Bob and Mandy? Hell, they cleared that wire with a foot to spare, and there they were, in on the kill again.

A man took his life in his hands when he rode behind the hounds of Uncle Bob of Hi Lo, but when he sped along with him in a wheeled conveyance it was a thousand times worse. Many mornings he would arrive at my house at daybreak, puffing, trying to keep his cigar lit and blowing a lot of frost instead, his ancient car steaming and rattling and ready to go.

He invariably knew where a coyote was hiding. Off we'd roar, me shivering in the winter air and him without gloves and his car window rolled down—for better vision—never feeling the cold at all. He chewed his dead cigar and stared hard and intently at every rise and fall, every bush, as he drove forward to that wonderful moment: the kill. When he spotted one he would floorboard the old Plymouth. It would lurch ahead, gaining speed until he figured he was close enough; then he would stomp on the brakes and yell at me, "Turn 'em loose!"

Out I would fall, and I do mean fall, for the old Plymouth would still be moving. Scrambling to my feet I'd jerk the trunk door open, and the bawling, wildly excited hounds would bail out, leaping high until they spotted the coyote. The next problem was to get back in the car before Uncle Bob took off after them.

Away we'd go, bursting into bear-grass clumps, dodging gullies and boulders, careening around dangerous slopes, and Uncle Bob swallowing his cigar an inch at a time. The old car usually held together, and we would be on the spot when the dogs nailed their victim. It was a very great sin in Uncle Bob's book, as well as a total disgrace and humiliation for his dogs, if he wasn't there for the climax.

We were not always lucky. There was one time we jumped an old white coyote that Uncle Bob had been running for three years. I turned the first team of dogs loose and jumped back in the coupe. For a while it looked as though they'd get him easy, but the coyote twisted through a mass of sharp rocks and lamed the hounds. We turned the next team loose. They didn't have a chance. The coyote circled a haystack and raced right through the middle of a herd of grazing cows and lost the dogs completely. But that didn't stop Uncle Bob.

We cut the coyote out into open country about three miles

from a canyon. It slowed us down, having to look for gates and places to cross cut-bank arroyos, but we kept the quarry in sight.

Uncle Bob yelled, "Get the gun ready!"

I levered a shell into the thirty-thirty, rolled my window down and started shooting. I fired one whole round and never hit within ten yards of the coyote. The coupe was bucking and pitching and weaving like a rodeo bronc as we flew across the prairie.

Then Uncle Bob got excited. "He's slowin'," he said. "Look! He ain't goin' to last much longer!"

It was true. The coyote had run with all his strength for many miles. We were gaining on him fast. I loaded up again. Then this fence loomed up. There was a narrow horseback gate right in the corner. Uncle Bob sized up the problem, knowing, as I did, that a deep canyon lay about a half-mile past the gate.

He gave the coupe all it had and yelled for me to jump out and open the gate. We could both see that the coupe couldn't go through at this narrow angle, though. However, I flung open the door and fell out rolling and firing one accidental shot up in the air. I finally got astraddle the whirling world and ran for the gate. At the same time I emptied my gun at the coyote, almost hitting him once.

Uncle Bob was gaining speed as he made a big circle. I got the gate open about a second before he hit it. He didn't quite clear the posts on either side, but his speed carried him through. One post snapped in two and the other cringed over like it was scared. There was a hell of a screeching of metal, but now Uncle Bob was in the clear and still going. The coyote was getting very close to the canyon, and for a minute I thought Uncle Bob might drive right on in after him. But he whirled the coupe to the side, slammed on the brakes, and tumbled out. The coyote was so tired it was barely moving. Uncle Bob grabbed a rock and took after him afoot. Just as the coyote got to the canyon's edge, Uncle Bob hurled the rock and hit the coyote right in the hind end. All it did was help him off into the safety of the canyon.

Uncle Bob fell down with the force of the throw and skidded a few feet on his face, doing nothing to improve his already much-scarred features. I saw him get up and run over to the edge of the canyon, raise his arm and shake his fist. He was cursing like a madman. But there was a note of respect in his voice, too.

The coupe was in bad shape. The fenders and running boards were crumpled and both door handles were scraped off slick as a politician's tongue. It's a lucky thing the windows had been rolled down. We crawled in and sadly backtracked, looking for our exhausted hounds.

We both had a severe case of coyote fever about this time. I bought an old army surplus weapons carrier to hunt in. It didn't have any kind of top on it, and the front windshield was missing.

Big Boy told us he had spotted a pack of coyotes just a little piece off the road this side of Hoover Young's place. He went along with us that day. We found them before we expected to.

We turned the dogs loose and took out after them at top speed. We had about a three-quarter-mile downhill run before we hit a snag between two hills. I didn't know it, but the radiator was low on water and by the time we'd run half a mile the motor was getting pretty hot. Then I saw smoke coming out of the glove compartment. I yelled at Uncle Bob to reach in and take out the box of shotgun shells before they went off.

He was standing, holding on to the steel posts where the windshield had once been, yelling: "They're goin' to get him! They're goin' to get him! Hurry! Hurry!"

I was hurrying as fast as I could, but at the same time I didn't want those shotgun shells exploding. Big Boy was bouncing around in the back, barely able to stay inside. I kept feeding the gas to the weapons carrier, at the same time leaning over and trying to get hold of the shotgun shells. I needn't have worried, though, because just then we hit a gully about three feet wide and three feet deep and the vehicle did a flip and the trip was over. Since there was no top to hold us in, all three of us were propelled toward the sky like a trio of big-assed birds.

It took a while to assess the damage. Uncle Bob had broken his right collarbone and added a few new wrinkles and contusions to his face. My left forearm was smashed. Big Boy had three cracked ribs and a busted ankle.

The weapons carrier wasn't fit for anything but scrap. But the worst of it was that we'd missed getting in on the kill.

Uncle Bob performed a service for the country that few people realized: he kept the varmints in balance. In other sections of the country the ranchers were always appealing to the state Game Department to come thin them out. As usual they did the job too well. With the coyotes gone, the rabbits and the gophers took over and did even more damage. Then the ranchers prayed for the return of the coyote. But none of this was true in the Hi Lo country—Uncle Bob's country. He kept things on an even keel, killing just enough coyotes and no more.

We used to take field glasses and sit up on a mesa all day searching the flats for coyotes. Once we watched one chasing a jack rabbit. He ran along behind perhaps thirty or forty yards, never crowding the rabbit. It looked intentional and of course it was. He chased the rabbit in a big circle, and all of a sudden another coyote raised up out of the grass and took up the chase. He circled the rabbit the way a good cutting horse works a yearling heifer. On the third trip around, the first coyote came back and nailed the rabbit in one easy burst of speed. The feast was on. Uncle Bob was breathless with admiration. "Never saw nothin' like it," he said. "Goddam things spell each other's names."

Another time we watched a coyote lie in a clump of bear grass a short distance from the hole of a prairie dog. He stayed there motionless for almost two hours. Finally the prairie dog ventured far enough from his retreat for the coyote to strike. With a swift, deadly surge he scooped the prairie dog up in his jaws and trotted off to a secluded canyon for his lunch.

One good winter Uncle Bob skinned out over a hundred coyotes. He gutted every one of them to see what they had been eating. "Only one of them had a domestic animal, a chicken it was, in its stomach. The rest were full of mice, rabbits, gophers, grasshoppers, and strings of cowhide from an already dead cow. Just like I told you boys a thousand times: you can't mess with nature. Them coyotes do more good than harm." Then he paused a minute to consider before he went on: "Of course, there can be too damn many of them, but your old Uncle Bob will take care of that."

It was curious. Here was a man who dedicated his life to the destruction of the very thing he so strongly defended and admired. But to Uncle Bob it didn't seem strange at all—just natural.

Big Boy and I drove up in front of Uncle Bob's rundown place, and dogs were barking from every post. Uncle Bob shuffled out pulling at the front of his bib overalls with one hand and yanking his hat down firmer on his head with the other. The dry wind tugged at us as we stepped out of the pickup.

"Howdy boys," he said.

We told him we intended to go coon hunting at the Adkinses', provided he would be kind enough to come along and bring his dogs.

His eyes lit up and he said, "Let me tell the old lady we're goin' and I'll get the dogs."

He loaded five flop-eared hounds of all colors in the back of our pickup and we took off north toward the Adkins place.

Uncle Bob said: "How in the hell did you ever get an invite to hunt down there? I've been tryin' to for fifteen years. Them are the wildest, orneriest hermits in all New Mexico."

Big Boy said: "I helped them gather a five-year-old steer out of the brush on Old Sorrel the other day, and they asked me if they could do me any favors. I remembered seeing all those coon tracks and it made me think of you, Uncle Bob."

Uncle Bob was so touched he couldn't say a word—just chewed harder on his cigar.

Usually we didn't drink on a hunt of any kind, but this time Big Boy had brought a pint along for the the Adkins boys. "They're real shy, and I thought this might limber them up a little," he explained.

Big Boy had arranged to meet them at the crossroads at eight o'clock. The November moon was up cold and sparkly as a two-carat diamond. We got there a little early, so Uncle Bob let the dogs out of the back and tied them to the pickup. All of a sudden they started fidgeting and growling. We looked up, and there stood two horse-faced men with rifles. You could tell it was an effort, but they smiled.

We all said hello, and Big Boy handed them the whisky.

"I'm Clem," said one. "This here is my brother Ake." They

both took about a third of the bottle each, and it must have pushed the talking button.

"Ake shore is mean," said Clem proudly. "Want me to tell ya 'bout the time he went to the big city with a sackful of coon hides?"

"Sure."

"Well," Clem went on, "Ake had this sackful of prime coon hides he'd trapped fer to sell. Them was the days when they was worth lots of money. Ake had got hisself a sale and was strolling down one of them concrete trails that runs all over them big towns, when a feller stepped out of a alley with a black rag tied around his face and a big black gun in one hand. This here feller says to Ake, 'Stick 'em up.' Ake asks him, 'Stick what up?' This feller told him to put his hands high in the air like he was pickin' apples." Clem started laughing, and for a minute I thought the story was over. But it wasn't. "Then this feller tells Ake to give him his money, and if he didn't he'd blow his brains out. Ake worked mighty hard, one whole winter in fact, to make that ketch of coons, and he didn't much take to this feller robbin' him. So he says to him: 'It's in my left-hand pocket. Go ahead and get it.' While the feller was goin' after the money, Ake was agoin' after his pocket knife. Show 'em your pocket knife, Ake."

Ake pulled a stick out of his pocket from which he opened a blade. It looked more like a cavalry saber than a pocket knife. Ake waved it suggestively in the air, now and then testing its sharpness with his thumb.

"As I was a sayin'," continued Clem, "Ake gets his knife out and takes a cut at the feller before he could get the money. This feller looks up sorta surprised like and asks Ake what happened to his gun. Ake tells him. . . . What did you tell him, Ake?" Clem queried.

"Told him it was a-layin' right there in front of him—to go and pick it up. Catch was, he had to use his other hand 'cuz the fingers of his gun hand was a-layin' down there along with the gun. I'm perty mean, all right." With this the two of them doubled up in gales of laughter. It was an interesting-enough story, but none of us laughed. However, we managed sickly grins for the sake of sociability.

The two suddenly straightened up and Clem asked, "You folks wanna go coon huntin' tonight or not?"

"We sure do," Uncle Bob said. "Say, before we go why not have a quick one for good luck?" With that we killed the bottle and untied the dogs.

"Mighty good," commented Clem after he had dried up the bottom of the pint. "Mighty good." He wiped his huge mouth with the back of his shaggy paw.

"Not too strong, but tasty," said Ake judiciously.

We moved out. Darkness was spreading its silent wings, intensifying the light of the full moon. Clem was carrying a lantern, and Ake had a powerful flashlight. We followed with the long-eared, low-geared, sad-looking hound dogs.

Clem was saying: "There's a creek aways up there that runs into the lake. That's where we'll hunt." Then he started telling us about the time he and Ake were seining for fish in the creek. A game warden had suddenly jumped out of the brush. Since seining of fish in this particular creek was on the shady side of the law, Clem and Ake had dropped the fish net and run like thieves.

"Ake was in the lead, him havin' the longest legs," said Clem. "He could hear me poppin' brush behind him. Ake thought all the time I was the game warden, and he run three miles afore I could ketch him. Ake sure is fast." Then he said, "We got to be quiet now, dammit. The dogs are beginning to work."

The hounds were circling, tails straight up and noses to the ground. The underbrush was thick as the hair on a skunk's back. The trees were silhouetted against the moonlit sky.

We spread out some now. A voice broke the silence. Ake said: "Two of them hounds has swum over to the other side, Clem. Think I'll jump across. The creek ain't very wide here, is it?"

"Naw, you can make it," replied Clem, adding for our benefit, "Ake shore can jump."

We could see the flashlight bobbing like a dizzy firefly as Ake backed off to make a run before the jump. He sounded like a herd of hydrophobic buffalo tearing through the brush. For a moment there was silence; then there was a splash that sounded as if the moon had rocketed into the Pacific.

Ake was making gurgling noises. Then he said thoughtfully, "Jumped fer enough, but guess I must of left the ground a leedle too fer back from the bank."

Clem said: "Ya had time to write a letter makin' that jump. Must've gone straight up."

Ake finally made it to the other bank. He crawled out looking like an alligator, and retrieved his flashlight, which he had tossed across when he realized he would fail to make the whole trip.

We were soon off again. The dogs, indifferent to the cause of the delay, had continued prowling and were now way out ahead of us.

Big Boy stopped short, cocking his head to the side. "Listen; what's that?"

"It's the hounds—that's old Bess and Blue bayin' coons. Come on, let's go," cried Uncle Bob.

The brush was crackling now like corn in a hot skillet. Clem was moving ahead fast. The rest of us tried our best to keep up with him. On the other side of the creek, Ake seemed to be skimming over the impeding brush. We caught glimpses of his dark scarecrow shape occasionally. He managed to disappear far ahead of the rest of us.

We had gone our thousandth weary mile through the thick brush that whipped, scratched, and tore at us at every turn, when we finally came upon Ake standing on the opposite bank, yelling at the top of his lungs. At the same time, our attention was drawn to a violent commotion taking place in the water. Ake trained his flashlight on the spot.

A fat, oversized coon, intending to escape the hounds, had taken a swim. He was much more at home in this element than the hounds, who were engaged in a watery pursuit. The odds were six to one, but the coon fought so hard, swam so fast, and knew so many devilish tricks that the hounds must have thought the entire universe was swarming with malevolent coons.

The coon maneuvered close to the bank—Ake's bank—where he intended to find sanctuary at the top of some high tree. What it actually climbed, though, was Ake. Now Ake was tall enough, all right, but I couldn't understand how a coon so well equipped for survival could have mistaken him for a tree.

This coon had the fighting qualities of a grizzly bear and the sinuousness of a snake, but right now he was in a dither. He was in good shape, though, compared to Ake, who was howling in anguish and beating about in all directions.

The hounds dragged their wet carcasses from the creek and made straight for him. They too attempted to climb Ake's frame. As a result, he was bowled over like a sapling in a tornado.

The coon dashed off to another perch—a real tree this time—and climbed up and up and up. Ake might have viewed the coon's mistake with a lenient eye if the six powerful, sopping wet, slavering hounds hadn't suddenly borne down on him. Intent only on their prey, they trampled every inch of his face, eyes, ears, and open mouth. This was too much for him. It was that coon who had started all this, and now Ake decided to settle accounts. He ran up to the tree flashing the light until he spotted the critter and then, yelling savagely, he made a mad ascent.

The rest of us cheered him on. Big Boy yelled, "Get the fat bastard and you'll have coon meat for a week."

There was one disadvantage working against Ake—the flashlight. It was difficult to carry it and climb, too. But gradually he made his way up. The coon was a much better climber, but the tree finally ran out of branches, and finally the coon was out on a limb—literally—and Ake was stretching out his hand for it. Ordinarily, he would have shaken the limb until the coon fell free to the waiting dogs on the ground. However, this had become a personal matter with Ake. Just as his hand touched the coon, he dropped the flashlight. The noise that followed was something to be remembered. The squalling of the wild coon, the ripping sound of branches and limbs— some of them Ake's—the bellering and baying of the hounds, and the assorted yells of our hunting party all shattered the night air.

Clem held the lantern as high as he could and barged headlong into the creek. The racket increased as he reached the opposite bank. The light of the lantern now revealed Ake at the foot of the tree, flailing one long arm as if pumping water. Attached to the arm was a live coon.

Clem yelled, "Is he biting, Ake?"

A painful croak came from Ake. "Naw, he ain't, you silly bastard. I'm just shakin' hands with the friendly little son of a bitch."

The dogs were in a great turmoil, all trying to get at the coon at once. In their anxiety they clawed Ake some and finally sent him toppling again.

The coon dived into the water. The hounds, seeing victory slip from their slobbering jaws so many times, gave up the chase then and there. There was no stirring them up again.

We made our weary way back to the pickup where there was a weak nightcap of water from a canvas bag. Some were wet, one was scratched and otherwise generally becarved, and all were exhausted and ready for sleep.

Uncle Bob remarked on the way back, "Should have brought more dogs." Then after a silence he added: "You've sure as hell got to hand it to that old coon. He whupped the whole damn bunch of us." And he began to laugh.

Chapter Sixteen

I took Josepha over to Ragoon and we played around there a couple of days. We got along just fine, and my feelings toward her were ripening, but the image of Mona still flickered between us. She read my mind on the way back to Sano.

"Pete."

"Yeah?"

"There's an awful lot of talk going around the country about Mona and Big Boy."

"I know," I said.

"But it's serious," she said, leaning up in the seat of the pickup and turning to me.

"I know," I repeated.

"Jim Ed Love has spread the word that Les Birk is going to get Big Boy."

"I've heard that one before," I said. "He hasn't got the guts."

"That's right," she said, "but Jim Ed will figure out a way so Les will go free and clear."

"I don't care how damn smart Jim Ed is, Les won't get away with it."

"What do you mean?" she asked.

"Because I'll get Les just like he gets Big Boy. Besides," I told her, "Big Boy's not so easily got."

"He has lots of other enemies, you know," she said.

"Yeah, I know. He's stomped hell out of a bunch of lice, and every damn one of them had it coming."

"Still," Josepha said, "they didn't like it. And another thing, lots of girls are feeling sort of let down. They don't ever feel too happy about a married woman stealing an eligible man."

I began to feel irritated with Josepha for the first time. "Sure, he's made a whole countryful of haters. That always happens when somebody's his own man and goes his own way. Sure, he's stepped on some toes. But I'll tell you one thing, Big Boy bothers nobody that doesn't bother him."

"What about Mona?" she asked softly.

Then I knew she had been leading up to this all along. "That's their business," I said. "They love each other and they intend to get together. I admire them for it. They've had something together that hardly anybody in the whole cockeyed, goddam world has feeling or guts enough to take. Even if somebody does get killed. And I'm not so sure it'll be Big Boy."

She was silent a while, gazing down the wind-whipped road. I knew she had wanted me to say something else, but I couldn't. It hung and ached in my throat.

My relationship with Josepha was something I couldn't analyze even to myself. When I looked at her I saw she had more actual beauty than Mona, and was just as poised. She was always clean, always pleasant, could show tremendous enthusiasm and yet somehow remain calm. It seemed she had merged the fire of her Irish and Spanish blood with the quiet acceptance of the older Latins. The lonely, isolated place of Sano was her birthplace, and she had remained there, giving much of her time to many sad, lost causes. She ran the store for her father while he was out in the hills at his old mine, looking for that rich, elusive vein. Not only was she his daughter but in a sense his wife and mother, too. She was the youngest of a large family, and the only one who hadn't left home.

I had first dated Josepha when she was a senior in high school, commuting daily the sixty-odd rutted miles by bus. I knew, as everyone knew, that she had many chances to get married. In fact, everyone expected us to marry right after her graduation, but then the war was upon us, and—well, I'd put it off indefinitely. She stayed in Sano while I was overseas, writing me faithfully, telling me all the news of Hi Lo and letting me know how much she missed me.

When I came back I felt sure I'd marry her. Yet I hesitated for some reason. She was, in all respects, just about perfect for a man of this unpredictable land—a complement to him in public, a source of peace, trust, and stability in private. But . . . was it Mona I had unconsciously waited for? I didn't know. I wanted to scream.

Who really knew Mona? Did even Big Boy know her, or was he caught, as I was, in a sex-baited trap?

Josepha was as clean and clear as a summer morning after a night's rain. All she was, all she could be to a man, was plunked right on the line. And why didn't I have the guts to admit she had thrown away a fair portion of her life waiting for me? God, she must hurt during the long nights alone. She had courage and patience, and here I was like a cheap bastard trying to get into bed with my best friend's woman.

Now Josepha was beginning to fight. Her claws, those women's weapons that sink deeper than a Spanish dagger, were extended and groping for a target.

We parted with nothing settled and both of us upset. As I drove into Hi Lo I saw Big Boy's pickup in front of Mitch Peabody's grocery store. I parked beside him. He came out after a minute and dumped an armload of supplies in the back of the pickup.

"Headed for the ranch?" I asked.

"Naw, thought I'd stop down at Lollypop's and see what's goin' on in this dried-up town."

I could tell by his unusual pallor and the way he gritted his teeth that he had heard talk. If he got drunk now there was liable to be a serious accident in Hi Lo.

I heard myself saying: "Listen, Big Boy, I was headed out to Tinker Grits' to see if he has any iron for a cattleguard. Why don't you come and keep me company?"

"How long you fixin' to be?"

"Just long enough to get the job done," I said.

"All right."

I knew he always enjoyed talking to Tinker. Maybe if I could get him in a good humor he'd go on back to Hoover Young's and stay out of town and trouble a while.

On the way out he said: "Haven't seen Tinker in two or three months. He must be working on some great new invention."

"He's always doing that," I said.

"You know," Big Boy said, "that old son of a bitch is going to come up with something one of these days that will rock the whole country back on its heels."

"I wouldn't be one bit surprised," I said. I was a little surprised by Big Boy's admiration for Tinker, since I knew that just before Old Man Matson died he had taken all Big Boy's savings, as well as his own, and invested them with Tinker in a worthless gold-mining operation. I also knew that Big Boy had been saving for four years to buy himself a new saddle. I said, "Say, just what kind of a mining deal was it old Tinker cooked up that time? I've heard fifty different versions."

"Well, it was an unusual type of undertaking," he said. "Tinker had planned to recover the gold from the Atlantic Ocean. He figured there wasn't any use bothering with the Pacific, because six months after operations started he would have so much gold he'd control the world's economy anyway. In fact, he said that tons of gold would have to be held in reserve or it would go down in value like pig iron. Damn, ain't that a real keen notion, Pete?"

I allowed this to be true, and Big Boy warmed to his yarn.

"Well, it's kinda hard to explain, but anyhow, he finally developed a chemical that would recover hidden gold heretofore beyond the reach of man. He figured that a certain amount of the metal was in a liquid-gas form, and when it was heated for fire assaying or smelting this liquid gold escaped and was lost in the fumes. His chemical grabbed the gold and pulled its parts into a whole. You know, don't you, that one of the most common methods for recovering gold is mercury-covered copper plates? Well, anyway, he would add a small amount of this chemical to the plates, and when the liquid gold came in contact with it, it grabbed it just like a magnet draws iron filings. Then by real slow, careful retorting he could turn the gold into powder and then melt it into the pure metal. Tinker proved this theory to the satisfaction of a bunch of people, including my dad, by assaying samples from old abandoned mine dumps and then testing them with his method. It never failed. His percentage of recovery was always much higher than the assay. All the investors tried like the devil to talk Tinker into getting a patent on his process. He just plain refused. He said: 'When you register an invention in the patent office, it is open to public inspection. Even though I could stop anyone from selling or claiming patent, the big companies could still use it in a slightly different form and it would be hard to prove damages.'

"Well, it was about this stage of the deal that he came up with the idea of recovering gold from the Atlantic Ocean. He claimed it was in the liquid form just made for his chemicals. His idea was to bend a reinforced copper sheet a hundred yards wide into a half-circle with a trough at the bottom. This trough would be filled with mercury and his own preparation. Then buoys would be attached to the top of the sheet and adjusted so that it could be pulled along just under the ocean waves. His plan called for a steamship to do the pulling. He figured that each round trip across the Atlantic and back to New York would recover several million dollars' worth of gold. Even though the ocean holds only three cents a ton, he knew the sheeting would come in contact with several billion tons of water on each trip. Hell, with ten steamships in operation, paying their own way with other produce, passengers, and such like, why it would only take five or six months to control the gold markets of the world. Lord A'mighty, just think of that!"

"I'm thinking."

"Well, anyhow, before he could get things going he'd used up all his original investors' money. So he formed a stock company. That was his mistake. He got carried away and forgot to register the stock with either the State or Federal Securities Commissions. He had raised about $100,000 and was on the West Coast trying to tie up an entire shipping company for his project. When the newspapers got wind of his idea, they splashed his plan all over the front pages—more as a joke than anything else: In three days this free publicity sold an additional $750,000 worth of stock for him. But another group had been reading the papers, too. On the fourth day the Federals picked him up and read the law to him. Poor Tinker spent eighteen months in a Federal pen. When he got out he put the formula for his invention in a sealed vault with instructions for it to remain unopened until thirty years after his death. Then he forgot it and went on to other things."

Tinker looked like a genuine drunkard. He had a large potato-shaped nose, deep-set watery eyes, and a scarlet complexion. His general appearance suggested a two-fifths-a-day man, which was wrong. He was a teetotaler. Big Boy's explanation was, "He's flushed that way because he's always drunk on ideas." He was about medium height. Even in the middle of the grimiest of work he wore a complete suit and necktie. This necktie seldom fit snugly but hung half done, stained and punched full of holes from various acids and chemicals. The rest of his drooping attire was in more or less the same sorry condition.

Then I said, "What did he do next?"

"Well, after this run-in with the law he recouped his lost fortune—all the money left from stock sales had been returned to the original owners—by selling beans. These weren't the pinto variety like we raise here in the Hi Lo country, but were large imported ones from South America. Tinker had long ago ruined his land by experimenting with odd fertilizers until now the toughest weeds had a hard time making a living.

"Well, he soaked these beans in a cheap perfume. Then he went around the country peddling them to housewives. 'Just think,' he'd say, 'a whole garden of perfumed beans large as the end of your thumb. All you have to do is rub one behind your ear or carry it in your purse, and the scent of the garden of Allah is with you wherever you may wander.' This appealed to the country women, and pretty soon Tinker was getting five dollars apiece for his beans. The rich part was, he'd go back once to each of his victims. They'd all tell him that the beans grew well enough but there was no scent. He'd say, 'Well, madam, that is a tragedy, but you must have bought a bad seed.

This is the only complaint I have had. To make it up to you, you may have two more seeds for the price of one. Adieu until next season.' Can you image that much guts, Pete?"

I shook my head respectfully.

Big Boy went on: "The women wouldn't report him after the second sale because they were ashamed to confess how they'd been hooked. Oh, he's done a little bit of everything. He's experimented with rockets, and cars that run on air, and thought machines—now there's one for you, feller: you think into it and the answer comes back out soundless but you pick it up in your mind. 'Knowledge beyond man's most fantastic wishes and deepest desires' was how he put it. The old bastard talks like a goddam poet along with everything else. Pete, I've heard my father expound on what a great mind Tinker has for hours at a time. Other folks could call him a madman and a moron, but my dad admired him plumb to the bone and believed to the end he would prove his genius."

It was plain that Big Boy had inherited his father's capacity for faith. Me? I just didn't know.

We drove up to Tinker's dilapidated homestead and stepped out in the earth-powdered wind. There were instruments, pipes, tubing, motors, bottles, and hundreds of other items piled in mountainous heaps all around the house. A thousand dreams were rusting into Tinker's ruined ground. We moved around the debris to the porch. It hung slackly, as if the wind would lift it to the heavens at any moment.

Big Boy ducked, stepped up to the door, and knocked. In a moment the door opened and was completely filled by the square, bulldozer body of Tinker's Indian wife. When she saw it was Big Boy she smiled and said: "Tinker, he's in the back pasture. He works."

"Thanks," Big Boy said. "we'll drive over and see him."

She closed the door silently.

As we drove up, we could see a huge boiler arrangement as big as a haystack with a funnel-like affair on top of it that would have made two stock tanks. Tinker was on top of the whole business, pouring a liquid into an iron barrel.

"What in the hell is that contraption he's working on now?" Big Boy marveled.

Tinker was oblivious of us until Big Boy yelled: "Hey, Tinker, what're you doing? Gonna blow up the world?"

He looked down at us, and his florid face broke into a toothless smile. He had all his teeth, but they were so black and stained they didn't show at that height. He finished pouring from the gallon bottle and climbed down. "Gentlemen, gentlemen," he said, happily extending a small fat hand with fingers that tapered like precision instruments. "It is a miracle of the gods that you have chosen this moment to arrive. You are about to witness my first full test on the greatest invention of this or any other age!" He was swaying in the wind, squinting his rheumy eyes almost shut against the dust as he talked.

"Having been gifted with the fine father you were, I know you will understand what I am about to say." He spoke directly to Big Boy. "I know that the import, the world-rattling immediacy of this experiment, will not be lost on so fertile and open a mind as you have so fortunately been bequeathed."

"What is it?" I asked, beginning to lose my breath out of sheer curiosity.

"What is it?" He looked at me as if I had just swung down out of the trees. "What is it?" he screamed, and his face turned from crimson to purple. "It is very simple," he said. "That, gentlemen, is a water-making machine! Water, the one thing man has never conquered or controlled. Even now, though he fingers outer space, he has failed ignominiously here on this earth. Water! Water! That's the answer to everything. Look! Feel!" he shouted, waving a hand in the dirt-filled wind. "Right here is the driest wind this side of the Mohave, but did you know it is filled with life-granting moisture all the way into the upper levels of space? Every square inch of it contains moisture that can never be destroyed. You can destroy nothing! This wind that howls like tormented wolves cannot destroy it. Man and all his follies cannot destroy it. It is there for the taking. And I, Tinker Grits, shall be the taker. If Shakespeare was a surgeon of the soul, then I am the doctor of the mind. What else is there but ideas, gentlemen, what else?"

I couldn't do anything but swallow and nod. Big Boy stood entranced.

"In a moment, gentlemen, you will be witness to an event that will make the invention of the wheel and the control of atomic fission look like the play of moronic babes. I shall turn a tiny spout, and chemicals will pass out of that vast funnel and a vapor will rise up into the heavens and condense and distill the water, pulling it from the sky down along this vapor trail and fill this container"—he motioned to the boiler—"and then it will spout out this pipe"—pointing to an eighteen-inch steel pipe like that found on the largest irrigation wells.

"It will flow like the nectar of the king of all gods into the arid land, and all shall become bountiful and the Garden of Eden will cover the face of the earth. Foliage shall grow so thick and ripe that this eternal devil-haunted wind cannot push through it and will die exhausted, never to molest us again. Imagine, gentlemen," he said, making a wide sweep with his pincer-like hands, "the mountaintops and the desert to the south will have row upon row of my machines like soldiers of peace and love lined up for the battle of good against evil. And from their spouts shall pour in unending streams that bountiful and luxurious fluid, water! Water!" he screamed and his voice almost failed. "Water!"

I was sure he was going to have a stroke.

Big Boy's expression was rapt.

"Peace," Tinker went on. "Peace. No more wars. Why fight, gentlemen, when there is plenty for all? Imagine the new rivers with lush banks of grass and orchards of fine fruits, lakes brimming over with powerful silver fish and forests full of animals of every kind. Yes, this is the answer. Not just a world of plenty but a world of bountiful abundance. No more blood or barricades or bomb shelters. No! All will be serene, all will be love, peace, and contentment."

Tinker paused a moment with one hand still flung in the air. "Listen," he said. "The howl of the wind softens. Now I must strike! Watch!" he said, "watch the spout!"—whereupon he whirled and scrambled up the steel ladder to the barrel and turned a spigot. For a moment nothing happened; then he yelled, "Observe, gentlemen!" and pointed up.

Sure enough, a vapor *was* rising from the boiler like a spirit headed for the final kingdom. We watched and waited. Tinker poured in more chemicals. The vapor grew thicker.

In a moment Big Boy said, "Look, by God, look! There it is!" And sure enough, a tiny drop of water rolled to the edge of the spout and dropped to the kiln-dry earth, making a tiny dark spot. In a few seconds it was gone.

About ten minutes later another drop fell. Tinker danced around in a transport of joy. "Success! Success! It worked! I knew it! The world is mine! Gentlemen, you have brought me luck. I am going to put you in charge of my great army. Big Boy Matson, you are my Chief of Staff, and Pete, you shall be General of the Army of Love and Peace. It won't be long now. I'm fresh out of chemicals and there will have to be a few slight adjustments made to increase the flow somewhat, but success is at the tips of our fingers. Soon we shall feel it heavy in our palms. Truly the streets of our cities will be paved with gold!"

On the way back to town we talked of the experiment. I said, "You know, right now the chemicals would come so high it would cost him a hundred dollars to make a gallon of water."

"He's on the right track, though," Big Boy said, his absolute loyalty to Tinker Grits strong in his voice. "If he doesn't live to perfect it, somebody else will."

"I reckon so. Someday," I said.

"The old son of a bitch is wrong about one thing, though."

"What's that?"

"Love and peace."

"What do you mean?"

"People *like* to fight," he said.

But it worked out as I'd hoped; Big Boy was in a good mood now, and he'd forgotten about the particular fight he was spoiling for.

Chapter Seventeen

Talk, talk, talk. Too much of it. From the stories circulating around Hi Lo, you'd think the chambered bullets of a hundred cocked guns were engraved with the name of Big Boy Matson. Jim Ed Love, the Felders, and a host of others had done their dirty work well. The ground-burning wind had set people more on edge than ever. They wouldn't blame themselves for what was happening to their land and their lives, so Big Boy was a welcome and convenient target for their bottled-up anger. There were plenty who listened, who'd never liked Big Boy because they were afraid of him.

I wondered how Mona was taking it. I hadn't seen her in quite a spell. I knew that Big Boy had, but he didn't say how or when. There was still a question mark in my mind about Josepha, and I couldn't get Mona completely out of it. if Big Boy could make his lick somehow and get enough cash to run off with Mona, get her out of the country, maybe I could settle down to my own future. If it had been any other woman in the world, Big Boy would have expected her to follow him penniless from one cow camp to another. But it was Mona. How could I criticize his reasoning when I myself was so in love with her I had actually considered killing him?

I asked Big Boy to go with me to Two Mesa, where the gambling was wide open. I suggested that maybe at the gaming tables he could hit that lick he wanted so desperately. I knew he had been making a deep study of gambling for some time now and all his homework, added to his natural luck, might just pull it off. But my real motive lay buried and unconfessed, like fused powder in a drill hole.

So we went to Two Mesa, that fabled mountain village of three cultures—Spanish, Indian, Gringo. A mud and viga town, hunkered to the earth between two mighty ranges of mountains, as a weary traveler might lie on a featherbed. It was full of artists, writers, and the usual run of businessman found everywhere else. But it had spark and it was different. And it was stiff with dice tables.

We took a room in a pueblo-type inn and started to shave and clean up. I noticed that Big Boy used an old-time straight razor. It half embarrassed me to use the electric one Josepha had given me for Christmas.

Big Boy said, "Here, hold this for me," and handed me the other end of a leather strap. He worked the razor back and forth, putting a fine edge on it and savoring the sound it made, as no doubt his grandfather and his father before him had done. They must have come to his mind too, for he said: "You know,

Pete, in the day of the horse I wouldn't be scrounging around raising a few dollars at a time. I'd get hold of another horse as good as Old Sorrel for Mona and we'd proceed to rob us a bank. In the day of the horse if you had guts and luck enough to get a bank robbed and get out in the hills without being caught, everything was *even* from there on. If the robber had the best horse and knew the hills, he was home free, feller. He could drop off down in southern Arizona or the Big Bend country of Texas, or even into Mexico, and nobody would ever know the difference."

He tested the razor and said, "But if I was to rob a bank today, within thirty minutes every local law in a two-hundred-mile radius would be looking for me. The state police would throw up road blocks; the telephones and Western Union would be full of my description; and if they didn't snag me the first couple of hours they'd call out the FBI and I'd be hunted with airplanes, motorcycles, and high-geared cars. And if *that* didn't get the job done, they'd have the National Guard out looking under every bush in three states."

"They've got a man by the short hairs," I agreed.

"Look at old Tinker Grits," Big Boy went on, getting the same far-off, thousand-yard daze in his eyes that Tinker did. "If he'd made that chemical to recover gold about forty years earlier, he could've raised ten million dollars and gone ahead and put it over. They didn't have all those laws then to kill a man who has ideas and guts. Hell no, a man could *use* his guts and his brains, and he knew that out ahead there somewhere was the double rainbow."

"Got to have laws," I said.

"Yeah, I know, but not these piddling little stifling laws." He looked out the window toward the mountains and repeated softly, "Little stifling laws."

We finished throwing powder on our flanks and went out to look the place over. The inn had a big lobby full of Navaho rugs, Spanish *santos* and oil paintings. There was a long bar, and just to the right of the bar a big room full of slot machines, roulette wheels, and dice tables. To one side, between the bar and the gaming room, was a small dance floor. The whole thing was visible and easy to reach from the bar. We had a drink, and Big Boy asked the bartenders when the gambling started.

"About eight o'clock," he said. "You got nearly two hours."

"Come on, let's roam around town," Big Boy said.

Some of the dives were already going, and Big Boy dropped about $20. I could tell he was looking for something to go on but I didn't know what it was. We made every joint; then we decided to head back to the inn.

The place had changed dramatically in the last two or three hours. The bar was busy and the drinking tables were half full. You could hear the slot machines whirring, clicking, and choking down. A couple of women sat at one of the tables. One was a tall blonde who looked about forty years old, maybe fifty. I kept staring at her because I knew I'd seen her picture in the papers sometime or other. For a while I thought she was giving me the eye, but of course it was Big Boy she was checking out.

He wasn't paying any attention to her but was studying one of the dice tables where a weasel-faced man handled the stick.

He leaned toward me and said softly: "Listen, Pete, when I move over to that table you go with me and stand right up next to that little bastard and glare at him like you was going to kill him just for kicks. At the same time you watch me, and when I push my hat back on my head you accidentally bump that little bastard hard enough to make his eyes spin. You got it?"

I nodded.

We had another drink, and Big Boy said, "Now."

We walked over to the table. "What's the limit?" he asked the dealer, at the same time pulling out a big crumpled wad of bills. "I'm goin' to buy my baby a new oil well," he said, laying $100 worth of chips on the table.

The dealer glanced at him and said, "Good luck."

Well, I leaned on the dealer and he kept shifting out of my way. Big Boy made eighteen straight passes. I was beginning to catch on to what was taking place. The dealer figured that Big Boy was a rich oil man, and he had given him a set of passing dice with no fives or aces. He couldn't miss. The dealer intended to let him win a while, suck him in good, then switch the dice when he started betting heavy.

The dealer was in a jackpot. I had scared him out of changing the dice so far. Big Boy had a hell of a pile of chips in front of him now. I kept motioning him to quit but he didn't pay me any mind. Then he pushed his hat back and I gouged the dealer in the ribs and grabbed him by the arm as though I'd had a few too many at the bar.

"Hey, mister, how do I get on this gravy train?"

Big Boy told me later what happened. He had watched the dealer carefully, and when he switched the dice Big Boy pushed his hat back. Soon as I knocked the dealer off balance, Big Boy switched another pair of tops in the game—his own.

He bet everything he had on a ten and won after three rolls. The dealer knew he was trapped and in trouble with his boss. He broke the mahogany stick and said, "The game is closed." A crowd had gathered and they started raising hell with him.

"The game is closed," he repeated. His face shone with sweat.

Big Boy cashed in his chips and took the money over to the bar. "Give everybody in the house a drink," he said.

"How much you think we've got?" I asked.

"I don't know, maybe two or three thousand."

"By God, that's pretty good. We can work that all over town and leave here with enough to buy in partners with Jim Ed Love."

"No, it's over," he said. "The same man controls the whole town, and the word is already out."

"Oh," I said.

We belted down a couple of drinks, then I saw the blonde get up and come toward the bar, leaving her plainer companion at the table. She moved like a bobcat after a fat sparrow.

"This is your night, cowboy," she said.

Big Boy turned his eyes without moving his head just like an old, tired dog.

"Every night's my night."

"Dance with me," she said, turning on so much charm that I damn near fainted just getting hit by it secondhand.

"Don't dance," Big Boy said, taking another drink.

I could tell the blonde was set back on her hocks a little at this. But she smoothed the squaw skirt across her lean model's figure and said, "Maybe you need a horse to dance with."

Big Boy swung around to her and looked her right in the eye. "Ma'am, my granddaddy told me that a man marries a woman, not a horse, but I'm beginning to wonder."

Well, with that I went over and sat down with the other woman. She knew I wasn't really interested in her but she was friendly just the same.

"Who's your friend?" I asked, nodding toward the bar where the blonde and Big Boy were still going at it.

"I'm her secretary," she said.

"What's her line of business?" I asked.

The woman laughed at me and said, "Her line? Well, she's an heiress."

Then I knew who she was: Sandra Compton, heiress to a fortune of over fifty million oil-soaked dollars. I swallowed two or three times and said, "She likes my partner, I think."

"I think you think right," she said.

I ordered us a drink and asked, "What's your name?"

"Irene."

"Mine's Pete," I said. "Glad to know you."

I watched the bar, and I could tell that Miss Compton was getting nowhere with Big Boy. I felt a little sorry for her; she didn't know the kind of competition she was up against. But even so it wouldn't hurt to dance with her. Hell's fire, fifty million dollars was a consideration.

All of a sudden Big Boy grabbed her by one elbow and marched her back to her table. She was cursing under her breath and her face was crimson. Big Boy sat her down hard, and when she tried to get up he bounced her down again.

"Now, you stay right there, little lady," he said, "before you get in trouble."

She started crying.

Big Boy said, "Come on, Pete, let's go."

I told Irene goodbye, but before we could leave, Miss Compton was on her feet and pleading with Big Boy: "Don't leave. Please. Please. I'm sorry. Let's talk." The tears had smeared her make-up.

Big Boy swiveled around and gave her a boot in the tail and we got the hell out of there. All the way over to Ragoon that night I expected to see one of those roadblocks thrown up ahead of us, but nothing happened. Maybe the heiress liked rough treatment.

We got to Ragoon in time to buy a fifth before the bars closed. We drained most of it on the way to Hi Lo. I couldn't remember much about going to bed that morning, but we woke up about noon over at Levi Gómez's place. He'd given us his bed and taken the old couch for himself. He had a pot of coffee going and cooked us a mess of scrambled eggs.

We spent about an hour doctoring our hang-over with black coffee, laughing and telling Levi about the night before.

We got to feeling so good that Big Boy said, "Come on, let's all us bums congregate at Lollypop's for the divine purpose of hoisting."

"Now you're talking like Tinker Grits," I said, "but it sounds good."

Horsethief Willy and a few ranchers were there. Horsethief could see we had been on a drunk, and when Big Boy told him about leaving Two Mesa sudden-like, he started telling about his own adventures the night before in Ragoon.

It seems he had run over a sign out in the middle of the street that said, ONE WAY—FIFTEEN MILES AN HOUR. (I didn't know he had ever had a car that would go any faster than that.)

"I stuck my foot in the carburetor and almost throwed the gallopin' rods out of the old Ford gettin' out of Ragoon. I had about two minutes to get away from the Ragoon law, and I gave them back one minute and fifty-nine seconds in change. I wasn't speedin' exactly, but I was flyin' dangerously low." At this old chestnut he slapped his wooden leg and yelled: "What the hell town is this? Give us another round!"

Well, somehow the word got out about Big Boy's winnings, and people began to drop in. Even those who lived scattered back in the hills got the message somehow. The bar was full before sundown. Big Boy was still standing drinks. The party was on.

"Let the goddam wind blow," Horsethief said. "Just give me a nice air-conditioned bar and I'm happy."

I thought about calling Josepha and inviting her up from Sano, but about the time I was looking for a phone a silence suddenly fell. It was the kind of silence you feel deep in a cavern. The crowd that had gathered around Big Boy thinned out. I could tell he was pretty drunk.

He lurched out to his pickup and took something from the glove compartment. He put it inside his coat and came in again.

He stood in the doorway with the wind behind him for a minute; then he closed it. I was scared.

He walked up to the bar and said quietly, "Give everybody a drink."

Lollypop came unstuck and went to pouring the booze as fast as he could. I knew somebody had spoken of Mona, probably just a casual mention. Nothing direct. But it had been enough for Big Boy. He hadn't picked out any one individual; he was mad at the whole damn community.

Everybody downed their drinks and one by one they slipped out and crossed the street to the Wildcat. Big Boy didn't look to the right or left.

"Give us another, Lollypop," he said, thrusting his empty glass forward. The last round didn't amount to much, for there wasn't anybody left now but Levi, Horsethief, and myself.

I started to ask him to let me have the gun, but decided I had better just keep still and maybe he would settle down. He didn't, though. He just went on running that whisky down.

After a while he said: "Come on, fellers, let's see how things are on the south side of the street. Lollypop's got a real keen place here, but I'm getting lonesome."

We stumbled across the street, feeling the liquor between our ears. But no matter what happened, the three of us would stick with him. Big Boy led the way in. Every head turned, and Nick Barnes stood stiff and big-eyed behind the bar.

"Come in out of the wind and wet your whistles, boy," he said, but his voice was strained.

Big Boy stood a minute and looked all around the room. Then he reached in his pocket and pulled out the thirty-eight special and whammed it down on the bar.

"Drinks for the house," he said. "All they can hold." And out of the other pocket he pulled over $2,000. Nick got busy. It was silent except for the forlorn wind, the heavy breathing, and glasses clinking on the bar and table tops. I had been on a lot of drinking sprees in Hi Lo, but this was the first that was like a funeral without the singing.

The sun went down and the wind continued to moan around the town, pulling and tugging at the stunted trees and the buildings like a talkative ghost.

I saw Lollypop turn out his lights, lock the door, and shuffle off down the street. Shorty McCullough, from Jim Ed's outfit, edged over by the door. Big Boy saw him in the mirror. He laid his hand over on the gun and, without moving, said, "Shorty, you didn't finish your drink."

Shorty hung there a minute and said, "That's right, I didn't," and went back to the table.

The wind gathered in force now, drowning out the heavy breathing in the Wildcat. Big Boy had downed twice as much as anybody else; he'd been on double shots all day. He turned around with his elbows on the bar, not looking or talking at anybody in particular, but pretending to address me.

"Now, Pete," he said, "I am one son of a bitch that can judge women. That's why I kicked that heiress up at Two Mesa in the ass. Not many men in this world can judge women. Lots of them can judge horses as far as soundness of limb and age is concerned. A man that really knows his horses don't have to even look at their teeth. He can tell that an old pony with holes above his eyes, a drooping lower lip, knobby knees, and a sunken butt hole is old, past the go-get-'em stage. But it takes a master to tell if a horse has got bottom. Some of the best-conformed horses in the world ain't got bottom. They will let you down when you get in that old bind.

"Now, a feller can't go around looking to see if a woman has got knobby knees or a sunken butt hole. Now can he? You got to be able to just sense it. A good woman is like a good horse; she's got bottom. Now, you take this Mona Birk. There's a beautiful woman. But that ain't all. She's got the same thing as Old Sorrel. Why, that old horse will go all day and half the night and still might buck you off, but when you are working cattle and the wind is trying to tear your head off and a wild cow cuts back through the brush, Old Sorrel's right in there running, turning, working his heart out to get the job done for you.

"Now Mona—this Mona that everybody seems to be so damned interested in, is going to make me a good pardner to go along with Old Sorrel, and there ain't no back-stabbing, gossiping bunch of yellow-bellied chickenshits going to stop me." He turned, put the pistol and the money in his pocket, and said, "Carry the message, you bastards!" He walked out to his pickup, weaving only a little, got in, and took off down the road toward Hoover Young's.

Everybody in the bar started breathing again, and the talk was so sudden and loud that for a moment it drowned out the shrill wailing of the wind.

Somebody said, "A man could get killed around here."

I said to Levi Gómez, "Yeah, somebody could."

Chapter Eighteen

During the long nights of howling wind I thought endlessly of Mona. She had not said No, but she had not said Yes either. I felt bruised and ashamed. On the other hand, if I had walked into the dance hall that night ahead of Big Boy, the situation might now be reversed. An urge to see her alone again became more irresistible each day. Somehow, the seething wind stretched my nerves until they throbbed.

I started driving into Hi Lo every day looking for her car. I waited for hours in the bars and pool hall, watching out the window for her. If I saw Big Boy's pickup instead, I drove on to Ragoon. I just couldn't face him right now. I let my ranch go to hell. For the first time in my life I was drinking without enjoying it. I cruised up and down the road to Jim Ed Love's, hoping to meet her. And all the time I felt guilty as a chicken thief for what I was doing.

Then at last, when I was positive I'd go out of my head and start tearing around the country shooting people dead, I saw her car coming down the road. My heart kicked against my ribs and there was a terrible pressure in my lungs. Now I would know.

I slowed the pickup. Then I saw that Les was with her. A coldness came over me like a north wind over frozen snow. I drove on a piece, then turned around and followed them into Hi Lo.

I drove straight through town and on out to my ranch, where the wind was tearing my land apart just as the thoughts of Mona tore at my emotions. And in both cases the worst was yet to come.

There was no use ignoring it, the drought was on. The winter winds, along with the desperate grazing of the stock, had left the pastures almost barren. There had been only two or three scant snowfalls, and this moisture had been dissipated into the dust and grime of that mighty lungless breath that eroded the features of the earth.

The cattle were thin and nervous, and so were the people that tended them. Actual losses were still light, but a heavy snow in the spring could finish them off. It was a weird paradox that nature set: if heavy snow came when the cattle were so thin and weak, they would die of the cold; if the snows failed to come and the spring rains were slow, they would die of starvation.

The people fought back, but it was almost too late. They had some good years at their backs and most of them could borrow money on their land. I myself borrowed heavily, considering the small size of my ranch. I used this money for hay hauled in from Colorado and for cottonseed cake from Texas. This kept the stock alive. But the fearful word was out that this was going to be another 1934.

By early spring I had exhausted all my credit and had only three days of hay left. Hi Lo had been forgotten for a long time. We only went into town to get what we had to have, and then hurried back to the ceaseless hauling of hay and cake. There was so little pasture for the cattle now that they stood in little bunches, tails to the wind, and waited for the hay wagon. The pickup was their pasture now. At the sound of its motor their heads would come up and they would trot forward on weak legs, bawling.

The day after I used my last forkful of hay I entertained the notion of going on my knees to Jim Ed Love, who had stacks of hay as long as two city blocks and the money to buy ten times that much more. As I was brooding grimly about this, two trucks groaned up the hill to the house.

The driver of the first truck stepped out and said, "You Pete West?"

"Yeah."

"Well, where do you want this hay?"

"What do you mean?" I said. "I didn't order any hay." I eyed it longingly.

"Well, Big Boy Matson did," the driver said impatiently, wanting to get his job done.

I pointed numbly to the stack lot. "Over there."

Big Boy had saved me for the time being, and in doing so he had set his and Mona's plans back a long distance. It must have taken two-thirds of his savings to buy that hay. The wind penetrated to the pit of my belly as I gave thanks to my friend. Without even being asked he had given what meant more to him than any herd of cattle. He was nicknamed right.

In spite of all the trouble the Hi Lo country was seeing, the annual rodeo came off as advertised. If the Russian army had been just across the Arizona border and poised to attack, Hi Lo would still have had its rodeo.

People came in from all the roadwebs to the hub of Hi Lo at this time. They came to gossip and tell their troubles to one another; Delfino Mondragon came to get drunk and raise hell; Abrahm Frink came to remind people he was mean enough to survive intact; Horsethief came to judge the show; Uncle Bob came to brag on his hounds; Big Boy and I came just to be in the middle of it all.

But this year I dreaded it. This was a bad time for Big Boy to be mixing with people. Tensions were too high. But there we were. The town was full. Hi Lo had gathered its sons and daughters back to its bosom for these two days and nights. Then it would spew them out into the desolated country again to fight their singular enemy.

The streets were lined with cars, pickups, horse trailers, and kids. The drought didn't mean much to them; their main problem was to down as much soda pop as their bellies would hold.

Most of the younger men and women had their horses groomed and shiny, ready to ride in the parade. And then it came down the street: the rodeo cowboys and cowgirls, the old hands and the young of the land in a pageant of the past and the present and the future that now looked so doubtful. But these people had conquered the land before and would again . . .

when the land wished it so. They sat their horses with pride, and the muscled animals moved down the street like a tangible expression of Big Boy's dream: that the day of the horse would return.

We all pulled at our hats in the skin-shrinking wind, and the same wind boiled the dust of the rodeo arena, reminding us of the problems we had shed for this brief space of time.

The crowd filled the stand and the show was on. The announcer had a hard time making himself heard, but no one cared. The local folk had little to cheer about that day. I was the only one that made a decent show, and that was by a trick.

Horsethief handed me a rope just before I rode my brown into the box, a heavily waxed rope that would split the wind and go unerring where the eye and wrist ordered. The fast pros, having little control of their ropes in the wind, missed or made bad catches. I rode out and fitted the loop over my calf's neck, got down, ran to him, threw him, and wrapped him up. The time was eighteen seconds, but it took the money. I had been slow but certain.

Big Boy's bronc was a runaway and left him out of the money. I bucked off just before the whistle. Art Logan got his revenge on Big Boy that day by taking the money in both the saddle-bronc and bareback bronc riding.

Now, Little Boy didn't like rodeoing much. In fact, he didn't care much for cowboying in general. It was only at Big Boy's urging that he entered the bull riding. He liked the pool halls of Ragoon and Hi Lo better than the grasslands. He was a throwback to some member of the family that Big Boy never mentioned. I could understand how Little Boy felt, because my main interest in the game was roping, and yet for years Big Boy had talked me into riding barebacks. About all I'd ever gotten out of it was a broken leg and a lot of bruises.

Big Boy drew a bull that hadn't been ridden in twenty-seven tries, and he spun off into arena dirt before he ever got with it.

Then it was his brother's turn. Big Boy was right there, helping him get the loose rope tight around the bull, giving last-minute advice and even opening the gate for him. The one-ton beast burst out, his white hide about the color of Little Boy's face, and he went up and around, striking the ground with a pounding twist that flung Little Boy to the ground with a thud.

The bull lowered his head and started mauling him. The clown tried to distract him, but the dust was too thick and the bull ignored him. Big Boy leaped in front of the bull and whopped him between the horns, yelling, "Haaaa! You son of a bitch! Haaa!"

The bull charged him, and Big Boy jumped at the chute gate, but the bull caught him, his horns splitting around each side of his right leg, and hurled him over the fence and into the chute. As the bull turned, the clown got his attention at last and lured him away from Little Boy's motionless body. His life had been saved and serious injury averted because he stayed limp on the ground and because Big Boy had risked his own life in that one crucial second. Little Boy was bruised, but that was all. Another five seconds and he would have been dead.

That night Big Boy and I stayed over at Levi's. Little Boy had other things to do. Big Boy spent the night rubbing liniment on his leg while the rest of the town was out getting drunk. His leg was in pretty bad shape. The next day it was all he could do to hobble, much less straddle a horse.

I took another second in the roping and won the average. Then it was time for my bareback ride. Big Boy was right there, giving me encouragement. I had drawn a wicked little horse named Dirty Britches—the same one that had broken my leg three years ago. I wanted to back out but of course I couldn't. I was scared. Cold scared.

"Pete West in chute number one," the voice of the announcer boomed across the dusty arena.

I pulled at my hat and strolled slowly over to the chute. I knew the rules in bareback bronc riding said, *Rider must be ready to ride in his turn, or be disqualified.* Well, I was as ready as I would ever be.

Big Boy said: "Don't think about the leg. This little old pony will buck you right into the money."

I wished he'd kept his mouth shut. Maybe, I thought, the leg would never have entered my mind. But I knew I was wrong. The fear had been there for years—not just the ordinary, empty-belly feeling, but a sort of cold panic.

I looked without affection at Dirty Britches. The little black gelding was quiet there in the chute with his head down low. He didn't look like the wickedest bucker in the Hi Lo country, but he was.

I checked the rigging that Big Boy had already buckled around Dirty Britches' belly. Everything was set. It was up to me now.

I crawled up on the chute and straddled the little black with my boots still between the chute boards. I looked at the small band of tough leather on top of the bareback rigging—room for just one handhold.

It was a lot different from the days when I'd ridden broncs out on the range. A man could take his time then about getting a horse saddled, and he mounted when he had him tied to a snubbin' post in a big corral. And he didn't have all these men, women, and children watching—people who had paid good money to see him crippled or maybe killed.

I pulled my hat lower on my ears, hitched at my belt, and eased down astraddle Dirty Britches' backbone. I slipped my left hand under the leather strap and said, "You gonna break my *other* leg this time, you bastard?" I grinned at Big Boy as I spoke, but I could feel the numb black fear and weakness that left me shredded as rotten rubber. If I had drawn any other horse it would have been all right, but no—I had to go and draw the one animal that really terrified me: old Dirty Britches. There'd been only one qualified ride on his bony back in the last seventeen tries, and that had been made by Art Logan, one of the best.

When I had first come off the range and started riding in little shows, I'd felt no fear, just an excitement that nothing on earth could equal. Man and horse were enemies here in the rodeo arena. The man's job was to spur with all his strength and skill, and the horse's job was to buck, kick, bite, fall, anything to rid himself of his rider.

In my early rodeo days, even when I began to get smart enough to be afraid, I had picked up a fair amount of cash. And Big Boy told me about the kind of money the top boys made, and so I kept going.

Though I could hear the announcer talking, I didn't listen. I settled my weight up as far forward on top of my left hand as possible. I felt Dirty Britches bunch under me—nine hundred pounds of leaping death.

Then the chute gate was thrown open and the show was on. The rules said—and you had to go by the rules to be in the money—*Rider must hit horse with spurs high in the shoulder first jump out of the chute and then spur both ways. One hand must be held high in air. It must never touch the horse. Rider has to stay for eight seconds.* The longest eight seconds in the world for the man on deck.

I noticed Dirty Britches' scraggly little mane where it sloped down to his wicked scarred head. I knew his plan was to throw me as high in the air as possible and kick as much of me before I hit the ground as he could. I wished at this minute I was back out on my ranch doing anything—even building fence or fixing windmills. Just anything.

Sweat made my hand slippery under the strap. I felt all gray inside, and my eyes blurred so that I could see nothing but the narrow wooden chute and the black bony beast between my legs. My stomach churned. I gulped and the muscles in my throat constricted. My heart was pounding like a horseshoer's arm, and my blood felt so thick and lumpy it wouldn't flow. I pulled at my hat again and gave Big Boy the nod.

There it was—open space ahead. Too late to back out now. It seemed like an eternity to me, that one flashing second when Dirty Britches swung his head and neck around and left the ground. The old habit of digging the spurs into the horse's shoulders raised my legs. I struck them there hard when Dirty Britches came down. At least I had balance. Many a good rider is thrown on the first jump, even if he does hang on for a couple more.

I felt all my weight thrown against the left arm where it was welded to the leather strap. The muscles pulled, and my elbow joint locked as far back as it could. I raked the spurs high again before we left the ground again. On the second jump my insides jarred so hard I felt a dull pain from skull to instep.

Then Dirty Britches snorted and whirled straight back toward the chute. I felt the momentum carry me almost over his right side. I had to contract the muscles in my right arm to keep from using it to regain balance. There was nothing out in front now but a whipping blur of black mane.

Dirty Britches turned back down the arena, and each time he hit, his hooves sunk deep into the dirt. The dust boiled up around us. My head snapped back and my hat jerked off like a missile. I clamped my knees, but my heels worked back and forth from the horse's neck to his flanks. The music of the spurs could be heard all over the arena—by everybody but me.

Then I felt it coming: the long jump and the wrenching back motion that had lost more riders than any other kind. My whole body snapped like a whip, and I yelled an old cowboy yell into the wind. Old Dirty Britches had put out all he had.

I rode loose and free now, with perfect balance, and every jar was more ecstasy than pain. Just as I sank the roweled steel in his shoulders again, hard, I heard the whistle that signaled the end of the eight seconds.

Before the two pickup men could get there to lift me to safety, I jumped off.

Big Boy came out to meet me, limping to beat hell, almost dragging his bruised leg.

"That's the way, feller!" he crowed. "That's the kind of ride I've been waiting for you to make!"

I couldn't tell him just then, but I was through. That ride had been my swan song. I'd never mount another bareback bronc as long as I lived, and nobody, not even Big Boy Matson, could talk me into it.

Chapter Nineteen

I was surprised and none too happy later when Big Boy said, "Come on, let's go to the dance."

Levi had bought himself a jug and was already halfway to the bottom of it. He said, "I'm ready." Whereupon he stuck a three-foot length of half-inch chain in his hip pocket.

"What are you doing that for?" I asked.

"Those bastards that stomped my head in the gravel will be there, and I'm not taking any chances."

I looked at Big Boy favoring his bruised leg; it was stiff and hurting him bad. "You can't dance on that leg."

"I can watch," he said.

With Levi half drunk and Big Boy half crippled, we were in no shape for trouble. And I knew we'd have it if we went to the dance at the high-school gym. But we went.

The place was full. It wasn't a real big gymnasium, but just the same it took about all the people in the Hi Lo country to fill it.

I looked around right away to see if Mona was there. Much as I wanted her to be there, I was relieved she wasn't. If our luck held, we might dodge trouble yet. The music was getting faster and the dancers were getting drunker and Levi Gómez was getting wound up. About eight inches of chain was hanging out of his hip pocket, and as he swung his girl it whipped around like a cutting horse's tail.

Then Josepha came in with her father. I swallowed, and the heat crawled up under my ear, I felt so guilty. They walked right by where Big Boy and I stood against the wall. There was nothing for me to do but ask her to dance. Her dad was so nice to me it hurt.

She moved in close, and it seemed as if the music slowed. By the time we had circled the floor once, her warmth thawed me out so I could speak.

"How've you been?"

"Oh, all right, I guess," she said. "I sort of hoped you'd come by and get me for the dance." She raised her head and looked me straight in the eye.

"I meant to, but Big Boy got hurt and I didn't think we'd come at all. Then too, you know how the weather's been. I didn't figure you'd want to make the drive up from Sano." I knew just how lame this sounded and I knew she wasn't fooled by it.

Then what I had prayed for and against happened. Mona walked in. She stepped out on the floor followed by her husband and a half-dozen JL cowhands. I saw the look of surprise on her face when she spotted Big Boy. She must have figured his leg would keep him away.

I had stopped in my tracks, and Josepha said, "Come on; you can dance with her next."

I didn't say anything else to her except a short "thanks" when I delivered her back to her seat. Then I went over and stood by Big Boy. That strange cold feeling I'd had earlier that day when I crawled aboard Dirty Britches was back on me.

Les was dancing with Mona, not looking one way or the other. Big Boy just stood with a cigarette hanging from the corner of his mouth, and watched. There was no particular expression on his face. Contrasted with the bronze of the others', his was like a white shadow.

The crowd was limbering up, and a few of the boys were beginning to yip when the music got to swinging. The other hands took turns dancing with Mona. She was obviously going to be on her feet all evening.

I turned to Big Boy and said, "Why don't we go on down to Lollypop's and get a drink?"

"There's a pint in the pickup," he said, his dark, marble-blue eyes never leaving Mona.

I looked at her too, and the same old hollowed-out feeling took charge of my chest. Goddam her, I thought. Maybe under all that softness, control, and courage, she *is* a bitch. A sharp, scheming, small-minded bitch. I didn't really know her. I had no good reason to feel this stabbing desire. If she could cheat on Les, she would probably cheat on the next man. I thought of the old Spanish proverb, *Dios que nos ayude con los serios.* (God help us with the quiet ones.) But I knew I was wrong. She'd be faithful if the man was Big Boy.

I saw her leave the JL bunch and go to the powder room around the other side of the gym. Suddenly Big Boy limped out across the dance floor, straining forward with his one good leg. He shouldered through the dancers, clearing a path almost roughly. He couldn't have attracted more attention if he'd been riding a Brahma bull.

He intercepted Mona. She stopped, and they talked quietly a moment. She glanced across the room at her group. Then, making up her mind, she moved into Big Boy's arms. Even with his dragging gait, it was the most obvious thing in the world that they fitted together like a well-thrown loop around a calf's neck. That part of my heart that belonged to Mona and that part of my conscience that was beholden to Big Boy hurt. I hurt all over.

Little Boy came and stood next to me. "God A'mighty," he said, sounding like an echo of his brother, "he's going to get himself killed, sure as hell."

My nerves started twitching and my breath hung in my chest. Crazy son of a bitch, I thought. He was just asking for it this time. It had to come sooner or later, but right now he was in no shape for a showdown. I looked around to see what help we could count on. The only friend I spotted was Horsethief Willy, and he was all the way across the gym telling somebody a long-winded yarn. Delfino Mondragon was dancing and raising hell, so drunk he'd be useless. Not much in the way of friendly troops.

It was a long set. By the time it ended, Big Boy was some twenty feet from the JL crowd. Levi was almost in front of them, and Little Boy and I were about halfway in between.

I was watching Les when the music stopped, and I saw him reach under his shirt. I knew he was coming up with a gun, but I couldn't take my eyes off his face. Hate was stamped on it like a skin graft. Then I heard somebody yell. It was Levi. "Big Boy! Look out!" And his arm came up with the chain and then down in a vicious arc. The gun went off just as the chain struck it, and the bullet went into the floor. Twenty tons of dynamite exploding wouldn't have caused as much reaction as the sound of that forty-four caliber pistol. Everybody froze, heads up, eyes staring. The gun smacked against the floor and skidded out in front of me. As I picked it up I realized I hadn't made a move to stop Les, nor had Little Boy.

Had I wanted someone to do my killing for me? How in the name of blazing hell can a man like, almost love, another man and still want him dead—all for a woman he knew so little . . . so very, very little? But one thing was a deadly certainty: she had a hold on me that was stronger than my friendship for my best friend.

. Then the full realization of what had happened hit Big Boy, and with a roar he charged. The JL boys moved in, and a lot of others with them. Men were hurled aside the way a mad dog strews a flock of sheep; the dark, terrible rage of Big Boy Matson smashed them apart like boxwood.

I fired the gun in the air till it was empty, then jumped into the middle of the crush. I cleared a small path with the butt of the gun, and felt bone crunch under the steel.

The injured leg was forgotten now as Big Boy knocked teeth from jawbones and opened the flesh of cheekbones. His mighty shoulders and arms worked with the crude and terrible power of a Neanderthal man. The numberless arms closed around us and smothered us. I was down, and I absorbed a lot of boot leather in my ribs and the side of my head.

Unaccountably, the pressure eased off. I looked up and saw Levi swinging his chain in a swishing arc. Each circuit was wider and more lethal than the last. Everybody cringed away from the hissing steel snake until a wide circle opened. Big Boy stood alone, his chest heaving, his shirt torn, blood streaming into his eyes, but there was a joy in his violence. He reached down and grabbed Les Birk, just as he had struggled to his knees, and gave him a smashing blow on the side of his face. Les' head snapped sideways, and Big Boy raised his arm and bunched his muscles for the final blow that would break his neck. Then a cry split the whole of the building, and Mona was clinging to Big Boy's upraised arm.

"No! No!"

I could feel the joints crunch and the muscles reverse themselves all over Big Boy's body. He looked at Mona for a long moment, and then let her husband drop to the floor, where he sagged limply, bent into a V at the middle. Then Big Boy's leg collapsed and he went down on his one good knee.

There was a small timid surge from the enemy, but it died as Levi rattled his chain. I got Big Boy on his feet and his heavy arm over my back. Levi helped us toward the exit. The crowd fell back, making a wide path for us.

As we passed Little Boy, where he had stood pale and unmoving during the whole thing, Big Boy said, "Where were you when the fan got hit?"

Little Boy looked down at the floor but stood his ground.

I led my friend out into the searing wind.

Chapter Twenty

Well, the day finally came when the four of us met alone. Thinking back on it, I can't recall exactly how it happened, but that day is as clear in my mind as fair weather.

We met in a little draw at the edge of a deep canyon several miles out of Hi Lo. No matter how you looked at it, the get-together was a hell of a risk. If Les Birk were suspicious enough to follow Mona, our picnic would turn into a pitched battle, and a lot of blood would mix in the sand.

Mona brought potato salad and deviled eggs; Josepha, fried chicken and a chocolate cake. Big Boy and I furnished the beer and whisky. It was nice down there, almost out of the wind. I say "almost" because you could never completely escape it. But we actually found a little patch of grass, and we spread the blanket and the food on it.

We ate. We drank. We talked.

"That's a lovely dress, Mona," Josepha said. "Did you make it?"

"Yes. Yes, I made it."

I wondered why in hell Mona had worn a dress at all out here in the hills. Josepha had on a pair of jeans and a boy's shirt, but she still looked plenty feminine.

"I like to sew," said Josepha, "but I'm not very good at it."

"It takes a lot of time for everything," Mona said, placing a hand in Big Boy's and, oddly enough, looking at me with the same softness that had shaken me that day in the motel room.

I took a big swig of Old Crow.

Big Boy said: "Don't be so goddam greedy with that whisky. Here, let me at it before it spoils." He tilted it up.

"How are the kids?" Josepha asked.

Mona looked at her quickly, then said without much expression, "Like all kids, I guess."

118

It wasn't much of an answer. I realized later that Josepha was making her *move*. There was a reason behind everything she said, and every word was directed at me. At the time, though, I was blind as a night owl at high noon.

The girls drank beer while Big Boy and I downed one whole fifth and started on another. The sun was warm. The wind hummed above us. Mona was getting relaxed, and started sharing the bottle with us. Josepha stuck to her beer.

Then Mona looked at me and said, "Well, Pete, when are you two going to get married?" She didn't even glance at Josepha.

It kind of knocked me back on my haunches and I stuttered, "I—I—don't know. Maybe she wouldn't have me."

"Oh, I think she would," Mona said, and there was no missing the unspoken words: but would you have her? I glanced at Josepha and was embarrassed for her. But then I figured, what the hell, it was just the whisky. Josepha didn't say anything, just sat straight and smiled.

Big Boy passed the bottle again and said, "I tell you what, one of these days before too long we'll have a double wedding and we'll enlist a whole damn regiment of Apache warriors to sing and dance for us."

"We'll more than likely need them for protection," Mona said.

I felt pretty healthy all of a sudden, so I jumped up, pulled Josepha to her feet, and yelled: "Come on, Big Boy, sing me an Apache song. We're going to dance right now."

He waved the bottle in the air, and sang. It was an Indian song all right, but I don't have any idea what tribe might have understood it.

Josepha pitched right in, and we leaped and whooped and were having a fine time. Then the whisky began to take over. I stumbled and grabbed Josepha, and we both went down laughing. I rolled over on her and kissed her, hard.

She whispered, "No, not here. Please. Later."

I lay beside her, getting my breath back, my eyes closed. The sun in my face, the earth beneath me, and Josepha at my side . . . it was nice.

Big Boy was quiet now. I turned my head a little to see what they were doing. I shouldn't have done it. A man's whole destiny can be determined by a little action like that.

Big Boy was lying across Mona with his head buried in the nape of her neck. Her dress rode high up on her naked thighs. All the old desire and pain crashed back through my body. I strained my body hard against the ground to keep from yelling. It was only my own heart pounding against the earth, but it seemed for a moment I could feel a heartbeat a thousand miles deep pounding against the tough crust of the world.

Josepha sat up suddenly and looked down at me.

I turned over and said, like a numbskulled idiot, "Hi."

"Pete," she said, pulling at me, "it's almost dark. Let's go see Meesa, the witch."

"What?"

"Come on. Please. It will be fun."

"Well, I don't want to know my future. I can just barely handle the present. But," I said, "if you want, I'm ready. Hey, Big Boy," I yelled, not turning around. "Josepha wants us to have our fortunes told. Want to come along?"

"Hell, yes," Big Boy said, "I've got some bad medicine I want made for some bad fellers. Lord A'mighty, Mona, maybe we can get that husband of yours dissolved and just wash him down the Rio Grande into Mexico."

"A fine idea," she said, straightening her hair and smoothing her dress. I had to look.

Mona took Big Boy in her car, and Josepha and I followed in my pickup. By the time we'd worked our way back to the Sano road, it was dark. I was glad. We were all pretty drunk, except Josepha.

"Here, have a little," I said, handing her the bottle. She took a light pull from it, more to please me than anything else.

"Pete," she said, "there's something I have to know right now."

"What's that, honey?"

"Are you in love with Mona?"

She would never know what happened to my insides, but I managed to glance at her and say: "What do you mean by that? She's Big Boy's woman."

"You didn't answer the question," she said. Her black eyes were full on me, straight and unblinking.

"To tell you the truth, I don't even really know her," I said.

"I only see her once or twice a year at dances and maybe a few times when she drives into town."

She waited a minute, then said: "If you won't answer me, Pete, I'm going to be forced to tell you something. You can think I'm vicious, cheap, whatever you like, but I love you and I might as well come out with it all. I've waited a long time for you—all of you. Now I have to know one way or the other. Mona is nothing but a cheap ex-prostitute and the biggest phony in the Hi Lo country."

I nearly hit her, but I caught myself and said: "What the hell. Are you jealous of her? Are you?"

"You're damn right I am," she said. "Where you're concerned. Now listen to me, Pete. Remember when I asked her if she made her own dresses?"

"Yeah."

"Well, she doesn't. That's a lie—a small lie but a lie all the same. She told me over a year ago where she bought that dress in Ragoon. And another thing: did you notice how she spoke about her kids? She doesn't even love them."

"Oh, come off it, for God's sake!"

"Don't you *see* she's a phony? Big Boy thinks she'll make him a wife that will sew and cook and take care of kids and wash and iron and make him a home. Hell, she's after him because he's a lucky gambler and will own a good cow ranch someday. And if something goes wrong, she's keeping you on the string for second choice," she went on.

I shoved the neck of the bottle in my mouth before I said something I didn't want to.

"Listen, Pete; now listen carefully. I had this woman checked out through friends in Ragoon who had friends in Denver. She was a call girl in Denver. That's where Les Birk met her. He convinced her he was a wealthy rancher and she married him, and before she found out any different she was pregnant and that was that. Now she wants out, and you and Big Boy are two possible solutions. She's had more men than a dog has ticks. Oh, you stupid, horny cowboys." She was breathing hard. "Well," she said, "give me a drink now. I've said all I'll ever say about her, and you're the only one who has heard it. I don't care about Big Boy. They might make it just fine. That's their business. But if I'm going to lose, I at least want *you* to know the truth about the woman that wins."

We both took a big drink. Maybe it helped me shut my mind to what she'd said. I don't know. I saw the car lights up ahead. Big Boy and Mona were already at Meesa's place.

I began to get the idea that Josepha felt the witch could reveal something about Mona that would back up her accusations. I said, "What tricks does this woman pull?"

"She can tell you just about anything you want to know. About *anyone*."

"What else?"

"Well, I've seen her ease childbirth with a mixture of raw eggs and onions. It soothes the pain and draws out the baby."

"I'm not pregnant," I said. "How does she cure hangovers?"

"Oh, that's easy for Meesa. It's eggs again. You just rub a hen egg on your stomach, then break the egg, pour it in a dish and place it behind your head."

"I'll try that first thing in the morning," I said.

"She can hex people, too. I think I'll have her make one for me." She smiled sweetly at me. I couldn't tell if she meant it or not.

"It's a good thing I don't believe in this stuff or I'd be scared to death of you," I said.

"The way to protect yourself from a hex is to hang a pair of open scissors over an open window. That cuts the tails off the evil spirits as they enter. An evil spirit without a tail is helpless."

"That's a good thing to know," I said, and took another drink.

We pulled up in front of the adobe house of Meesa the witch. It sat alone—no other home was within an eighth of a mile.

Josepha said: "I'll go in and tell her what we want. We'll have to enter one at a time. I'll be last. You'll have to decide which of you will be first."

"We'll roll high dice for it," Big Boy said.

While Josepha made the arrangements, we hunkered down in front of the car lights and rolled the dice. Naturally, Big Boy won. I was next.

In a few moments Josepha came back out and said, "She's waiting."

Big Boy went in, and we all huddled behind the car, trying to get out of the wind that was growing stronger all the time. Mona and I took another drink. Josepha refused. She was standing very close to the left of me. Mona stood on my right, her arm just barely touching mine.

After a while Big Boy came back. He was very white.

"Give me the whisky," he said, and took about five swallows.

"Lord A'mighty, I'm sure glad I don't believe what that woman said."

I could hear Mona begging him to tell her as I left to take my turn.

The old woman sat at a tiny table with nothing but a black cloth on it. There was a strange acrid smell in the room, mixed in with the scent of burning cedar. I could see a cracked mud pot oozing a little smoke under a window.

"Enter, my son," she said, rising and to my surprise giving me a good solid handshake.

I had heard of her for many years. Everyone in our country had, of course. But this was the first time I'd seen her up close. In the dim lamplight she appeared much younger than I had expected. There were no wrinkles in her face. Her age showed only in the tight skin across the jutting cheekbones and around the large sunken eyes. Even the skin of her hands was smooth, but thin as onionskin.

"The cards or the crystal?" she asked.

"Crystal?"

She removed the black cloth from around the top of a small crystal ball.

"That'll be fine," I said. The smell came stronger from the pot and seemed to permeate my whole being. I was sure that even the high wind of Hi Lo could not blow that scent away.

"What do you wish to know most of all?" she asked.

I thought of Mona. Then a cold prickling went up the back of my neck. What if Josepha had planned this whole act and made a deal with the old woman? It was possible.

I said, "I'd like to know if all of us here tonight will live and be prosperous through the next year."

The old woman looked at me, and I was sure she could read my every thought. Then she put her hands around the ball a moment, warming it, and when she pulled them away her huge black eyes burned into the glass.

I waited.

Silence.

The wind talked to us, and the smell of cedar grew even stronger. Finally, just as I thought I was going to pass out, her voice came to me.

"Ah, yes, here it is. It comes now. Clearer. Clearer."

I wanted to scream, *What! What!* but kept my mouth shut.

"Yes, young man, yes. It is large and clear. It is the sign of death. Death will come."

"Death? Whose?" I croaked. "Who?"

"Quiet," she said. "Now you have destroyed the vision. It is gone. It is done."

I lighted a cigarette with a shaky hand.

"Put it out!" she screamed. "Put it out immediately. Something else comes in the glass. It is something you must do in the next hour of our universe. Something you must know."

"What?" I asked.

"Ah, it must be your decision," she said. And so saying, she folded the cloth back around the glass. "That is all. Go."

Brother, I went. For the first time in my life I wanted out in that wind. I wanted to tear this smell away from me and cleanse my lungs. But it was still now. Very still.

I met Mona walking up the path toward me. "I saw you come out," she said, and brushed lightly against me as she passed.

My head was whirling dizzily; otherwise I would have run to the car.

"Where's Big Boy?" I asked Josepha.

"Passed out in the back seat," she said. "He's dead drunk."

"Don't use that word," I said.

"Drunk?"

"Never mind. Give me a drink."

She handed me a bottle from the front seat of Mona's car. It was two-thirds gone. After I drank I could still smell the cedar. It was so still. . . . I stood breathing in the unusually sluggish night air and looked up at the moon smiling down at us. Or was it scowling? I squinted and decided it was neither.

"Josepha, the moon is laughing at us."

"It has its own way," she said, and leaned full-length against me. I almost went to sleep holding her. Then I saw the door open and the light jump out of the house for a moment and jump back in.

"Go on, Josepha," I said. "It's your turn."

She went.

Mona came toward me with her sinuous walk and her tight blue dress. She was as pale as Big Boy had been, but the moon gave her face a blue glow several shades lighter than the dress. That goddam dress! Why did she have to wear it? The memory of her thighs and the movement of her hips penetrated through the alcohol, and I wished again for the wind to come and fill my lungs with fresh air. It was hard to breathe.

She said in a whisper, "What did she tell you, Pete?"

I took her by the arm. "Let's walk a minute and I'll tell you."

We came to a little sandstone gully. I set the bottle down and turned to her.

"What did she say, Pete?"

"This," I said, and pulled her to me. It was as before. No giving, no refusing.

Suddenly I threw her to the ground and fell on top of her. She rolled away, and I thought crazily, Good! Resist me. I'll rape you anyway, but please, *resist* me! But it was only the slope of the ground. She rolled into a gully and I scrambled madly after her. Then my arms were around her and I pulled her down against the flat stone. My mouth found hers, and my breath rasped in my throat. I ripped the buttons from the front of her dress and tore the brassiere from one breast.

It was over very quickly.

She lay as still as the stone beneath her. I raised my head and looked into her face. Her eyes met mine . . . saying nothing, just looking. I felt numb.

And then things became extremely lucid. She had not even given me the satisfaction of destroying her resistance. For a moment my hand tightened around a rock and I fought the urge to bash her head into the ground with it. Then the hand loosened. I got up and walked a step or two away.

I looked down at her. Only her eyes moved. They stared up at me—through me. The laughing moon gleamed along her thighs; the naked breast, with my teeth marks on it, gleamed like another little moon. I had not had the pleasure of raping her—hurting her. She had denied me that. Everything that had gushed from me—everything—had simply been absorbed. Not a shred of it had been returned. She lay there as if she waited for the next in line.

The only thing that had been violated was the honor and trust of two friends. I reached for the bottle, but I didn't drink. Instead I hurled it away from me, and it smashed against a rock, the liquid dulling its crash as it shattered to pieces.

I bent and picked her up and struggled back to level ground. I had to get her to the car before Josepha came back or Big Boy woke up. I had to. She rested her head against my shoulder, and I thought I felt her sigh.

There before us stood Josepha. I couldn't speak. I put Mona on her feet and her eyes opened. She swayed a moment, then righted herself.

Josepha said dully: "Come with me. Meesa will give you a shawl to cover yourself."

Chapter Twenty-one

The death of Big Boy Matson had been delayed these last few weeks by Providence, Levi Gómez, and the silence of Mona Birk. It would be delayed still further by man's struggle with the elements. Man had no time or strength left to fight his fellow man. I knew the battle I was waging on my own ranch was being fought all over the Hi Lo country.

The winter snow had been light and the spring rains had been few and far between. I rode across the pastures searching for green. It was almost nonexistent except along the draw leading to the water hole. No question about it, the drought had its teeth in our throats. The grass had dried, twisted, and shrunk by the hour.

My face felt eroded, wind-ripped, wrinkled. It was a hot dry wind now as spring spilled into summer. It rapidly gathered in strength and whipped the fast-drying grass back and forth, shriveling it further, taking the green life from its thin tips where they broke away—shortening the stems and shortening the life of the valley. Around the roots of the grass the earth was torn loose, gradually exposing the tender shoots to the ceaseless inferno of the burning wind. The air filled with millions of minute particles of dust and vegetation. The intense blue of the sky gradually changed to a dull yellow. The water hole became coated with filthy scum.

Each day I rode out into the pastures. I tied my hat down with a red bandana and wrapped another about my face to filter the dust from my nostrils. The horse pasture was scoured clean and barren. Perpetual clouds of red-brown earth swirled upward. The horses had long ago been turned in to the main stock pasture. It wouldn't last long, but as yet they were in fair shape.

The cattle foraged in the foothills where the wind had done the least damage, but in the late afternoon they stood abjectly in the poor shelter of the scrubby piñon. Some of the mother cows, whose weakened calves had been eaten by coyotes, bawled forlornly. Their bones showed more prominently every day.

Mid-August, and things got neither better nor worse. But now the very thought of winter was a threat. God, how many winters we'd endured with the one idea: *Hold out till spring, just a little while now till spring.* And then at last the spring greenness, the lush summer, and the early fall when the hay was stacked in the lot next to the barn. Let the snow fall then. But now . . .

My saddle horses fared a little better than the cows. Their longer, sharper teeth enabled them to eat the grass much closer to the ground than the cows could. Even so, they showed the wear. Their ribs were beginning to look like barrel staves along their sides. I could feel the spring missing from Old Baldy's fast running-walk. I rode him, though, with a feeling of confidence born of our many hard-working years together.

Then hope returned on one of those few days when the wind let up a little. The stock moved about, foraging harder than ever for survival. The sky retained its dirty hue, but the dust settled and the wind sank to a barely audible whisper.

I rode down to check the water hole. I had been aware for a few moments of the slow monotonous bawling of a white-faced bull moving closer and closer. The bull came up the draw toward the spring, plodding straight ahead. His mouth was open and his nostrils were scenting the air. A two-year-old unbred heifer grazed near the water hole where there were still a few sprigs of grass. Her tail arched slightly from her hips. She was in heat. The bull had caught the scent, and he moved forward telling the world of his intentions.

He stopped where the heifer had urinated, and smelled the froth-covered spot. His upper lip curled and his eyes rolled back as his head went up. He pawed at the ground, first one forefoot then the other. The earth sent up a puff of dust at each stroke, and a deep, throbbing sound burst from his lungs. Then he moved to her, smelling her hips, snuffing, tasting. He pawed again, his bawling rising in pitch until it was almost a shriek. The great knotted muscles in his shoulders rippled. The massive red shaft came out from his underbelly. He raised up, his forelegs split across her back. There was life yet.

If the rains would just come.

I rode back to the house, hitched up a work team, and made for the hills. I might as well haul some wood, I thought. It would sure as hell be dry enough to burn.

I swung the ax with automatic precision. It ate through the gray outerstains of the dry dead piñon and exposed the fresh, cream-colored inner wood. Each downward flash of the blade widened the V of the cut and a smooth chip flew into the air. I made a last swing, then broke the log in two with the butt of the ax. Each piece was short and light enough so that I could load it onto the wagon by myself. Later I would shorten it further for use in the cookstove and fireplace.

I undid the lines from the wagon wheel where they had been tied so as to pull back on the horses' mouths if they tried to move forward while I was away from the wagon and crawled up on the load.

I yelled, "Giddup, Bob. Giddup, Bill." The two horses strained against the traces and put the wheels in motion. I held the reins not quite tight, not quite loose, for best control.

I looked out across the pastures beyond the valley above my home. A few weeks more and the stock, the feed, the whole valley would be destroyed. I gritted my teeth and swore softly.

The wind had blown so hard and so long it was impossible to remember a time without wind. It slacked slightly now and then, but these periods of quiet were of little comfort. All the growing things in the meadows and hills had already given themselves to the eternally sucking, consuming wind.

In a way the wind itself had kept me from breaking. The necessity for physical action had given me no time to think. Day after day I rode out into the dust-choked valley. I rode with my head down, raising it only when I was in the foothills. I found one old cow down and on the lift. I got off and took hold of her tail.

"Come on up, baby," I said, straining with all my strength. The old whiteface cow turned her dirt-brown face to me but she couldn't get up. I had to leave her.

A little farther on I found another, and this one I managed to tail up. She breathed hard and went lumbering off, wobbling from side to side. I knew she wouldn't last another day.

The next three I found were dead. Their stiff legs stuck out straight. The dust was piled up against them in delicate, shifting little dunes.

Dust pneumonia was killing them. They were so weak they couldn't get up, and with every breath they breathed dust into their lungs.

The herd bull stood with his huge head bent low. His once thick neck was thin and weak. He no longer went about his breeding duties, but stood motionless, his strength draining away, and bawled low and coarse into the wind.

Then I found a mother cow with her calf half born. She had been too weak to shed it. Along with its mother it had died, never having seen the new world it sought.

I rode up into the jumbled boulders beneath the rimrock, hunting grass I knew I wouldn't find. Old Baldy labored, but he had some strength left. The white slobbers ran down the long shanked steel bits and turned to mud in the boiling dust. His thick dark mane showed a line of dirt where it parted along the top of his neck. I stared from bloodshot eyes out over hollow cheeks, searching the crevices for patches of grass or dead cattle. It was hopeless, but I knew I had to try to keep trying.

Old Baldy worked his ears back and forth when I talked to myself, as if he understood every word. We threaded our way through the boulders, through the gullies and oak brush, and finished working the canyons, but it was no use. We headed back each day a little before dark.

There was home—the house and the water hole. All of our lives depended on the water hole, the womb of the valley, the wet, life-giving mother of us all. But now it was dirt-covered, and twigs and bits of grass and dry manure fouled its once clear blue surface. Its water was muddy and had to have the vileness strained out before it could be used. There had been life at its sides in the past. The birds, the cattle, even the coyote sometimes crept cautiously up and drank from its depths. Life had been started there and life would finish there. Now the water hole seemed to me like the festering womb of a diseased prostitute. I thought of another spring, when my love for Josepha O'Neill had been a wondrous, flourishing thing. I wondered if *that* spring was dying too. Or had I killed all the love in me that night with Mona?

The dark was neither restful nor soothing. It was like the spreading shadow of a giant, evil vulture. And the wind howled louder at night.

I decided then to make my move. I opened the gate into the haystack pen. There was only a little of Big Boy's hay left now, six or seven days' supply, but I was glad I had made up my mind.

"There's not enough hay," I said aloud, "but I can drive them from the haystack to the water hole without draining too much of their strength. With luck we can hold out right here within a hundred-yard circle for maybe ten days. Then . . . then if it does rain I'll have horses and cattle enough to start again."

Early the next morning I rode out again. The herd was scattered between the muddy water hole and the foothills. About half of them were already dead. The rest were dying. Now the buzzards had found the carrion. They circled in the sky, making a black speckled funnel in the still, hot, yellow dust-laden air. Now and then some of them landed and pecked away at the carcasses of the cattle. The black-and-white magpies came out of the forest, crying their sharp piercing cries. They too joined the feast.

The sun took the moisture from my lips and tongue. My throat was taut, raw. There was no escaping the August sun.

I listened to the low, mournful bawling of the cattle. The old white-faced bull still stood, his head too heavy for him to hold erect, his legs splayed to keep from falling, his large, useless testicles swinging under his shrunken belly. He bawled occasionally from deep inside his weak frame, but the sound was not that of a thick-muscled, virile breeding animal: it was only a whisper cast into the wind.

I gathered the living and walking stock into a small herd, then slowly moved them toward the haystack just across the draw from the water hole. Each day I drove them to the water hole and back to the diminishing haystack. I lost three more head, and the coyotes moved closer at night to feast on fresher meat. I didn't stop, though.

On the morning of the seventh day white clouds gathered in the west, but I couldn't believe it was anything but bluff. Then their bottoms turned black and they moved swiftly across the hills and out over the ranchland. The first rumbling of thunder sent all the wild things seeking cover. Then the very air turned dark, and stabbing flashes of lightning scorched the sky.

The rain came in torrents, cascading down the crevices, soaking into the dried earth, washing the dust from trees and bushes, roaring down the draw, clearing the dirt and grime from the water hole, filling it with muddy water—clean new mud. Along the banks below the draw, tender pale shoots of grass unfolded and reached for life.

The cold wonderful wetness shocked me into action. I ran from the house and drank from a depression in the rocks. My mind and body ached terribly as yet, but I could feel my heart beat and pulse the living blood through my veins. I ran to the corrals and turned all the cows and horses loose but one. This one, Old Baldy, I saddled and rode across the draw. The rain had come and gone. The sun came out—warm but not hot. The sky was washed blue.

The mud was already settling in the water hole. In a day or so, I thought joyfully, it would be clear, cool, and fresh again. The creatures of the forest would come down to drink, and the free flying things of the air would dry their feathers on its lush green banks.

Chapter Twenty-two

The heavy rain further scarred the earth. With so little protective cover left, the torrents cut through the topsoil in thousands of places. New arroyos were formed, some of which would in time be deep canyons. But the grass returned. It was a reversal of seasons. Now in late August, when the grass and weeds should be preparing to cure, the land glowed green as early spring.

During this spell of peace, when even the wind subsided, the ranchers counted their losses, pulled in their belts, and prepared for winter. The Hi Lo country had been hard hit. There was at least a 30 per cent stock loss on the average, and it would take years for the land to recover its peak productivity.

Almost everyone was in debt. I was no exception. My losses stood close to 60 per cent, and the bank had cut off my credit. The few steer calves I would have to ship in November would be too light to bring much. Those who could would hold some calves over to start replenishing their shrunken herds.

At shipping time about the only herd of any size in the area belonged to Jim Ed Love. His surplus stacks of hay had hardly been touched, and his stock, though lighter than usual, weighed out enough per head to show a profit. Even with the last grass coming, the ranchers could take no chances. They had to have hay and cow cake in advance. If the snows came early, with only short grass for feed, the loss could be total.

Jim Ed had the hay and he sold it for a price; he was charging thirty-five dollars a ton and taking mortgages on everything loose. Until the land recovered from its devastation, Jim Ed was the lord and master of most of the Hi Lo country. His holdings would grow like the belly of a bloated cow. All across the land the wolves and vultures fed on the cattle carcasses, fattening off the misfortunes of man. Jim Ed was indistinguishable from them.

I had nowhere to go. It was all over for me. Rather than make a lopsided deal with Jim Ed, I decided to give the whole thing up. I listed my place for sale in Ragoon, threw all my thin cattle on the market, and moved into the hotel in Hi Lo for a while.

I had reached the last of my credit, and a winter without feed reserves would have been insanity. But it hurt.

It was a late fall and everyone had a new breath and, more important, new hope. Some would lose and some would win. It was all a question of courage and luck. But nature wasn't going to make it easy. This brief lull in the battle was as deceiving as a woman—some women, anyway.

After a while I moved out to Hoover's place, agreeing to work a while for just my room and board. I wanted to give myself a chance to think. And somehow, sometime, I had to have a showdown with Big Boy Matson. I would have to tell him the truth, no matter what. All this time Mona had apparently kept silent.

It was a good outfit. Mrs. Hoover had the sure confidence born of a thousand overcome disasters, and she handled the house, the meals, and her men like a West Point colonel.

Big Boy and I rode the hills looking for grassier places to shift the cattle to. The red-brown oak brush and the golden aspens higher up gave us a smile now and then.

Big Boy was restless. He seldom mentioned Mona, but when he was quiet, looking off in the distance, I knew he was thinking about her. I had repaid most of my debt to Big Boy out of the money from my ranch sale, and I expected him to make his move at any time. When he told me it would be early summer before he could leave Hoover's, I was puzzled. There were plenty of hands looking for work now. In fact, I was willing to take the job on, and told him so. But he shook his head and said: "No, I can't leave now. I have reasons."

Thanks to Mrs. Hoover's good cooking I was picking up a little weight and feeling about half contented. In the evenings we would sit around the fireplace and listen to Hoover tell tales of the old-time cowboy days. His tight, weather-aged face would glow and his eyes would sparkle like snow in bright sun as he talked. Big Boy listened, entranced, not moving, reliving in his head and heart every story Hoover told.

It got colder, but the snow still held off. We started easing the cattle back down to the home pasture, so they would be in ready reach of the haystacks. It was a good time, too good to last long.

The morning the storm struck we were riding about five miles from the house, pushing fifteen head of cattle in front of us. Hoover had gone into Hi Lo for supplies. First there was an almost invisible grayness, something you felt instead of saw. Then from the west and north long fingers of clouds, like the spear points of an attacking army, appeared over the mountains. They advanced swiftly, silently, shoving the sun from the sky and killing its blue, like the tentacles of a ghostly flying octopus.

The wind came. A white wind. And with it the billions of flakes of blinding, freezing snow.

We spurred our horses back and forth, keeping the cows together as they moved out ahead of the storm. Within an hour the drifts had begun to pile next to every tree.

Big Boy was worried about Hoover. "I hope he was already on his way in before this hit," he said. "In another hour the drifts will cover the road from Hi Lo and there he'll be, stuck for sure."

But Hoover got back before we had unsaddled.

"Keep the horses up, boys," he said; "we're sure as hell going to need them in the morning."

Night had come an hour early, and the trip from the barn to the house seemed like a mile with blinders on.

Oh, it was warm in the house, with the old cookstove throwing out the heat and the homey fragrance of Mrs. Hoover's hot biscuits. But you couldn't forget the cold; the snow-laden wind rattled the windows and ate at the corners of the house.

We all turned in early. I lay in my bunk thinking how lucky I was to have cashed in my chips. The cattle out there, standing with their tails to the wind and shivering, were not mine. But I felt guilty, too, and couldn't sleep. I wanted to be in the saddle, saving as many head as possible. The storm did a lot of talking that night. As it lashed in icy fury it seemed to say: *You can't escape me. You have to face up to me. But I will win in the end.* And then the terrible voice would be lost and only a great sighing and moaning could be heard. Then it would come again, as if it had circled the earth, picking up all the moans of torment in the world, in order to hurl them all in the white, frigid face of the Hi Lo country. Well, the coyote would understand. Just as the forces of the storm could understand his timeless howling at the moon.

Next morning we gave it everything we had. Leaving the ranch-house kitchen was the hardest part of all. It smelled of safety, comfort, home—the things that only a woman can create. But we left it and struggled through belly-deep drifts to the barn. The horses were skittish, and it was difficult to spur them out into the weather.

We hit a fence line in single file, the horses' heads low, nose to tail. Their eyelashes turned to strings of ice, and their nostrils coated with frozen breath. We had the collars of our sheep-skinned coats turned up, and one bandana tied our hats on and covered our ears while another was tied about our faces, leaving only a slit for the eyes. Every few moments the ice had to be scraped from the handkerchiefs where our breathing had frozen in the cloth.

It was Hoover's guess that most of the stock in the open country to the north would drift to this five-mile fence line, and hold. There was a gate every mile. The idea was to push these cows through the gates and into the home pasture, where a lot of brush-covered draws afforded some protection. At least the strongest would have a chance for survival if the storm didn't last too long. Then we could work them on into the haystacks, which were their lifelines.

It was hard to stay together as the horses breasted drifts that plugged their nostrils one moment, and hit hard frozen ground the next. The cold sifted in under our coats and down our collars and finally straight through to the marrow of our bones. It seemed to strip the flesh away and leave a naked skeleton exposed to the raw, unthinkable air.

We found most of the cattle in little bunches where they had drifted to the fence. They stood with heads lowered, their tails curled under their bellies, all humped up trying to withdraw into themselves. It was hard to get them to move, and the horses were half-blind. But one by one we fought them through the gates. Time seemed to stand still, frozen stiff, but after a while the unseen day was gone. We had probably saved fifty or sixty head, but we were now five miles from the house and it was getting dark fast. The Arctic Circle had suddenly up and moved to Hi Lo.

We relied on the horses to keep near the fence; without its guiding line we were done. We moved a drift at a time back toward Mrs. Hoover's warm kitchen.

I don't know now how it happened, but topping out on a little rise where a gully cut under the fence, my horse stumbled. He must have stepped on an ice-coated rock. He fell heavily into the horse in front of him, and we all went down in one big heap. I didn't know whether it was Big Boy or Hoover until I felt someone lift me and heard Big Boy's voice through the howl of the frozen gale.

"You hurt?"

I stood up. "No," I said, "I'm all right."

"Hoover's got something broke, and his horse's leg is busted to hell."

I looked for my horse. He was gone.

"Where's my horse?" I asked.

"Probably lit out through one of the gates into the home pasture. No use looking for him now."

"The dirty son of a bitch," I said.

Hoover sat next to his fallen horse trying to untie the heavy wire pliers from his saddle.

Big Boy said, "Here, let me do it."

He got them loose and with a savage swing embedded the tool in the base of the horse's skull. The animal kicked into the snow a moment, and then was still.

"Come on, Pete," Big Boy yelled, "help me lift Hoover on Old Sorrel."

We picked him up, but something must have wrenched, because he made a grating noise in his throat and went limp.

"Do you think he's dead?" I shouted.

"I don't know, but he will be if we don't get him on in."

We got him up behind Big Boy; then I took a catch rope and

lashed them together. Hoover's head dangled to one side and his arms flopped like dry clothes on a line.

"Get Old Sorrel by the tail and hang on," Big Boy yelled.

I did, and we moved out into the ever-increasing white darkness. Old Sorrel plunged into the drifts carrying a double load and half dragging me besides. I was down and up and off to the side, and sometimes I fell forward into the hard hoofs of the horse. The effort to hold on soon had me breathing so heavy that my lungs were afire with pain. Then instead of white I could see only the red and orange flashes of lost vision and strength.

Finally my arms numbed and my hands slipped from the horse's tail and I fell in the snow. I no longer gave a damn.

Hell, this is a soft warm place. I'll just stay here for a while until I feel better.

"Get up! Get up, you crazy bastard!"

It seemed so far away. Then Big Boy's voice drilled through to me. "Pete, get up and listen!"

I strained to my feet and held to the mane of the horse.

"Listen now, Pete. I'm going on in with Hoover. But I'll be back. Your only chance is to keep moving. Hear me? Keep moving down the fence line. If you turn loose you'll lose your direction and I'll never find you. Try to keep from gripping the wire too tight, Pete, or you'll cut a hand off. Pete! Pete!" he screamed. "I'll be back! Just keep moving."

I mumbled something and took hold of the wire.

Then I was alone. It was all up to me now. I kept saying over and over to myself: *"Keep moving, moving, keep moving. Post to post."* That was the idea. If I could just keep going from one post to another, I would finally make it. The drifts were higher around the posts, and time after time I wanted to stop and rest just for a minute. Even ten seconds would help. But I would hear Big Boy's voice echoing in my skull, "Keep moving, keep moving!"

Time froze forever. The whole world was just a fence that went on and on and never stopped, and there was nobody left but me. My hands were so numb I could no longer feel the wire except when my weight fell against it. The mittens were worn through here and there and the wire had cut to the bone across my palms. The blood clotted and froze in the rips as fast as it oozed.

He won't ever make it back, I thought. The horse will founder under the double load. I'm sure he knows about me and Mona. Now he can have his revenge. And then I fell into the opening of a gate—and centuries later, another. This time I couldn't get up. I just lay back and kicked feebly with my legs and shook my arms, hearing Big Boy's warning to the last.

When I woke up next morning I couldn't reconcile myself to the idea of being in bed. I decided I was dead and gone to heaven. Then the reality of pain brought me around. My hands throbbed as sleep left me. They were bandaged. I got up, and it was quite a spell before I could get dressed because of the hands.

I went into the kitchen. Mrs. Hoover was boiling some strong-smelling something on the stove.

"How's Hoover?" I asked. "Where's Big Boy?"

"Hoover's in a bad way," she said. "Broken hip, I'm afraid. Big Boy's down in the pasture driving the stock to the stacks."

I noticed that the sun was shining, not a cloud in sight. I looked out the window at the glittering stillness. The land was a desert of white stretching on and on. I shivered.

"Here," Mrs. Hoover said, "take this coffee. Your hands were pretty bad cut up, but they'll heal if you're careful."

I gulped the coffee, scorching my throat. I said, "Don't you think we'd better get a doctor for Hoover?"

"Can't," she said. "It's twenty miles into Hi Lo, and even if a horse were to make it, old Doc Mullins is too old and feeble to get out here. We'll just have to wait and hope till the roads are cleared."

"That might be days," I said.

"I know," she said, "but it's all we can do." She strained the boiled liquid out into a tall glass and took it in to Hoover. I followed her.

Though he was in great pain, he said, "Thanks for the help, Pete. I think we saved the most of them."

I felt rotten. "Hoover," I said, "I think I was just in the way, and if it hadn't been for me you wouldn't be in the shape you're in."

"Hell, son," he said, getting half sore, "it's nobody's fault. Blame it on the storm if you want, but not on yourself. We're lucky to get out as easy as we did."

Big Boy came in after a while. I could vaguely remember now his returning for me, and saying, "Hold on, feller, just hold on and we've got it made."

He took his hot coffee and went into Hoover's bedroom. I could hear him say, "Well, Hoover, we've only lost seven or eight head as far as I can tell. Most of them had found the stacks, and I got the rest of them in now. We can make it till spring, Hoover."

But Hoover didn't make it. He died the day the machines plowed open a path through the snow to the ranch house. Clots formed in his blood, and the old man went on his last ride in terrible pain.

It had been a disastrous storm to say the least. Over on the Diamond-Two outfit three hundred head of two-year-old heifers that had survived the drought started drifting with the blizzard and walked off a sheer bluff into a two-hundred-foot canyon. The snow had piled in on them, and it would be spring before even the coyotes could get to them. All across the range cattle lay stiff and frozen with their legs sticking out like cedar posts.

Jim Ed Love had called his forces together. His own machinery had cut a road into Hi Lo, and within a couple of hours an army regiment in Colorado had started the forward motion of Operation Hay Lift, while the county and state bulldozers, road graders, and snowplows fought the drifts. Gradually, one by one, the ranchers were freed. The army flew in hay subsidized by the government and dropped it to the isolated, starving cattle. It cost more than it saved, but the ranchers felt that at least they had not been deserted.

Mitch Peabody extended credit, and his wife even kept her teats off the scales for a while. The bank in Ragoon lowered interest rates. After the government had declared Hi Lo a disaster area, Federal funds on long term pay-out were made available to the ranchers for restocking. It would take all the time they had been allotted for full recovery, and then some.

Abrahm Frink, who had butchered what few cattle he had anyway, just sat around and blamed the storm itself on the government. He said that it was a plot and that the politicians had hired Tinker Grits to make this storm with his rain machine so they could show how generous they were with the army airplanes paid for by the citizens. All this would be good publicity, he figured, and garner a lot of votes next election.

A couple of days after the storm Uncle Bob saddled his hunting horse and called his dogs. In the deep drifts the long-legged hounds caught and killed six cattle-gorged coyotes. It was one of the best days of his entire life.

It was too bad that Hoover hadn't made it to see Jim Ed Love's bulldozer plow right up into his yard and then open a path to his grave.

I felt pretty bad about that, but Big Boy told me: "Hell, he lived more good lives than a city full of deacons. This is the way he would have liked it. He died fighting for his land and his cattle."

Maybe because I had quit, maybe because of Hoover, maybe because of Mona, maybe because of my guilt around Big Boy, I don't know, but anyway I left Hi Lo. I decided to go south and take a job on a ranch near Santa Fe. Before I left I stopped in Sano to get Josepha. Suddenly I knew I wanted her and needed her very much. All my doubts had gone with the storm.

Sano was the lonesomest place I ever saw. The snow lay frozen in the shade of the buildings, and only one car was parked on the street. I walked into the store, and her father shook hands with me. He asked about Hoover, and I told him the news and we hashed over different ranchers' losses.

Finally I asked, "Where's Josepha?"

He paused a minute, then said, "Didn't you know?"

"Know what?"

"About a week before the storm she left on her honeymoon."

"Honeymoon?" I said vacantly.

"Yeah, she married a boy from Ragoon. They're going to live in Los Angeles. He's got a good job out there in an aircraft factory."

"I didn't know," I said. I told him goodbye and stepped outside. The wind had died for a minute. It was very cold.

Chapter Twenty-three

I liked my new job, but it took some time for the years at Hi Lo to begin to dim. There were five hands besides myself and the cook. The food was good and there was always plenty of it. I started getting acquainted with the neighboring ranchers and their cowboys, but you don't get to know men in five months unless you are thrown into extreme situations with them.

About half the Two-Bars outfit was in rough country and had to be worked horseback. The balance was down on the flats and could be covered in a day with a pickup truck.

I had heard through people who had kin in the Hi Lo country that the spring rains had been plentiful and the grass was coming on.

I spent many hours trying to forget a lot of things and many more trying to remember everything. A lot of pictures crowded my mind: the night Big Boy whipped half a dance floor with only a little help from Levi and me; the evening in the desert with Josepha; the drought and the brief but deadly blizzard. And Mona. She was the most vivid of all.

Some of the ranches around us had already started spring roundup and branding. The foreman told us to get our gear ready to begin the following week. I suppose this started me thinking more and more about Big Boy. We had made so many brandings, rodeos, and drunks together that a whole chain of memories ran through my head.

I decided to write him a letter. I told him about the kind of outfit I was on, what kind of horses they had, the grub, the pay, the whole works. I told him about the country dance at a neighbor's when I had held a skinny gal so close I thought she was standing behind me, and a lot of other meaningless stuff. I finished the letter by asking about Mona. Then I wondered if that was why I had written.

I had already crawled into the pickup to take the letter into town when the foreman came out of the main house and yelled, "Pete! Long distance!"

I got out and walked over to the big frame house, trying to guess who in the hell could be calling me.

The operator said, "One moment, sir, and I'll get you a better connection."

It wasn't much of an improvement; this was a privately repaired line and was always bad.

I finally heard, "Pete, can you hear me?"

"Yeah."

"This is Levi."

"Why howdy, Levi. How the hell are you, boy?"

"Pete—" He hesitated a minute.

"Yeah?"

"Big Boy was shot and killed yesterday."

It was strange how calm I was. Levi said they were burying him the next afternoon at two o'clock. Then the connection went bad. I yelled into the phone, trying to reestablish contact, but it was no use.

I hung up and stood a minute without moving. Big Boy dead. I'd lived with the idea a long time, but even so I couldn't take it in. It was as hard to accept as the idea of the sun not coming up every morning.

I made arrangements with my boss and took off for Hi Lo. I had sworn never to return, but now I wanted to go back and get whoever was responsible for Big Boy's death. That would probably mean Les. Maybe even Mona.

It was a long drive, and by the time I got to Ragoon it was late at night. I was drained emotionally by then, feeling all hollowed out, like a rotten log. I decided to stay in Ragoon and go on to Hi Lo the next day. I could make it for the funeral and do what I had to do before sunset. Somehow I didn't want to spend a night in Hi Lo. I couldn't really say why.

The next day I took my time, not admitting it but secretly hoping I would be late for the funeral service. I didn't figure Levi would go either. I was right. He was leaning in the door of his shack, waiting for me as I drove up.

As usual, he didn't greet me with any formal hello but simply pointed to a chair. He poured us both a cup of coffee, and we sat down across the table from each other. Through the window we could see the crowd gathering at the church a couple of blocks away.

"Who did it?" I asked, feeling the blood drain away from my face.

"Little Boy," he said.

"Little Boy?" I was prepared for anything but that. "Little Boy? Well, God A'mighty. How?"

So he told me about it.

"You know that Little Boy never did measure up in Big Boy's eyes. He wasn't much of a cowboy and didn't even take any real interest in the ranch. He spent most of his time in Hi Lo and Ragoon playing pool and such. Fact is, he didn't seem to be a Matson at all. It wasn't his fault, Pete; it's just the way he was made. Big Boy was like his pa and his grandpa. You know, old-time, roughhouse bastards that just plunged into everything with guts and muscle. Well, thinking back on it, Big Boy gave his brother a pretty rough time, trying to knock him into something he just wasn't meant to be. About a month ago Big Boy was telling me how sore he was when he found out his brother hadn't even made an effort to get out to the ranch when the blizzard struck. He just stayed here in town, drinking and playing pool. The old woman and the youngest brother had it all alone. They lost pretty heavy. In fact, figuring it on a percentage basis, they lost heavier than almost anybody around. Big Boy just naturally blamed it all on his brother. He told me, 'Levi, I'd knock that boy's brains out if I knew where to hit him.'"

"That sounds just like him," I said. "But God A'mighty, Levi, remember the Hi Lo rodeo last year, when Big Boy just flat-ass risked his life for him?"

"I know," Levi said, "but I always guessed that Little Boy held that against him. His big brother was everything in the world that Little Boy could never be."

"How did it happen?"

"Well, Big Boy went home to help with the spring branding the other day. Since you left he'd taken over Hoover's outfit and had got himself an interest in it. It seems that Big Boy had cussed Little Boy out at the branding, saying he couldn't rope and never was in the right place at the right time. Which was all true enough. Then the day of the killing Little Boy had walked off, saying he was going to town. Big Boy followed him and told him to look at the yard fences. They were all down and full of weeds and the barns needed fixing and the corrals repairing and, by God, Little Boy wasn't going anywhere until this outfit was put back in shape like it had always been."

We could hear the singing up at the church: it was the Marine Hymn. I had completely forgotten that Big Boy had once been a Marine. He had been so much else.

"Well," Levi went on, "Little Boy told him he wasn't his boss and he would do as he damn pleased. It must have taken all the nerve he had to face Big Boy and say that. Anyway, he claimed Big Boy hit him then and knocked him up against the car and picked up a board and made for him. Little Boy must have been scared right down to his socks. He ran around the other side of the car, jerked the door open, and pulled a thirty-eight out of the glove compartment. The way he and his mother told it, Big Boy came around the fender with the board raised in front of him. Little Boy pulled the trigger, and the first shot went through Big Boy's elbow and chest at the same time. He kept coming. Little Boy pulled the trigger as fast as he could, and on the fourth shot Big Boy spun around and went down on his face. The fifth and last shot went between his shoulder blades."

I sat a long time without saying anything. They were bringing Big Boy out of the church now, and the car engines were beginning to start.

"There's just one thing wrong, Levi," I said finally. "Big Boy wouldn't have used a board. You know he wouldn't. How could the whole family swear to a lie like that!"

"Listen, Pete," Levi said, "whether it's true or not, his ma had to do it."

"Why?"

"Well, look at it this way. Her whole life had been lived on the thin edge of tragedy. Her father-in-law and her husband and now her son had all died violently, from gunshots. What did you expect her to do—throw her next oldest into the gas chamber?"

I thought a minute, then nodded. I don't know when I ever felt so tired.

The hearse was turning down the main street of Hi Lo now, and the wind was rising, whipping the little flags tied to it.

I got up and said, "Well, I guess I'll go on up the hill, Levi. Want to come?"

He poured himself another cup of coffee and rubbed his hands along the back of one of his cedar statues. "No, I'll go afterward," he said.

I started to ask about Mona, but something kept me from it.

I waited until all the other cars were on their way, then followed along behind. It took a long time, it seemed to me, for everybody to wind up the hill and unload.

Jim Ed Love was there. I saw him give his condolences to Mrs. Matson. I knew it was all hypocrisy, but maybe she didn't know the difference. The Felders were there. Young Martin couldn't keep the relief out of his face.

The old-time cowhands Big Boy had worked with, loved, and understood, gathered in a group apart with their big hats off. They stood stiff-jointed from all the blizzards, droughts, bucking horses, tail drives, and hell raising of their younger days. There weren't many like them left.

There were a few others that truly grieved, such as Uncle Bob and Tinker Grits, but all in all, the rest seemed anxious to get it over with and call it quits. I was one of those. I had been the last to climb the hill and I was the first to leave.

I drove back down to Hi Lo intending to drop by and visit with Levi again. But I just didn't belong here anymore, so I turned right down the highway. Then it hit me—Mona hadn't been there. I would have bet anything in the world that nothing could have stopped her. I found out later that on that very day she had given birth to Big Boy's only son.

About five miles out of Hi Lo I noticed my letter to Big Boy lying on the seat beside me. I pulled off to the side of the road. I got out and took the letter with me. Then I tore it into little pieces. The wind caught them one by one and sent them dancing across the rolling hills of Hi Lo.

PART TWO

■■■■■■■■■■■■■■■

Bobby Jack Smith
You Dirty Coward!

*These few chapters of fun
are fondly dedicated to
Charles Ford, C. W. (Dusty) Dunbar and Brian Keith,
keen and loyal amigos;
and especially to
Sam Peckinpah's trailer house at Malibu.*

Chapter One

If it hadn't of been for that big-titted school marm, I don't reckon I would've become the educated son of a bitch I am. There's times I wished I'd stayed stupid.

When I first spotted her, I was punching cows for Gravy King. Gravy, the richest cowman with the biggest spread in this whole country, was called Gravy 'cause he always had some of it on his vest. This didn't mean he was dirty, just careless.

Me and three other hands was moving a bunch of cows down from the hills to winter pasture and stopped to water at the country schoolhouse. It was recess time and the school yard was swarming with little ranch kids running, jumping, hollering and playing games. Right smack in the middle of them, waving her arms and giving instructions, was this here teacher, Della Craven.

I sat there on horseback staring at her, but about all I could see was teats. When she raised her arms, they bounced. When she walked, they bounced, and when she just stood still and talked, they bounced. A feller's eyes just couldn't help being drawn to all that movement. I would of liked to see some more of her parts, but her dress hung almost to the ground.

I reined over to her and said, "Howdy, miss . . . ma'am."

She looked up with that pretty face tilted sideways like a half-breed pup's and said right back, "A good day to you, sir."

This sorta rocked me back on my haunches. I'd been called such like as, "You numb-headed, jacked-off, piss-complected, bastard of a dumb cowboy," and a hundred variations on that, but never "sir." I was mighty pleased.

I ranted on. "Uh, the grass looks good, don't it?"

"It certainly does!"

"The cows are lookin' good, too, ain't they?"

"They certainly are!"

I took a little closer look at the cows and, sure enough, they did appear better than usual.

I ranted on, staring across the playground at the kids. "Kids behavin'?"

"Of course. I insist on discipline. It's the *only* way to an education, and education is the *only* way to success."

Now even at this time of my life I wasn't as dumb as most folks thought. I asked a right smart question of my own.

"Success? Jist exactly what does it mean?"

She eyeballed me a spell, and even staring straight ahead them titties shook and quivered in all directions. They reminded me of a wild cow I'd penned last week that just kept running at different parts of the corral till she finally broke loose.

"Well, who acquires all the money in the world?"

"A crooked crapshooter!" I answered feeling plumb smart-ass.

"Surely not. There's always one more crooked than he."

I stared.

She ran on. "The bankers and the politicians, that's who."

I stared some more. In the meantime she grabbed Johnny Watkins by the ear and twisted it till it looked like a little piece of catch rope and then batted him up beside the head, saying, "I told you to quit pinching Mary Lou there."

Johnny stumbled off holding the sides of his head with both hands. This here was a woman of action. I could tell just by looking.

She turned back to me using the same perty smile.

"The bankers and the politicians get all the money because they can outfigure everyone else. And the reason they can do that is because they can read and write and add and subtract. You've *got* to have an education to be a success," she said again.

I was beginning to savvy what that word meant. However, this didn't do me much good because I didn't know how to do any of them things she mentioned.

I said, "'Bye," and rode off, suddenly feeling like a failure. If she'd taken one of them big, shaky blouse-fillers out and waved it at me I doubt if I'd uh had enough guts to look back.

We moved the cattle towards home.

She kept right on running through my skull all the time—even at night after I'd been in the saddle so long my tailbone showed through my hide. I got bucked off twice 'cause my mind was on grabbing her instead of the saddle horn—and they are two entirely different shapes. Finally it come to me clear, that sure as my name was Bobby Jack Smith I had to have this here woman.

One night I waited till all the other hands were asleep in the bunkhouse before I slipped out. Nobody would have paid any attention 'cause somebody was always stumbling out in the fresh air to take a leak. This was a private matter, however.

I saddled up the night horse and set out the five miles to the schoolhouse. The cockeyed bugs was buzzing all over and ever' now and then a coyote would howl, sounding just like I felt. I hadn't been into Dirty Town for over a month, and I was sure enough horny. The closer I got to the schoolhouse, the harder I breathed. I'd done forgot I didn't have no education. I rode up to where she stayed in the back, tied my horse and knocked on the door.

She came to the door, opened it a crack, peeked around asking, "Who is it?" I told her and she said, "Just a minute. Let me get decent."

I watched her turn the lamp down low. When she bent over to do it, the oversized nightgown dropped down and both of them quivering beauties flopped out free and bouncing.

I had a hard-on that a cat couldn't have scratched.

If my balls had been tied with barbwire to a thousand-pound rock, I'd uh still made the same run. Without stopping I ran right through the door and across a chair, falling hard up against her just as she was rearranging the nightgown. She fell back on the bed and I fell on her. The bed broke somewhere around its middle and as we hit the floor her big, long legs flew apart and she spread both arms trying to break the fall. That left her wide open. I was trying to stay between those kicking legs, trying to keep her claws outta my eyes with one hand and tear off my boots and pants with the other. I was a right busy cowboy there for a minute or two. While I was doing all this, she was trying to throw me off. It's true I ain't got much learning in lots of departments but riding anything that bucks is my business. I finally got a little in her and this seemed to give me some leverage—like having both feet in the stirrups makes staying in the saddle easier.

I got her arms spread and held them. The more she bucked, the better it got. I was now well stirruped and in a minute I had time to watch them titties flopping around like two crazy moons. First she was screaming for help and calling me some of those names I've been called so often before. The louder she hollered, the harder she bucked. Finally she was all damp like she'd been hit in the butt with a wet mop. She wasn't cussing me anymore. She just moaned a little and it was all over.

She lay there under me, and I just waited for her to start cussing. Instead she rolled me off and sat up in the dim light of the room and stared at me, sort of caressing her long white thighs slow, like rubbing down a hard-run horse. I sat up against the side of the busted bed and stared at her, already wanting another ride in that saddle.

She said, "Why did you do that?"

"Mainly 'cause I ain't got no education, Miss Della. I'm just so dumb I don't know any better."

"Would you truly like to better yourself?"

"I truly would, ma'am, if I just had somebody to teach me."

She quit rubbing, got up and pulled a towel off the wall rack, and stood there in front of me drying herself off. She got down to her big round belly and even lower, spreading her legs to get a better swipe. Me and everything else just stood straight up again.

She said, staring hard at my best lick, "Well . . . well, I'll instruct you in the three R's but you've got to promise never to do that again till . . . till . . ."

"Till what?" I croaked.

"Till I get my nightgown off. It damned near strangled me!"

I laughed and bent her over on an old worn-out divan and gave her a long, slow cowboy ride.

The next morning I had to lead my horse up to the porch to mount. I was so weak I couldn't raise my foot all the way up to the stirrup. Course I *was* out of training.

Chapter Two

Now I had quite a time convincing hardheaded ol' Gravy King of my craving for an education.

"All you need to know is how to keep a horse between yore legs."

"Now, Gravy, you know there's better things than a horse to fit between a man's legs," I shot right back, smartin' off.

It didn't matter what I said, though. He said, "No, you cain't be ridin' over to Della's schoolhouse ever' night and still do an honest day's work. It'd just wear you out till you cain't even talk sense to a horse."

Then one of them flashes of brilliance I was to become noted for later on whacked me good.

"I tell you what, Gravy, I'll ride one of them green broncs out of that new string over there ever' night."

"You will?"

"Hell yes, and sure enough."

"Without a hazer?"

"Right, old pardner, without a hazer."

"Well, if you're that big a damn fool, then so am I."

It was pleasing to hear. Course I did have some trouble arriving sometimes before she went off to bed. Riding raw broncs without another cowboy along to haze 'em out of fences, canyons, tree limbs and gully holes can lead to a rough life. I was peeled all over from broncs running me into all the aforementioned hazards, and I was clawed and bruised all over from paying my tuition in Miss Della's broken-down bed.

It was a trying time for a dumb cowboy, but I just figured it all as part of *working* my way through school. I had learned the letters of the alphabet from an old aunt of mine, but had just never learned to sort 'em out into words. It did help, though, and it wasn't long till Della had me reading . . . and writing.

"This here is a dog. Look at that fast dog run. Watch that goddamned son of a bitch catch that rabbit."

I never in my life saw anybody with as much patience as Miss Della. It wasn't so much that I was a slow learner, but it was mighty difficult to keep my mind on studying when she was around. I reckon she sorta figured this out because she would read me a little bit of a story, enough anyway so's I'd get interested in knowing what was going to happen next, then she'd just quit. No matter how I begged her she wouldn't go on. I had no choice but to work like hell so I could find out how the story ended. It was sorta like throwing a kid out in a pond to teach him to swim. He either learns right there and then or drowns. Sometimes she'd say, "Now Bobby Jack, it's not just the letters, it's also the sound." Then she'd make noises showing me all the different ways the ABC's could be read. She'd even draw me little pictures of lambs, cows, rabbits and such like, then write the word under it. She called this last "identification of words related to objects."

As much as I liked funnin' around in the back room with her, I was also catching on to something brand-new to me—some women are good for things besides screwing and sewing. This here revelation was a shocker. I kept wondering how come I'd never noticed this before. Not that she wasn't a fine hand with a needle and thread, but she was also a good cook. She had ninety-seven ways of fixin' pinto beans, all of 'em good. "You didn't learn this in school," I said once, as I swallered the last of the best bowl of chili beans ever made. She didn't say anything back at this, acting like she hadn't heard me. She even made bean pie with molasses that tasted better'n Christmas dinner.

One night we'd studied hard, ate a big bean supper, and celebrated the whole damn thing with some nice warm loving. We were laying there staring out the window at the moon, listening to all them blabbermouth bugs outside keeping one another awake. I said, "You must be awful proud to be educated so much you can teach other people. That's just about as high as you can go."

She took hold of my hand and said kinda soft like, "No, darling, you mustn't ever think like that. Sure, you must acquire some kind of education to get started, but then there's no limit. This," she said, waving her arm in the blue night air at the schoolhouse ceiling, "is only a start."

Now that was hard for me to believe. But then, that's what I was studying for. To use Miss Della's own words, "An education is to make the heretofore unbelievable, believable."

I really didn't know what she meant exactly, but someday I damned sure would.

I rolled over and blocked her view of the moon. The cockeyed bugs probably went on chirping as usual just like they owned the whole damn world, but me and that great lady under me didn't hear them anymore.

I tell you I was becoming a fast learner considering I was getting about a half-hour's sleep a night. I sure was glad for the weekends 'cause Della went off to Dirty Town to visit relatives. Anyway, that's what she told me. Even on weekends I broke horses during the day and studied at night. Us cowhands didn't make enough money to go into Dirty Town but about once ever three or four months, so I always had plenty of company in the bunkhouse. Sometimes I'd get to reading and writing and working things out in my head and forget all about the lamp. This was resented on occasion by the other hands, especially when they'd been digging post holes or stacking hay all day.

Cranky ol' John Benson kept yapping off such things as, ". . . Ass, now let's see, how would you go about spelling Big Ass Della? I know how to spell Ass . . . it's A—R—S—E. Now let's see, how would you spell Big Titted Schoolmarm? T—Y—TT—Y?"

They'd all laugh and I'd feel a little heat rising, but I stayed with my studies.

Then that cockeyed Jose Fernandez said, "Maybe the way Bobby Jocks [that's what he called me, *Bobby Jocks*] is studying, he can geet in the first grade by the time he ees feefty."

Then that blabbermouthed Indian bastard named Half Storm said, "All he's got to do to pass is just keep *harrrd* at it."

Well, now *that* was private business. I threw down my book and kicked Half Storm way across the bunk on top of Ole Benson and splatted Jose Fernandez in the mouth right where I'd knocked out two of his teeth the last Fourth of July. I hadn't gave Ole Benson *his education* yet. So soon's he scrambled out from under the Indian I kicked him in the balls. While he was down on his knees pissing and moaning and holding his sore spot with both hands, I up and gave him a lecture.

"Now, if you spider-brained bastards want to stay out here the rest of your useless lives breaking out Gravy King's three-dollar horses for nothin', fine! That's just fine. You hear? Fine! But not me, I aim to elevate myself!"

I went on awhile longer; then when I saw I really did have them listening I pulled the real clincher. "My old aunt read me out of the Bible once where it says, 'Them who seeks, gets!' " I just rared back and let that soak in awhile. I could tell by the nice expressions on their faces I wasn't going to have no more trouble.

However, the next Monday night I was having another kind of trouble. A little black, stocking-legged horse had been giving me problems with tree limbs and trunks. He just seemed to have a hell of an itch and kept wanting to run into trees to cure it. I was busy fighting him and was right up beside the little white schoolhouse in the meadow before I saw somebody else's saddle horse tied there. I got down and tied the reins to a tree. I also took a catch rope from the saddle and tied it to my bronc's foot and then to the bottom of one of those trees he loved so much. Now if he broke the reins he was going to be in for a jam-up surprise when he hit the end of that forty-foot rope. I didn't aim to be left afoot this far from home with competition setting in.

I eased up and felt the brand on the bay horse. It was a BR and then I knew it was that goddamned educated Brad Ross, a small rancher from over north, that'd also gone to school.

I wondered if Della had run out of lamp oil. It didn't make sense them visiting in the dark otherwise. Well, soon as I got up by the window I could hear them visiting plain enough. "Oh! Oh, Brad! There! There! Right there!"

Well, I reached down and pulled my gun out. I'd make 'em both know where "right there" was, all right. Then some of that new learning took ahold of me. I couldn't revert back to my old style. I must not allow myself to go backwards. Not now, when I was so close to graduating.

I went back out and untied my horse, did up the rope, and eased him away chocking hell out of the saddle horn and chocking hell out of my gizzard, at the same time fighting to keep my wild, crazy self under control.

I rode on north a ways and got on the trail to Brad's place. I followed it till it came right up close to the rim of a canyon that dropped straight off several hundred feet into a bunch of sharp boulders. I took my bronc up ahead past this spot and tied him in plain view of the trail. You think I ain't a figuring fool. If I hadn't done this, Brad's horse woulda smelled mine and boogered, letting Brad know something was hiding by the trail. This way his horse would booger, but Brad would think it was from my bronc up ahead and he'd ride cautiously on by me.

I gathered me up a five-foot limb about four inches thick, picked out a nice pile of rocks to hide behind along the edge of the rim, and waited. And waited. It was hard to stay awake just sitting still like this, but I stayed hooked by thinking about the way Della yelled, "Right there!"

Them same old bugs and coyotes and owls made all their same old noises as always. I waited some more. Then way to hell off over the world, I could see a little violet light shoving up in the sky running from the sun. Right after that I heard horse's hoofs coming *cloppity, clop, clop, clippity clop.*

I peeked around the rocks and could see Brad's bay with his head up and his ears thrown forward towards my little black. Ole Brad was staring hard, and just as he was about to pass me he pulled his gun out. I let him get on by just about a yard. I made a right good swing with the limb. It caught him *splat* across the shoulder blades and away he went off the horse, over the rim. Not much time went by till he quit all that hollering he was doing on the way down. I walked over to the edge of the canyon and looked down where old Brad was spread-eagled in the top of a juniper tree on a little ledge. By the time he figured out how to get down out of the tree and out of the canyon without killing himself, he'd have time to think over the foolishness of foolin' with my teacher. It ain't that I'm jealous or too stingy to share, but Brad Ross had gone to school for nine years and I'd only been studying a few months.

I untied the black and rode on back over to Della's and just crawled on her and the next thing she was hollering was, "Oh Bobby Jack, right there! That's it! That's it! Right there!" I was pleased she could tell the difference between me and Brad Ross in the dark.

I just barely got out of there before school took up. I rode towards home, though, feeling good that my education would continue.

I studied hard and gentled a lot of broncs that winter. It was a fairly mild one, not dropping more than thirty degrees below zero over ten or fifteen times. I kept up my duties with Della. She never did mention ol' Brad to me even after they found him wandering around talking to himself like those millions of night bugs. That lady teacher was a high-toned, fancy-stepping, brain-massaging son of a bitch. You just can't say much better than that about a person.

Chapter Three

Now I'd worked for a lot of son of a bitches in my day, but none of 'em compared to ol' Gravy. I don't know what made me reflect back on the last few miserable years I'd spent slaving for him, but I did. Maybe it was because I wanted to get all the good reasons in my head I could for leaving the King spread. Anyway, as the feller said, "I dipped into the past to see where I'd been." Like one time he bet me, just for fun, that I couldn't eat a quail a day for thirty days. I'd heard this ever since I was a little button, but there wasn't any money up so I bravely called the bet. It wound up that I was spending what spare time a cowboy has trapping quail. I built this little box and would prop one end up kinda delicate with a stick. Then I'd tie grain on the stick and when the quails started pecking and pulling at the kernels, they'd jerk the stick out and the box would "plop" right down over 'em.

Yeah, I ate a quail for thirty days all right. In fact, we had quail ever day for six months. I reckon we'd still be eatin' 'em if their population hadn't shrunk so. That conniving, greedy bastard had saved a lot of beef this way. It had taken me a spell to catch on, but hell, once I see a thing it makes me smarter. Gravy gave me enough help along this line to make me the true genius I later became.

One day he said, "Yuh know, Bobby Jack, if a man would take a baby calf and pick it up ever' day till it was grown, he'd be the strongest man in the world."

I said, "Huh?" All the time, though, my brain was really putting out. If a feller was the strongest in the whole world it would give him lots of advantages. I was perty damned powerful to start with.

"Hell," he says, "a calf grows so gradual that a man'd never notice the gain atall."

Well sir, I gave it a try. Sure enough that little ol' milk pen calf was just as easy to lift after one week as it was to start with. My muscles just simply grew the same amount as the calf. Hellsfire, anybody could have figured that out.

I got to talkin' about this to Gravy, and he said he admired my spirit so much that if I could pick that animal up off the ground when it was a mere yearlin' he'd give me three months' extra wages. "Course," he said, "if you turn chicken and quit I'm naturally gonna expect you to give up three months' pay."

Naturally. One thing I ain't is chicken, so I agreed right there to his generous terms. The first three weeks I just walked out to the milk pen and jerked that calf a foot off the ground, and didn't even squint my eyes doing it. At around six weeks I ran into a problem. It wasn't that the calf was so heavy—it had just growed a mite taller. It was a little bit more of a lift to get him up that high. The calf had taken a liking to me and waited ever day just like a dog for me to do my trick. I kept feeling my muscles to see if they were still growing. It seemed they all were except those in my back. Somehow or other they'd taken to aching all the time. Soon, the calf was so tall I could no longer reach down over him, but with a fair show of wisdom, I just crawled under and lifted him on my back. That worked fine for a few days even though it felt like I might be bustin' a gut now and then. Mine, not the calf's.

The other hands kept cheering me on, giving dumb advice such as, "Don't feed the bastard an' he'll quit growin'." "Give him an enema once a day. That'll keep him light." "What you need, Bobby Jack, is boots with higher heels." "You might jist teach him to jump straight up when you grunt."

I appreciated their concern but nothin' worked out. It happened one day after I'd put in ten hours and thirty miles in the saddle. I really blew the plug, but the best I could do was get three legs off the ground. Then a few days later I could only lift two legs. I grunted. I farted. I cussed. I was whipped. Like the feller says, my mouth had overloaded my ass. There went three months when the other boys would be goin' to town, getting drunk and running whores. Three months that I'd stay on the ranch and fight back the tears. It's the law of the land. Everbody knows a cowboy cain't cry anyway. It was no wonder I later made the move I did with Miss Della Craven to get some learnin' in my head before it was too late.

Well, by damn, I might have been rooked a little on account of my back muscles deserting me, but I got even. There was a widow woman with seven kids over East. I'd seen Gravy's horse parked there lots of times. Shirley Mae wasn't the pertiest thing in the world, but she was a little more appealing than a she-cow. Things on her body kinda drooped. The point is, though, she at least had them things.

Ever' chance I got to ride and check the east pasture, I took. Part of the kids were in school, but there was enough left that we never did get to use the bed. She would just ask me out to look at the hogs, chickens, and milk cows, and my advice on their care. At the same time she'd put the rest of the kids to work cleaning the house. I will say this about Shirley Mae, she might of been a poor widow but she kept a sure enough clean house.

Not only was I enjoyin' the lady in the hay barn, but I was getting even with that goddamned Gravy King. One day I met him coming while I was going. The sweat popped out right in that freezing wind like I'd just finished diggin' a ten-foot hole in solid rock with a tablespoon.

"Howdy, Bobby Jack. Did you get a good count on the cattle in the east pasture?"

"Hundred percent," I choked.

"Good. Good. How're they winterin'?"

"'Bout usual."

"Good," he said, riding off leaving me setting there like a

cockeyed cedar post. There was something wrong, but even my quick mind couldn't get to it.

It wasn't much longer till he pulled another surprising thing. "Bobby Jack," he starts out, "a cowboy has a lonely life, and seein' as how you ain't had relaxation in town like the other boys, I'm goin' to do you a special favor."

I perked right up at this good news. My later education showed me that favors that are given cost twice as much as those you buy. I smiled and waited, seeing myself in town drunk with a whole week off and a pocket full of money. There was girls, perty girls hangin' all over me.

What he was offering did concern the female sex, all right. By God! He said he was goin' to take me over and introduce me to a fine upstanding widow, Shirley Mae. Even though he was giving me a present that I already had, it was generous of him just the same. Maybe he did have a little feeling in that rawhide heart, after all. He smiled at me like I was his favorite son.

The introduction had me sweating in that freezing wind again, but Shirley Mae acted like she'd never seen me before. Well now, it was right nice. I could ride over there and whack her down in the hay any minute I could steal. It was a comfortable feeling and a hell of a lot more fun. The next month was the best I ever spent on any ranch.

One day me and Shirley Mae had come back from inspecting the livestock, and the kids was sent outside to repair the porch. We were alone. She poured us a cup of coffee, and sat down across from me. "Bobby Jack," she says, looking mighty serious for a woman who had just been happily screwed, "there's something I got to tell you."

Folks don't often hesitate to lay good news on you, so I kinda braced myself in the rickety chair and waited for the blow. I sure hoped she wasn't wanting to get hitched.

"I'm in a family way," she sneaked out.

I tried to swaller. I tried to grin. I tried to keep my breathing steady and healthy. Nothing worked. Then she started bawling and saying such things as she had all the kids one poor helpless woman could raise, and I was just going to have to take care of this 'un. She blabbered on and on. What she really meant was she wanted half my wages. I stuttered some weak lies and told her I'd see her in a few days and we'd settle the whole thing.

Even with all the brains I had in my head there just didn't seem to be any way out. Cowboys get paid just enough to buy one pair of boots and two pair of Levi's a year, and take a cheap day in town once in a while. Now that's the average cowboy. I wasn't average in no way. In fact, Gravy had me in such a hole I couldn't have got out if I was a bird. I figured. I thought. I worried and I cussed. Nothin' worked. I wanted to help Shirley Mae, all right, but I was helpless.

I was riding along plumb sick all over. If I'd had to fight a grizzly bear with a pocket knife I woulda done it. But this here situation had my head rattling as loose as goose shit. I was numb.

My horse stopped all on his own mind under this overhanging limb. I noticed my hand was fingering my rope. Even the horse knew what I had to do. I took the rope off and tied it around my neck. Then I threw the other end over the limb and tied that in the same place. Now all I had to do was spur the horse out from under me and there'd be no more freeze-ass winters and burn-ass summers. There'd be no more pregnant widows to worry about, and best of all there'd be no more Gravy Kings. At the thought of him that bright brain of mine that had been so addled started pulling itself into shape. Why, Gravy had seen Shirley Mae twice as much as me before the introduction. . . . What if . . . what if he . . . my God mighty! I might be hanging an innocent man!!

I untied that rope and coiled it up, tying it on the saddle without taking a breath, praying all the time that ol' horse wouldn't booger. Whooee!

Chapter Four

What with Gravy working me perty near to death and the widow hounding my ass for money, those were not the good

old days. I was one harassed cowboy, but I was also alive.
There is a lot to be said for that condition.

Now there was *one* thing that really got to ol' Gravy. That
thing was the biggest wild steer that ever lived. Old Randy, as
we called him, stood higher than a horse, and had to weigh in
at about eighteen hundred pounds. His tracks were eight inches
across and far between. He was twice as wild and three times
as smart as the deers and coyotes. It took a lot of Gravy's grass
to keep that belly full and moving. Old Randy was six years old
and every time Gravy had a thought about all those years of
free feeding he would—Well, there ain't no use going on about
it, the proof of his deep feeling is the fact he offered a
twenty-dollar reward for the outlaw's capture.

The trouble was, about all you ever saw of Old Randy,
besides those huge tracks, was one eye staring at you through
a hole in the thick brush, or a noise where you knew he was.
I bet I'd ridden a thousand miles after those tracks, and all I
heard was the sound of him runnin' over things way out ahead.
Sometimes I doubted he existed.

I decided to put a loop on him. It was the only way out. In
spite of my many problems I was thinking beyond the reward.
My brain had gotten tougher with the troubles.

Ever' chance I got I cut across country looking for Old
Randy. It was amazing the ground he covered. One day I'd
latch on to his tracks and the next day find 'em twenty miles
away. You could see where he'd ripped through the brush,
breaking limbs. Twice, when I thought I had him headed for an
opening where I might get a go at him, he'd backtracked quiet
as a mountain lion, losing me., It was enough to drive the
dumbest cowboy nuts. What it did to a high thinker like me was
just pitiful. Ever' white-face cow that was half hidden got to
looking like that yeller-hided Randy. I dreamed about that steer
having me hooked on one horn and getting ready to throw me
off in the same canyon I'd tapped ol' Brad into. Just the
cockeyed same I kept after him.

Then it happened. I outsmarted the smartest. I admit the top
side of my brain didn't tell me how to do it. The top side being
about one-hundredth as smart as the bottom side, I thought it
was luck. But those real bright lower regions knew better. You
just can't fool those lower regions. I'd tracked him half a day,

staying far enough behind so he wouldn't break and make one of his famous five-mile dashes. I was downwind and I don't believe even now that he knew I was really after him. He'd lost me in the mountains so many times he just got overconfident. The fact that I might have been just a wee bit underconfident probably brought about our meeting.

I was riding the biggest and fastest bay horse on the ranch. Even so, Old Randy must've outweighed us both put together by at least four hundred pounds. I was easing quietly up the soft sandy bottom of this little dry creek bed. There was good brush cover on the banks to hide us. Then I saw him through a small hole in the limbs. Just as I did, he threw his head up and spun halfway around, looking, smelling, sensing, but he hadn't located us yet. He had been grazing high up against a horseshoe bluff, where the grass was long and rich. God uh mighty, my heart started knocking splinters off my ribs. I felt the bay feel me and bunch his muscles. I undid the rope and made a real big Mother Hubbard loop. And then I whammed the spurs to my horse. At the second my mount busted out through the brush into the opening, Old Randy charged for the edge of the bluff. Now he had to come back a little towards me to make it. So with his coming towards me, and me going towards him, we were getting right swiftly to a confrontation. We were also cutting across on him. The bay horse was just as tired of tracking this son of a bitch as I was. He really built a fire to the steer. We all got to the corner of the bluff at the same time, moving just as fast as animals can move. I just threw the loop out there somewhere and said eighty-seven different prayers in one-half second. I prayed I'd catch him and was scared to death I might. I prayed that if I did he wouldn't jerk me and the horse out of sight in the sky. I prayed that he wouldn't tear the saddle off with me riding it, to my death in a bunch of sharp rocks. I prayed the rope wouldn't break. I prayed Randy wouldn't drive those horns into my horse and then pitch me off in that canyon like I'd dreamed. I tell you I was one praying bastard!

The loop just moved out there slower than constipated dog doo, and after what appeared to be four or five years, caught that damn steer right around the horns. I had 'im! Now that was my *lower brain* working again. Any kind of cow animal is easier to handle by the horns than the head or neck. The pressure of the rope squeezes some nerves or something.

Now this good bay cow horse was trained to slap on the brakes when he felt a weight on the other end of the rope. If he did that now, the air surrounding us would have suddenly been full of shit, hair, blood and corruption, and a few pieces of leather. What I did is brilliantly spur him forward with Randy not getting a chance to put his full weight on the rope. Even so, we were jerked about like a little six-inch trout on whale tackle. Then he went on one side of this tree and us on the other. It spun him around facing us. That's when I let the bay whip on the stops. Randy was snorting and blowing, and I'll always believe I saw sparks flying off the tips of his horns. He tried to charge us and this spun him around the tree twice more till he was wrapped up almost against the trunk. I took another rope, and latched it onto his neck, tying it up short to the saddle horn. Then I took a third rope, dismounted, and caught one of his long legs and tied the rope across to another tree. Then I sat down on a flat rock trying to coax some air back in my lungs, just staring at the impossible done made possible. When I got over the blind staggers I took the rope off the saddle horn and tied it to another tree. I had him three ways now. All he could do was shake his head and blow snot.

I rode back towards the ranch, one happy and proud cowboy. I gave credit to the horse, too, and told him so. Now all I had to do was leave the beast tied to that tree for three days till he got so weak I could fulfill my final plan. Course, I did have to sweat that some other cowboy wouldn't ride up on him and claim a free victory. I felt sorry for Randy, but it was the steer or the cowboy. I chose me.

It was a hard wait, but finally the sun said hello and good-bye three times and put the coup de grace to Gravy King. I didn't know those fancy terms then, but I learned 'em later from my studies of Napoleon.

I tromped over to Gravy's office. Most of the time when you take this long walk, Gravy is going to shove it to you. It may not always seem like it, but the results have been made known to many a sorry cowboy. Not this time, though. I had him by the left nut, and the right one had gone into hiding.

"Come in, Bobby Jack. Come on in and make yourself to

home. How is Shirley Mae? Fine woman, that. Make a man a good wife, and he'd have lots of ready-made hands for the ranch."

"Yeah, she's a dinger, all right," I threw right back to him.

"You're lookin' good, Bobby Jack. There's nothing like outdoor work to keep a man healthy and happy. Especially if he's got a woman to share these benefits with him."

"Yeah," I said. "I never felt better."

Gravy gave me one of his funny looks. I could see I had him rattled to the gourd.

"I just feel so full of life and energy, Mr. King, that I'm jist goin' out tomorrow and fit a loop on Old Randy."

He gave me an even funnier look, and then smiled like he was my great-great-grandfather.

"Well now, son, that would make me happier than a whore at a brand-new gold strike."

"Me, too," I agreed.

I rared back and laid the wood to him. "I don't figger I'll ever get so full of 'rarin' to go' stuff in my whole life again. Why, I'd be willin' to bet I can deliver him right here to headquarters by noon tomorrow."

"You don't mean with a thirty-thirty rifle and in pieces?"

I was way ahead of him. I knew he'd ask that question, trying to hedge his bets. "No, I mean alive on the end of a rope."

You could tell by the way his neck swelled up like a ruttin' buck's that he wanted to laugh till his pocket change rattled. I gave him credit cause he made out like he was thinking it over.

"How 'bout three months' wages?" he asked, knowing my weakness for that number.

"That'd be all right," I said, "but there's just one more thing." It was my turn to pause, and his to sweat. When I gathered he had all he could take, I socked another one in to the quick. "I want the steer, too."

Gravy had a few light convulsions and laughed out loud, telling me the steer wouldn't be fit for a vulture to eat.

I said, "Gravy, I wasn't aimin' to eat Ol' Randy, I just want to make a pet out of 'im."

That did it. We shook hands on the bet, and I could see in Gravy's sneaky eyes that he felt he'd pulled off another cinch.

I took three more ropes to make it look good, and headed for the hills in the middle of the night. I didn't give a damn about the cold or nothing else. By sun-up I had that steer tied so many ways he looked like he was caught in a giant spider web. He was drawn down and so weak he kinda leaned over against the tree while I was putting the fancy twine to him. The bark was peeled from the tree where he fought, horned, and pawed. The ground was powdered a foot deep and he'd shit and pissed half his life away. He was skinned and peeled all over—in some places to the bone. I had to love the big bastard—but I loved me more.

I left one rope tied from Randy's horns to my saddle, and headed downhill. He made a few attempts to fight, but me and the horse were stronger now. That steer hadn't gone slick-free for six years being dumb. He knew he was whipped, and soon just moved in the easiest direction and that was downhill towards Gravy King's headquarters.

I stopped out behind the barn and left my horse there holding him. Then I went up with a worried look on my mind and asked Gravy if I could have a little talk with him, real private down by the barn. He looked me over, and observing the strain I was forcing in my eyes, and the worried wrinkles I was having hell screwing up on my face, he lectured, "There ain't no backin' out of a bet of honor. A man's got to stay with his words no matter how bad it looks. We all pop off once in a while. Get ourselves into things we want out of."

"Yeah, I sure enough agree with you there, Mr. King . . . but . . . but . . ."

"Now, now, Bobby Jack. No need to try and talk your way out of it. We all have to face up to bein' a man once in a while no matter what the cost."

Just as he said "cost," we rounded the corner of the barn. I didn't look at the steer. My interest was elsewhere right then. Gravy stood and shook and looked at Old Randy and then at me and then back at the steer. His mouth was kinda slack, moving without words, and his eyes looked like a skunk had fresh sprayed 'em. He even took his hands out of his vest, and dropped them over his belly like he had the cold-water cramps. I had felt good that morning, and I'd had some joy in me on occasion when I'd swallered the fifth shot of brown whisky on some Saturday night. There'd been the fine feeling after two days in bed with that little red-headed whore five years ago, but all of that combined couldn't start the joy that whizzed through my body right this second.

Finally he gasped, "It ain't fair. That steer's sick."

"You feelin' all right, Mr. King? Would you like a drink of water, or maybe just standin' out here in this fresh outdoor air awhile will help you get your health back. Anything I can do to help, just let me know."

Well, he slobbered and groaned and paid me the cash. I stuck 'er deep in my pocket and drove that steer right on over to Shirley Mae's. I gave her the money and told her that if they'd keep the steer tied up a few days to a hay stack they could butcher him and have meat for a year. Since I knew I couldn't get the lady pregnant again in her present condition, I gave her a goodbye screw in a pile of old Randy's hay. Then I rode off never looking back again. She seemed right pleased and satisfied with the whole deal.

It was a few months later that I met Della and started preparing for my great future that would make history in our country for a hundred years. I don't think it should be too difficult to understand my wantin' to better myself, and get on in the world. Anybody that could outwit the steer and Gravy King, too, just had to win the world someday. Still, there was times when I wondered—just for a second, mind you—if what I'd done was pay for Gravy King's seven-pound boy.

I decided not to—how do they say—"reminisce" anymore. The present was more pleasant than the past.

Chapter Five

Finally the tiny green grass began to shove its way up through what was left of the brown winter grass, and the prairie dogs, the coyotes, and all of them damn bugs started sniffing one another and mating. It wasn't long till school was out for the summer.

Then one night after we'd broke the bed again flouncing around playing grab-ass, Della gave me the good news. She handed me a book with something wrote on the front of it. That something was *Napoleon—His Rise to Power and His Conquests.* She said if I'd read every word of that I would feel myself ready to leave the ranch and seek a richer life in town.

"Bobby Jack, you are one of the few people left in the world who is truly trying to better himself. Oh, I don't mean that many aren't desperately hunting wealth and prestige, but you're after pure knowledge. Do you know how rare and precious that is?" she finished, looking me between the horns, waiting for my answer.

I stumbled around the room, flipping the pages of the great book, my brain rotating so fast I couldn't pin down a single thought.

"Of course," she went on, "certain circumstances can exist in one's life where money is a need, a salve for survival, and it is a true and lasting comfort to know that one has fought for the high ground, won, and then used it well. Do you know what I mean, Bobby Jack?"

"Yes 'um, yes 'um," I said. One thing I did know for sure, this here Miss Della lady had as much going for her as any woman I'd ever met, and more than any man. I just don't know what would of become of me if I hadn't run into her, and I knew that I was the luckiest cowboy that ever got kicked in the head. By damn and rat turds, if I didn't finish that book in less'n two weeks and reported to the schoolhouse to hear Della's congratulations. All I found there was a note saying:

"It has been a great pleasure teaching you, cowboy. Someday maybe we'll meet again. All life is *the word.*"

"Well, I'll be a broke, pricked boar," I said out loud, and here I not only knew how to read, but spell "the word."

I was gonna miss that gal, but I'd soon be in Hi Lo where there was dozens of women to help me forget. I read her note over and over on the way back to Gravy King's. The note gave me no clue to Miss Della's whereabouts, or why she'd left so suddenly. She was sure enough a mysterious woman in some ways, but the note did say that "maybe" we'd meet again. Maybe.

Chapter Six

I saddled my horse, put the thirty-thirty in the scabbard, tied the little roll of my belongings on the back of the saddle, stuck a few things in the saddle bag, including the Napoleon book, farted and walked over to Gravy King's office.

"Come in, Bobby Jack. What can I do for you?"

I looked down wanting to reach over and scrape some of the crud off his vest and said, "Pay me. I'm quittin'."

He rared back from his desk, stuck his hands in his vest pockets and stared up at me like I'd just kicked his dog.

"Nobody quits the King ranch. Nobody ever has . . . lessen I fired 'em."

"Some few has been worked to death. I call that quittin'."

"You gettin' smart with me, boy?"

"Just pay me off. I got five months comin'. Twenty-eight fifty per month. Jest pay me."

"This here is the biggest ranch in five states, with the most cattle, water, grass and timber. Nobody quits that kind of an outfit and gets paid. That's the law of the land."

"That is also the biggest string of bullshit ever laid on mankind." I thought about what Napoleon would have done and jerked my pistol out and shoved it in his mouth so's I wouldn't have to listen to all that useless blabbering.

"Now, Gravy," I says softly, "I know that's a hell of a lot of money—even for you, but jest do as I say. Reach in that desk and give me my pay."

He started to gurgle out some more of that product made by bulls and I just shoved the barrel a little deeper. He quietly reached in and got the money. I counted out what I had coming and left.

As I walked proudly out I heard him mutter, "Should've known better'n to let you get half-educated. Ruins everything."

I would've gone back and shoved the pistol sideways up his rear end but my mind was already on the doin's in Dirty Town. I rode out of there to a better life with five months' pay in my pocket and a thousand years of knowledge in my head. I rode right on by that little schoolhouse so empty and quiet, and I sure saluted hell out of it and all that happened to me there. Someday, after I'd built a vast empire, I'd return and make a speech to the kids, I decided, on how to go up in the world. I'd come up with that "vast empire" idea reading Napoleon. Those two words seemed to fit exactly what I wanted for myself. Well, my God, what else? Like I said before, I had a brand-new education and a hundred and forty-two bucks and fifty cents in my pants.

A little further on I could see the stage road winding through the hills. As the stage went by I waved at the driver, the shotgun rider, the two young lady passengers, all of which stared at me. Then I followed along in the dust knowing that where they went was where the money was. That was Hi Lo, New Mexico, mining and cattle center.

I rode way up on a piñon-covered hill and looked down on the town. It was just after sundown and I could see a few dim lights coming on here and there. I could also see wagons and teams, horseback riders and people afoot, and dust boiling up out of the street, hanging like a dirty cloud in the air above the town. All out around it was just space full of cows, buffalos, coyotes, bugs and Indians. It looked small all of a sudden, and then sure enough BIG all at the same time.

I reined off downhill towards her. Just before I got into town, though, I stopped and put five dollars in my boot and five in my hat band. This just shows what a really smart son of a bitch I was getting to be. Naturally the first thing I did was ride up and down the street listening to saloons. Finally I decided on the loudest one. It was called The Double Garter. I tied my horse and entered.

Now, there was a lot of fun going on in this here place. That's the main reason cowboys always head for these places. People was dancing and hollering and playing cards, and the joint was just full of fancy women with two garters on their left legs. That seemed like a hell of an idea to me.

I crowded up to the bar between a double-gartered woman in a dress with almost no top atall, and an ol' miner with a sackful of nuggets. He was just barely hanging on the bar. By the time I had given them double garters and other double things a fast glance and then looked back at the ol' miner, he'd done spent his money and fallen down on the floor. I knew this because his bag of nuggets was gone and I stepped on him as I turned around. I'd come to the place of fast action, all right.

I said to the smiling woman—I assumed she was smiling; I'd never really got up that far yet—"That old man is the fastest spender I ever saw."

"You know what they say, honey, 'Fast come, fast go.' "

"Yeeeaaaah!" I sure enough agreed.

I then stared into the purest, kindest-looking set of blue eyes I'd seen since Miss Della's. I ordered us some drinks, and reached over and gave her a great big kiss. She drawed back like she was surprised—and maybe this never had happened to her before.

She stuck her titties right up in my face. I was beginning to notice that certain women used those things somewhat like a bank robber did his forty-fives. Both of them looked like they was about to bust out. In fact, she gave a fancy little twist and one of them did. I reached over like a regular gentleman to help her put it in place, but she didn't seem to appreciate it like I thought she would. She stepped back and did her own putting, saying, "Talk about fast!"

"That's me, all right," I says, grinning mighty proud. "I learned to read and write in seven months."

"Ohhhh," she says, snuggling up close to my side. "I just love educated men. They're so smart."

"More drinks," I yelled, throwing another bill on the bar.

"How long are you in town for, cowboy?"

"Till I own this place and two more like it," I says, meaning ever damn word.

"Ambition, that's another trait I like in my men."

I grabbed her up and whirled her around saying, "I like the way you used them two words on me."

"What two?" she asked.

"'My men,'" I yelled.

Boy, I'm saying that I liked the way that woman felt dancing up close and wiggling around so's you could feel her all over at one time or another. I was thinking that I was never going to leave this life. Never!

I pulled out all my money in a wad so she'd know I hadn't come to town broke and says, "Who owns this here place?"

She looked up at me again, hesitating a minute, then saying, "Gradell. Gradell owns over half the town and they say half the mines, too. Hey . . . he owns . . . you hear me—owns the stage lines—the freight lines—" She squatted just a little and ranted on, "And maybe lots of other things."

"Half ain't enough for me. I want it all. Where can I find this Gradell?"

"Well, that's just it, honey. No one has ever seen Gradell."

"No one? Somebody has to have seen him! How'n hell can he know what's goin' on in the world—what's goin' on in people's minds—if he don't get out among 'em? Somebody has to be taking messages to him."

"Well, I suppose so, but if they do they sure never speak about it."

"That can wait for tomorrow," I yelled and whammed the money down in front of the bartender. We had two more fast drinks and I just took command, reaching down, grabbing her plump little soft hand and leading her astray.

She followed along, out the back of the saloon, in the alley and then said, "Come with me, darling." It was as soft as a whispering breeze over a tank of cool water. I damn near peed my pants right there. I followed her down the alley, reaching out and feeling them buttocks of hers moving up and down and sideways till I just couldn't stand it no longer. I grabbed her up and grabbed her other places and things.

She gently pushed me away and said, "Right here," and reached for a door, motioning me to follow.

Did I!

She lit a rose-colored lamp and there was this fancy room. I stared, jerking off my gun belt, boots and pants all sort of at the same time. Then I plunked her down on that big soft bed, and gave her a hell of a feel all over. But when I started to unbutton her dress she just held my hands and said, "Wait, wait, darling, there's something you must do before we take it all off!" She reached down and pulled one of the garters up and let it thump against her thigh. "Put it on the other leg," she said.

I did.

She raised her legs and moved them in and out to help. I was trembling so that I thought I was going to shake the nails out of the floor.

"Now," she said, and started helping me remove the costume. The big tits flopped out happy to be free and when I grabbed them they felt like homemade butter wrapped up tight in white silk. I started on off with the rest and she whispered, "I always leave the stockings on when . . ."

I croaked out. "That's fine with me. That ain't the part I'm after anyhow!"

Just as I was about to mount this beautiful mare, something went wrong. I went out! Now I remembered later that I'd heard a noise behind me but figured it was the back of my skull cracking apart with passion.

Well, it was cracked and caked with blood and swelled up and hurting like hell when the sun woke me in that alley. I was also broke in the pocketbook. I stumbled up, puked, and then sat back down. I did all this so's I could properly think things over. I finally figured that for such a smart son of a bitch I hadn't done as well as I could've my first night in town. I felt in my boot and got the five dollars there. And I looked in my hat and did the same. How could a feller figure that far ahead and then mess it all up in less than two hours. Well, this here wasn't enough money to get me started on my vast empire, but it would sure as hell buy me a saw and a sledge hammer.

I got some breakfast in my belly at a little cafe full of hungovers like myself. I took my horse down to the stable, got him rubbed down and fed while I went shopping for the two items aforementioned. Then I rode out of town with conquest on my mind. I'd take care of that bitch . . . that bitch . . . oh hell, I'd forgot her name, if I'd ever asked for it atall.

Chapter Seven

I rode out of that Dirty Town a determined man. My horse felt good and I was feeling some better, too. The cockeyed blue jays splatted about through the dark green piñons, and the magpies hollered at the sun. My old pony walked out of there fox-trotting a little and now and then breaking over into a running walk—the best gait of all, a mile-eating pace that doesn't shake a man's liver loose and doesn't kill the horse off.

We passed a prairie dog village and I watched the little ones all head for the holes as the boss dog barked his warning. Some of them just stood up on their hindlegs and flat insulted me after they found out I meant no harm. Twice I reined off the trail and hid in a clump of trees when riders came along. I didn't relish no witnesses today.

It was a few minutes after top sun when I found the bridge. I set about hiding my horse so I could later ride off behind the trees and brush, out of sight all the way.

I took the saw and sledge hammer off the saddle and headed for the bridge. It stood about five feet above the shallow creek. I took off my boots and waded down under the bridge. Then I started sawing on one of the timbers. I sawed it plumb through, took the sledge and started smacking the timber over along the cut till there was only a tiny hold on the edge. This here was just a guess. What I wanted was the heavy stagecoach to mash the timbers off and the back end fall into the water, trapping everybody right there.

As I say, I was just guessing. It might not fall at all and the horses might just *clippity clop* right on into Dirty Town with me sitting there feeling somewhat silly. Course, the weight of the first horse might collapse the thing, in which case there would be one hell of a wreck. Many things such as these were whipping through my skull as I stood by my horse and waited.

Pretty soon my horse threw his head up and his ears forward and I jest barely caught the nostrils in time to keep him from nickering our position away. It was a horseback cowboy on his way into town. God uh mighty, was I sweating as he rode out on the bridge and sure as frozen turds melt in the sun, the bridge fell down. His horse boogered and jumped off into the water, and this person fell beside it.

With my mind working swiftly, I jerked my gun out and raced to the edge of the stream, caught on the horse's reins as he got up, and pointed the gun at the person. He stood up kind of addled, wiping water out of his eyes. He didn't stand up very far for he wasn't very tall—maybe five feet. He was a mean-eyed little fart, maybe twenty-two or -three years old, but the way his nose was broke I could tell he'd been places.

I said, "Howdy."

He said, "Howdy. What are you pointin' that gun at me for?"

I said, "Because this here is what you use to kill people with, and when you aim to kill 'em, you point it at 'em."

He smiled and stuck out his little hand, saying, "That makes sense. I'm Runt Jackson."

I cocked the hammer back and solemnly said, "Well, Runt, before I shoot you, we are goin' to pick that bridge back up and put it where it belongs."

"Ain't much of a bridge if'n it won't hold up a little feller like me."

"You was on an animal considerable heavier than you," I advised this dumb little bastard.

I tied his horse and we got down in the water and sure enough put our backs to it. I kept the gun on him all the time to make him lift better. We finally got it back in place.

Runt stood staring at it and finally says, "You was aimin' on robbin' the stage, I can see that from way over here." Which was six feet away. I was a little bit rocked at his sudden wisdom, and I stared at him right hard.

He swallered a few times and then spoke out fast, "If'n we wuz to tie our catch ropes together, and then tie them to the bridge timber, and then pull it around behind that brush and tie it to your saddle horn, and you wuz to spur the horse the other way just as the stage wuz on the bridge . . ."

"Whoa!" I yelled, never having heard so much bullshit come

out of such a small package in my whole life. "Whoa! Whoa! Whoa!" It hadn't taken me but one-third of an instant to see that this here took the risk out of the bridge falling wrong. No sirree, I figgered that one out. So I says, "Get your rope and tie it to mine," and I went right on telling him how to hook it all up, knowing he didn't have enough sense to do it by hisself. We got 'er all fixed and then I suddenly started having another thought. *What in hell was I going to do with Runt Jackson?* I recocked the gun.

Runt was trembling and swallering, but he didn't beg and he didn't turn away. I stood there, the pressure growing on the trigger finger and then I let the hammer down easy.

"There ain't no way you could have been smart enough to have figured out this rope deal less'n you done it before."

He nodded his head. "Yes," and smiled like a dog that had just sucked a dozen setting eggs.

I don't know what made me do it but I put away my gun and said, "Glad to have you in the wagon, Runt."

He liked to have jerked my arm out by the roots shaking hands and said right back, "Hey, ol' pardner, I can tell me and you are crazy in the same corral."

We got our handkerchiefs ready to pull up around our faces and did some more of that waiting. Soon we could hear the stage creaking down the road, and through a crack in the trees it came into sight. Now Runt had hooked the rope down into the creek bottom on a tree root so's the stage driver wouldn't see the rope. Still, he could if he just happened to look, but he didn't. I'm telling you, it was perty!

The driver slowed the stage down to cross, the team pranced right on over. I spurred my horse, the rope tightened and the bridge fell. The rear end of the stage dropped hard into the creek, throwing off the driver, and the shotgun dropped his shotgun. Before they could think atall we was on 'em and had 'em disarmed. There was a little screaming going on in the coach, but that soon quieted down.

I told the driver and the shotgun, "Don't jist stand there, you impolite bastards, take care of your passengers."

They helped them, one after another, out on the creek bank. When I saw these two big-bellied, bowler-hatted fellers with huge gold watch chains hanging out, I knew we had 'er cut.

There was a good-looking, whore-type girl there and a gambling-type man that just might have some money on him, too.

I threw my brisket and my Adam's apple out, standing as straight up on my bowlegs as I could and snorted, "I'm an educated son of a bitch and I need financing."

I motioned my head at Runt and he began to rob them. It sure worked keen. We got a bag of gold coins from each of the big-bellies, about half that much from the gambler, two watches and a big ruby ring from the whore-type. They was squawking and taking on like buzzards in a dead cow's belly, but me and that Runt didn't pay them no mind atall. To tell some truth I wasn't even listening to their gripes.

Then Runt got up on the back of the coach and threw the baggage down to me. We found some nice straight razors and all kinds of stuff we could use, like fancy clothes. The whore-type had some of the pertiest feeling cloth I ever laid a hand across. There was a black box in one of the bags. In it was a book. I flipped it open and read out loud to everbody. The name on the cover was *Translated into English for the first time, HOW TO MAKE LOVE AND OTHER THINGS, in French*. This made me feel right worldly. I could tell which one of the whey bellies it belonged to by the way he ducked his head and twisted one foot into the dirt. The gambler and the whore-type laughed.

We started sacking ever'thing up, and that little Runt Jackson was sure enough gleeful. I've seen little colts and baby lambs buck about with joy but nothing better'n him.

I unhooked the horses and ran them off. We needed some time to get into town ahead of them. Then we rode around out of sight and broke into a long lope, laughing our asses off and feeling plumb chesty. They hadn't seen our faces and hadn't got a glance at our horses. We were clean as a nurse's blouse.

We got in to town and I rented us two rooms in a hotel across the street from the Double Garter. Then I put *Napoleon and His Conquests* in the black box with the French book. By damn, I aimed to continue my education soon as I took care of a little chore across the street. I told Runt to pay no attention to what I was going to do unless somebody pointed a gun at me or tried to knock me in the head with something hard.

We walked in and that place was going just like before. I saw the woman standing there at the bar putting the hustle on another drunk cowboy. I knew damn well without her help I'd never find the bastard who robbed me.

I walked right up and got her by the hand like I was going to crush it into mush, which I halfway did. Her eyes widened and when she started to holler I gave her one of them looks that said, *"Be quiet, bitch, or I'll break your goddamned neck."* She was quiet. I led her around the room looking ahead and ole Runt follered, backing me up. I was watching eyes. We got plumb around, over by the door, before I saw the man. He was playing poker and I saw him drop the cards and give her the look, waiting for her signal. I cleverly ignored him and walked right up by his side and dropped a gold coin on the floor by his chair. When he bent over to pick it up I whacked him across the back of the neck with my swiftly drawn pistol. He fell over on his face and didn't move around much after that.

With my pistol sorta casually pointing at the crowd, I picked up the gold coin, saying, "Damn thief tried to rob me. Somebody better tell him to leave town 'fore it gets catchin'."

Me, the girl and Runt waltzed out. Runt stopped in the door and yelled back, "Better get him outa town 'fore somebody else catches it!"

I pulled this girl across the street to my hotel room, took her clothes off, putting both garters around her neck and snapping them. Then I made her lie there in bed and suffer for me while I continued my education.

I started reading the French book. When I was about halfway through I came to a sudden stop. There was no use in reading further. My education was complete. I put the book away to be sure this here girl—said her name was Melee—wouldn't see the title.

I bent over, leaning on one of them titties and whispered in her ear one of the lines I'd read in the book. She grinned plumb around her face and her eyes opened up wide, just spurting out signs of love. I ripped off my clothes and leaped in that bed for a night of delight as it promised in the book. Yes sir, it sure does pay to have an education. Miss Della woulda been right proud of me.

Chapter Eight

I woke up wore out. I couldn't figure whether it was going to be harder to get up than it was to get up a hard. But I whispered them words in Melee's ear just the same and that settled that there. Her eyes flew open and her legs flew apart. She might be a bitch but she sure was fun, and there are cases where a man can overlook failings in other people—especially if he's educated like me.

Soon as I got enough air back in my lungs I told Melee, "Get your little fat ass out of here right now. I got worlds to conquer today."

She sorta pouted a minute, but I gave her a push with my foot and she got the idea. While she was dressing she asked me if I'd do it again—say that thing to her once more, please.

I said, "Not again right now, honey. We both need our strength for the day's struggles."

"Tonight?" she begged, and then seeing she might be pushing a little she sorta apologized. "That is, of course, if you get everything conquered today."

I said, "Well now, honey, you just take care and keep things clean till you hear from me."

"I will! I will!" she said, blowing me a kiss as she went out the door.

Goddamn them Frenchmen! Why, just think where I'd uh been if I'd uh come upon that masterpiece earlier in life. I washed up and shaved, then went over to Runt's room to get him up and at 'em. He wasn't in that bed and never had been. Goddamn him, too!

I walked across the street to the Double Garter Saloon and whorehouse. I went upstairs to the latter department. There was hungover, red-eyed, bushy-haired miners and cowboys roaming all about, sneaking down the stairs to get another start at the bar or trying to make it to work on time. None of them was Runt.

I asked the madam if she'd seen him.

She grinned at me with a smile so old and slow I didn't ever know for sure if it happened, and said, "Why, honey, all these cowboys and miners look alike to me."

"Not this'n. He ain't but about this high, and he's got a nose that mashes two ways at once, and he's got little bitty eyes meaner than a constipated hog's and he don't have a whole lot of smarts."

She batted her eyelashes and said, "Sounds fairly normal to me, and like I said, honey, they all look alike."

I tried two more whorehouses and he wasn't there. Then I asked the bartender in the Wild Goat Saloon if I'd run out of places to look.

He said, "No, there's one low-down place left, out on the edge of town. But hardly anybody goes there but winos and bums."

"Well, that's got to be it," I said. "I sure thank you, amigo. You have answered my question and soon's I buy this place I'm gonna give you a raise."

He stared at me like he'd been whacked in the backside with a tubful of cactus.

I went over to the stable, got my horse and headed out to get my pardner. Hell, everbody knows that old Napoleon said, "Never attack till all your forces are in order."

I rode out to this long, low building shaped like a square horseshoe with lots of different rooms that didn't connect. It was sorta hidden by a bunch of half-dead trees. I heard a yell and then saw three unclean, mostly undressed girls dash out ahead of them yells, and suddenly I knew that bartender's information was right. Then a shot came busting through the roof of the house and out stumbled my pardner, plumb slick-ass naked except for his boots. He had a six-shooter in one hand and half a bottle of whiskey in the other, and he was yelling, "Come back here, you little wenches. I done paid for three whole days!"

He stopped right out there in the middle of the courtyard, turned around slow-like and shot another hole in the side of the house. The girls was running and screaming in three different directions and others were peeking out windows in great fear, but I didn't hear anybody fall or holler inside so I guess he missed. I did spot a change in the action, though. Some male customers were running outside, changing rooms and taking new positions. I knew right then they were going to take the side of the whores.

It didn't take me long to figure out that Runt was wasting ammunition and a lot of valuable conquering time. I spurred over, untied Runt's horse and charged right out in the middle of the upcoming battle. I had to get my little army out of there. Hellsfire, there was a weakness showing in his armor. I yelled, "Mount!"

Runt spun around wild-eyed and yelled, "Where is she?"

I said, "No, no, the horse, you stupid bastard!"

Still holding the bottle in one hand and the pistol in the other, Runt tried to get in the saddle. I saw a gun barrel peek out around one of the open doors. I swiftly unholstered my gun and busted a cap right behind it. It ripped through the thin wood. The gun dropped and I heard a yell. Then I cleverly shot the bottle out of Runt's hand so he could get hold of the saddle horn. He wasn't all the way on as I spurred away still holding the reins of his horse. Runt and other things were flopping all over the saddle, but he hung on and even managed to return a shot at the whorehouse where bullets were now zinging out at us. We escaped.

I spurred hard down an alley and just as we stopped behind our hotel, Runt fell off. He might just as well. We were home anyhow. I got him in the back door, through the lobby and up the stairs. A few impolite bastards stared hard at us, but they had to look fast 'cause we were really moving. I got him in his room and while he jerked on some clothes we talked things over.

I finally had to ask, "What in hellsfire was you doin' in a cathouse with your boots on?"

"Safety."

"Safety?"

"Yeah, Pa told me to watch out for them communicable diseases when I went to them dirty places."

"Co—co—communicable?" I finally got out.

"Yeah, he said that there athlete's foot sure is painful."

If I wasn't so short on troops I'd uh killed the little runt and skinned him for a watch fob. There was no use trying to sober him up this late in the day so I went and got us a bottle. He seemed to feel better after he chugged another drink. I walked over and took the bottle away from him before he got drunk again, and decided I might as well have one just for the thirsties, 'cause there was no way I was ever gonna catch up with him. I took a big swaller. It cleaned out my throat so's I felt like expounding great truths.

"Runt, ol' Napoleon always said that upon entering enemy cities one must immediately overcome the local government and the rest of the pop—populace was easy." I rared back to watch that sink into his malpais skull.

He went to the window and looked out as if he was having a deep thought. I knew, of course, he was faking that. The deepest thought he could possibly have was the bottom of that quart bottle.

I went on, while I was waiting for his turtle mind to move. "Nap also said, 'When you strike, put your best weapons in front.'"

I could see something had penetrated the little idiot's head by the way he squinted his beady little eyes. Well, he wasn't very old and he did lack experience. He held out his hand for the bottle in such a pitiful manner I gave it back to him.

He used the bottle properly and finally spoke. "Your best weapons, huh?"

"Uh huh, yeah . . . well . . ." I said.

"And now what's that? Huh? Huh?"

"Well . . . well . . . I guess it's my secret love words," I said, being crudely forced by the little mind robber to reveal my own private thoughts out loud.

"Secret love words?"

"Of course. Don't tell me you haven't noticed my astounding success with women. Well, you might say it's due, in part—only in part—to my secret love words."

He didn't answer, but took some more advantage of the bottle.

Now ol' Nap had plainly said that the best manner in which to take over a captured town was to get control of the head honcho. That way the regular citizens would follow his advice, and it would be unnecessary to execute them. He had added that the easiest way to get that control was to accuse the town leader of falsifying and hiding official reports and the misuse of public funds. Then threaten to expose the miscreant to the public. Since ninety percent of men in high government places are guilty of at least one of these, the odds were nine to one in favor of total success. This was an encouraging thought to sashay forth into enemy territory with. We moved about talking to cowboys, miners, winos, whores, barbers, blacksmiths, and whoever else would visit. It wasn't so difficult to loosen tongues. We took along a bottle of whisky which was appreciated by most everyone. There was the caretaker at the funeral parlor, for instance. I asked him if he would trust the sheriff of Dirty Town, a section of the town of Hi Lo, with his life.

"Not on *your* life," he answered, and took another swallow of the nice wet brown.

When I said to the livery stable attendant, "It looks like Mayor Caldingham has done a good job of governing the town," he answered, "The mayor has a beautiful wife."

See what I mean about sly hints and suggestions? Any damn fool could see that there was a vast undercurrent of distrust here. That the faith in their government had seeped out of the people. Something was rotten in Dirty Town.

"See there, Runt. We can't just let the people go on being lied to and cheated like this."

We stood looking at the mayor's seventeen room mansion out on the edge of town. We had heard quotes all over from the mayor about his need for a refuge from the daily cares and responsibilities of his office. A sanctuary to hide and heal himself from the wounds of public service.

I went on, "A man just can't afford to live in a place like that on his salary."

"You don't ride thoroughbred horses when you make burro money," Runt said, as if he knew what the hell I'd been talking about.

"That's what I said. The mayor's where it's at. Now we gotta come up with a way to get to the mayor."

"The mayor's got a beautiful wife," stated Runt.

I walked back to our room as fast as I could, holding back

my justified rage until we were inside away from witnesses. Runt had to run ever' other step to keep up.

I took about three circles around the room snorting and trying to control my wild self. "I know that! I KNOW that!"

"What do you think I'm gonna do?" I moaned in misery at his ignorance.

"You've got it," he says. "Through her you uncover the mayor's dirty linen and kick him out of office! You've got it," he yelled.

Course I had it. What did the dumb little nut think I'd educated myself for in the first place? "Course I got it!" I said, not a little bit proud of my fast and deep thinking. Now I'd really lay it on him. I pulled out my pocket knife and cut a map on the wall.

"This here place is sometimes called Hi Lo and part of it's sometimes called Dirty Town. We're goin' to rename it Our Town."

"A very good name," says Runt.

"Now, I've already explained to you how we are goin' to take over the mayor, right? Savvy?"

"Right. Savvy."

"After that . . . the next step."

"Uhhh . . . ," he says, looking up as if he expected me to give him all my wisdom and learning at one time. I looked back at the map on the wall and said, "Next step's next."

"I know you done thought of it, and it embarrasses me to even bring it up."

I stared at the little mind thief, wondering which part of my brain he'd picked now. Then he told me.

"That Melee looks much more like a lady than a whore. If you was to tell her to go to the mayor's annual Saturday night party and seduce 'im . . . which she no doubt has already done many times in the past . . ."

"Whoa!" I yelled.

"Jist a minute!" he rudely yelled back just like any other uneducated bum. "And you was to be there in disguise to see that the mayor's wife caught 'em in the act . . ."

For a full minute I stared at the little window two stories up and cogitated on whether to throw him out the window, jump out myself, or both.

"I wish to hell you'd quit wastin' our time spoutin' off about things that's done been thought of!"

"I'm uh tryin' to learn."

"All right now, we're goin' out here and turn the world inside out, and we ain't gonna spill a drop of anything while we're doin' it."

Runt nodded his head in agreement. If he just hung around awhile longer he just might—might, I say—start catching on.

Chapter Nine

I didn't have no trouble with Melee at all. I just promised her I'd whisper them words to her later on that night if all went well. Right now though we had to spend a little time getting her lady-like clothes and all that fixed up.

She said, "Heck, a lot of ladies are secretly whores so why can't a whore secretly be a lady?"

She was absolutely right and as far as ol' Bobby Jack Smith was concerned there was no problem either. All the time I'd been coming to Dirty Town I was generally running whores, drunk, bloody and in jail. My appearances and acquaintances had been limited to those establishments that take care of these here activities . . . and needs. So if I got all dressed up in brand new clothes from hair to boot-sole not even ol' Runt would know me. I'd get me some long skinny cigars to smoke and three or four gold pieces to rattle in my pocket and spin around through my fingers and just head for that party with the best-looking prostitute in the West hanging on my arm. She'd be just as well disguised as myself. It would be plumb easy. This here was my lower brain clicking again. Anyway, I remembered Della's advice about THE WORD, and I sure as hell had one to drop on these here society people tonight. After that I could walk in with a naked woman and bang her on the dining room table and those people would act like we were just doing a slow waltz.

That's the way it worked, too. I ain't the smartest cowboy in the world but I'll make do till they find him.

Now the mayor was fat—like most mayors should be. He had long white hair hanging down over his ears like a judge. In fact, he'd once been a judge. His eyes were a little red and watery and had a round circle of sick blue somewhere in them. His face was one of them tender-looking things that hinted the blood was going to bust out any minute and run down on his starched white shirt. In fact, it had damn near done it in a few blotches scattered around on his cheeks and nose. He had a permanent grin that made him look like he was chewing tobacco but didn't want anybody to know it.

His wife, Dorothy, wasn't bad atall though, with a small waist and some of that front hardware that made a feller think of Della, and I sure didn't mind that. I just wished she could of been here to share the conquest with me. Dorothy had a round face that never would wrinkle much except a little around the eyes, and one of them laughing red mouths that was sure wasted as far as her husband was concerned. Plumb perty.

The sheriff, Asa Digby, was there and he eyed me and Mclee a little but not too much. The fancy clothes she was a-wearing had thrown him off. He wasn't even as smart as Runt. He was as fat as Mayor Caldingham himself in the belly, but where the mayor had a few angles in his face the sheriff just had a face, that's all. Anyway, I didn't pay too much attention to him because I'd fire his ass soon's I took over from Caldingham. That there would not be long either.

A couple of the directors and owners of the local gold and silver mines were there from back East. A Reverend Balcomb was present, talking to the banker. I made a note in my head of this. If I went to church I damn sure aimed for it to be where the banker went. I remembered all them things Della had told me about bankers and politicians.

One of the mine owner's wives sidled up to me and Melee after the mayor's wife had seen to it that we had drinks. She shook her tail and rolled her eyes and said, "And what might your business be here in this glorious Western land?"

I rared back and said it as loud as I could without yelling, "I represent Gradell!"

There was one of them silences that happens after you've been bucked off ten miles from headquarters and the horse is done out of sight and hearing. It wasn't long till everbody was just falling down on us. Hell, I might just as well gone ahead and said I was the president of the United States and the king of England combined. Everybody went for the source of power. It sure was right keen.

Melee moved in on the mayor and I moved in on his wife.

"Oh, we hear so much of Gradell, but this is the first time he's sent one of his emissaries to one of our parties. I'm deeply flattered."

I said, "It's nothin'. We intend to branch out in many areas."

"I'm so pleased you chose our home to begin with," she said, and she looked up smiling like she'd just learned how.

Sure funny what the right name put into the right words at the right time will do. And it was even funnier because I had less of an idea who Gradell was than anybody here. But the magic was in the name and I sure used it like any other phony.

It wasn't long till Dorothy had introduced me to everybody there and I could see Melee getting that mayor drunk and wobbly. Things were hooking up fast.

I did all them dumb acts you do with these kind of people, like saying: "Yes, we are goin' to branch out and help build the country for the benefit of all." "Yes, it is a community spirit we're after, a glorious goal to riches we'll all reach together." Shitfire, I was sounding just like a politician or a preacher—take your choice. But I learned all this from Napoleon himself, The general, by God!

It wasn't long till everybody was getting loud and silly. Folks who had been stiff and sorta backward were now half tongue and half stagger. That's just the way we wanted it.

I saw ol' Caldingham slip a feel on Melee's behind with one hand and her crotch with the other. She just leaned right in there doing her natural duty. Bless her beautiful whore's heart!

Dorothy had taken quite a little bit of a liking to me. She was escorting me around the big, two-story house showing me treasures they'd imported from the East and everwhere. It was hard for me to concentrate on the silly statues and the fine china when I wanted Melee to get that mayor nailed right to the top of her.

I did say now and then to Dorothy, "That's sure perty." "Well, who woulda thought it." "Now, if that don't beat the wildcat's bite," and such-like.

Then I saw the mayor look around like a deacon that had farted in church and lead Melee swiftly upstairs with his arm planted around the part of her that followed when she walked.

As I say, things were turning out right keen. I grabbed Dorothy around the waist and asked if she would guide me upstairs and give me a tour of the upper regions.

"Surely," she said, and up we went.

I caught a glimpse of the door closing behind our fated two. For a minute I was boogered, thinking we might arrive on the action before it really got all churned up. So I stopped at the head of the stairs and started admiring a nude statue of a young girl frolicking about like she'd just lost her blessed virginity to the richest man in town. Dorothy kindly explained to me that this handsome thing had come from the land of Napoleon. I was mighty pleased to know this. I looked at other objects, admiring them completely, with my sharp ears straining for the right sound to come busting out of that closed room. It took longer than I thought, but Mayor Caldingham was perty old and perty drunk too.

Dorothy was now showing me the room next to theirs. Then I heard the giggling and the sighs and knew the yelling part was about to begin so I asked to see the next room. Dorothy was mighty pleased at this, saying, "Oh, I'm so glad you insist. This is our elite guest room. Only the maid and very special guests ever enter there. We feel something should remain inviolate for our overnighters. But in your case I'm thrilled to make an exception. In fact," she went on beaming, "I'm positively aghast that I'd do it."

She sure was that, all right. There was old Caldingham with his fat rear right up in the air, taking a plunge downward on Melee, and she had her legs thrown wide and straight up. She was peeking out around him at us as we stepped through the door. And she screamed, "Now darling now! Just like you always do it!"

Oh, it was a perty sight to behold and stare upon. But even

more beautiful was the look that gathered on poor Dorothy's
face. Her eyes just sorta glazed over and she swallered and
swooned at the same time. We staggered out of the room with
me tenderly holding her up like any real sure enough gentleman would do. I guided her down the stairs, through the
people, explaining that it was just a little case of nerves.

"Overplanning, she's overplanned," I explained.

They all said, "Oh."

We went into the study and I locked the door. I got her
settled down on a nice soft couch and took her silk dress up and
wiped the tears out of her eyes.

She sobbed, "How could he? Oh, how could he?"

"I just don't know," I said sadly, "and with my fiancée, too."

She started bellering again and laid her head over on my
chest. I patted her nice soft hair and caressed the back of her
neck with much kindness and consideration for our mutual
plight. I rubbed her neck good and moved up around her ears.
It seemed to me this was easing up her grief and hurt some. The
sobbing slowly ceased, and then when I could feel her leaning
on me for more comfort I said THE WORDS in her delicate
little ear and one minute later we were on and off the couch and
she was moaning like Melee just had and doing her best to give
me some of that comfort back. I took it with appreciation as
any real gentleman woulda done—just like it told me how in
the French masterpiece.

She straightened up and pulled the silk skirt down over her
legs. My lightning brain was flashing fiery thoughts. The
smarts were taking over. I just couldn't help it. While she
sighed and snuggled up against me, no doubt wanting to hear
me whisper to her again, I was staring at the safe.

Then I said, "Now, honey darlin', I'm goin' to take care of
us. Just tell me the number of that safe so I can get your
marriage certificate and prepare our case. We've both been
done wrong and it must be corrected."

She just mumbled the number out and snuggled closer. I
tenderly stretched her out on the couch, gave her a big kiss and
told her not to move till I got back. I whizzed that knob around
on that black iron monster like I'd manufactured it, and there
it was as wide open as Melee's crotch. There was a neat stack
of gold coins in canvas bags and since I was sure it was stolen

I just returned the favor. There was too much to shove in one pocket so I crammed it down in my shirt which was new and had all the buttons on it. I spotted a nice leather folder and knew that's where all the papers would be that would landslide me in as mayor of Dirty Town.

I went back over to Dorothy feeling so good that I whispered in her ear again and in less than half a minute this time we had another romp around, up and down and all about that nice soft couch.

When she screamed, "Now, darling, now! Just like before!" it had a familiar jingle to it.

After I assured her that all was in place, and that we'd now see justice performed, and promised her more of what we'd just had, I up and left.

Outside, I felt of the money, and stuck the pouch in there with it—right next to the hide for safekeeping. I took a lung-spreading gasp at the clear night air and looked up at the heavens, wanting to thank somebody. It didn't take long, for out of some brush stepped that Melee, grinning at me and saying as she grabbed me just below the money, "Now, keep your part of the bargain."

It was a strain but I took her home with me and did all I said I'd do besides giving her a nice pair of gold coins for a bonus. Them damn words were the best in the world but I was beginning to wonder if I was horse enough to live up to them. I slept right solid that night. In fact, I was working so hard at sleeping, I didn't have time to dream till I woke up the next morning.

Chapter Ten

I was standing back grinning at Runt with pride like a greedy banker who'd just foreclosed a mortgage.

"And then I told 'em right out loud that I represented Gradell."

"Oh," grunted Runt.

It didn't seem like to me he'd grabbed the importance of what I was telling him so I went on some more. "You shoulda seen 'em after that. They just fell down all over me."

Runt pulled at his ear, looked at his boots, stared at my map on the wall, got up and looked out the window, and turned and spoke. "What if one of them people was Gradell?"

I pulled at my ear, looked at my boots, stared at my map on the wall, stumbled over and looked out the window, and turned around to speak. There was no voice. Just silence. Finally I figured there was no need to carry on like this about something that didn't exist, so I talked of things that were really important.

"We got the money now to buy our own place."

"Which un?"

"This un." I pointed at the floor we were standing on.

"That makes sense," says Runt.

I was proud of him too for just a second. By damn he was beginning to catch on to what I'd been telling him. Let me state he was getting smarter by the breath.

Runt rambled wisely on. "We got to remember what you've said ever since we met."

"What's that? What's that?" I could barely wait to hear what he was gonna quote me on next.

"Well, first off, you got the mayor by the *huevos*."

"Damn tootin'!"

"Second and third, as you always said, the way to control the money of the town is to control the whiskey and the women."

"Rooter tooter, that's exactly what I've always said. You recollected exactly!" Now I took charge. "I'm goin' down and take over the mayor's office. You get out of here on a spyin' mission. I want to know how we get to the Number One Bootlegger in the country. These mining and cowtowns all have one."

"Done!" Runt yells standing straight up five feet.

"Soon's we take care of these here chores I'll personally take care of the women."

"Can I help?" he sorta begged.

"Well, it will be a little strainin', but I feel it's *my* duty."

We moved into action, me and Runt. I rode over by the mayor's house to check out my position with Dorothy. It was the same as last night only I had to say them words again and do all that went with 'em. Later she just lay there on the couch with a nice smile on her face and her legs still spread while I tried to talk business. Between looking at her and thinking about creating a vast empire, I might say that I had to show what ol' Nap called *fortitude in battle*! I showed it.

Finally I got her mind on the business at hand and she said she'd given ol' Caldingham my messages. She'd told him he would be asked to resign and he was to do it. Otherwise certain papers and pertinent information I had in my possession would wind up in the hands of the U.S. Marshal in Santa Fe. Also his memory was to be refreshed about the papers showing false assay reports from the mines and reminded how those people enjoyed a little lynching party whenever they'd been mistreated. There had been a lot more, but it wasn't really needed. He would also be moving out of the house so's I'd be at liberty to come anytime. I had to agree. Besides, I sorta liked her here and there. I gave her a nice caress where it counted and left to keep an appointment with the mayor.

It didn't take long with Caldingham. In fact, he was already packed.

He said, "Do . . . do you think there might be a place for me later? I've been in public service most of my life. I don't know what I'd do if I didn't have a public to serve anymore. I'd probably get sick."

I rared right straight up six foot three, stuck out my forty-five-inch chest, and said, "After askin' a man to his home and then seducin' his fiancée in front of your own wife, I'd say the chances was goddamn thin. It's just a good thing you resigned in favor of me. Anyway, I'm goddamned tired of hearing you government bastards talk about *serving* the public. You assholes *use* the public. You *use* their money. You *use* them for your power. You *use* 'em plumb up!"

He took his little bag in his thieving little hands and scooted to hell out of there. The town was better off already. I called Sheriff Digby in, and told him that he could stay on till I could find somebody better.

"Yes sir," he said. "Yes sir." He bowed and ripped out the back of his shirt where them rolls of fat looped down over his kidneys.

"Now," I ordered, "next week we're closin' down the whole damn town for remodelin'."

"But . . . but . . . but what about Gradell?"

"Do you know 'im?"

"No sir, I don't. Nobody does."

"Well then, this'll be his worry, right?"

"Uh . . . yeah . . . yeah. I'm sure he'll be . . . er . . . concerned."

I sat down at my new desk, put my new boots up on the top and took a cigar out of the humidor that the ex-major had forgotten. I was a happy cowboy. Hell, I wasn't no cowboy no more. I quickly corrected my thinking—hellsfire, I was the mayor. Yessiree, the mayor of a town—and that was just the beginning. Oh well, what else could I expect from such an educated son of a bitch as me.

Ol' Runt musta been doing a good job of spreading the news, cause I had all kinds of visitors. Even the banker and the preacher came by. I assured them that a new community spirit would start the very next week and they shouldn't worry atall. The town council gathered and wanted to know when I was calling the first meeting.

I pulled out my gun and calmly sighted down it like I was fixing to shoot a rabbit and said, "We just now had it."

The meeting was adjourned and without any more wasted bull. Three madams dropped by just to make sure that all was well, and though two of them said they were employed by Gradell, they just wanted me to know they'd be cooperating all the way. I assured them that they didn't have any idea how cooperative they was gonna be after the remodeling of the town. By damn, I had no idea that a mayor had so much to do. It didn't matter. I'd gather me in a bunch of right effective assistants soon's I had time.

It was getting along towards the shank of the day, so I decided I better go gather up Runt. I knew by now he'd be in some kind of trouble. I knew he'd be getting drunk, too. I wanted to get that information about the bootlegger out of him and get him passed out early. We'd need to feel good for the bootlegger visit tomorrow. Being a town official takes lots of careful planning ahead.

I strolled down the street of Our Town and it didn't take me no time atall to spot him. A six-horse stage was parked in front of the station where a great noise was busting out. Most of it came from Runt. A crowd was gathered on the porch. I snuck up behind the stage. Runt was standing in front of a miner half as wide as a wagon tongue is long and about as tall.

Runt was popping off big. "I can whip your butt in any size circle you care to draw!" and he pointed down into the dust.

The miner just shook all over with laughter. I didn't blame him, no siree, not atall.

"Mess with me and I'll flog you till you look like smoke comin' out a chimney," Runt continued.

I could tell it had finally gone too far cause the miner quit laughing. I slipped my pistol out so's none of the crowd could see, and just as Runt jumped straight up off the ground trying to reach the miner's jaw, that miner took one step back behind the stage trying to avoid the mighty blow. I whacked him just under the base of the skull and he went "whoomp." I swiftly reholstered the gun.

Runt stood over the fallen miner, looked back at the crowd and asked, "Any you other toughs need a lesson?" None of the other toughs moved and then Runt saw me. "You got here too late," he scolded, "I mighta been outnumbered for all you know."

I tried to ignore this and helped the miner to his feet. He was still wobbly but stuck down his hand to Runt and said, "I've been a foreman in ever' boom town in the West, but pound for pound I ain't ever been hit like that."

They shook hands, and Runt patted him on the small of his back saying, "It's all right, just behave yourself and I won't do it again."

We took Foreman Dooley inside the Double Garter and bought him a drink. He congratulated me on being mayor and having such a fine assistant as Runt. I accepted this and told him if there was anything the miners needed, just to let us know. I had plans to take care of their *needs* before long whether they realized it or not. Just as I was feeling a little expansive over the day's success here comes Melee. I knew there was no way out. A man's got to fulfill his obligations if it kills him. There ain't nothin' on this earth a man can be so far behind on and catch up with so quick.

I just yelled, "Give the whole house a drink! There's a brand-new time bein' born in Our Town!"

This pleased Runt so that he just grabbed him a girl and danced. He sang songs, and talked to clouds and horses—all indoors.

Melee just shoved herself upon me and said, "Give it to me, darling. Give me the words."

I had no choice, bein' the man of wisdom and honor that I am. It was a real keen night.

Chapter Eleven

That Runt was turning into a pretty good spy in spite of being a copycat and ignorant in most other departments. He'd found out that Bootles Bodkins was the only bootlegger around that amounted to anything atall. He also found out exactly where Bootles' house was in the foothills of the Sangre de Cristo Mountains.

We rode now, up a little blue-green stream, clear and perty as a virgin's eyes. A feller could feel a zing in the summer air. It cleared the smoke and whiskey fumes out of a man's lungs, and I was perking up considerable. Bugs was still buzzing around a mite, and the goddamn magpies was hollering through the trees with flashes of their black and white wings streaking now and then through the deep green of the piñon trees. Along the edge of the creek we saw the tracks of raccoons, deer, bobcats and coyotes. Well, shitfire, this here creek was perty near as busy as Our Town.

"Runt," I says, "we're doin' all right for two dumb-ass cowboys," not really meaning but half of the last.

"I ain't had so much fun since Pa run me off for screwing Cousin Alice."

"I don't savvy that. Lots of cousins married up in my family."

"That's what made Pa mad. He said I should have married 'fore I mated."

"Well, you know how the older generation is about them things."

"Narrow-minded I'd say," says Runt.

"Naw, just behind the times that's all."

Blam! A bullet smacked into a tree right alongside my head. We retreated swiftly to take up a more secure position behind a great big jumble of rocks. I stared and I stared, but couldn't see a thing moving.

Runt explained. "I know it's Bootles. He don't like nobody around but Indians."

"Yeah, and we ain't Indians," I wisely concluded.

Runt says, "Well, I'm a quarter Mexican. You'd think that'd count for something."

"How come he don't like nothin' but Indians?"

"I'm gonna leave that up to him to tell."

"Well, I may never hear then."

I studied the terrain like Nap woulda done. In fact, I tried to think just like he woulda thought.

"Runt," I said, "move out ahead till we can tell just what the range of his rifle is. Ride slow now so's you don't get too close and get hit."

I could tell Runt didn't like this, but he had no choice but to obey his commander. He mounted his horse sorta gritting his teeth and squinting his eyes.

"No. No, leave the horse tied here. We cain't take no chances on you bein' left out here afoot this far from town."

He stared silently at me again as he dismounted and tied his horse. For a minute there it looked like I might have a little mutiny on my hands.

"Now listen close to the plans. Soon as you get within four or five steps of the fartherest he can shoot, just stand there and let him blast away."

"That don't sound safe to me."

"Come on now, pardner, course it is if the bullets can't reach you. He'll either run out of bullets or I can sneak up behind and capture him."

Well, a great leader is not called that for nothing. I just stepped out and marched swiftly forward. When that first bullet grazed my leg I marched swiftly backward. Then the bullets was plunking into soft sand a few yards in front of me. I marked the spot with a stick and told Runt to stand there. He didn't move.

"You ain't scared, are you?" I asked, being the considerate commander at all times.

"Naw, just got a little watery stuff running down into my boots."

"That's good," I said, "now take your position so he'll fire again. I'm gonna circle and surround him from the rear."

I swear that spineless little bastard moved three more steps backwards, but he did draw fire, and I pinpointed the thick clump of piñons surrounding a pile of rocks where the shot came from. I moved out with stealth and cunning. As I scrounged and clawed my way through the brush I could hear a shot fired ever' now and then. My only worry was that Runt would break and run out on me. It took me a lot longer than I thought. Them thirty-thirties shoot quite a distance.

After a while, I was behind the firing and crawled over and peeked through a clump of bushes. There he was all hunkered down looking along a rifle barrel. I waited till he fired and just as he did, by damn, I attacked. I jerked the rifle from his hands. As he stood up he dragged a pocket knife out of his pocket. I kicked him in the balls instead of shooting him. Shitfire, we couldn't afford to hurt this man. We needed him too bad. As he dropped to his knees, I took the pocket knife away from him and yelled for Runt to come bring the horses.

When Bootles finally got to where he could stand up without moaning like a buffalo cow in heat, I spoke kindly to him.

"Howdy there, friend." I also gave him a big grin to clinch the deal.

"There is something wrong here," he said.

"What could that be?" I smiled again.

"You jist don't approach a man like a tried and true friend, that's all."

"Well there's been a little misunderstandin' all the way

around. We just rode up here to make you rich, and you been tryin' to shoot my assistant. That could cripple a man."

"You're right. I shore do apologize." I smiled my sweet acceptance and then he added, "I tried to hit 'im right smack between the eyes." Then he got back down to business. "Rich, you say?"

"Richer than fourteen yards up a bull's gut."

Well, that money talk gets to them all. Runt rode up with our horses, and I told Bootles that I was the new mayor of Our Town and that ever'thing was going to be different from here all the way to the vast empire. Then I got down to the real castrating.

"How come you only sell whiskey to the Indians?"

"Cause Gradell sent people out to tell me not to sell anywhere else: It's his way of keepin' me and the Indians both down."

My lower brain told me this was "control by commerce." Well, I'd just have to converse with the Indians about this when the right time loped by.

"You seen Gradell?" I asked.

"No, they'd come at night. Two of 'em. I didn't believe 'em at first, but after all my fences wound up cut, my haystacks burned, and the waterhole poisoned, something jist plain told me they meant it."

"Well . . . well . . ." I said. "I see."

Runt butted in, "Bobby Jack is the new mayor. We done leased us one saloon which we'll turn into a pleasure house right off. In a week we'll have another. We'd like to use your whiskey exclusively."

I thought for a minute he'd ruined everything, but then I didn't realize that Bootles was smart enough to overlook a soldier who was no doubt in shock.

Bootles just grinned all over and said, "Come on up to my house, and we'll test out the product."

Now his house would not be called that in lots of places. It looked like he'd fixed it up about twenty years ago by painting one of the windowsills. It leaned over to the east away from the west wind and it was propped up from that side by logs of different lengths. The reason for this was that the house had probably blown over, three or four different parts at a time. I kept noticing I was tilting my head to the east to look at it on even terms.

"Get down and tie yore horses, men."

We did. Bootles might not of made much money out of the Indians, but he still had considerable livestock around. There was dogs, too, all over. Some asleep, some lazily pissing on trees and some smelling our legs. There was a big old sow pig asleep under the porch and a bunch of little ones rooting around everywhere. Chickens and goats were all over the place including on the porch and in the house. There were turkeys and ducks and younguns mixed all up in the rest.

Bootles introduced us to his wife and said for us to visit while we went down in the brush to the still to get some fresh product. I could smell the product ever'where as well as other scents in the summer breeze.

His wife had a baby chewing on one long floppy tit. It didn't look like the baby was getting much out of it. She pushed some stringy hair out of her eyes with one hand and tried to talk.

"Ya'll jist watch now, you gonna enjoy Pa's stuff. He makes the bess stuff you ever laid a thirsty lip over." She sorta weaved about for a minute. Two little runny-nose twin boys about seven apiece ran up and pulled at her skirt and peeked around both sides of their mama.

"This here ugly one is Ned," she said, "and the other one—the perty one—is Fred."

It was hard for me to see which one was pertier 'cause they were both so damned ugly it would have turned a copper-lined stomach to look at either one of 'em straight-on. They were weaving right along with their mama. I reckoned they was just weak from undernourishment, and I felt plumb sorry for 'em.

I walked off a ways studying the distant landscape where Bootles was heading, and left Runt to do the talking. He was more their caliber anyhow.

Suddenly I heard this here voice say, "Mister."

I looked around and there peeking around a tree was this little ol' gal. I guessed her to be around sixteen. Her hair was stringy too, but thick and long. If she'd ever washed her face jist once she woulda looked pretty damn good. She wore a thin little ol' dress that there wasn't nothing under atall but her. I could see where the nipples were trying to tear two half-inch holes in the front of her dress.

"Whatchall doin' here? Gonna get drunk with Papa? Huh? Huh?" She twisted one leg so that the tree was smack dab between both of hers, and that put me to thinking and looking too.

"No . . . no . . . honey, we're . . ." She rubbed up and down on that damned tree and I forgot for a minute what I was going to say. "We're here on business."

"Oh, I been wantin' to meet a real businessman all my life. Could I jist shake your hand?"

"I—I—reckon so."

Poor little thing, she came walking over to me weaving from weakness just like the rest of the family. I began to wish we'd brought along some grub. She took my hand and looked up at me, and I looked down her dress which had stood out in front all the way now and what I saw down there sorta gave me the staggers. I weakened. She just moved everything up against me, and gave me a sure enough juicy kiss. My God! I could taste the bootleg whiskey all the way down to my hocks. These people were all drunk! I shoulda known they weren't weak from hunger. Hell, they had enough livestock to feed 'em for two years.

"Always wanted to jist get close to a businessman," she panted right into my brisket.

Over the top of her head I saw Bootles riding back. I moved away with her sorta hanging on to me. I tried to act like it wasn't happening and walked back over with Runt, the twins, and the missus.

In order to make talk, I asked, "Do you folks all drink this here product of Bootles'?"

The missus grinned like a shit-eating dog and said, bragging, "Shore 'nuff, all but the baby, and he spits it out."

I was sure glad when Bootles got back and we all got hunkered down on the porch sampling everything. I took a couple of drinks faster than I should have because that drunken little gal was leaning over the porch so's I could see down her dress again. The way she was grinning kinda bothered my gizzard, too. There was nothing to do but get on the whiskey and business and stay there.

"Now," I said, taking another drink, "tell me where the rest of Our Town gets their whiskey?"

"They have to buy it from Gradell," says Bootles.

"Well, where does he get it?"

"Over by Taos. He's got a big still over there he supplies the whole county with."

The missus spoke her piece. "They calls it Taos Lightnin'" over there, but when it's shipped over here it's known as 'fine imported whiskey.'"

Just as I had things going right that cockeyed stupid Runt had to butt in again.

"We could undersell him by a big margin, huh? And 'sides that we can shoot a few holes in their barrels 'fore they get to Our Town. That sure oughta put us in control. Anyway, that's what my boss thinks," he said just in time, glancing at me swiftly.

"Do you say that?" asks Bootles.

I rared up to my most majestic height and, looking straight down the middle of that little gal's dress stated, "I always say that," and snorted like a grizzly bear with a bee in his nose.

Bootles took a drink of his own poison and looked at me a long minute. Then he busted out with, "Talk's cheap. Hit takes money to buy whiskey."

By damn I had him there. I whacked a stack of six gold pieces down on the porch. The whole family encircled the gold like a pack of hounds killing a coon. We had us a deal that would conquer the world, and I put the signature on it by slipping my hand up under that little gal's dress and putting a thirty-eight-year-old period on her sixteen-year-old piece of paper.

She wiggled like she liked it and looked up and smiled at me, saying right tenderly, "My name is Mary Lou."

I couldn't think of what mine was, but I shook hands with her just the same.

We stayed all night.

Chapter Twelve

I spent a whole day reading *Napoleon—His Rise to Power and Conquests*. It was not only good for my mind, but it also helped my body overcome the night spent with Bootles Bodkins and family. I rested without a woman that night for the first time since we'd hit Our Town.

Next morning I got up ready to do total battle. It was a trying but glorious day. First I had Bootles deliver the ordered barrels of his product to our newly named place—The Cat's Meow. He'd put his whole family to work, including two cousins imported from Sante Fe who could double as guards and gunmen—if we needed them. This now gave us a five-man operating army with a number of supply troops behind the lines, mostly women and kids. Still, we were gaining.

Melee helped with the first move. She started sowing dissent among the whores working for Gradell. At first, the thought of Gradell chilled them to frosty silence but after Melee promised and hinted at THE WORDS a great thawing took place. All I had to do now was move in on the madams. I did this with a great burst of energy created from my night of rest. It wasn't any time atall till we had all the first- and second-class prostitutes moved over to The Cat's Meow. I was taking a drink of Bodkin's Product, sorta relishing the fact that we had girls all over the place—two and three to the room.

Runt took a drink with me, then ran and grabbed an eighteen-year-old from the Oklahoma Territory. He sorta got a bulldog hold on her and shoved his mouth up against her ear whispering fast. She held still just a second then broke loose and busted Runt across the side of the head, hiked up her dress, shook her tail and trotted off upstairs.

Runt stumbled back over to me, holding the side of his head. "Bobby Jack, please, tell me the right words. Please."

I put a fatherly hand out on his shoulder and told him in solemn sound, "Soon's you age a little, son."

"I'm twenty-three, comin' twenty-four right now."

I shook my head saying, "I know. I know how you feel, old and full of wisdom, but you're just not ready yet, son. When the time comes . . ."

"I keep tryin' to guess," he almost cried. "I musta used two hundred combinations of words and nothin' works for me but money."

"That's a right keen substitute for words, and brains too, so why worry?"

"I reckon I'll just have to keep tryin' on my own," Runt says.

"Now you're talkin'. That's the only way."

All of a sudden he forgot about his stinging face and said, "You know, Bobby Jack, I been thinkin' about what you said this mornin'."

I glared at him like he'd just robbed his blind grandmother. He ranted on.

"There's no question about you bein' right, Bobby Jack."

I cleared my throat, and pulled at one ear and listened to more of his talk.

"We got too many girls in this here place. There ain't nothing' private about it."

I pulled at my other ear and scratched under my arm. He continued. "We're goin' to cater to a certain class here, not exactly the highest, either."

I farted softly, took off my hat and scratched the top of my head.

"Yeah, Bobby Jack, we should take the higher-class gals over to Dorothy's place and let her handle 'em."

I walked out, got my horse and rapidly rode to Dorothy's. I had to be sure she'd go for my bright idea. Before I could tell her much, she was leaning on me saying she was a little worried about the ex-mayor's silence.

"It's unnatural," she said. "I just know he's gone to Gradell and they're plotting together to destroy us."

Well, I knew it had to be done so I leaned over to her beautiful ear and did it. She undressed right there in the hallway. We made love around the corner and into the parlor without hitting either side of the archway, right on out into the main drawing room and up seven stair steps before I got her sold on establishing Dorothy's House of Pure Fun. I sorta lost my hold and slipped off, but a fast grab for her breasts saved me from a crippling fall. I stayed there snug with my head on her belly while I gave her the final instructions. I had to pull myself back up even with her on the stairs before I clinched the deal.

By nightfall we had half of our girls moved into the new place. Of course, they had a lot to straighten out so the only guests allowed that night were the banker and his dear friend the reverend. They appreciated the special treatment so much I felt we'd sorta pulled a "political coup," as Nap would have said.

It wasn't too long till I'd acquired "the place on the edge of town"—that's as close as we ever came to naming it. I really didn't need it, but it had sentimental values. After all, I'd pulled a daring rescue when I'd fought my way in and out to save Runt from certain ruinous diseases. I gathered him up and told him it was time we made an official inspection of our main source of income. Actually, we had two places on the edge of town—opposite edges, of course—and the Cat's Meow right smack in the center of town. We had this particular market pretty well cornered.

I decided we'd start with the worst first. That way the day was certain to show improvement as we worked our way up. The madam of that place was the best-looking thing there. She weighed two hundred and twelve pounds. She had four teeth on each side of her mouth. It was said that her gums were so tough, though, she could chew a raw buffalo steak. Her main asset was the fact she was friendly and cheap. She was also fast, or so I heard. Her name was Tess.

"Tess, honey," I said, "is there anything we can do to help?" She looked around the room at the other girls. "Well . . ." was all she said. I took a look where she just had, and knew what she meant. There was room for improvement in the girls' appearances. Their dresses seemed to be made from old worn-out curtains, and the curtains looked like they were made from old worn-out dresses. I was about to suggest some improvements when two customers entered after having done their do. One looked like he'd been given birth by a smoke-stack, and had been weaned on cheap wine.

The other had slept in his overalls for at least twenty years without taking them off except right here. His face looked like he used fresh pig dung for soap and washed it every thirty minutes.

Runt read my head again. "Won't do no good to waste money fixin' up this place."

The girls were beginning to grin and sidle up to us. I was determined to treat all my people the same. There wasn't going to be any discrimination in our organization. So we just backed our way out smiling right back at 'em. When you go to the grocery store, there's many different grades of meat, but if you're with real poor folks, you take the lowest-priced cut just like it was the best.

Things were really perking over at The Cat's Meow. The curtains were dull-colored but clean, just like the beds in the various rooms. The divans had a couple of pillows on 'em, and had nearly every rip sewed up. Most of the girls had most of their teeth, and they were lounged around the waiting room. The little tables here and there might have lost a chip or two, but they were clearly polished. Some old prints of English foxhounds hung about on the walls. The place smelled pretty good too. That is, if you like the smell of middlin' clean whores and whorehouses. Melee had every right to be proud of her girls.

"How's business, hon?" I asked, smiling around in a circle so nobody would feel left out.

"Dandy. Just dandy. The mine payroll's getting bigger. The cowboys' deportment's about the same."

"Good, good. Is there anything you need? Any complaints?" I asked, really meaning it.

Melee thought hard. "Oh, yes, the number-four bed's got crabs. We need some bug killer for that . . . and . . . we'd all feel more comfortable if we knew you were going to keep your offices here. Here, where there's a warm welcome for you. Where you can feel at ease in your work, and not uptight like the pressure of Dorothy's place is bound to make you."

"Rest assured," I said diplomatically, "that we'll keep our

central location to expedite all matters concerning our team and our town."

All the girls stood up and cheered along with Melee. It made a man feel proud to be their leader. I wanted all my girls happy and secure and they sure as hell were that. Whereas "the place on the edge of town" operated on volume, low prices and speed—a 'get 'em in and get 'em out any way you can' basis— a tired cowboy or miner could come here to The Cat's Meow, bring his bottle and take an hour if he wished choosing the lady that fit him best. No one was ever rushed out of bed, but the girls here were so efficient in their knowledge of satisfaction and pleasure that they could comfortably and leisurely service three or four customers a night. The price was set according to the wages that the cowboys and miners drew. All in all, everybody profited in many ways from the arrangement.

Runt popped off early again with, "A good paint job would really pay off here."

"God uh mighty, of course, of course. Ain't I done told you to paint this whole place, Melee?"

She nodded yes, as any good madam would. I decided to get Runt out of there before he thought up something I'd said when I was five years old, and embarrass me in front of my employees.

I migrated on over to The House of Pure Fun. I knew Runt would never fit into these high-class surroundings, so I left him at headquarters.

Hellsfire! There was a welcome mat that covered the whole front porch, and a knocker on the door made outa pure brass.

Dorothy let me in smiling wide, and sure enough I felt welcome just like the doormat read.

"Darling," she says, "I'm so glad you're here. There's something I've been dying to show you."

"Whatever it is, I been uh-dyin' to see it," I answered.

She took my hand, leading me through the waiting room. It was some kinda room! Heavy red velvet curtains hung plumb down to the floor, and there was "objects de art," as Dorothy called them, hanging on the walls, and little statues of naked girls, frolicking about, setting around on white marble tables. Best of all, of course, was the real girls. Ever damn one of 'em was a Jim Dandy Piss Cutter, and as I've always maintained, you just cain't get no better'n that. They all smiled like they had fresh-brushed teeth and wiggled just a little to let a feller know there was real red blood pounding through their veins. They were all dressed different, but scarce. Some had on little frilly soft things cut so's a leg or a tit peeked out just enough to make a man wanta see more. There was this smell about, sorta soft and warm, like fresh-made summer honey. It was enough to make an old dog throw up his head and sniff into the wind. These were women to match the velvet curtains on the wall.

Dorothy must have felt how much appreciation I was showing for the scenery because she damned near jerked me upstairs to the main bedroom. She pushed the big oak door wide open and said, "See!" Well, what I saw was a bed big enough to hold a Fourth of July celebration on with a New Year's dance thrown in. It had a purple spread over it that you could hold a revival meeting under. But that wasn't the capper. No sirree. Over the bed was a painting of Dorothy leaning back on a pile of pillows, naked as a baby in a bathtub.

"Where'n hell did you get that?"

"It's for you, darling."

"Well, thank you a bunch, Dorothy, but where'd you get it?"

"Oh, I had this artist come all the way from Taos."

Being the fine businessman that I am, my next question was plain natural. "Must've cost a fortune."

"No, darling, he took it out in trade."

"Well, now, that's what I call smart, hon. I'm right proud of you."

"Thank you, Bobby Jack."

After looking at the picture again, I was also thinking that those artists wasn't as dumb as everybody tried to make out either.

She ducked her head down shy-like. I looked again at my painting. It was so real a feller might get confused. So I grabbed Dorothy up close so I would know what was which.

I could tell by everything, beside and around me, that our high-paying clientele would continue to grow here at Dorothy's House of Pure Fun. I spent a whole hour of a very busy schedule proving to her how proud I was of all she'd done and was doing. A man owes something to loyal help.

By zingos, we had things moving out! A high-class, a

middlc-class, and a low-class whorehouse, all in the same town. And we had the whiskey market cornered too because we ambushed and shot holes in every shipment of Taos Lightning before it reached Our Town. Bodkins' product was in heavy demand. We were selling it for half what the other places were forced to charge and making huge profits. The business and the money was coming in so fast that I had to hire Mary Lou Bodkins to count it. She had a real talent for that. I was glad to know she had other thoughts in her head than sex. With a body like hers, this only went to prove how difficult that was.

She had just finished stacking up several rows of money and figuring the total when she looked up and smiled that way she does and said, "I always knew I was going to have a knack for business."

I said, "Yeah, it just seems to come natural with you."

She stood up in her new silk dress and gave me a hug. I patted her down the backside a little and pulled away saying, "I have to go make a speech to the town."

She pouted and asked, "When're you goin' to whisper to me like you do to some of them other girls?"

I replied as I was leaving. "Honey, they need it, you don't."

She ran and grabbed me, saying, "That there's the nicest thing anyone ever said to me."

My mind wasn't as clear as it should've been for a man who was about to make a speech to his very own town, but I moved forward anyway with Runt limping along beside me.

As we walked toward the courthouse, I looked at the double line of weatherbeaten buildings.

"Runt, observe this here main street—four inches of dust to walk through. Why, it's a disgrace to Our Town. Not even the mayor can walk from the Fun House to the courthouse without needin' a shine."

Runt interrupted as usual and asked a silly question that had nothing to do with the importance of the upcoming speech.

"Do you think Mary Lou would go out dancin' with me tonight? There's a cake sale down to the schoolhouse."

I answered without hesitating. "Cain't have 'er runnin' around all hours of the night. She's got money to count all day."

"I'd help her catch up."

"Hellsfire, Runt, you cain't count."

He hung his head, quit limping and said sadly, "I forgot." Then he brightened up. "Hey, I could learn!"

I ignored this ignorance and said, "Speaking of reading, look at them signs. Cain't hardly make 'em out. They're uh-hangin' at bad angles and covered with dirt. This town has got to be straightened up. I'm ashamed to let anybody know we own it."

Well the word had been spread around about the speech all right. Everybody was there. I told them, "Folks, what we got to have here is a community spirit. I want this town painted, and painted bright. None of them old dull colors that look like rat turds to start with. I want some reds like fresh blood, and oranges like a full risin' moon, and some blues like the noonday sky. Yeah, and some yellers that match the settin' sun. And, by God," I said, "these signs are gonna have to be nailed up straight, and ever' loose board in town nailed tight. The water wagons are gonna water down the streets ever'day before and after folks have their nooner. Hellsfire, when you're a mile out of town you cain't see nothing but the dust boilin' up out of our streets. If we don't think enough of the only town we got to take loving care of it, at least we oughta have respect for our lungs. When you get to where you cain't breathe, life becomes difficult, the joy goes outa things. And if a feller cain't have a little joy now and then, what's the use? Huh? Huh? And another thing: If you don't have enough goddamned simple-minded sense to keep people in office that'll help you take care of your town, then you deserve anything you get! You hear me? What if someday we was to have some high-class out-of-town visitors? How you gonna feel? Huh? Huh? This is OUR Town, and we want to be really proud of it."

I leaned off the courthouse porch and pointed right at them all. A roar went up, and I could tell I'd get their cooperation. All, that is, except one woman in a purple dress and a heavy veil who stood right in front of me and never lifted a hand. She just walked away while everybody else was clappin' to beat hell and giving me my just dues. While all this roaring was going on, I suddenly blacked out.

Runt dragged me into the courthouse yelling at the crowd, "Just overenthused, that's all." He told me this later 'cause right then I didn't know anything—which is very unusual for me. He poured a bunch of water on me and a bunch of whisky in me, and I sorta came around. Then he showed me the big rock with the note tied to it. There was a knot on the back of my head the size of that rock. The note said: "GO ON AND HANG YOURSELF. I'll cut you down." And it was signed "GRADELL."

I jumped up and weaved up against the wall yelling, "Come out and fight, you sneaky coward! Come outa your hole and I'll tear you up and feed you to the red ants!"

Runt pulled at me saying, "Gradell ain't here in the office, Bobby Jack. We're the only people in here."

After that little incident I cut the price of whiskey another nickel a shot, and soon Gradell didn't have enough business left in his bar to pay the swamper.

The citizens pitched in and started painting and nailing.

The town blossomed out like a ranch wife's flower bed on a wet year. It was pertier than peppermint candy. Gradell refused to paint his place so we just did it for him. Twice a day the streets were watered down, and the air was so clear you could see a fly on a window half a mile away. The fun houses were working at full capacity, and the whiskey was selling so fast that Bootles had to put in three more stills. Word spread around the country and we even had people coming from as far away as Santa Fe and Albuquerque just to *taste* our whiskey, *feel* our gals, *breathe* our special air and *look* at Our Town! Just shows what good folks can do if their leaders are truly dedicated.

I walked in to see how Mary Lou was coming on her money counting, and there Runt was holding her down on the floor telling her how much he loved her. They weren't doing anything but feeling around, but I could tell by the enthusiasm they were showing that other things were to follow. I backed out quietly and went to my room. I sat down and studied the floor for a long time. I didn't learn a damn thing from it either. I called Melee in and told her to go down to Mary Lou's room and tell Runt I wanted to have a conference. She had to make three trips before she caught Runt *un*busy.

I told Melee, "Mary Lou's in love with me, of course, but I'm gonna sacrifice her for my number one assistant and amigo."

Melee agreed totally. "Surely. I could tell it was you she was thinking of when she chewed on Runt's ear till it bled."

That's what I'd always like about Melee, she saw things as they were.

Runt came in grinning. I bet he had that same look on his face the time he seduced his cousin Alice. I motioned him to sit down. I poured us a drink and handed him a cigar. We drank and fired up. He still had that silly-ass grin all over his face. I cleared my throat four times, scratched my shinbones, pulled at my nose and said, "My friend, I've reached a decision that has to do with your future." Goddamn, I did wish he'd quit that grinning.

"Yeah?"

"Yeah, now you know that Mary Lou is young and innocent? A new flower in the garden, so to speak."

"Yeeaaah."

"You also know that her father is a very important business associate of ours?"

"Yeah! Yeah!"

"And he has completely trusted his delicate, inexperienced little daughter into *my* hands?"

Runt just nodded his head up and down so hard he almost slung off the silly grin.

"Well, amigo, pardner, number one helper, I am hereby exchangin' *my* hands for *yours*—like any real gentleman would do."

"Yeeeeeoooooow!"

He ran over and shook *our* hands for about two minutes, then turned serious on me.

"Bobby Jack, you know what you was tellin' me last night before you went off to bed with Melee?"

"'Course I remember," I insisted, feeling cold and sick somewhere between the north and the south part of my stomach.

"Well, I jist knew you would, and you're damn well kerrect when you say we ain't plumb done-in Gradell yet."

I rubbed one boot against the other and felt around in my pockets looking for something, and then I coughed three times for no reason atall.

"He's still got an ace in his hole," Runt said.

I threw my head way back and stared up at the ceiling, trying to count the places where uncouth flies had shit.

Runt says, "What are you doin'?" as I counted the specks out loud.

"Nothin'. Nothin'," I said, "just plottin' what I told you last night."

"Oh. Well now, you did say that he still had control of the mercantiles and was still makin' a fat profit sellin' beef to the hungry miners?"

"Of course, of course," I yelled, "but it was my next words that were important. Bet you don't remember 'em."

While the little brainless bastard was trying to remember what I'd said next, I got up, looked out the window and down the hall, too. Then I looked the other direction down the hall thinking all the time what a slow thinker the poor little moron was. He finally did remember, though. Got to give him a little credit there.

"You said if we was to rustle Gravy King's cattle and cut the price just like we done on the whiskey that we could wipe out Gradell and ruin the King Ranch at the same time."

"Runt," I said in agony, "how come you've waited so long to do what I told you? Go get our horses, and a lot of new catch ropes. Get Bootles to bring his wagon and team to haul the butchered beefs in."

"Damn right, boss!" And he jumped up and took off.

God uh-mighty, if I wasn't around to tell him what to do, he'd starve to death on the toilet.

We went to work on that end of the business just like we had with the other booming enterprises. Ever'time I'd think about old Gravy King coming up short on a cattle count, I'd just lay down in bed with Melee or Dorothy and laugh till they cried.

Chapter Thirteen

Dorothy kept warning me, "Be careful. That Gradell will make a sneak attack at an unknown moment."

I figured, though, with me already in control of the town and educated like I was that Gradell didn't have a shot. My romances with Melee and Dorothy perked right along on both axles. The town was painted and cleaned up so perty that we had a regular tourist business going. I tell you it pays to keep things clean and pure. The money from the whiskey, whores, and Gravy King's free beef was stacking up so fast that Banker Zilch had taken me in as a pardner and put me on the board of directors. Gradell had lost face—it's hard to say that when nobody had ever seen his face—to the point he only had one joint left open. That was the Double Garter Saloon, and hardly anybody went there but the bartender and a drunken swamper.

Runt had taken to the romance department perty heavy. When he wasn't stealing cows and Mary Lou wasn't counting money, they were off on buggy rides into the sunset, eating box suppers and dancing at socials. They were acting plumb silly—seemed to me.

I was sitting in my official office and Melee brought me this letter from the Territorial Governor. I'd made Melee my secretary at the courthouse. The town council had raised strong objections, saying that it was unheard of for a lady to be a secretary to one of such high rank as mine. That it was standard all over the country for a male to hold this position. "Well," I'd stated, "to hell with the rest of the country. Since we're pertying up the outside of Our Town we might as well do the same good for the inside. Besides, by God, ladies are people, too."

They were just barely wise enough not to contest this wisdom.

In fact, I got to feeling like Melee had the potential of a Della Craven. I don't mean bedwise, I'm talking about doing difficult things with money and stuff that took brains, by damn.

Anyhow, the letter said, the governor had heard about this display of community spirit and he and his aides were arriving in three days to inspect Our Town as a model city—whatever the hell that meant. It sounded like a brag so I was mighty proud, and we set about preparing a big welcome for the governor. When old Nap attacked Russia, he had said that was his crowning achievement. I sorta felt this might just be mine. One damn thing for sure, the governor wasn't coming to see no faceless Gradell! It was an educated, go-getting son of a bitch known as Bobby Jack Smith he was meeting.

We did it up correct. We watered down the streets and hung welcoming banners across from side to side. A band was ready, and lots of the girls were lined up to do a high-kicking dance. The buggies were washed down and the axles greased to escort the royalty around our great town. To cap it all off, I was going to make a speech.

When the day came, Runt stood beside me soaking up the excitement in front of the stage station. A crowd had gathered to watch the important events.

"Runt," I said, "we've finally reached the top."

He had his arm around Mary Lou, and he didn't hear what I said. Here I'd given him this girl out of the pure sympathy of my soul and he didn't even appreciate it enough to listen. That's the way with the younger generation, they just don't listen to the wisdom of their elders. Just think about having fun all the time.

A big roar went up and there came the stage. Only a tiny puff of dust rose from our well-cared-for street. I stood proud, as the horses came to a stop with the stage door directly in front of me. Runt did turn loose of Mary Lou long enough to jump off the porch and open the door for the governor.

I was a little surprised by his appearance. I'd expected a great big bear with a walrus moustache and bushy sideburns. Instead, out crawled a medium-sized, hundred-and-sixty-five pounder. He had blondish hair cut fairly short and thinning on one side. He wore glasses above a thin little mouth that looked like he'd been raised on dried prunes and alum water.

We shook hands and then shook and shook and shook. The aides shook, the whores shook, everybody shook hands. I never did get to make any speech. As the dancing girls finished their stuff, the scrawny bastard stepped up on the porch and clapped like hell. Then before anybody could say anything, he raised his hand for quiet and told how he had suffered and fought for the economy of this area all his life.

He went on and on about his desperate struggles for Our Town and country. And he ended by saying with a wave down our colorful and clean streets, "And now I stand here humbled to know that you folks have heeded my lessons and my dedication to your town and country. I know that I can return now to the capital and report that my unceasing efforts have not been in vain."

You know something? That goddamned crowd clapped like it was all true. Talk about your sheep! I even caught myself doing the same and tried to break both hands by hitting them up against a barber pole out of shame.

I felt a little better, however, when we all got seated in the buggies and I was in the lead right next to the governor. We rode along with me proudly pointing out different color schemes and how every board in town was nailed down and ever sign was clear and spelled right so that even the weakeyed would know where they were going.

He leaned over to me in the most confident of tones and said, "Mr. Smith, I really appreciate what you've done in this area. Nothing would have happened without you. I appreciate it, Mr. Smith, I really do."

Then it hit me that all this bragging had been for nobody's ears but mine. He sure as hell wasn't going to give up any points to the public that way but was still trying to make them with me.

He kept on smiling and nodding at everthing I said, and then finally leaned over again in that way that made me think he was fixing to reveal to me the date of the second coming of Christ, and said, "I've heard a lot about the wondrous art collection and the advanced architecture of a house here in Our Town. I believe it's called . . . er . . . Let me see, I believe it's . . ."

"The House of Pure Fun," I finished for him.

"Yes! Yes, that's it." He slipped the words out through thin lips as dry as a droughty wind over a dead stick.

He had sorta topped me on the speech-making, but I'd figured days ahead of him about going to Dorothy's. This was one trip he was going to make whether he liked it or not.

We dismounted and, as previously planned, Dorothy opened the door and all the best gals in this part of the territory yelled in unison, "Welcome, dear Governor!"

He licked those dry, thin lips and pushed at his mousy, thin hair. His milky blue eyes gleamed out through his glasses till I expected them to melt. It certainly wasn't going to be any trouble to entertain the governor.

We all gathered in a circle around a big table in the main drawing room and partook of Bootles' Best Product. The governor chose a big-bosomed, black-headed Mexican girl, explaining that he was partial to Mexican women. Everyone giggled to be polite and make him feel good. He had made a pretty damn good choice in Maria Sanchez. I'd tried her myself before we hired her and found her a lot of fun in or out of bed. Course, this didn't hurt the governor in politics any either. I got the notion after a while that he would have mated up with a cross between a polecat and rattlesnake if the boys in Washington wanted it.

We had some more drinks and the banker and the Reverend and the whole town council all took turns running up to the governor to shake hands and tell him how honored they were to have him here.

The governor had five quick Bodkins' Specials, and after that he just said the same thing to everybody. "I'm honored to be here, and I love Mexican women whether they're whores or not." He had one hand under Maria's dress and the other down the top of her blouse and he was still able to say, "Yes, it's my honor," although it did limit his handshaking some.

I got down a considerable amount of the product myself and did a few dances with Dorothy. She looked up at me right sweet-like and said, "I'm *so* proud of you, Bobby Jack. You've pulled off a big thing for Our Town and *our* place."

Oh, everything was perfect. Dorothy had a three-piece Mexican orchestra playing some of those old love songs that make you want to cry and you don't even know what about. I was just raring back, feeling like I'd swallered the world and found out it was all chocolate.

Then it happened!

Dorothy saw it first. I know 'cause I was staring at her when that perty face just pinched up all over. Her mouth flew open, she stopped dancing, and pointed down at the floor. Seems like everbody there saw the same thing at the same time.

Mice! There were mice everywhere. The beady-eyed little bastards just ran and stopped and turned, not knowing what to do or where to go. The girls were screaming and jumping all about and climbing on top of the table, the staircase, the statues and the governor.

This was not only happening downstairs, it was up as well. Two naked girls came sailing down the stairway, and then when they got to the bottom turned and ran right back up into the arms of two naked governor's helpers. The aides needed help themselves but there was nowhere to get it.

Turning those mice loose on both stories at once had been carefully planned. With my lightning mind flashing fire again, I turned my wild, crazy self loose in a dash for the out-of-doors. Sure enough, I got out just in time to see two riders topping a hill into thick brush about half a mile away. I knew it was Gradell and one of his assistants. I was mad! I was also helpless. I had been underselling this Gradell.

The screaming was still going on. Everybody was running out into the front yard now from the ground floor. Several naked—and half-naked—people were skinning down the vines from the second-story balcony. Some had taken time to wrap up in a bed sheet. Others hadn't.

The governor was in a rage! He was yelling at everbody. "Do something! Call out the militia! It's my honor! God, I love Mexican women! Where did she go?"

Well, this panic would not do. I herded everybody out to the barn and made a few soothing comments. But there was no way to get the girls back in the mood. I even brought a small barrel of the finest product out there and pointed out different hay-covered parts of the barn, but the girls just weren't in no notion to play. They just couldn't do their work properly after such a scare.

I ordered Runt and the council to get going and confiscate every cat in town. While they were out on their mission, I returned to the barn and got the little orchestra playing again and that calmed things down. There's nothing like whiskey and music to take people's minds off current problems. A little bit of loving was starting up. I could see the governor had found Maria and was finally going to make it with her if he didn't pass out first.

About that time Runt and his troops got back with three boxes of cats. He said some of the local citizens had resented the taking of their pets, but he'd just told them the town was under martial law by decree of the governor. I thought I'd recalled telling him to say that but couldn't believe he'd ever remember to do it. There was still hope for that boy.

I jumped into a commanding position at the front door and gave the order.

"Release the cats!"

Three boxes, one right fast after the other, were emptied in the front door. Never in the history of Indian wars and madhouses has there ever been such a noise. The yowling and screeching and scratching was more than the average man could stand. Even I walked away and looked across the far mountains with my fingers in my ears. I cussed that Gradell like I never did even Gravy King. I took my fingers out of my ears to test the air. It was still full of sounds.

The governor finally gathered up his aides and requisitioned one of our buggies and left, taking Maria with him, saying, "By damn, I'm taking her to Santa Fe where a man can get a little piece in peace."

I hated to lose a good working woman, but who can deny His Honor? Hell, he'd soon be a senator and that's important.

After a while it became obvious that the mice were done in, but now the cats were so full that they couldn't eat any more and they were fighting each other over the remains. I tried to get in and kick the cats out, but the blood lust was upon them and I got a bone-deep scratch. Would this siege never end?

I sent out emergency orders to Runt to gather up all the loose dogs he could find. Away he and the council dashed to get a covered wagon. It didn't take as long to deliver the dogs as it had the cats. In fact, a few dogs had gathered on their own, whining and wanting to join battle in the House of Pure Fun!

I remained calm and made them wait till Runt returned with a whole wagon load. I wanted to attack with full force as Nap always insisted was proper if you expected to win an overwhelming victory.

There was no trouble pointing out the direction of attack to the dogs. The only problem was getting the door open. They were leaping at it so hard and fast that I finally had to call for help. The noise that had come before was nothing like this. Cats were coming out windows, leaping off the balcony, climbing up on the roof, and here from where I held the front door open there was just streak after streak of fur zapping past.

Finally the job was done. All we could hear was dogs yapping in the distance where they had treed the enemy. All was silent in the house. It took three days to clean up the House of Pure Fun, and there would always be scratches here and there that were too deep to cover with paint.

The word had spread lightning fast about Gradell's lick. We were laughed at a lot—even out loud. And it was for sure, the governor would never return to Our Town. Even though the word spread all over the country about our downfall, I was not concerned about the governor saying he had witnessed it. He just wouldn't come back, showing the rest of the state what fine taste he had.

My God uh-mighty, after he became senator, he might get to be president. A fearful thought, sure enough! I remembered what ol' Nap had figured out—ninety percent of the politicians were third-rate men. First- and even second-rate men did other things. The whole damn nation might just go plumb flat-ass to hell. A fearful thought. Right now, though, I had to solve something else.

There was no question about it. Gradell had timed his move perfectly. It was hard to hold a feller's head up, but we must carry on and fight back. But how do you strike at something you can't ever come face to face with?

Chapter Fourteen

Everybody on our team was a little bit let down. To get wiped out by six hundred mice is kinda hard to take. When I think how long Gradell had been planning, trapping and finally turning those mice loose at *my* supreme moment, I just wanted to run my head through a rock wall and keep going till I found another one. If he had shot me or knocked me in the head with a post I could have taken that, but this mouse thing really hurt. I could tell that the fun girls weren't putting all they had into it anymore. The doubt had been cast as to who would wind up the great leader. Our business was still good, but even with Gradell's higher prices a few customers had gone back to the Double Garter and three or four of our sorriest whores had gone along with them. I don't mean that we still didn't have business, it's just that it wasn't booming like before.

The only two people who didn't seem to care was Runt and Mary Lou. They had even announced their engagement. The less money we had to count, the more time she had to hold around on Runt. That just goes to show that a man has little to gain from generosity.

Then other little things started happening, like somebody broke into the courthouse and stole the papers that I'd stolen from the ex-mayor. Somebody painted on the front of our saloon BOBBY JACK'S OUTHOUSE in letters four feet tall. Then one night somebody painted a sign all over the side of The House of Pure Fun that read: IS THIS A CAT HOUSE OR A MOUSE HOUSE? I tell you it was getting to be humiliating for a feller in my position. I kept looking round for something to hit, but there was nothing there but air.

Then we had another bad break—the weather turned cold and it started snowing. It soon melted in the flats but up in the foothills and mountains it hung like cockleburs to a wool saddle blanket. It was getting harder to steal cattle because of all this snow. Old Gravy had hired some mean cowboys, and they damn near ran us down in the snow one time. If I hadn't shot the leader on a narrow mountain trail, they might have got us. We had to keep on rustling though 'cause we had already committed this meat to the miners for the winter.

I was sitting in my office listening to the wind piss and moan across the snow-covered mountains, with my butt to a hot wood fire. Melee was sorting out some papers and now and then she'd glance up at me and then run her hand across her breasts like she was cleaning off strawberry jam. I knew better though. She was just drawing my attention. She got it. My lower brain went into one of those thought storms I was getting famous for.

I said, "Melee, honey, come here."

She got up smiling and walked over to me with movements that showed me she was a whole bunch of woman. I put her between me and the fire and began to smooth her clothes up against her real tight. Soon they were almost hot enough to scorch. Man, that put the wiggles to her.

Then when I'd played around long enough for her to get out of breath and start horsing like a mare in heat, I said to her, "Honey darling, I know you know something about Gradell you're not telling me."

Well, I could see these tactics were not going to work so I just pushed her down on the floor and gave her a good un. Damned if she didn't tell me while I was laying there plumb exhausted.

"I did sleep with him one time."

I cheered up, and sat up pulling my pants back on.

"Tell me, tell me!"

"Well, it was in total darkness and I never did get to see him."

I tried to hide my disappointment. Melee, being basically kind and madly in love with me, saw this and tried her best to help.

"He was big-bellied and a lousy lover," she said, as if I cared a diddly shit about that.

"Was there, I mean . . . did you feel any identifyin' marks?"

"No," she said sadly, then brightened, "but he does snore like a boar hog."

After all I'd done for this girl, and this was the best I could get out of her!

Melee pouted, "You don't love me anymore."

"Yeah, I do, it's just that I got this Gradell crap on my mind all the time. If I could get him by the throat . . ." And I grabbed off out into the empty air feeling like a damned fool, which is very rare for me. "Well, there ain't a bit of use sittin' here taking on, we gotta get beef for those miners. Winter won't last forever, then rustlin' will be easy again. We cain't quit now."

I pulled ol' Runt out of Mary Lou's bed and she called me a "mean ol' man." I thought to myself that before the wedding took place I was going to show her what an old bastard I really was. I could tell she was mad 'cause she was having to marry

Runt instead of me. Hellsfire, there ain't no telling what a jilted woman'll do or say.

Runt did a little griping, too. "Cain't we wait a day or two till the wind settles?"

"That wind is comin' all the way from the North Pole and it ain't ever gonna settle."

"We get up in the mountains we ain't even goin' to be able to see the cow tracks much less the cows."

Here he was defying orders in front of one of our hired help. That'd never do. By zingos, I had to teach this young man some manners. I quoted the Bible to him like my old aunt had read to me so long ago.

"*The Lord giveth and the Lord taketh away.* Now you run down to The House of Pure Fun and pick up the week's payroll from Dorothy. Then we're headin' for the mountains."

He didn't act much like he wanted to go. I yelled after him. "No foolin' around with Dorothy, you hear?"

There that Mary Lou lay in bed half propped up, and the cover just somehow slipped down off one pointed titty. She eased one leg out from under the covers at the same time. She looked up that way she had that said, "*What next, cowboy?*"

I just kinda leaned over and so doing one of my hands accidentally slid underneath the covers to her other leg. I hadn't actually meant this to happen, but there my hand was under those nice, warm, feather quilts and I plumb lost control of that hand before I knew it. She just closed her eyes, sighed soft and low-like and slid down in bed raising the cover and pulling it over me just as I got the last of my clothes off. That's the warmest place I'd ever been.

The wind whistled outside and we whistled inside. In fact, we sang right out loud an old, old song. A man ought to know what he's got before he goes around giving it away. Well, I was glad I'd taken it back for a little while. I would always respect and admire my generosity a lot more.

I got up and locked the door, then crawled back into bed. Mary Lou was fooling around with the back of my neck when I heard a loud noise all the way down in the bar. I knew something was really wrong. I jumped up and had most of my clothes on when Runt started beating on the door. Then I heard them terrible words:

"THE FUN HOUSE IS BURNING DOWN!"

I jerked open the door, ran past Runt, across to the stable, got my horse and spurred to the scene. The girls were all standing out in the wind freezing, and poor Dorothy was trying to scoop up snow with her bare hands to throw on the inferno. It was no use. Most of the water in town was frozen and so was the pump at the Fun House. It was the perfect time to burn a whorehouse.

Dorothy was crying and still raking her fingers raw in a hopeless try to put the fire out. I finally dragged her away and held her up close trying to give her what comfort I could. A crowd gathered even in the half blizzard. I told Runt and Sheriff Digby to get the rest of the girls over to The Cat's Meow out of the cold. For a minute I thought Digby was grinning from his deadpan face—but maybe it was just twisted up from the freezing cold.

The house burned right down to smoke and ashes. Then everybody left but me and Dorothy. I was still holding her up close. We walked around behind the ashes and sure enough, there in the snow were the tracks of two horsebackers coming up to the house and then riding away. The wind had already nearly covered them and I told Dorothy, "There's no use tryin' to follow the trail. It'll be gone in five minutes in this here wind. What kind of a cheap bastard would set fire to a whorehouse when all the water's frozen? It ain't fair," I added, "it's dirty pool."

"It had to be Gradell," she said, "and no doubt my 'ex' helped plan it."

"The war is on," I said into the wind. "It's now officially declared!"

"What is your first move?" asked Dorothy.

I kicked at the snow and pulled my hat down over my ears, and then I turned in a half circle with my tail to the wind so I could think better. Dorothy realized that my silence signaled great thoughts, and she wisely asked me no more questions. I walked with her up the street, leading my horse, and held her as close as I could to protect her from the wind. She still shivered there in all that whiteness.

My vast empire was taking one hell of a beating, but now I was mad and when you get a general mad . . .

I gathered up that Runt and went by Bootles Bodkins' to pick up the rest of our army. The trouble was they were all down passed out drunk, all except Bootles who had been that way so long he seemed sober.

Bootles said, "Them two cousins of mine are passed out from workin' six straight shifts of guard duty. They'll be okay when they have another little drink." We all had a taste of Product and Bootles continued. "We was raided and the stills shot full of holes twice last week, that's why Matt and Elmer had to do extra guard duty. Course there ain't no danger of raids in weather like this." He took another drink.

I squirmed around on the bench trying to avoid a couple of loose boards in it and told Bootles, "Bootles, you make the best whiskey in the world considerin' the speed with which you have to turn it out."

Runt said, taking himself a little warm toddy, "That is true, it's raw but you appreciate it more for the struggle to swaller it."

Bootles hung his head, grinning, and said, "Awww, hit ain't much."

Then I told him the bad news. "Just a little while ago Gradell burnt down our best whorehouse."

"Nooooo."

"Yeeaaah," said Runt.

"Now you realize that will not only cut our income in half, but we'll lose half our gals cause we don't have enough room for 'em."

"Goddamnit," Bootles said and grabbed the jug. He took at least six big gulps before I could wrestle it away from him, and take a drink myself.

"War! War is declared, men!" and I whammed my hand down on the tabletop and started to stand up and give the general's salute. But one of the loose boards in that bench had slipped, and my balls were caught in a bind. I didn't get over three inches towards standing up till I plopped right back down, screaming in terrible pain.

Runt went sorta wild and was trying to drag me free which made it hurt worse. Bootles, always helpful, jumped up around the table, pulling out his long-bladed knife, saying, "Don't worry, Bobby Jack, I'll have you loose in jist a minute!"

I had no choice. From a sitting position I picked up the jug and hit Bootles between the eyes. It went "thunk" and he fell flat. Then in great pain I instructed my number one helper to take that fallen knife and throw it as far into the storm as he could. While he was doing this, I carefully took hold of one of the boards and with great courage moved it so I could stand up without the bench coming along. When Bootles came around and sat up feeling of his head, I told him, "You really oughta do somethin' about that slick floor. If you keep fallin' down and bumping your head like that, hellsfire, feller, you're gonna kill yourself."

He looked carefully at the floor and stepped lightly around the table and eased into a chair.

We all took another drink and I said, "They have attacked us in the winter. Old Nap himself would advise strongly against that, and if anybody knows about that, he does. Gradell has made a tragic mistake. Now we'll counterattack."

If they hadn't been drunk, I doubt if they would've followed orders. However, both of them were drunk. Of course, I hold my liquor real good and was sharper than ever.

We finally got the wagon and horses hooked together. We all mounted up and headed out into the wind. It didn't take that wind long to chill us plumb numb. Actually I was about half glad I couldn't feel much for a while. My balls had taken one hell of a beating in the last few hours, one way and another.

Runt asked me, "What'n hell do you think ridin' off and freezin' ourselves to death is gonna do to Gradell?"

I blew my nose, blinked my eyes, reached down and scratched my ass and said, "Just you wait and see."

We rode on about another hundred yards with the drifts getting deeper and all of a sudden Runt popped off. "Awwww hell, I know. You figger he'll laugh hisself to death."

I broke a limb off a dead tree and was just raring back to whack ol' Runt where it would do him some good when my horse stumbled and I had to drop the stick to hold on. It saved his life.

We rode damn near half a day and never saw a cow's tracks. The storm was getting worse. I rode over to the wagon where old Bootles was all humped up and said, "How you doin'?" always showing concern for my troops like a good leader should.

Bootles tore some icicles off his eyebrows and worked his jaws for a minute before he could talk. Then he said, "Since you asked me, I might as well tell you the truth."

I stared at him wondering if he had the measles or something else catching.

Bootles added, matter of factly, "I'm cold, tired, wet and hungry, and I got up a hard and need to shit."

That did it! I knew by that we were done for the day. So I led them back down, out of the hills towards Pedro Martinez' place. We could stop there for some hot coffee, thaw out and head on home. Pedro was a bachelor who kept a few sheep and goats around for milk and meat, and every summer he'd brew up a few kegs of chokecherry wine for his own use and entertainment. When I used to work for Gravy King I'd stop by and visit Pedro quite often. No special reason, of course, but friendship. Today I was hoping maybe he'd still have a drink or so of that fine wine left. Bootles' Product was rapidly wearing off.

We rode up to Pedro's place, and I could tell by the way the drifts were up against the door that nobody had been out of the house for a day or two—or longer. The sheep and goats were all right because the stack-lot gate was thrown back and they had plenty to eat. There wasn't any smoke coming out of the chimney, but I said, "We'll go in and build us a fire anyway. It's the law of the land."

I had to get a pick from a shed to dig the frozen snow loose so we could open the door. It was colder inside than out. There sat old Pedro, with his back to us, at the only table in the shack. Beside him was a gallon jug. By God, he was stone-cold drunk.

"Pedro, you old sot," I yelled good-naturedly and whacked him across the back. I was in for a surprise. That friendly gesture goddamned near broke my hand. Old Pedro was frozen to the gut.

Being the mayor of a town and all, I took charge of the investigation. It didn't take me long to figure out what happened, but that rude Runt butted in and quoted me before I had a chance to say a word.

"He obviously got drunk and went to sleep at the table. The fire went out and he jist flat froze to death before he woke up."

I said, before Runt stole it, "You can tell by that grin that he was dreaming he was fornicating the second he went."

"He do look happy," added Bootles.

I picked up the wine jug to test my theory. Sure enough it was half empty. "Two quarts missing," I said. "Just enough to pass a man out. I gotta be sure he wasn't poisoned," I said, and threw the bottle up and took a big slug. "No, it's the same old wonderful, bittersweet product as always."

Bootles took a drink and said, "That man was a damn fool for not selling this stuff." That was from one pro to another—a regular compliment.

Runt took a long pull and said, "Yeah, he might still be movin' about if he had."

I looked around the place and found another jug. This encouraged me to think some, but again Runt said exactly what I had on my mind.

"We cain't build a fire. He might melt and run all over the place."

I said snorting, "Course not. We got to get him into town where he can have a proper funeral."

Bootles and Runt both nodded in agreement. We took another drink and lifted poor old Pedro up and tenderly dropped him in the back of the wagon. Bootles said to lay him down easy or he'd break off into a bunch of little icicles.

As we rode along I realized that the day hadn't turned out too good. The best whorehouse in the West had been burned down. We'd lost half our income and half our gals. We'd drawn a blank on stealing cattle, which was going to put us in a bind with the hungry miners. An old friend was frozen to death, and I damn near got castrated. I took a long pull out of the jug, trying my best to cheer up. I passed it along to the rest of my troops. They eagerly accepted. We did a toast to Pedro Martinez.

Bootles gave him the supreme compliment. "Hell, ol' Pedro made wine most as good as I make whiskey."

We all agreed.

By the time we hit town it was getting dark and the wine was gone. Runt says, "Oh yeah, Bobby Jack, what was that you said you was gonna do to Gradell? I'm so cold I cain't remember."

I looked off into the darkness until my eyes watered over. I slapped the leather chaps on my leg and felt of the butt of my pistol and said, "Foller me, men."

We rode right up in front of Gradell's stronghold, the Double Garter Saloon. I bravely dismounted and my men copied me. We tied up our horses and the team and walked right in. I could tell that Runt's interest was picking up. He knew now that his leader had something going. I waltzed right up to the bar and called for a drink for everybody. That wasn't too big an order, for most of the girls that had deserted us out of desperation were in bed from overexposure. Two of the earlier deserters were hanging around, along with a couple of town winos that didn't care what kind of a place they bummed drinks in. When the girls sidled up grinning, I said, "I'll buy you drinks, but my body will never again touch yours. Goddamn traitors!"

Al the bartender was skinny like he'd been mashed between two boulders. Even his eyes were set so close together that I kept thinking there was no nose between. I could tell by that he was a mean son of a bitch, and I insisted he have a drink out of the bottle before we did.

"You think it's poisoned?" he snarled.

"Naw, we just want to be friendly and make sure you have a drink 'fore you get too busy."

Well, things began to feel better. Even the third-choice girls were beginning to look good. Runt danced around the room with a tall, thin one, and Bootles chose one on the chubby side. I just kept buying drinks and hoping something would happen to Gradell. Nothing did far as I know. The boys were getting out of control again. They started yelling, dancing faster, drinking more and loving up those gals like a couple of horny kids. I looked on in a fatherly way, keeping calm myself and thinking tough thoughts.

Finally I told the bartender, "The next time you hear from your boss, tell him I'm extending a public invitation for him to meet me on the street at the first thaw in the weather."

The bartender just glared, and if I hadn't been an important mayor I know he would have thrown our asses out in the cold.

Suddenly Runt comes over to me and says, "Me and Bootles been talkin', and we agree with you all the way."

"Yeah?" I said, doing things to the top of the bar.

"Yeah, we don't feel it's right for Pedro to have to stay out there in the cold. This here may be the last celebration he'll ever be in on."

"What celebration?" I asked.

The little smart aleck came right back with, "Why, this'n here. The one we're havin' on account of what you're doin' to Gradell."

I sorta made a noise that didn't say nothing and shook my head up and down and sideways too. Bootles and Runt slapped me on the back and ran outside. Then here they came carrying old Pedro into the saloon and sat him right up between us.

The bartender said, "We don't serve nobody that's passed out cold."

"Don't worry," I said, "I'll be responsible." It's hard to turn down the mayor of a town, especially when he's holding a gun and is rattlesnake fast in both hand and mind like I am. Drinks were set up right spritely for all.

We had three more after that, and then I could see that the bartender was wondering why Pedro didn't touch his.

"Drink your drinks," he says.

I said, "Whoa! Whoa! Whoa! He's just takin' your advice and tryin' to sober up."

"Besides," chimed in Runt, "he's deaf and dumb." Runt moved right up beside him and made sign language. Then he told the bartender, "He said to tell you he shore thanks you for your kindness and in just a minute he'll drink 'em all down."

The bartender smiled a tiny bit at this consideration, and I could tell the dumb bastard didn't even notice that Pedro hadn't made any signs back. Now Runt ran over and jumped up on a table and fell down on the floor and kicked and yelled to get the bartender's attention so I could get rid of Pedro's whisky. I was gulping them down so fast that I no longer felt very thirsty.

One of the prostitutes got drunk and slipped up and gave Pedro a feel in the crotch. Her eyes flew open and her mouth issued a "Whee!" and I could hear her telling the other whores "*what a man*" that was sitting there deaf and dumb as a frozen post.

Runt was watching this and he must've caught my eye, because he and Bootles picked up Pedro and took him over in a corner and sat him in a chair. Then they gathered the women back up to the bar and kept them there.

Well, we had some more drinks and suddenly the bartender went over to stoke up the big pot-bellied stove. That's when all our well-laid plans bore winter fruit. Old Pedro was sitting a little close to the fire. His clothes had sorta melted a little and the water had run down between his legs out on the floor. I was watching the bartender in the mirror. I saw him straighten up and sniff the air. He slammed the stove door so hard it almost knocked the chimney loose and then let out a great cry of rage.

"Get up from there, you deaf bastard, and get out of here! Up, I say!" He looked down and stepped back from where the wetness had moved along the floor under his feet. Then he really got mad. "I'm tellin' you for the last time! OUT of here! OUT! OUT! OUT!" He looked down again and then yelled, "Piss on my floor, will you!" And when he looked up and Pedro just sat there with that frozen grin on his face, he made a vicious lunge at him and swung the poker as hard as he could.

Poor Pedro was only thawed on the surface and when that poker hit him in the neck his frozen head just naturally broke off and rolled clunking up against the wall.

I can't remember giving Runt the orders but I know I had to. He would never have had enough sense to do what he did. He got Bootles and everybody in the place—the whores, the winos and all—to witness the brutal beheading and then yelled to the rafters, "So this is the kind of rotten, murderous place that Gradell runs! He is responsible as much as this bartender. You are all witnesses to this!"

Everybody yelled "Yes!" and then I took charge in my customary efficient manner.

"Get the bodies, I mean . . . the pieces out of here."

Runt stuck Pedro's head back on and they carried him out to the wagon with great dignity. They came back inside, and when the bartender wouldn't move from the spot on the floor, Runt just poured us all a drink and said, "Well, Boss, you said all day you had a lick figured out for Gradell and you sure as hell wasn't lyin'."

I said, "All the drinks has been on the house. That's the least that murderin' Gradell can do."

Everybody agreed.

It was a happy funeral. I'm sure that Pedro himself had a laugh somewhere, and he sure as all hell had come through for his old friend. We had music and dancing girls and the preacher got drunk and instead of saying "ashes to ashes" he said, "asses to ice." We would have to buy him deeper as soon as the ground thawed a little more.

It was still a fun funeral.

The word got around that they were knocking deaf and dumb sheepherders' heads off in Gradell's place, and we got through the rest of the winter way out ahead of him in every way. I felt kinda proud of my swift and brilliant comeback so soon after the Fun House fire. The sign of a champion for damn sure.

Chapter Fifteen

That old sun started warming things up. The snow moved closer to the tops of the mountains, and the damned bugs buzzed and crawled about getting friendly with one another again. The birds were chirping, singing and hunting the bugs. Hellsfire, it was spring. It sure felt good.

I had Our Town back in full control now. It was a time to "consolidate our position" as Nap's book said. I had promised Dorothy we'd start rebuilding The House of Pure Fun as soon as the ground thawed. I already had some men digging ditches for the foundation this morning. I decided that before I called all those other official meetings, I'd go by and tell Dorothy about it and pep her up.

Nearly all the girls were gathered in the lounging room where the customers made their selections.

"Good news, Dorothy," I said. "They done started rebuildin' this morning." I whapped her on that bountiful ass and nearly made her hair fall down. Since she'd been forced to live over at The Cat's Meow, for some reason, she'd worn her hair all piled up on top of her head.

She turned, glancing at Melee, and said, "That's nice. It'll be good to get back to a first-class operation."

Melee snorted and went on with some sewing she was doing.

I visited around with the girls, asking Shirley the blonde if her crabs were cleared up.

She said, "Yeah, I gave 'em all to Shagnasty the miner."

Everybody enjoyed that.

I patted Rose the redhead on the neck and asked if Half Storm, the Indian cowboy who worked for Gravy King, still did his war chant while he was doing it.

"Not since he jumped off to dance and had his big moment on the floor."

"What's he do now?"

"He stuffs a handkerchief in his mouth and makes love from the bottom side."

"Jist shows, them Indians don't trust nobody no more. Not even theirselves."

I asked Melee, "Whatcha makin'?"

"New curtains for my room," she said kinda sharp-like.

"That there's real nice," I said, trying to please.

"Well, some people—*some people*—think it's the decoration that makes a place first class, when it's what's in the feathers that counts," Melee said rather loudly, and for some reason Dorothy stomped out slamming the door. By zingos, there was something going on around here that I didn't know about.

"Now, gals," I said standing tall and rared back out in the middle of the whole damn bunch, "if there's a whey-bellied bastard ever comes in here that falls to sleep and snores soon's he's done, and don't allow no lights on atall . . ." I stopped a minute thinking, ". . . with an outfit the size of a peanut, and a man who's really over the dead pecker line, I want you to jump up and come after me. You hear?"

"If we was a charging by the inch we'd all starve to death," said Shirley, and everybody laughed and was in a good humor. That's about the best feelin' a man's gonna get in this here world.

That's the way I like my whorehouses—good humored. It's just plain business sense. Old Nap always said you got to keep the troops happy and well fed to have good fighters. I wished Dorothy had stayed for this final scene. It might have done her some good.

I told Melee she didn't have to go to the office today. I already had set the meetings myself.

"Good," she said, "maybe I can get my room looking decent." She said the last word like she was spitting out spoiled mush.

Mary Lou followed me out, saying softly, "Bobby Jack?"

"Yeah, honey, what can I do for you?"

She hung her head looking up at me in that way, and said, "I . . . thought you could come down to the room awhile." And she rubbed both legs on the side of mine like she'd done that tree the first time I saw her.

"Where's Runt?" I asked.

"Out stealin' cattle. He wants to get caught up 'fore the weddin'."

"Oh, yeah," I said, "good boy. He's showin' a little sense there."

"I know you're a busy man," and she moved around on my leg till we were face to face, belly to belly, and . . .

"It's the experience I need," she said, breathing hard. "I want to make Runt a good woman and the best little homemaker and business person the world has ever known." Then she broke loose, stepped back and turned real thoughtful a minute. "Marriage is a serious business, you know."

By zingos, she had me there. This kind of love and growth could not be denied. I just followed her down to the room and helped her prepare for the wedding. God uh-mighty, the sacrifices I've had to make for that dumb little Runt Jackson.

I was somewhat late for the appointments with the town council. I explained, "I was held up."

They all sat in a circle holding their bellies with locked hands, ever' now and then clearing their throats. I asked if they had any recommendations about improving on my work at Our Town. Several cleared their throats again and one or two got out with, "Well . . . ughhh . . . let me see . . . well now."

"Good," I said. "Good. Thank you, gentlemen, for your help and cooperation. Meetin' adjourned." And I hit my fist on top of the table because I'd lost the gavel.

Next came Asa Digby, the sheriff. There wasn't any way he could lock his hands around his belly, but he could hook his thumbs in his gunbelt.

"Asa, you've surprised me and done a good job."

He twisted about a bit and said, "Awww, I haven't done nothin'."

"That's what I mean. You *are* keepin' on the lookout for Gradell, ain't you?"

"Oh yes, Mayor, all the time. Day and night."

"Fine, fine," I said. "That's the right time to look out for him. Now I've got an important mission for you." He leaned forward over his belly till he lost his breath. "You know how I've cleaned up this town, beautified the buildin's, planted trees, watered down the streets and all, so we don't have to ruin our lungs breathin' dirty air?"

"Oh, yeah, yeah."

"We've got to keep lookin' after the health of all our citizens, right?"

"Oh yes, I agree."

"That is good."

I leaned over at him and pointed my fingers like a gun. "Sheriff, you've got to stop them drunks from pissin' in the main street." He slung his head about and tried to roll his eyes, but there was just too much fat for either to have much effect. I continued. "It draws flies, and flies carries diseases, and diseases ain't good for folks' health."

"What do I do?" he asked.

"You make 'em go around to the side of the bar or plumb back in the alley. That way we can keep this place sanitary and be proud of Our Town."

He got up and stumbled off to do his sworn duty. To tell the truth I didn't really know if Digby had enough going for him to be piss controller or not. But to justify his salary I had to give him *something* to do.

Banker Zilch came over. He was almost as fat as Digby, but there's where it ended. His brown eyes were always moving and looking—even backwards up at his own brain. Every now and then you could see little gold flashes of light jumping out, giving away the main color of his thoughts.

He politely inquired about The House of Pure Fun. Since his interest seemed right sincere, I assured him that it'd be done up and ready for action by the time the grass ripened this fall. That got our meeting off to a good start.

He showed me the profit-and-loss sheet, and we were way out in the black. He wanted to know if there were any investments I'd like to make with my share and I explained, "Uh huh, there shore is. I want to buy out Gravy King."

The banker took both of his little soft hands and rubbed them down the sides of his face. I could tell he was doing a deep think.

"That . . . that will not be easy," he said.

"Why, I heard he's had big cattle losses lately."

"True. True, but he does have a very *big* ranch, and lots of cattle left."

I stared a long time at Zilch. Then I got up and went over and looked in the pot-bellied stove. Since it was warm weather, I didn't build a fire. That's what kind of a thinker I am. Then I went over and opened and shut the office door, but I didn't go out because I was in a meeting with the town banker. After that I took my hat off the hanger and recrushed it. A man needs a properly crushed hat in a windy country . . . even when he's inside. Hellsfire, a window might blow out any minute. You gotta be able to think and think ahead.

Then it came to me—one of those lightning flashes that few men ever know. I'd remembered Runt remembering something I'd thought of. I stood up, way up. My chest was so far out there was no way I could have seen my belt buckle. In fact, I couldn't have seen the toes of my boots.

"Zilch."

He rolled his eyes up in his head telling his brain to hear good.

"Zilch, if you cut enough boards off the biggest tree in the world, it finally gets down to a single splinter."

His eyes quit rolling up. They rolled down, and with much admiration in his voice he said, "I never thought of that."

"That's the difference in me and you. Well, you see that's what I'm doing to Gradell. He ain't no bigger'n a single piece of kindling right now," I said, and having that taken care of, I took up other matters. "I reckon you've heard about the showdown between me and Gradell?"

"I've heard rumors, of course."

"You've now heard facts. On May the first at straight up noon I'm walking down the main street of Our Town to have

it out with Gradell. If he don't show up to face me in front of
all the citizens, then he's got something to hide, right? I've
already sent the challenge. The local paper is printing it and
we're sending invitations to everybody around."

"What if he refuses to come?"

"Hey, Zilch, he cain't! His whole honor and position is at
stake! I aim to shoot 'im down in the middle of our clean
streets like the sneaking coyote he is."

"Good luck," says Zilch, not showing the enthusiasm the
event deserved.

As he walked out, I yelled, "Hey, come on out to Bootles
Bodkins' house tomorrow to the wedding. Your friend the
Reverend will be doin' the honors."

"I'll be there." He smiled and left.

Somehow I didn't like that last smile. It's unnatural for an
old died-in-the-goat-hair banker like him to smile.

Chapter Sixteen

It was a right fine day for a wedding. Runt and Mary Lou
had gone on to her folks' house ahead of us. I drove out in a
two-seater buggy with Dorothy and Melee sitting side by side
not saying a word. I didn't much care—I had too many
thoughts on my mind. I had reasoned that to ever have the vast
empire I'd set out to get I needed Gravy King's Ranch. If Runt
kept on rustling cows the way he had been, and didn't let his
marriage vows get in the way, it wouldn't be long now.

I was sure surprised at the big crowd that had already
gathered. The banker and the preacher and ever'body was
there. Younguns were ducking and running and yelling all over.
A considerable number of these were Bootles'. The eating,
drinking, hand-shaking and back-slapping was going full blast.
A make-do table, forty feet long, was out in the front yard, and
it was piled high with all kinds of things to eat. I'd given Runt

a bag of gold to buy grub for the feast. Bootles had two barrels on the front porch, and all a feller had to do was turn the spigot. A lot of folks already had. I could tell that by the noise, having had lots of experience in these things.

I dismounted and helped the gals down like a real gentleman would have done. As I walked towards the crowd with one on each arm, I suddenly had a feeling like I was tied between two runaway mules, one going north and one south. It was good to break loose a minute while I got us a drink.

Bootles' twins were having a profound discussion. One said, "In jist four more years I'm gonna be a dozen." The other one did some serious thinking. "When I'm big I might even be a thousand dozen." It didn't take his brother long to solve that. "Naw," he said, "that'd be older'n granpa."

Here came Runt with something on his mind. I knew that was a helluva strain so I stepped aside with him a minute to try and give him some relief.

"Bobby Jack?"

"Yeah?"

"Bobby Jack?"

"Yeah? Yeah?"

"Bobby Jack?"

"Yeah? Yeah? Yeah?" I was beginning to get a mite impatient but being the thoughtful and forgiving man I am, realized that the pore little ninny had probably forgotten what he was going to say. He finally came up with something though.

"I . . . I . . . know I done asked before, but I gotta do it again."

"Lord uh-mighty and big frog turds, get it over with!"

"I just wondered if you might tell me . . ." He looked all around. ". . . tell me the secret love words to use tonight."

I kicked a big rock and, though it hurt like hell, I was man enough not to let it show. I took a cigar out and lit it. I broke the match up in four pieces and put them in my pocket. I puffed on the cigar then took it out and pointed with it over to Mary Lou where she was talking to the preacher.

"Son," I said, quietly. Runt was looking up at me with hope gleaming out of his eyes like a baby pig watching his first bucket of slop just before it was poured. He was twisting his nose trying to make it straight, which was impossible. He pulled up on his brand-new wedding pants. I put my hand out on his little shoulder and advised, "I just cain't do it—for your own good. Why, it would be a vile insult to that pure, unsullied little flower. Don't you see?"

"Well . . . when you put it that way."

Then I was rescued by Mrs. Bodkins. She had on a dress that was so new it was still struggling for its first wrinkle. There were places that it didn't exactly fit, but then there wasn't any way to do that. Her usually stringy gray hair was up in little curls tighter than sailors' knots. She took me by the arm and dragged me towards the house.

"This is better'n taters and gooder'n snuff," she said, beaming like a fish in a barrel full of fat worms. "I gotta show you our new improvements."

First she pointed out the three new prop-poles holding up the house. I bragged like hell on these.

"Mrs. Bodkins, I don't believe I ever saw three poles any pertier than those in my whole life."

"Thanks, Bobby Jacks." I knew I was prominent in the area, but this was the first time I realized I was thought of as more than one man. It sorta pleased me.

We moved on around to the back door and there it was. Just as new as the poles. That wasn't all—this new door even had a regular store-bought latch on it.

I said, "Now if that ain't keen."

"And lookie!" she said, grinning so all nine of her teeth showed at once. And sure enough there it was, a sight to stare upon in great wonder—a new washtub and rubboard, too. It was just too damned much, and I told her so. Then I added, "I never saw a place shapin' up like this'n before in my life."

"We'uns owe it all to you, Bobby Jacks."

Being the modest man I am, I said, "No, that ain't atall true. I have a little help here and there."

Then another side of life showed up. Melee now called me off behind a bush, just busting right out with, "I'm getting tired of taking that phony Dorothy Caldingham's insults."

"Insults?"

"The bitch sneaked over to me a while ago and whispered that I was nothing but a whore."

"Well?"

"I told her if it wasn't for embarrassing you I'd of jerked all the hair out of her head and shoved it up her ass till she looked like a walkin' buzzard's nest."

Was that any way for a genuine lady whore to talk?

There were many things I would have liked to be doing at that minute in my illustrious career. I looked off · at the snow-capped mountains and thought how nice it would be to turn into a snowshoe rabbit.

"One of us has got to go," she continued. "If I can't be number one, then I'll have to seek employment and companionship elsewhere."

"Now, honey," I says.

"Don't honey me, when you been honeying *her* ever chance you get."

It struck me as odd that a woman who was bedding down for money with two to ten men a day would get all upset with me for doing my own duty, but there it was. As wise as I am in many ways, with a fine education and all, I was a little bit puzzled.

My luck still held for *now*—it was time for the wedding! Since I was the best man, it was necessary for me to be there. Besides, I had a speech to give. The preacher got us all lined up and then I raised my hand for quiet. It was amazing how nice that bunch of drunks was. All chatter stopped. I noticed that Dorothy and Melee were standing as far apart as they could get, glancing at one another then at me like a horny badger that had mistakenly tried to make love to a porcupine.

"Folks, we've all worked hard under my leadership to shape up this country and not only make it pay but keep it ·perty. I think a good job has been done." A cheer went up that would have scared all the deer and bears clean over into Arizona—if they'd been listening. I rared up a little more and went on. "Now our company is growing so fast that the burden of handling it all by myself is beginning to wear on me a mite. Now, mind you, I could do it alone, but for the best efficiency and continued improvement I think I will accept some help. I am hereby announcing a new vice-president! This here is him!" I said, and picked Runt straight up and held him about a yard off the ground. Well, that mean, little dumb cow-thief had tears in his eyes so I put him down and ordered the preacher, "Get to marryin'."

The preacher had his book out but he couldn't concentrate on the words. Mary Lou's wedding dress was cut so tight around her crotch she looked like she was about to pop all the way out into the fresh air ever'time she took a breath, and the preacher kept looking down. He stumbled through a few words, then finally said, "Aww heck, do you younguns take one another for man and wife?"

Just at that second I felt a painful tingle on my right ear and as I reached up to touch it I glanced at the preacher. His eyes were opened wide and I saw a small black hole right between them. Then I realized I'd heard a shot. The Reverend fell over on his face downright dead. That bullet had been meant for me! In fact, you can't come much closer to blowing a man's brains out than shooting him in the ear.

Everyone got a little upset and wanted to take off after whoever had done it. Being a calm and cool man under all trying circumstances I asked them, "Well, now where do we run to? What do we run after? Does anybody know which clump of trees the shot came from?" I didn't get a single answer from that. They calmed down like their leader then.

Bootles had enough sense to drag the preacher over in the shade of a tree and prop him up. As he was coming back, Runt bleated out, "We could get into town and get hooked up by the judge!"

I said, "He's sick in bed with the gallopin' crud."

Bootles backed me up with, "Besides, he's so damn crooked hit wouldn't be legal nohow."

That Bootles was no backward bastard when it comes to making whiskey, but he was faster'n a double dose of salts when it comes to performing a wedding. He just took a hand of each of them, and put them together, and said, "I now declare you common-law man and wife."

That's what plain common sense'll do for you. Another great and hearty cheer went up from the crowd. The three-piece orchestra started playing and everbody was soon eating, drinking, yelling and dancing again. I did my part of that, too, cause I've had lots of experiences in those fun-type things.

Then Dorothy waltzed me way off and said, "I can't stay another night in the same whorehouse with that Melee. She works for Gradell anyway, so I can't figure out how you can be so blind and unfaithful at the same time." She pouted then added, "Why, she's got underarm odor right now!"

I wasn't aware of this affliction on poor Melee, but then Dorothy was a very sharp woman and maybe she had a better smeller than mine. I was horse enough to admit that she might.

I looked way off over and past the snow-capped mountains this time and thought how nice it would be if I was an Aztec prince and was standing all alone on top of those pyramids down in Mexico. I told Dorothy, "Honey," I says, chomping at my tongue while saying it, "this wedding has got my bowels in an uproar and I'm gonna have to head for the brush right now."

As I dogtrotted off I heard her snort, "Honey?"

Just the same I'd come up with one of my usual fast thoughts. I got down in that grove of trees and picked me a stump to sit down on. There was a little clearing, and it sure was quiet. Not even a bug buzzed. It was peaceful for a while, but perty soon a goddamn little chipmunk peeked around the trunk of a tree at me. Then a bluejay started flying from tree to tree squawking out loud, tearing up the quiet. A squirrel busted out chattering and a yellow butterfly flew around like he'd fallen off the sun.

I studied some black ants swarming and working on a dead log, and they just didn't seem to give a shit for nothing. All of a sudden I didn't either. Hell, I had to plan hard ahead for the walk-down with Gradell. The goddamned women would just have to fight it out till I got that settled. I was going to shoot him just like he'd done the Reverend, only I was going to put six holes where he'd put one. This soothed me and I rared back and looked up at the sky thinking that all those noisy animals weren't doing anything to me atall. Hell, maybe they were trying to tell me that they knew more than people. I started trying to talk back, but realized that I'd never taken time out to learn animal talk, except to outlawed horses and wild women. There was still part of my education to be filled in after all. Shitfire, I had something to look forward to.

Chapter Seventeen

The first of May did come. Now we'd find out who the head honcho, the mayordomo, the king gun and the big boss was going to be. I'd been going out in the woods practicing getting that forty-five out and blasting away fast. I had given myself many talks. It would have been my greatest pleasure to sneak up behind this bastard and shoot his backbone in half. But the best shot in the world can't kill a hidden ghost. No, there just was no other way except a public gunning. Another thing, it would stop anybody else from getting the same kind of foolish notions as Gradell.

I left The Cat's Meow around ten o'clock that morning feeling confident of the "ultimate victory." Runt, Mary Lou, Dorothy and Melee all wanted to come and comfort me while I was waiting. I rared up half out of sight and said, "No, here's some things a man—even a man who owns three whorehouses—has to do alone." I took out my gun, spun the chamber, sighted it, and pulled my hat down low and added, "There's gonna be a big crowd after the fight. Somebody has got to have 'em prepared for the celebration."

I strolled over, unlocked the office door and just sat down and stared up at the clock. How could I lose this after coming along so far? Hellsfire, I was mayor, bank director, business-man and entertainer, and before the summer was up I'd surely have the King Ranch. Ever since I had reread that part of Nap's book that said "never put all your supplies in one depot," I'd been hiding out a lot of gold in a cave up on the side of the hill about a mile beyond town. Why, some dirty crook like Gradell was liable to rob our bank any minute.

The clock kept ticking and I kept thinking. The first thing I knew it was five minutes till twelve. Well, I'll be damned! Here I thought this two hours would go on forever and it had only lasted two hours. I couldn't hear a sound from the crowd. I guess they were just too awestruck to talk.

I checked my gun again, put my desk chair back in place, cleared my throat, and at exactly high noon stepped bravely forth into the main street. I'd worked it so the sun would be a little behind my back and somewhat in Gradell's eyes. I didn't figure it would be slanting in enough so that anybody but Gradell would notice it, and by then it would be too late. A man in my position has to think of everything.

I'd walked along for quite a piece before I took a chance on glancing at the crowd. I would never have done this, but it was plain to see the other end of the street was empty. By zingos, so were the porches and the windows and the whole damn town. I bet that fun-loving Runt had gathered everybody up around Gradell, down some side street, so they could hoot and make fun of him. That had to be it! I felt better.

As I walked confidently along I thought of how clever it'd been to have the end of the street I walked on watered down the day before. Gradell's end was dry and powdery. I wanted the dust to sure enough boil when he hit the mother earth. I kept walking, wondering now if he'd really chickened out. Course, that would kill him just the same as a bullet.

I came to a cross street, stopped and looked both ways as fast as I could sling my head. They were as empty as a church on Monday. Well, I guess they were all down at the end of the street where it would be closer to the graveyard. I walked on past the cross streets, then I saw some of the crowd ride out towards me from the end of town. I grinned good-naturedly till I saw that these people were strangers and all of them had their guns out. I didn't grin anymore. I looked behind me and here came another bunch. Then they began to step out of doors and up on roof tops. I just stopped and stood there because there were just two ways for me to go—up or down. Now, I ain't no mole so I couldn't dig down and I ain't no bird so I couldn't fly up. I would have liked to do either one but being the man of wisdom I am, I didn't even try.

They just rode up all around me, and didn't have the polites to speak when I tipped my hat like a real gentleman would do and said, "Howdy." I spoke this in a voice that guaran-damn-teed I was friendly. They didn't do anything but point guns and stare. I stared back, not knowing anything else to do but maybe shit my pants. Then it got to the point I couldn't see anything clear but a million horsebackers with ten million guns. That's when I knew for sure I was outnumbered.

I started to raise my hands but before I could, somebody roped me and spurred off down the street. It was a relief to know that in about one-half more second I would have my face up out of the dirty part of town and would be dragged through my own clean part. It was comforting because that's all I had to take pleasure in at this time. I could hear, even with my ears full of dirt, a lot of loud laughing, hooting and hollering. Then I figured they must have run my head into the side of the jailhouse because that's where I woke up.

Runt was there with me in the cell. For a minute I was wobbly and just figured me and Runt had been on a little party and he'd accidentally locked us up. I leaped at the cell door jerking and screaming, "Let us outa here! Free us! Free us, you hear!"

Then from down at one of the other cells I heard a drunk yell back, "I cain't do 'er, amigo. I'm locked up myself!"

I wished I had never come back to my good senses. I might not have if that interrupting Runt hadn't said, "Gradell has done gone and got us."

I grabbed him up and was stuffing him through the bars when I remembered the whole event on my own. It was not a pleasant thought. I dropped Runt on the floor, saying, "We have got to stay calm and do hard thinking."

"You wasn't no sooner heading for the office yesterday than I seen Gradell's army riding in," reports Runt. "Right then I told Mary Lou to scat home to the hills and tell Pa and his crew to move the whiskey stills way back into the brush."

"I was meanin' to instruct you to do that," I said, "but I had my mind on the showdown."

Runt said, "The only chance we got to escape hangin' now is Dorothy and Melee. Mary Lou cain't show up nowhere in sight."

I did my best to give Runt confidence as I rared back, saying, "Goddamnit, little buddy, we must learn to respect the impossible!"

Just about then we started getting some answers about our problem. Here came old Caldingham and the sheriff waltzing up to the cell door. Caldingham had Dorothy hanging on his arm, and she never did even look at me. That's when I learned that the most beautiful creature in the world can look like the bottom of a monkey's cage in less'n a second. Digby had one of those big grins on his face that meant he was thinking funny thoughts. Something told me that they would be just the opposite of mine and Runt's. They just stood there talking about us like we wasn't present atall.

Caldingham says, "Sheriff, I've already spoken to the judge and he feels we should have the hanging on the Fourth of July. The governor would like to be present, and we can have a regular countrywide get-together."

"Sounds perfect to me, Mayor," says Digby. "We could have a big barbecue and all."

"Good idea, Sheriff. I know Gravy King would be glad to donate the beef."

I was trying to catch Dorothy's eye, but she wouldn't look up from the floor. If only I could have whispered those magic words to her just once she would have done something. I don't know what, but she would have.

The sheriff went on, enjoying himself considerably. "They tell me Melee is back at the Double Garter doing right well."

"Yes. In fact, Gradell has promoted her to the number one madam of that establishment."

"Well, after all the hell she's been through it's good to know that things have tilted better for her," the sheriff shoved down our closed-up throats.

I could see Dorothy sorta quiver at these last words, and it gave me a second or two of hope. They rambled on awhile and left laughing plumb out loud.

Runt stretched out face down on the bunk, and I looked at the rock wall trying to see through it and maybe hear birds singing and bugs buzzing. It was not a good place to be. Lord uh mercy, we would have to spend over two months here taking insults before we were hanged. All my women had gone over to the other side, not figuring they'd ever hear the secret words again. There was no way that Bootles could rescue us. They had enough guns in town to start a revolution.

"Runt," I says, "let us pray."

Even that didn't do any good. After that we were left plumb alone except for the two guards who wouldn't even talk to us about the weather. I kept yelling at them to hang us and get it done with. They would just go on playing checkers or oiling their guns like we were already dead. The food was dry bread, dry prunes and dirty water. It was altogether enough to make a man sick at the stomach. That's why it was a sure enough welcome sight when this woman with a heavy veil and a purple dress showed up and the guards handed us a couple of loaves of bread with a chunk of meat stuck between them. I couldn't tell if it was Dorothy or Melee the way she was dressed, but the overall build could have been either one. Anyway we bit into the food like it would be our last decent meal, which it probably was. I was halfway through mine when I bit down on something hard. I ripped that sandwich apart, quivering like a fresh-fornicated sheep. I just knew it was a gun. Well, it was the next best thing. It was a half pint of whiskey!

"Looky here, Runt," I yelled, "a whiskey sandwich!"

"Probably poisoned," says Runt.

"Naw, they're not going to miss out on the fun uh hangin' us."

I turned her up and swallered half of it and handed the rest right over to Runt. He did the same. For about thirty minutes we felt real close to being human again. Then it wore off. Still, it gave us a mite of hope.

It was getting along close to the Fourth of July and everbody who passed by our cells mentioned the hanging as if it was the inaugural ball.

Then it finally got around to the night of the third of July. You could just sense the festive feeling busting out all over. I especially felt it in my gizzard, like an old worn-out laying hen with the croup.

We were just sitting there trying to think of something cheerful to say without any success atall when this woman came in and spoke so softly to the guards we couldn't hear it. She was dressed in purple and the guards leaped up and nodded their heads. By God, this had to be the mayor's wife. Nobody else could carry that kind of authority. She had on that same veil so thick I wondered how she could see through it.

She walked over and stood right up next to the cell bars, and slowly pulled up the front of her dress. Well, a striptease was as good a trick to have as a last thought as anything else. Me and Runt stood staring at those beautiful legs like a hypnotized rat docs a snake. She pulled the dress right up over her drawers and reached down in there to a big bulge. Damned if she didn't hand us a gun apiece through the bars, all the time hiding everything she was doing with the rear end of that lovely body. We took them quickly and shoved them under the mattresses.

She turned and left with me staring hard at her shaking hind end, trying to recognize it under all those skirts. There was something familiar about it, but I just couldn't decide for sure whose figure it was.

As soon as the guards were busy playing checkers again, we examined our guns. They were fully loaded and there was a piece of paper rolled up and stuck in the end of mine. I pulled it out and read: *After you escape, come to the old boarded-up house behind the mercantile. Two horses will await you there. Your pardner must ride away then, but you must knock on the shed door that is attached to the house. That's the bargain! It must be kept!*

I would have knocked on the gates of hell till my fist was bloody to get out of this place. All my life I'd been celebrating the Fourth of July, and it looked like I might have another chance at it.

I hid the gun in my belt under my shirttail and stalked around the cell laying clever plans. I looked up at the tiny window and tried to see a star that might smile down upon us. It just looked dark, that's all. I went over and leaned on the rock wall and belched, tasting nothing but dirty water and dried pruncs. Then I made three fast circles of the cell and sat down rubbing the top of my head, coaxing at the clever thoughts. Just as I opened my mouth to say them, Runt stole them.

"Just tell them I've died. That's the only thing'll booger them. They want us to live long enough for the hangin'."

I glared at the little thought-thief and went over and yelled, "My pardner's done died!"

It got to them all right, just like I figured it would.

They ran over scared-like, knowing that one of them might be the replacement, what with all the plans that had been laid statewide. They were so nervous that one of them had to take the keys away from the other before they could hit the hole. When they finally did get the cell open, things happened fast. I whacked one in the back of the head as he bent down to examine Runt. Runt kicked the other one in the balls from where he was lying dead. Soon's he dropped to the floor to moan I repeated the old gun-barrel trick on him. It would be quite a spell before their checker game would get back to normal.

Being the man of action and forethought I am, we went out the back door of the office and down the alley behind the mercantile running pretty goddamn good for a couple of cowboys who'd been cooped up for two months.

By zingos, there were those two horses. I gave quick instructions to Runt about the location of a cave—the one I'd buried my gold in. I said I'd see him there soon, I sure hoped. He mounted and took off. I dashed to the shed door looking back half the time, expecting many bullets to enter my back.

I knocked. I waited. I knocked again. Then I waited some more, damn near dying standing there. The door opened a squeak and a female voice whispered, "Come in." I did. Then a soft hand led me through the shed. In the dim light I could tell there was a buggy and horse in there. This was funny 'cause everbody in town thought this house was empty. It was supposed to belong to somebody back East, and there was talk about it being haunted and inhabited by ghosts. The shed was nailed on to the house and we entered that right quick.

She led me along a hall and into a room. It was really fancy, this room. In fact, I could tell that it had taken a lot of gold to fix this room up like it was. Heavy purple curtains, the color of her dress, hung down and the chairs and divans were covered with velvet almost as fancy as the curtains had been at The House of Pure Fun. Silver and gold things were all over and fine paintings hung on the walls.

Before I could do anything else, she blew out the lamps. I stood there waiting for instructions from my lifesaver. I could hear clothes dropping on the floor. It was that quiet. Being a man of experience like I am, I just dropped mine, too. I could see her some in the dark, but only enough to make out the main features like tits and ass and perty long legs. That was enough for now 'cause she just floated across the room and grabbed me up all over, whispering, "Ohhh."

Down on the bed we went and got after it!

Again she whispered, so I couldn't quite recognize the voice, "I just had to hear the words everyone keeps on talking about."

Well, I knew I'd heard that voice before but couldn't place it, but I never whispered those words sweeter than I did right now. It sure was nice.

After a while, though, she touched me on the temple and said, "That's all now. Go and don't ever return or Gradell will bury you."

I said, "Thanks," put on my clothes, snuck outside, got on my horse and spurred like hell for the hills, hungrily breathing in that clean Dirty Town air before they got it all polluted again.

Chapter Eighteen

It took me awhile to find Runt in the dark. He put away the gun he'd drawn on me, and I entered the cave. There was a little split in the rocks over the cave that made a fine chimney. We could see by the smoke on the ceiling that the Indians had used this cave for centuries. We built us a little fire.

Runt asked, "Who was she?"

I didn't want to get his little mind too confused so I just answered, "A friend."

He grunted and put some more wood on the fire. "We done outa business."

I didn't answer that either. He went on, "We're broke. We ain't got no arms but two pistols. We're outgunned fifty to one."

I'd now heard enough of these falsehoods. I took a stick of firewood and crawled back into the cave, turned over a flat rock and dug up the gold. Then I crawled back and tossed those bags of beauty right out in front of Runt.

"What's that?"

I motioned for him to look and see. When the gold spilled out in his hands and the fire light started dancing around on it, I could tell a difference in Runt's attitude. His little pig eyes gleamed almost like the gold coins and he looked up smiling under his busted nose, pushed his hat way back on his head and said, "We done back in business!"

"You remember when Napoleon returned from exile and took over France again for a hundred days?" Runt tried to act like he did but being the student of human character I am I could tell he was faking it. I continued, "Well, by zingos, I'm goin' to return for ten thousand days!"

Even if Runt didn't savvy, he still had spirit. He jumped up, shook hands and says, "When do we start?"

I threw some more sticks on the fire, pulled off my boots so I could warm my feet better, looked off outside to see if I could spot an owl that was hooting and picked up two rocks and cracked them together.

Runt says, "Well, why don't we round up our people and set up headquarters right on top of this here hill in plain sight of the enemy. It might put the boogers into 'em."

"Takes too long to build a town. Winter'd get us," I said.

"What did Napoleon use for headquarters when he was on a big campaign?" Runt asked.

"Tents."

He started shaking my hand, congratulating me. "You done thought of it again! Why, we can have a whole temporary town made outa tents."

"While we organize for the counterattack!" I wisely expressed.

"Whoooeee! We can shore enough hurt Gradell's business while we prepare."

"Course," I snorted, "anybody'd know he'll raise his prices outa sight since he thinks he's got everything sewed up now."

"Right again!" yelled Runt, throwing his hat down in the dirt of the cave.

"To quote the great general himself, 'An enemy without funds is weak in battle.'"

"That there's what I call good di—dip—"

"Diplomacy," I said, saving the little idiot any more embarrassment.

Now I took complete charge and instructed Runt in his duties. I told him as plain as possible to go get Bootles and his bunch. At the same time, Bootles was to send some of his Indian friends into Sante Fe for tents, rifles, ammunition and anything else it would take to build and hold Temporary Town.

Bootles had been forced by Gradell long ago into trading with nobody but the Indians. But he had liked and gotten along real well with them. They trusted Bootles and would be delighted to have a chance to be part of the country again. *We'd* been shit on by Gradell. *Everybody* but Bootles had taken a crap at the Indians. By God, I wanted everyone to share in our good part of the country according to their abilities. In the meantime I would have a talk with our miner friend, Foreman Dooley.

At daybreak the next morning, the morning of the Fourth of July, we set out. I had to reach Dooley before he went into town to celebrate. Runt took off in one direction and me in another. I knew that there would hardly be anyone out in the hills hunting us today and by the time they got sobered up and their hangovers cured we'd be well entrenched.

As I rode along from one clump of brush to another I sorta chuckled out loud thinking of the dampness we'd spilled on the annual Fourth of July festivities by breaking out of jail.

I rode down into the mine camp like I owned it. It didn't figure Gradell had had time to get any reward posters out on us yet. I rode right up to the mine shack that was Dooley's home and office. Sure enough, he was outside washing up. I just rode up and handed him some gold coins so he'd know I was a sincere man. He took them in a sincere manner and his first words were, "Now what do I do?"

I explained that I wanted to hire a dozen of his best, most trusted men, and I wanted him to get into town and spy for our side. This tickled him some for he shook hands so hard he damn near jerked me off my horse. It seemed to me we had us a deal.

"There's a lot of us miners that knows Gradell has a big interest in the mines," Dooley said.

"Course, that's why the pay is so low," I said.

"You gotta promise to get us better wages after the . . . the . . ."

"The revolution," I helpfully finished for him. My God uh mighty, I don't know what this part of the country would have done without an educated man like me.

Chapter Nineteen

Well, it doesn't take a genius long to get things organized and moving. We already had out tents and other supplies. The dozen miners were there ready to dig. Bootles and his bunch had set up to guard the operations. Now there ain't nobody that can dig trenches like a miner, and when they asked me "Where?" I looked around and motioned for Runt to come over. I knew he was an expert in what was needed.

"Runt, we want our outermost defenses all around the rim of this hill." I could see Gradell's men barricaded and watching us with guns cocked way down below.

He just stood there looking at the town like it smelled bad.

"Get it done," I ordered, and he snapped to work.

Ever' now and then a shot zinged at us from below. We were out of range but the bullets were still close.

We dug trenches all around the circle that made up the top of the hill overlooking Dirty Town. We put up tents of every size. A tent for the bar and private tents for the girls that were bound to come. Bootles moved his stills over and started right out manufacturing.

With the high prices on beef, booze and bordellos in town, it wasn't any time atall till things moved our way. The miners were already beginning to come up and get drunk on our low-priced product. Bootles, being the artist he is, said he didn't feel too good about serving this whiskey till it had time to age.

He says sadly, "Don't you think hit's a little raw to sell to our friends?"

"Nawww," I explained. "They'll just get more of a taste out of it. Last longer, too."

Now, there was one thing I'd been secretly worried about. My books! They were hidden under a board in my old room at The Cat's Meow, but that goddamned double-crossing Melee knew where they were. It could be a disaster if these valuable documents got into the hands of the enemy. Course, I tried to comfort myself that they would be unable to understand the deep meanings anyway. Still, I worried.

Then one night Dooley comes leading Melee over to my tent. She had a bag of clothes and stuff with her. I wasn't too friendly. On the other hand, I hadn't had a woman now in a spell. She was a woman. She was wearing that same dress I'd first seen her in. That there revealing design sorta weakened my thought of revenge.

"I was virtually a prisoner," she reassured me, and bent over smiling right in my face in the dim light of the tent. When she opened that bag and handed me my precious books, I just took her in hand and straight to bed. The girl had sure as hell made her point. By zingos, I'd ride a lot of muddy rivers with her.

In less than two days we had most of the gals in Hi Lo working their little hearts out in Temporary Town. Now, where the beef, booze and women are cheap and plentiful that's where you're gonna find the men. Ever' kind. The word spread around and we had scoundrels from all over. There were bank robbers and stagecoach robbers from out of the great mountain wilderness to the north, gamblers and con-men from the mining camps to the south. They fit in right well. Since we had a fine platoon made up of the Poles, Mexicans, Italians, Welsh, Blacks and Irish from the mines led by Dooley, and our own elite bunch led by myself, there wasn't much trouble. The wild activities were mostly fun. When we weren't training for the war, we were partying. Besides the regular spur-of-the-moment dancing, drinking and loving, we had organized concerts twice a week when the girls would give us special songs and high-kicking dances. These were received with some of the loudest applause ever given.

Even with our low prices the volume was so great we were making more money than ever. The Indians heard from Bootles about these advantages and started coming around. When I was told that it was against the law to sell them drinks, I asked, "What law?" and that settled that. In fact, I told my vice-president, "Runt, let's see that we get a few tepees up right away for the Indians. If they don't have some of their own housing here, they might get to feeling discriminated against."

"Yeah, and besides that," Runt agrees, "they're good fighters and we need 'em for *our* war."

I wanted to, and in fact started to run my fist through the wall at this, but then when I remembered it was made of canvas I controlled my wild-ass self and put the hand in my pocket and felt many gold coins. This soothed me and I finally was able to calmly state, "Course, course, I've already been looking for the leader of the Indian platoon."

At first the Indians got far drunker than anybody else because they drink faster. There was a reason for this, too. They figured that if they didn't get it down in a hurry somebody was going to come along and take it away from them. After a while, nobody was robbing them or rushing them, and they relaxed a little and didn't get any sillier than the rest of us. Well, maybe one of them did, but he was that usual exception that always shows up. Hellsfire, ever'body knows that that knows anything atall.

This one was Chief Big Dirt Road Maker, and he felt right at home among all these tents and tepees. In fact, he imported several of his own women to keep the family outlook up. We sat in the main entertainment tent one night visiting. I wanted him to know he and his people had friends here. I figured that if I shared some of his customs he wouldn't mind sharing the load of battle so much with me. We had us some good drinks like good combat veterans will do. He had traded me three hides—two coyotes and one bobcat—for a full bottle. I was going to announce to him that night he was to be the leader of the third platoon—the big red platoon.

Big Dirt was having a good time, and he was more talkative than ever. "Many moons ago when duh fadder sun blessed duh land with much corn, and the buffalo were fat, my fadder *do* my mudder in corn patch. Cum sabby? Dat make it me great lover, great drinker, and great warrior. You sabby dat made it me?"

That I could savvy.

"I gonna go *do* Little Jump and Squat—tonight. Make nudder great lover, drinker and warrior."

Now Little Jump weighed a good two hundred and had been secretly drinking ever since she'd been here. Unlike the chief she felt out of place and couldn't understand how all the gringo and Mexican women could just *do, do, do* all the time with different men. She belonged to the chief. It gave the poor girl an understandable case of the confusions.

I rared way up and put my hand out on the chief's shoulder. He handed me a drink from his bottle, sensing, like Indians do, a moment of great importance coming up. I took the drink. He took one. Then I said, speaking with a voice that anybody would have recognized as being that of a gentleman general— that's what I hoped history would call me, like they called Napoleon the Little Corporal—"Chief Big Dirt, I hereby appoint you as full leader of the big red one platoon and give you all power and privileges thereof."

He looked at me with his dark revolving eyes, took another drink and spoke, raring up a little himself. "Dere, brudder, I take 'em! I do 'em!"

By the Lord uh mighty, here was a man of quick decision. I led him outside in the bright moonlight, and pointed him in the direction of his tepee. He made a small full circle, now and then, on his way. I figured this was his natural warrior's caution, checking signs to see if there was an ambush anywhere abouts. I watched him carefully to make sure nothing happened to one of our leaders. Wc officers stick together.

Suddenly he stopped and looked hard at a lump on the ground. That lump was Little Jump. She was flat out on her back. Fact is, she was just out all the way around. Big Dirt studied her hard a minute, even bending over slightly to look. He acted like he wasn't sure it was Little Jump. Hell, I could tell that from plumb over here. But then I had to remember that unlike me, few men had the eyesight of an eagle, and could hold more whiskey than a cow can fresh hay. It was plain that Big Dirt wasn't real sure.

He looked up at the moon, lining it up, then got her by the moccasins and pulled her around in about a quarter circle. Then, when he lifted up her long skirt, he had the moon shining in a direct line that made his examination more efficient. Since she had on lots of skirts, there was some difficulty getting everything cleared. However, I figured an officer in Bobby Jack Smith's brigade is not going to be deterred by a minor problem like this. He wasn't. He pulled them all up together and bent far forward making a close-up examination. I heard him say in complete knowledge and revelation, "Awwwrrruh. Arr! Arr . . . rrrrrrr!"

Now Little Jump would never know when it happened, but Big Dirt went to work and made him an heir right there in the cool blue of the southwestern moon. No telling what kind of Indian chief would come out of a *do* like that. Hell, he might even be president of the United States or mayor and general like me. I knew that all the way around it was a good sign though.

Things were moving. Bootles had his product machinery going twenty-four hours a day in three shifts. Runt was stealing cattle and trying to screw himself to death with his new bride. He was getting a little pale and wobbly, but Mary Lou just seemed to fatten up and get healthier. There was no question about her being the best money-counter anywhere, and a couple of times, just out of pride, she had to show me how well I'd trained her for her marriage duties.

"I jist wanna make sure you know how good I learned," she said and did that rubbing trick of hers on my leg. Well hell, me being human to some degree, I gave her the test. I just did it to please her, and keep her confidence up. Anyway, it was the code of the West. It seemed to me that she'd improved herself a whole bunch. We got to bucking around the money tent and dislodged the center pole. The tent fell down. I crawled out to come face to face with Melee.

With one of my typical, lightning flashes, I said, "We was uh addin' and subtractin' too fast."

Melee grinned a little teeny bit and said, "Go on to your war. I'll help straighten up the tent."

I appreciated that and decided it was late enough in the day to go through our military training. So I had one of the miners blow a blast on a bugle. The miners under Dooley fell into the second platoon. The Indians under Big Dirt into the third, and the first under my vice-president. There was no lining up in a row here. I didn't believe in it. Shitfire, these were modern times and all that lining up was old-fashioned and made an easy target for the enemy anyhow. Like the old saying, "Getting all the ducks in a row." It didn't make sense atall.

I stood out there and ordered, "Check your guns."

They did. Fortunately most of them had their own weapons—that being their nature and survival anyway. The way I looked at it, we had here sort of a citizen's army—free to farm, ranch, steal cattle, pray, play and whore around, like folks have always naturally done, and at the same time regimented and dedicated to throwing the bastards out of Hi Lo. I say it made sense.

A few of our men had to be held up between others as a result of the previous night's activities. I had no way of controlling this. If I did, Mary Lou wouldn't have any money to count. And that would never do.

As soon as my platoon leaders had made a count and reported that at least ninety percent of our men had their guns with them, I prepared to make one of my usual stirring announcements. However, Big Dirt gave me a small problem first.

"Sirs," he said to me. There it was again, just like Mrs. Bodkins calling me Bobby Jacks. Folks were always thinking of me as more than one person. Well I couldn't help that. "Sirs, some Indian brudders don' cum sabby dem rifles. Sirs, some of dem Indian brudders wanta use spears and bows."

"Chief," I said, "tell our dear Indian brothers that I wish I knew how to use those weapons myself. There ain't anything I'd rather see than Gradell pinned up against an eight-foot pile of fresh hog manure with one of those spears.

He spoke in Indian to his troops. They all raised their weapons and their voices in a right rousing cheer. It made my heart warm and contented. It also gave me confidence which, of course, I always have anyway.

I went on. "Now, men, take a little time off from your training and have a little fun down in the entertainment tent. In a couple of hours I want to meet all the leaders for a war council."

Melee followed me off to one side where I'd walked to face up to my enormous responsibilities alone. She'd had a hard night. Those north country bandidos had left her sagging a little here and there this morning.

She excused herself, saying, "I've been overworked lately."

"I savvy," I said gently. Having a full understanding of such problems myself, I showed proper sympathy.

"Bobby Jack, when we attack I want your promise that you leave that bitch Dorothy for me to take care of." When I didn't speak, she said, "Well?"

I took three steps forward, picked up a rock and threw it plumb out of sight down the hill. Then I picked up a dead stick and broke it in four pieces and dropped them in a pile. I walked around that pile of sticks five times humming a war song of the French Revolution. If I'd known the words I would have sung out loud.

"You know she's a traitor and a deserter and a . . . a . . . lousy lay!"

"Course, course, course. I was just goin' to say that."

"Well?"

That was all those goddamned "wells" I could take. "She's yores, honey, but don't do her plumb in, she might come in handy for a cleaning woman or something. You know how I am about keeping our country neat?"

Melee ran over and gave me a hug. If *anybody* has to, a general must keep cool under fire. I had a big conference to hold so I just took her for a short walk and didn't do anything but hold her hand and say consoling words to her, like, "When the battle's over, you will be the number one madam in charge of all houses and operations." This tickled the piss plumb out of her. Or I reckon it did, for she just upped her skirts and downed her bloomers and went at it. Any other time I would have given her a lecture because she was squatting smack dab in a patch of wild dandelions. They wilted right before my eyes. In her enthusiasm the girl had forgotten how strongly I felt about keeping the land beautiful and natural. I turned my head away from this sin and stood looking off across the distant mountains thinking of my vast empire.

Chapter Twenty

It was time for a council of war. I had spent several hours going through the book again. I might have missed something, being the busy man I am. There was one special trick that ol' Nap pulled over and over that I wanted to get down.

I had Big Dirt, Runt, Dooley and Melee in the headquarters tent, listening.

"Dooley, would you give us the report on your spyin' activities 'fore we go into the final plans?"

"Aye, and I will, Bobby Jack."

Dooley explained that business in Hi Lo was bad except for Gradell's hired guns, and they didn't pay half the time, anyway.

"Good. Good," I said, and everybody else nodded that it was good.

He went on to tell us how the paint was beginning to peel on the buildings, nails were coming loose, and the horse-shit ground into the street dirt was causing a breathing problem because Gradell wouldn't allow any watering of the streets.

"That's bad. Real bad," I said, and everybody else agreed that was real bad.

There was no piss controller on the town council atall according to Dooley. Flies were all over the place, and not just in the back alleys where they belonged.

Lord uh mercy, this last hurt, after all I'd done to keep things pure. Seems like folks drag things back down the mountain faster than you can pull them up.

"Is Gradell hisself in town?"

"Some of the lads say he is."

Then I wanted to know why Gradell hadn't attacked Temporary Town with all the guns he had available. Dooley reported that as far as he could find out, Gradell just figured the winter cold and wind would do away with the tent town anyway.

"That ain't too bad uh figurin'," I says. "Course, he don't know we are soon goin' to be livin' down there in those nice warm wood buildings ourselves."

That brought about applause from my bunch.

I sorta rared back and up a goodly piece and said, "Now here's the plans." They all gathered around a big map. "I drawed this here myself," I said. Hell, hadn't I studied the master's maps for month after month? 'Course I did have ideas of my own. Some that might even be better than his. I pointed out the town, and our hill, and the things in between.

"Now," I says, "I don't want the town tore up." Everbody looked at me, waiting. I let them hold on a spell so they'd hear better, and then I laid it on them. "Big Dirt will attack straight downhill at the town. Some of his men will be carryin' torches like they was gonna set the place on fire." I looked at Big Dirt and he looked at me. I could tell we was communicating. "Now, Gradell may be a dumb son of a bitch, but even he's gonna know that a burned-down town just don't make much money."

Runt got all excited and butted in, saying, "That way the Indians will only move down far enough to suck the gunmen out of town. Then the Indians'll turn and retreat back up the hill."

"'Course, 'course!" I yelled. Didn't the dirty little turd know I'd just read what he said less than an hour ago? In fact, I wondered from his talk if he hadn't been sneaking around and stealing some reading out of my book.

Runt ranted on, just jumping up and down and still trying to twist his nose straight. "Then we could ambush 'em from both sides uv the hills and save the town! Right?" He looked around at us all with his eyes spread wide open.

I took a deep breath, smoothed out the map, cleared my throat, and pointed to the valley they would chase Big Dirt up, and explained how Runt would hide behind the rolling hill on one side and Dooley and his bunch on the other till they reached a certain point. Then, WHACK! It would be simple. Soon as the battle was over I'd lead a select group into town to finish the job. I didn't expect much resistance in there, knowing the weak character of its steady citizens already. Melee was to follow right behind with all the women and children as a mop-up and clean-up unit. I wanted the town back in order with the saloons and gals ready for business that day.

"Everybody got it?" They had it. "One more thing. Dorothy belongs to Melee, by agreement, but Gradell is Bobby Jacks Smith's!" By zingos, maybe all those people were right. Here I was calling myself more than one person.

The meeting was over, and now I had to go make a close personal inspection of everthing before the battle. It would give folks confidence to talk to their leader in person.

The saloon was a right lively tent. I could tell that business was good before I entered by the noise. I went around to various of our members and did the right thing. Old One-Earred Smith—no kin of mine, of course—was sitting there with one of my gals on his lap, and when I asked if he was prepared, he tilted a bottle up, drew his gun and shot through the top of the tent. He didn't say anything but I could just tell it wasn't necessary. That one-earred bastard was ready! I patted him on the shoulder and said, in a voice to soothe any doubt, "Fine, fine."

To the same question, Killer Joe Newton grinned, showing a perfect row of red gums, both upper and lower, and said, "Yaaaarrrr." He then rammed his fist right through the bar top. I stopped to help him pull it out. A leader must let his followers know that he's right in there with them. There was no use wasting any more of my precious time. Things were just about as good as you could get them here.

I moseyed over to check the Product stills and visit with Bootles and his group. His cousins smiled and sorta pulled at the brims of their hats, not unlike a regular salute. Bootles had things perking, and to see that the Product was always as near perfect as possible, he constantly tasted it. To verify his opinion and be sure he wasn't just prejudiced, his help took samples ever' little bit, too. I told them how much I admired their constant concern with the Product. Bootles ducked his head, pulled at his nose and said, "Much obliged to yuh. We do try."

One of the cousins agreed. "We shore do that."

Another one added, "We do do dat."

I took a sample myself and said, "Ahhhhh. Ah. Perfect."

Bootles pulled his long nose and said again, "You know . . . I'm near bein' over the dead-pecker line, so I gotta make *this* end of the business work like the other'n used to."

Mrs. Bodkins was in charge of the kitchen. She had pumpkin pies outside the cook tent cooling. They were everwhere—on posts, stumps, on rocks and wagons. When I asked her about it she wiped that mousy hair out of her eyes, gave that nine-tooth grin, rubbed at the apron across her slightly bulging belly and explained, "Jist figgered, Bobby Jacks, that a good bait uh punkin pie "fore thuh fight'd put a little starch in the boys' backbones."

Now if that wasn't pure dedication and bright thinking, a feller is not likely to witness it in this lifetime. I wished I had a medal to pin on her but instead I just leaned over and gave her a kiss on each cheek. This pleased her so that she ran over and took a drink of Product, explaining, "Jist felt a mite faint there for a secont."

I could tell she felt better after that 'cause she went right straight to stirring a big pot of stew, looking down and sideways at me, giggling in her craw. She gave me a big bowl of stew and a slice of pumpkin pie. I swallered it like I was starved to make her feel good. She did. I could tell this by the way her giggling speeded up. It got louder, too.

I could see I had no worries about our field kitchen, so, I dog-trotted on over to talk to Mary Lou. She started giving me those looks between counting and I just got to hell out of there saying on the way, "Put the sack in the money, honey," and when she yelled "Huh?" I loped out of hearing range like any thoughtful leader would do. Hellsfire, I had to have all my strength from here on.

Chief Big Dirt nailed me right out in the middle of the compound.

"Bobby Jacks."

"Yeah?"

"It comes to me a big vision."

"Yeah, yeah?"

"Me think it to me, me better tell it to you." I stood listening politely. He went on, "Me think it you better come in with me."

When one chief speaks to another, I feel some attention

ought to be paid. Some respect should be shown. So I up and followed him to his tepee.

He said, "Arrrr. Arrrrruuf." And his women scattered out of there like hens from a chicken hawk. "Medicine man meetum great spirit with me last nights. Me, he, see many things."

I squatted down on some rugs, trying to act Indian. He took some fresh cedar leaves and threw them in the little fire in the middle of the tepee. They sure did smell. When they'd burned to ashes he dipped them into a bowl and held them under my nose. The smoke made me choke but I covered this by saying, "Just a slight cold."

He chanted things, moving the bowl back and forth under my chin. When he'd finished all this, he squatted down beside me and handed me several pods of gray-looking stuff about the size of a sunflower center.

"Peyote," he says. "Make it you hear my vision. Maybes so make it you see 'um, too."

I chewed this bitter damn button and swallowed it. Now I say right out into the fresh, smoked air of the tepee that it took me some while to do this. On about the third one, I jumped up and ran outside and puked up against the side of the tepee. Things were spinning and nothing seemed solid to me. A dog showed up and he was standing in my former lunch. It struck me a little strange when I suddenly thought to myself that I knew where I'd got the pumpkin pie and the stew, but I couldn't anyway figure when I'd swallowed that dog. The chief gathered me up and dragged me back inside the tepee. I felt better, and finally got down half a handful of those things.

We sat there now and way off somewhere I could hear him saying, "Very soon, you find it, big town, big ranch, many cattles, many golds."

"I see it! I see it!" I yelled. Hell, this wasn't a difficult vision atall.

"I see it this person. This person split in two like um santipede bug. Sabby um?"

Well, that was a dumb question especially for a chief. Shitfire, my old Bible-reading aunt had told me long ago that if you cut a centipede in half it would grow right back. To really kill one, you had to mash him plumb dead.

Big Dirt sang a little song while I was seeing forty-four

million cattle running over New Mexico and parts of South America and those parts all belonging to me. I saw wagon-train loads of gold being pulled away from the mines and that belonged to me too, along with a river full of Product flowing into countless bottles. By zingos, those visions were sure enough coming on. Then I saw Gradell.

"I see that there snake-screwin', shit-eatin', whore-deceivin' son of a bitch!"

The chief quit singing and says, "Good for it you."

It was around sundown before I quit having visions. I was sorta glad they were over. We had a lot to do before we attacked in the morning.

Runt came wobbling up and says, "I reckon you and the chief talked over the war daince."

I blew a bunch of peyote fumes out of myself, straightened up my gun belt, leaned up against a cedar tree and said, "Lord, uh mercy, course."

"You told 'im, too, that since we won't be able to sleep tonight anyhow, a war daince would keep Hi Lo awake and nervous same as us." I glared at him so hard, he just up and admitted, "I should uv known you would. Sorry."

I took care of that matter right away. I ordered Mrs. Bodkins to hold supper back as late as she could. I marched right in and informed the bartenders that they were to start watering the whiskey heavily. We didn't want anybody passed out the next morning. I told the chief that the dance couldn't start till after everybody ate. We built a big fire and dragged up lots of wood to keep it going all night.

I called Melee off and asked her how many gals were working right now.

She looked at the tents and counted with her hand in the air. "Ten. No, eleven. There goes Shirley and One-Earred Smith right now."

"All right, that's it. Get the word to the girls that there'll be no more action tonight. Course, we'll make an exception of them already playin'. It's only fair."

"Certainly," Melee says, and adds sweetly, "Bobby, I just want you to know how proud I felt when you told the others Dorothy was my meat."

"Awwww, don't think nothin' about it, honey. You deserve it."

"I hope I get to show how *much* I appreciate everything real soon."

"Tomorrow night, honey."

"Do I get the words, too?"

"The words, too."

"Oh, oh, ohhhh!" And there she went popping one of those perties out slick naked again. I swiftly looked away and up at the moon and damned if it didn't look just like that beauty of Melee's. I jerked my head hard back down at a dark patch of ground to get these kind of thoughts out of my busy brain.

I placed guards out in the right spots and then Mrs. Bootles Bodkins rang the dinner bell. Everbody took two or three helpings of that stew and finished off with a great big slab of pumpkin pie and it was time for the pow-wow.

First we had the friendship dance where everybody joins hands and dances in a big circle around the fire to the beat of the drums. Then the Indians started chanting. It was slow at first but got faster and louder as the night flittered on. We sat watching, feeling the blood pump around in time with the drums. The wilder they got, the wilder we felt. It was hard not to attack in the darkness.

I sneaked off with my telescope and spied on Hi Lo. Yes sir, I could see them scattering about with their own torches, moving wagons out in front of the town and piling up all kinds of stuff to get ready for the attack. That was good. They wanted to keep the battle outside of town just like I'd wisely planned. I went back to the dance. The watery whiskey was just keeping spirits alive, that's all. Everything seemed to me to be just about perfectly planned. Well why'n hell not, after all my study? An educated man like me don't aim to make many mistakes.

I thought hard about Gradell. Now that I'd seen him in the vision there was no part of the world I couldn't find him in. That didn't make any difference anyway. I'd get Gradell in Dirty Town before noon tomorrow.

I told Mrs. Bodkins that there would be nothing else served to eat till after the battle and the town was cleaned up again.

Hell, everybody knows that humans and coyotes run and fight better on empty stomachs.

The Indians were screaming and dancing that stiff-legged dance, bending over and back up screeching at the sky. The night was wearing away.

Chapter Twenty-one

Just a bit before daybreak I started my move. I rode down and got Runt and his bunch located on the right flank. They scattered out and got their guns ready. I took Dooley and his assorted miners and north country bandidos and lined them up the same way on the left flank. It was a good thing the Indians were still dancing, otherwise a big movement like this might have been spotted from down below. I gathered the women and younguns behind the entertainment tent. They were armed with brooms, mops, towels, pitchforks and stuff like that for a quick cleaning up of what would soon be called Our Town again. Melee took charge of this with Mrs. Bodkins and Mary Lou second and third in command. I reached out and patted each of them solemnly. No words were necessary. We all knew what we had to do.

The Indians danced and sang on. They were at that frenzied state now. I couldn't figure how they'd gained strength dancing till daylight, but they sure seemed to. I was going to have to study up on these people more. This was another tiny little crack I'd discovered in my great education. Well I'd damn sure take care of that soon as I got my town and country back in order.

I was watching the east hard. Sure enough that old sun eased up near the top of the world and shoved that gray coloring out of the way. The Indians really knocked holes in the ground with their moccasins now. I signaled the chief and he signaled his tribe. All was still. Still. Nothing moved. Just our hearts pounding like hell, yelling inside us, "Go, man, go!" I waited a good ten minutes to move. I wanted those scums down below to have fainting spells and dark whizzing spots before their eyes.

Then I walked over to the edge of the hill. The Indians mounted their ponies and faced around in the right direction. I rared up the tallest in the sky I'd ever stood, with one long arm up and my chest shoved out big. I felt that the full spirit of ol' Nap was there beside me, wishing me the best, knowing I'd studied him well. I brought that arm down with, "Charge!"

The horses' hooves pounded past me. The Indians were screaming, waving spears, torches, rifles, and bows and arrows. It was a downhill run and I mean it was swift and quick besides. The enemy was so surprised that hardly any shots were fired for a spell. Our men started cracking away. That's when Hi Lo opened up. We were losing damn few men because they were riding in circles, shooting and yelling in front of the barricades. It was enough to make the enemy not only dizzy but a little deaf. Then Chief Dirt rode out behind and let out some kind of shout. The tribe could hardly hear him but somehow they did. They turned, made a circle and retreated like they were the cowardliest bastards from hell. The Hi Lo troops fell for it, like I knew they would, and most of them were charging, afoot, up the hill. A few did have sense enough to come on horseback, but not many.

Now I was standing in a spot so that both my right and left platoons could see me as well as Chief Big Dirt. I waited and waited till the enemy was way up the hill and there'd be no way back. Again, I rared majestically up, and down came that arm like a chopped pine. Out over the hill roared my men from the right and from the left charging in behind. The Indians turned suddenly and raced back. We had 'em!

I made another motion at the women, untied my horse and charged my own wild self down the hill with spurs ringing like trumpets in the wind. Right into the battle I rode shooting with absolute accuracy, trying to line up two at a time. They fell like shit-hunting flies. I motioned good and true men to follow me. The battle was being wrapped faster than even I'd imagined.

The women and younguns had skirted around the main center of fire and were well on their way to town when me and my bunch ripped out around them. We thundered down that main street. I motioned my men into various buildings, while all the time I was heading for the mayor's office. Up on the hill the shots were already slowing, and only two or three cracked through the streets of the town. These were mostly just to get attention and respect, I wisely figured.

I came to a sliding stop in front of my old office, jumped from my horse and kicked open the door. There I saw this sight! Caldingham was climbing upon the window ledge on his way out. I just shot what I saw as he disappeared over the edge of the sill. The judge was hunkered down in a corner smiling and waving timidly at me. I didn't have no time to wave back.

Dorothy was cowered down behind the desk and when I jerked her up she says, "Oh, Bobby Jack, I thought you'd never return, my darling!" and grabbed me around the neck so hard I dragged her plumb through the office and outside in the street before I could tear loose. She fell down in the street. I could see Melee advancing on her and knew that that would soon be under control.

I raced back inside and told the judge not to worry, he would still be alive for a while because I had a wedding for him to perform—maybe two. He waved again and thanked me with what I thought was a slight show of appreciation. I could have been wrong, but it is not likely since that seldom happens.

I kicked in another door and there stood the sheriff with his hands up. I strolled over and took his gun, but that was only to compliment him for he didn't really know how to use it.

I said, "How come you ain't in the battle?"

He said right back, "Oh well, you see . . . you see . . . someone had to stay and protect the women and children."

I admitted that this needed to be done, but when I looked around the jail cells and under the desk I couldn't find a single woman or child. Oh well, shitfire, he'd still make a good sheriff. He would exactly fit the needs of our pure, clean town. There wouldn't be a cockeyed thing for him to do but oil his gun, shine his boots and maybe now and then he might have to take a message or two from me to the street-watering boys and the piss controller.

I walked over to the bank and there was told by the president himself, "We're sure glad to see our board of directors properly filled again. Besides that, deposits have been off lately."

I felt sorry for them, to tell the truth. Of course, big winners like me can afford this generous emotion more than others. I assured him that the deposits would start rising by the next morning, especially in my own personal account. He thanked me so hard I got embarrassed for him and left.

I strolled down the street. It was working alive with the clean-up crew, scrubbing, painting, nailing down loose boards, trimming trees. Right in the middle of them was Dorothy, on her hands and knees, scrubbing like hell on the porch of The Cat's Meow. I could see where patches of her hair were missing. Somehow she just didn't look near as elegant as she had when I first met her.

I spotted a member of the town council hiding behind a coal bin and told him to get the rest of his group off their dead asses and see that the streets were watered down.

"Now! Now!" I stated.

I didn't have any worries about the pleasure gals. I knew they'd be setting up house for the night's festivities with great speed. Hellsfire, they were pros.

About the time I decided to change the name of Hi Lo to Our Town to MY TOWN, I realized I'd slipped up on one detail. The most important of all. Gradell! I broke into a trot and headed down a side street and up the alley to the old boarded-up house. I could hear a commotion inside the shed. Then the door flew open, and out came the buggy with a big fat man driving and a woman in purple beside him. That same woman I'd seen so many times, hidden under the veil.

I raised my mighty arm and yelled, "Whoa! Whoa! Whoa!"

The bastard just laid the whip onto the horses and tried to run over me. He really shouldn't have done that. As soon as he was past, I jerked my gun out with that faster-than-the-human-eye speed and shot him in the back. He fell off. The woman in purple grabbed the reins to the runaway horses. I blew in the end of my gun just in case there was any smoke or dirty air in there and strolled over to have a talk with the gentleman—if there was any of that left in him. The lady reined the horses in a circle and pulled up right by the fallen man. She clambered down and knelt beside him. He lay on his side facing away from me.

She put her finger right by the hole in his back and said a sad soundin' thing to me. "Bobby Jack Smith, you shot my ace in the hole!"

I rubbed one boot in the dust and answered, "He just happened to be goin' the way I was uh-shootin'.."

"Shooting a man in the back is a cowardly thing to do," she moaned.

"No ma'am," I insisted, "it sure ain't. It's jist safe."

This she didn't seem to understand, as true as it was. She broke out to sobbing, moaning and taking on something awful over this man. I walked over hoping to console her and pulled the man flat out on his back.

"Howdy, Gravy King," I said happily.

He tried to spit in my face but couldn't seem to gather up enough of a wad to let go. Then the woman jerked off her hat with the veil and there was my Miss Della Craven, the educator. By zingos! Gravy . . . Della—the two names put together made . . . Gradell! It was so simple my hard-thinking mind had overlooked it.

She tenderly put the hat under his head while taking on some more. I am a very tender-hearted man for one who can fight and figure like six tigers. This bawling was tearing at my insides.

I pointed my gun at her head and said, "I cain't stand it. Please shut up."

She choked a minute, looking steadily down the gun barrel unafraid. She said, "Go ahead, my heart is with God."

I said, "Your heart may belong to God, honey, but your ass belongs to me," and with that I jerked her over close and whispered THE WORDS in her ear like no ear on this earth ever heard.

I expected Della to fall down and gap open her legs. She didn't do either one. Instead she looked at me like I was a big piece of standing shit. I never did care much for that kind of attention. I twisted my other boot in the dirt trying to figure where I'd failed for the first time. Since I couldn't come up with any answers I asked some questions, "Where'd you go, Della? How come you up and disappeared? Huh? Huh?"

She gave me another one of those dirty looks, saying, "It's none of your damned business."

"The hell it ain't! You left me out there in the cruel pastures, half educated. That ain't no way to treat a good pupil like me."

She looked over at Gravy and then back at me. I could tell by her eyes that she wasn't too happy over recent happenings. I reminded myself again of those words of the great Napoleon Bonaparte, "When in doubt, attack!"

"Now you lissen here to me," I said, tiptoeing in my boots, "not only did you desert me in a time of need and trust, but you took off just as I was beginnin' to care for and respect you."

She gave me a different look now. I could tell my fancy phrases were working again.

"Well . . . I guess I might as well tell you . . . seeing that Gravy is . . . I joined up with Mr. King . . . it seemed like the thing to do, you know. He had all the cattle . . . money, power . . . That's what I wanted."

She stared way off through my clean air at a flock of sparrows looking for a place to land, then started up again, "My folks starved almost to death on a little hard scrabble farm to get me educated so I could go in the teaching·profession."

"Well, now, they did a hell of a fine job," I said, feeling helpful.

"It wasn't enough, Bobby Jack. My folks' health is gone. They're helpless out there on the farm now. Just two sad old worn-out people on worn-out land waiting for someone to come along strong enough to dig two holes so they can go ahead and die. A teacher in a one-room schoolhouse is barely paid enough to feed and clothe herself. There was nothing left over to help those two who had literally sacrificed their lives for me—me!"

Her eyes were full of sad water. In fact, I was swallering a little more than usual myself, flapping my eyelids down over my eyeballs about ten times as much as regular. She had this tone to her voice, like one of those brush arbor preachers. I half expected her to pass the collection plate.

"I just couldn't take it, Bobby Jack. I had to try and make their last painful months as passable as possible."

"I can savvy that," I said.

"I'm glad you can see my tribulations clearly. It helps to know one has comforting thoughts cast about them in moments of distress. The calamities calm with this caressing knowledge."

She went on and on like this. It got to where I wasn't seeing a goddamn thing but her eyeballs, and all I heard was a head-numbing hum. Finally I sort of woke up in time for, "So now you know. That's why I joined forces with Gravy King. It would have all worked out if it hadn't been for you. I never expected you to self-educate so swiftly."

"I can sure enough savvy that," I said, feeling better than I had at any time during the last five or ten minutes.

She sort of ducked her head over to the side, saying sweetly, "And then, of course, I never really forgot you, Bobby Jack. That's why I showed up in the veil to warn and help you all those times. I guess, when I face it now, I wanted to win it all and still not lose you."

There she was—just like ol' Runt—stealing thoughts out of my head, and words off my tongue. I yelled, "Me too! That's jist what I was gonna say, Miss Della! I've always had this here—this here—'liking' for you too."

"Oh, I'm so relieved," she said, smiling with enough white teeth showing to make an alligator jealous, "I was afraid you'd forgotten me."

"After all you done for me," I snorted. "No, sir, Miss Della, I want to take good care of you. Look after your folks and all that. When they get ready to go, I'll even send Runt over to dig the holes. Anyway, I'm the winner around these parts."

Old Gravy set about moaning and mumbling again.

I continued, "Seeing as how your future with Gravy is going to be perty short-lived, how about jumping in the saddle with me."

She moved over, belly to belly, looking up, saying, "What is true is true and what you just said is true."

I was so pleased that we both knew the truth when we saw it that I just leaned over next to her ear and tried my luck again.

Her eyes fluttered up at me, she blushed and patted at the back of her hairdo, and said, "Oh, Bobby Jack, it's always been you. Just you." Before I could do anything else, she was grabbing me and loving me all over, saying, "We'll join. We'll join up. Just you and me."

Well, I would have joined her right there in the street if I hadn't respected a dying man's anguished eyes. I finally tore away from her and Gravy got our attention.

He raised up with a great struggle and said to me, "THE WORDS, please, before I go."

I looked at Della. Then squatted down by him saying, "Gravy, you poor dumb-ass bastard! Don't you know that women ain't cattle? You cain't just herd 'em into one pen where they all look and act alike. You say different words to different women at different times."

He looked at me like he'd been puked on. "You mean that's all? That's all there's been to it?"

"Yep, exceptin' the *way* you say it. That's what I learned from the French book on love."

He let out a bull-shaming beller, and instantly flattened out plumb dead. Me and Della got up, arm in arm, and walked over towards My Town, which I decided to just call Hi Lo once and forever like it'd always been and always would be. I glanced back at Gravy, and there was a huge frown frozen on his face as if something had puzzled him all the way to hell.

We turned the corner hugging and smooching up a little. Then I saw Runt and Mary Lou doing the same. Since there were no more shots to be heard and everthing was getting the polish put to it, I said, "Come on, you two. You're goin' to the judge and get rightly married."

"How come?" that dumb Runt wanted to know.

I just stopped and gave Miss Della a big juicy kiss and a big hug around the hindquarters, then I said, "'Cause it ain't legal for a vice-president to sleep with a woman less'n they're properly hitched."

"It ain't?"

"Nope, and one thing a vice-president has got to be is legal," I says, knowing that for once I had the stupid little bastard by the short hairs.

"What about you and your lady?" he ripped right back at me.

"Look, Runt, *I'm the president,* and everbody knows they do as they damn please." There was nothing for him to say to that.

I could see the water wagon coming towards us, wetting down the street, keeping our air clean and pure like we all deserved, and I glanced back to make sure Runt and Mary Lou were following. They were. Slow. But then, they couldn't help that—it was just their natural nature.

After the Fun—
The Facts

"Hey, Max, *Bobby Jack* is going to be a best-seller!"

That's what the publishers elatedly told me back in the seventies just two weeks after *Bobby Jack Smith You Dirty Coward!* was published. It sold several thousand copies in its first two weeks—even before reviews had been printed. And there had been no advertising. The only help it had received was: I had done one national radio interview and four minutes on Mickey Hargitay's TV show. He was Mr. Universe and Jayne Mansfield's husband. The reps were calling in begging the publishers to get ads out fast before the momentum died.

A few days later I was in Hollywood doing whatever a high-desert rat does to raise book writing funds when they excitedly called me to come and see the artwork on the ad. I excitedly did so.

Now back in the late sixties, a group of young New York editors convinced a certain Mr. Nash to pioneer a general trade publishing firm in Los Angeles. He had made a fortune in text books and other endeavors. They were a bright, ambitious bunch, and right off had two best-sellers. Oddly, best-sellers became their downfall. This encouraged them to publish too many books too soon. Mine was the last one.

My editor at Nash Publishing was Janet Shepard. She had been with a major firm in New York before moving to L.A. and was tremendously excited about the marketing possibilities for the cowboy-turned-pimp, Napoleon enthusiast and entrepreneur of women extraordinaire, Bobby Jack Smith. However, since Ms. Shepard was a deeply committed feminist, I asked her why she liked the obviously part-time chauvinist Bobby Jack. She looked at me like I had spoken my first words ever and said, "Bobby Jack is dumb, dumb, dumb. He uses other people's thoughts for his own."

I stared at her, waiting, not daring to speak for the *second* time in my forty odd years on this earth. She accepted the vapidity of my stare. "Besides," she continued, "who was manipulating him all the way through his stupid labors?"

I had no choice now but to give voice to *her* thoughts. "The woman . . . Della," I pushed from my voice box.

Janet continued and ended this remarkable and fearful exchange with one more question for the creator of Bobby Jack. "Who won in the end? The woman."

"The woman." I quickly verified.

She had nailed the thrust of the book and my feeble little brain to the cross with sharp nails and a heavy hammer. Later she said in an almost whisper, "Well, it does have several levels of humor."

Anyway there I was in the offices at the very end of the business district on Sunset Boulevard staring at the great artwork for a big advertisement in *Publishers Weekly, The New York Times,* the *L.A. Times* and several other publications. The art director and Janet were beaming like a couple of suns. I was smiling as big as a chimpanzee with a tree full of bananas. We could not miss now. The ad would hit just as the reviews came out. I was trying to calculate all the royalties that would accrue from 10,000 then 100,000, then 300,000 copies being sold. Maybe Bobby Jack could have added that high, but it was far too massive for my tiny bean counter.

Then . . . then everyone seemed to hear or, more likely, *feel* the ominous noise, or silence, moving toward us—office to office, down the hallway of the entire floor of the Nash Publishing firm. I didn't understand the exact words as they were delivered, but Mr. Nash had called the editor-in-chief and instantly shut down the firm. THAT instant. It was over.

Afterward, the reviews came out, mostly raves, even if a majority missed some facts that I'll end this with. But first: Fred Engel, producer of *Lilies of the Field,* the film that won a long-shot Oscar and made Sidney Poitier a star, optioned *Bobby Jack Smith You Dirty Coward!* with much elation. Later, he got mad at me when I would not renew the option for free. Sam Peckinpah was working on a screenplay for *The Hi Lo*

Country and sent it to an old friend of his, director Tom Gries. Tom loved it. I was deeply fond of Tommy and respected his talent very much. He had made a first-rate Western feature with Charlton Heston's first-rate performance in *Will Penny*. He told me that he had to direct a film on Muhammad Ali in order to include a contract on *Bobby Jack*. He would do it next. The day after wrapping the Ali film in Florida, Tommy was relaxing playing tennis and fell over dead. Now forget the shock of losing someone you respect and love at the age of fifty and stay with the book. I naturally held back publishing the paperback rights so I would get more money when the filming was set. After that, I simply forgot it and went on to other works, never submitting it for paper publication until now.

Let me finish with a couple or three sincere thoughts. Since I was raised mostly by old-time cowhands—respecting, working and playing with these old cowboys for many years—I can tell you that this book, according to the ones who were there, is closer to the truth about the "Old West" than most historians care to imagine. I can tell you with dead certainty that the beginning of the book comes directly from real ranch work and pranks that I have lived. The giant-steer roping incident happened to my cowboy cousin, David Evans, on a ranch near Las Vegas, New Mexico, in the 1960's. I embellished the sequence with a few of my own experiences. The fun in the book is as true as an emperor's emeralds—it had to be then, for survival, and it still is now.

"*Amen*"